THE WORLD'S CLASSICS

THE ROMANCE OF TRISTAN

PROFESSOR RENÉE L. CURTIS is a world authority on the *Tristan* legend and well known for her three-volume edition of the Old French *Prose Tristan*. She has also written a book of essays entitled *Tristan Studies*, as well as countless articles, many of them dealing with aspects of the *Prose Tristan*. She has given lectures on the *Tristan* legend at Universities all over the world. Professor Curtis has taught Medieval French Literature at the University of London for most of her life and is currently Professor of French at Queen Mary and Westfield College.

CW00820179

THE WORLD'S CLASSICS

The Romance of Tristan

THE THIRTEENTH-CENTURY
OLD FRENCH 'PROSE TRISTAN'

Translated with an Introduction and Notes by
RENÉE L. CURTIS

Oxford   New York
OXFORD UNIVERSITY PRESS
1994

Oxford University Press, Walton Street, Oxford OX2 6DP

Oxford New York Toronto
Delhi Bombay Calcutta Madras Karachi
Kuala Lumpur Singapore Hong Kong Tokyo
Nairobi Dar es Salaam Cape Town
Melbourne Auckland Madrid
and associated companies in
Berlin Ibadan

Oxford is a trade mark of Oxford University Press

British Library Cataloguing in Publication Data
Data available

Library of Congress Cataloging in Publication Data
Roman de Tristan en prose. English
The Prose Tristan / translated with an introduction and notes by Renée L. Curtis.
p.   cm.
1. Tristan (Legendary character)—Romances.   2. Romances—Translations into
English.   3. Arthurian romances.   I. Curtis, Renée L.   II. Title.
843'.1—dc20   PQ1542.E5C877   1994   93–41829
ISBN 0–19–282792–8

1 3 5 7 9 10 8 6 4 2

Typeset by Pure Tech Corporation, Pondicherry, India
Printed in Great Britain by
BPC Paperbacks Ltd
Aylesbury, Bucks

CONTENTS

TRANSLATOR'S NOTE

THE aim of this book is twofold: firstly, to provide a translation into English of those parts of the Old French prose romance of *Tristan* which link that work with the *Tristan* legend; secondly, to give the reader an overall idea of the whole of this enormously long romance by including a synopsis (printed in smaller type) of the sections not directly concerned with the traditional story. This means that I have translated a large part of the three volumes of my critical edition *Le Roman de Tristan en prose*[1] as well as of the fourth volume which is as yet unpublished. These four books contain most of the material which French scholars have called *les parties anciennes du Tristan en prose*. After our hero goes off to Great Britain near the end of volume iv, he undertakes innumerable knightly adventures, becomes a companion of the Round Table and even participates in the Quest of the Holy Grail; the story is now no longer based on the *Tristan* legend, and this part of the romance has been summarized. I have however translated in full two episodes in this section which are clearly linked with the legend: the scene of King Mark in the laurel-tree and the account of the lovers' mutual death. I have not included in this book the long description of Tristan's remote ancestors, nor the story of the *Vallet a la Cote Mautailliee*, in neither of which Tristan plays any part whatever, and which, though added early on, did not, I believe, form part of the original prose romance.

In this translation I have endeavoured to be as faithful as possible to the Old French original,[2] whilst at the same time producing an idiomatic English version which would be pleasing and enjoyable to read. It is therefore not a literal, word for word translation, which would have resulted in extreme clumsiness as well as in a notable lack of clarity. In order to avoid any awkwardness of style, I sometimes felt it necessary to alter the word

[1] Reissued Cambridge, 1985. In order to make it possible for this translation to appear in one volume, I have occasionally included a passage not central to the story in synoptic form.

[2] The base manuscript that I used for my critical edition was the excellent MS Carpentras 404; see 'Introduction', vol. i. 22 *et seq.*

order and the syntax, especially when faced with the perpetual
repetition of clauses beginning with *quant* and *et sachiez*. I have
tried to cut out all unnecessary duplication of words and phrases,
and only maintained these when their use was clearly rhetorical.
The constantly repeated phrase *fet il* has been freely translated as
appropriate by *he said, he replied, he asked*, etc. To eliminate
ambiguity, I have on occasion felt obliged to substitute the
relevant proper name for a personal pronoun. Old French proper
names can vary in their spelling from page to page, indeed from
line to line; I have chosen the form most commonly found and
used it throughout the book. I have given the English equivalent
of well-known proper names: e.g. Mark, Arthur, Gawain, Kay,
Tintagel, Camelot. I have replaced the historic present by the
past tense in my translation as this sounds more natural in English,
except in the synopses. The story has been divided into chapters,
not present in the manuscript, in order to facilitate the reading of
the text. The section numbers in square brackets at the end of
each chapter refer to my critical edition or to the MS used.
The paragraphs of the critical edition have not necessarily been
adhered to. Finally, I would like to stress that whatever modifications I may have made, I have always tried to remain faithful to
the meaning, the tone and the mood of the original.

The text is preceded by a Select Bibliography and by a short
Introduction which is intended to provide even the most unin-
itiated with the necessary background for the full enjoyment of
this romance, without being, I hope, entirely devoid of interest
to the scholar. The text is followed by Explanatory Notes and by
an Index of Proper Names. The Notes are designed above all to
clarify the text by explaining medieval practices, customs and
institutions, as well as names and places; and by referring the
reader, where relevant, to other versions of the *Tristan* story or to
sources outside the legend. The Notes also point out linguistic or
structural ambiguities in the Old French text. An asterisk *
indicates the presence of a note.

R. L. C.

ABBREVIATIONS

Analyse	see Löseth, *Analyse*
BN	Bibliothèque Nationale
fo.	folio
fos.	folios
Löseth, *Analyse*	E. Löseth, *Le Roman en prose de Tristan, le roman de Palamède et la compilation de Rusticien de Pise, analyse critique d'après les manuscrits de Paris* (Paris, 1890)
MS	manuscript
MSS	manuscripts
OF	Old French
OUP	Oxford University Press
Tobler–Lommatzsch	A. Tobler and E. Lommatzsch, *Altfranzösisches Wörterbuch* (Wiesbaden, 1915–89)
vol. i, ii, iii	*Le Roman de Tristan en prose*, ed. Renée L. Curtis (3 vols.; reissued Cambridge, 1985)

INTRODUCTION

The Tristan Legend

THE medieval legend of Tristan and Iseut is undoubtedly one of the greatest love stories to be found in world literature; I would not hesitate to say the greatest. For well over eight hundred years it has enthralled audiences in all parts of the globe. What is the secret of its powerful impact and its lasting appeal? I hope the following pages will go some way towards answering that question.

Scholars nowadays all agree that the legend has its origins in Celtic tradition. Even though no early Celtic version of a *Tristan* romance has ever been found, there are numerous factors which make this assumption more than likely. It is surely not a coincidence that the action takes place in Celtic regions, Cornwall, Ireland, Brittany, and that the names of the principal characters—Tristan, Iseut, Mark, Brangain, Gorvenal—are likewise Celtic. Moreover, a number of 'primitive' episodes are clearly not devoid of significance, such as the curious incident in one of the French versions[1] where a dwarf reveals, when his head is pushed into the hollow beneath a thornbush, that King Mark has horse's ears; this is doubtless linked with the fact that in Celtic *marc* means 'horse'. One should mention also the allusions to Tristan (Drystan) in the Welsh Triads, which list, in groups of three, names of Welsh heroes and exploits of early times. Although none of the extant manuscripts pre-dates the thirteenth century, some of the references at least suggest that Drystan belonged to an early tradition.

It is generally accepted that the first written version of the *Tristan* legend was a French verse romance dating from the middle of the twelfth century. Unfortunately this has been lost, no doubt sharing the fate of so many medieval works which were burnt in the Renaissance, or torn up to use as covers for registers or records. Countless hypotheses have been made concerning its

---

[1] See Beroul's *Tristan*, lines 1306 *et seq.*

authorship, none of them conclusive. What is clear however is that the success of this first romance about Tristan and Iseut must have been immense, for the story of these two lovers evidently so appealed to audiences that from the second half of the twelfth century onwards authors all over Europe felt inspired to write their own version of this tragic love.

This is the period when the courtly verse romance became popular in France, eclipsing the epic poems which had been in vogue in the first half of the century. The central core of this new type of literature was what we now call 'courtly love', a code of rules no doubt devised by the noble ladies at court stipulating that the man must strive to be worthy of his lady, should serve, revere and obey her, in return for which he would be granted his reward. Discretion, secrecy and outward respect for social conventions were an essential part of courtly love, especially as the lady was often already married. This type of relationship must not however be confused with an 'affair'; it was an all-embracing and loyal one on both sides, bringing with it much suffering but also much joy. It was above all a positive force, leading to the ennoblement of the lover. Although writers of the period did not in their works adhere to all the tenets of the code, the overall result was that women characters, from being almost absent in the earlier *chansons de geste*, now played a leading role in the courtly romance, and love became the primary theme. It is not surprising therefore that the love story of Tristan and Iseut should have had a special appeal at this time, and several of the French poems date from the last quarter of the twelfth century.

The Tristan Poems

Beroul's *Romance of Tristan*[1]

Beroul was a Norman poet whose name is only known to us because he mentions it twice in the course of the narrative. His romance of Tristan (or Tristran, as he spells it) is preserved in only one manuscript, unfortunately very incomplete, containing probably only a fifth or a sixth of the complete story. It describes

[1] For editions of the *Tristan* poems mentioned, see the Select Bibliography.

the lovers' plight in Cornwall after Iseut has married Tristan's uncle, King Mark; their secret meetings fraught with danger, their discovery and escape to the Forest of Morroiz, where for three years they live in hiding; and finally their reconciliation with King Mark based on the condition that Tristan must leave Cornwall.

It is a measure of Beroul's gifts as a writer that in spite of the fragmentary nature of his text it makes very enjoyable reading indeed. Beroul was a born story-teller, and the pages are full of drama and suspense, horror and humour. The characters are drawn by a masterly pen. The three main protagonists are complex and convincing: King Mark, the jealous husband, who really knows perfectly well what is going on but till the very last moment clutches at every straw to convince himself that his wife and his nephew are innocent; Tristan, whose uncontrollable passion forces him against his will to betray the loyalty he owes to his liege lord and the love he feels for his uncle; and finally Iseut, whose Freudian dream of two starving lions wanting to devour her, each seizing hold of one hand, shows that subconsciously both men, Mark as well as Tristan, presented a threat to her which she feared and resented.[1]

The artistic merit of Beroul's poem is in no way diminished by the fact that it constitutes a less polished version of the *Tristan* story than others, and in many respects is no doubt closer to the primitive legend. This can be seen not only by his forceful and dramatic style, so full of exclamations, curses and little asides to the audience, but also by the unconventional and at times uncivilized behaviour of the characters, even though they belong to the highest nobility. It is not just that the lovers are forced to live an outlawed, hunted existence in the forest; even when at court their conduct is instinctive and natural rather than refined, and indeed quite brutal where the vengeance on their enemies is concerned. Their lies and ruses, too, and the evident delight they take in them, convey a somewhat lax code of behaviour. It is Beroul's great originality that during a period when most writers succumbed to the influence of courtly ideals of refinement, he should have produced a work so fresh and so free from any stereotyped forms and feelings.

---

[1] Lines 2065–74.

Beroul's version is often linked with the Middle High German poem by Eilhart von Oberge, also dating from the late twelfth century. Although most of the German romance is lost, we fortunately have a fifteenth-century redaction of it which has kept quite close to its source. Beroul and Eilhart seem to belong to a separate family, often referred to by scholars as the common version. What above all distinguishes these two poems from the other *Tristan* romances is their different portrayal of the philtre. All the versions agree in making Iseut's mother, the Queen of Ireland, brew a love potion which she intends her daughter and King Mark to drink on their wedding night, but which is mistakenly given to Tristan and Iseut on the boat taking them from Ireland to Cornwall. Beroul and Eilhart are alone in limiting the duration of the philtre's effectiveness, which loses its force after three years in Beroul's text, after four years in Eilhart's. Does the idea of the philtre's abatement go back to the original *Tristan* poem? The problem has never been resolved.

Thomas's *Romance of Tristan*

The romance of *Tristan* by the Anglo-Norman poet Thomas, although written more or less at the same time, is completely different in conception as well as in style. This poem too has come down to us in a very incomplete state: only eight fragments of it have been found, some of which are very short. The two most important relate Tristan's marriage to Iseut of the White Hands in Brittany after he had been banished from Cornwall, and the simultaneous death of the two lovers. As can be seen, what is left of Thomas's poem concerns mainly the latter part of the story, thus complementing Beroul's text. All in all, the eight fragments constitute about three thousand lines, a section long enough to enable us to assess the essential qualities of Thomas's work.

There can be little doubt that Thomas was a learned man. His style and treatment of the subject-matter show that he must have enjoyed a very thorough education in clerical logic and literature. His mind was essentially rationalistic, no doubt both by instinct and training. Over and over again he insists on truth, moral and psychological, and on reason. He criticizes earlier narrators for telling the *Tristan* story in an illogical way. 'Thomas is not prepared to accept this, and is ready to prove rationally that it could not have been like that.'[1] Perhaps the most notable feature of the Anglo-Norman poem is the depth and subtlety of the psychological analysis. Hundreds of years before the birth of this science, Thomas was aware of the complex and contradictory impulses which are responsible for human behaviour. In his quest for truth, he probes into the innermost recesses of the human heart. Unlike Beroul, he is less interested in the outer action than in the inner life of his characters. Thus, when he deals with the theme of Tristan's marriage to the second Iseut, it is not the ceremony, the banquet, the festivities he dwells on, but Tristan's tormented and tortuous state of mind before and after the wedding.

As for the episode of the mutual death of the two lovers, it is a wonderful example of narrative skill and precision, for it is extremely moving without ever descending into sentimentality or melodrama. It makes a most powerful impact on one, and must be considered as one of the finest monuments of medieval literature.

Thomas's poem has been described as the courtly version of the *Tristan* legend, and in some respects this is a useful way of defining his romance. However, one has to remember when using this term that the relationship of Tristan and Iseut cannot be thought to conform to the courtly code. Symbolized by the magic potion, their love is an uncontrollable passion which must needs bring them into conflict with society, and which can only end in tragedy. Thomas has in no way changed this central and basically uncourtly theme of the traditional story; nor is Iseut the typically capricious, haughty lady who imposes her will upon her lover. None the less, it is true that the Anglo-Norman poet seems to have undergone more noticeably than Beroul the influence of the courtly society in which he lived. His poem reflects the fascination with love's problems and intricacies that we find in court circles at the time. The wealthy Count Cariado, even though he turns out to be an unpleasant and cowardly knight, is a very courtly figure as he tries in vain to win Queen Iseut's love and engages her in highly sophisticated conversation.[2] The invention of the *Salle aux Images* likewise has a very courtly aura about it; here the exiled Tristan had placed the life-like statues of Iseut and

---

[1] Fragment Douce, lines 862-4.   [2] Fragment Sneyd[1], lines 791 *et seq.*

Brangain which a craftsman had sculptured for him, and here, in this kind of temple of love, he regularly retired to indulge in his meditation and communicate to his beloved his doubts and sufferings, his hopes and his desires.[1] But above all one can consider Thomas's version courtly because he consistently modifies or even completely changes the primitive episodes found in the common version and the uncivilized behaviour of some of the characters.[2] The extent of the courtly influence is perhaps not quite so evident in the eight fragments which have survived, but fortunately we can refer to a number of translations of Thomas's poem:

1. The first and most important is the *Tristan* by the Middle High German poet Gottfried von Strassburg, more an adaptation than a straightforward translation, written at the beginning of the thirteenth century. The poem is not quite complete, though 19,552 lines of it have survived.

2. A prose translation into Old Norse, *Tristrams Saga ok Isöndar*, at times very abridged, composed by a certain Friar Robert in 1226.

3. The Middle English metrical romance of *Sir Tristrem*, written *c.*1300; only 3,344 lines long, this is a drastic condensation, sometimes very free, of Thomas's romance.

These adaptations show how popular Thomas's version must have been all over Europe. It is with their help that we must study his work in order to appreciate fully his genius and his originality.

The Episodic Poems

Apart from these verse romances, we have a number of episodic poems about Tristan and Iseut. Two are particularly well known, both anonymous, written at the end of the twelfth or the beginning of the thirteenth century. The episode described in each case is the same—a visit by the exiled Tristan to King Mark's court disguised as a fool in order to escape recognition—and they are known today as *La Folie Tristan de Berne* and *La Folie Tristan d'Oxford* after the place where the unique manuscript which has been preserved of each is kept. The shorter *Folie de Berne*, 576

---

[1] Fragment de Turin[1], lines 1–50.
[2] e.g. the theme of vengeance and the brutal murder of Tristan's enemies; the lepers; the lovers' harsh existence in the forest, etc.

lines long, has some links with Beroul's version; the *Folie d'Oxford*, almost twice as long, is closer to Thomas. The subject-matter is treated very ironically, for Tristan disguises himself so well that Iseut does not realize who he is and indeed refuses to acknowledge her lover, whereas his faithful dog recognizes him at once! The theme of disguise is of course inherent in the *Tristan* legend, for in Thomas's romance too the banished hero is drawn back twice to Cornwall to see Iseut, dressed up as a leper and a penitent; and in Eilhart's text we find a series of returns to Cornwall culminating, in lines 8655–9032, in his last journey there when he is in fact disguised as a fool.

In this context one can mention also the Middle High German episodic poem *Tristan als Mönch* (Tristan as Monk), based probably on a lost French source. This poem of some 2,700 lines, composed before 1260, tells the story of a funeral procession bearing the supposed corpse of Tristan to Tintagel, accompanied by a monk who is in reality Tristan, and who thus gained entry into King Mark's court.

Marie de France's lay *Chevrefoil* (Honeysuckle) about a secret meeting of Queen Iseut with the exiled Tristan is another example of this type of episodic poem. Only 118 lines long, it is the shortest of her collection of twelve lays[1] (end of twelfth century) and tells how Tristan, hiding in the woods, throws a stick of hazel-wood with his name carved upon it on to the path where the royal company was passing in an attempt to alert Queen Iseut of his presence. She pretends to feel indisposed and declares her intention to take a short rest in the forest. The title *Chevrefoil* is symbolic: when Tristan saw the honeysuckle twining round the hazel-tree, he realized that he and Iseut could no more be separated and survive than could the honeysuckle and the hazel.

The Prose Romance of Tristan

The Development of Prose

The works mentioned up till now have all been narrative poems written in the metre popular at this period, namely the octosyllabic

[1] Marie's *Lais* are short narrative poems based supposedly on Celtic songs.

rhyming couplet. They were recited by *jongleurs* or professional
performers, more often than not no doubt of an evening in the
lord's great hall in front of an audience of barons, knights and
ladies. Before the thirteenth century, prose was considered unworthy as a medium for writing literature. It was freely used in
the domain of law, business and religion, but romances were
written in verse. Gradually, however, at the beginning of the
thirteenth century, this attitude was beginning to change, due in
part perhaps to the fact that many more people were able to read
for themselves: whereas verse lends itself better to recitation,
prose is more suited to being read in private. Literary prose now
became fashionable, the most popular topics being the themes
already treated in the earlier poems: the story of the Holy Grail,
the siege of Troy, the heroes of Chrétien de Troyes and of course
the legend of Tristan and Iseut. But one only has to look at the
Prose Erec and the *Prose Lancelot* to realize how different these
prose works are from their poetic models. With the growth in
trade and commerce and the rise of the bourgeoisie, there was a
gradual tendency away from the rather narrow preoccupations of
the aristocratic society of the twelfth century, so interested in
discussions on matters of love. Chrétien de Troyes in his poem
Erec et Enide relates the story of a crisis in the marriage of this
couple, but in the prose romance of *Erec* the name of Enide is not
even mentioned! Similarly, in Chrétien's *Lancelot*, the hero seeks
to liberate Queen Guinevere, whom he loves, from the hands of
a felon knight who had abducted her; the *Prose Lancelot*, often
referred to as the *Lancelot-Grail* cycle since it is made up of five
romances, is an enormous work, a large proportion of which deals
with the adventures of numerous knights of the Round Table
and has no connection with Lancelot at all. Seen in this context,
it cannot surprise us that the *Prose Tristan* is not merely a prose
rendering of one or other of the poems about Tristan and Iseut.

The Manuscript Tradition

Before examining the place of the prose work in the *Tristan*
legend, it might be useful to establish a few facts. Begun probably
between 1230 and 1235, but expanded and reworked after 1240,
the *Prose Tristan* was extremely popular in the Middle Ages,
witness the eighty odd manuscripts in which it has been pre-

served. Despite this, it has remained until recently the least known of the *Tristan* romances in modern times and is the only one of which we still have no complete edition. This seeming paradox can no doubt be explained by the complex manuscript tradition, as well as by the enormous length of the work which fills two huge, closely-written tomes of manuscript. Fortunately the first three volumes of my critical edition contain the parts of the story which link it with the traditional legend. In the absence of a complete edition, our knowledge of the *Prose Tristan* is based principally on a summary of the romance made in 1890 by the Norwegian scholar Eilert Löseth.

The Authorship

The authorship of the *Prose Tristan* is problematic, for two men claim to have written the work or rather, as they maintain, translated it from Latin into French, a statement we need not take too seriously (see below, note to p. 3). The Prologue is composed by a certain Luce, a knight born in England and lord of Gat Castle near Salisbury. His name however is not associated with any other medieval work, nor is there any trace of a castle called Gat (variants Gast, Gaut, Gant, etc.) near Salisbury. The author therefore may well have invented this name to hide his real identity. The language shows no obvious Anglo-Norman influence, and one wonders whether he pretended to be an Englishman in order to forestall criticism of possible imperfections in his style. In any case, unless some document is found proving the existence of Gat Castle near Salisbury, the true identity of Luce has to remain shrouded in mystery.

The claim to authorship is made also in the Epilogue, not however by Luce, but rather by a writer who calls himself Helie de Boron. Helie was presumably a knight, since he tells us that he has 'left all knightly deeds' in order to devote himself to the writing of this book. In a slightly longer version of this Epilogue found in some manuscripts he refers to himself as a relative of Robert de Boron, the well-known author of the verse versions of the Story of the Holy Grail and of Merlin (end of twelfth century). There is no indication however that Robert had a relative of that name, and Helie is now usually regarded as an imposter who wanted to exploit the poet's fame.

The Epilogue by Helie de Boron is found already in the oldest manuscripts, and there is no trace of an epilogue written by Luce. Helie states that he put much effort into completing this work, but that Luce 'first began to translate'; and the most logical conclusion which imposes itself is that Luce started the romance but left it unfinished, and it was continued by Helie de Boron. This hypothesis is confirmed by the abridged Prologue found in four of the *Prose Tristan* manuscripts[1] where we are told that both Luce and Helie wrote the 'Story of Tristan', and that it was begun by Luce 'who spoke briefly while he was alive'. This suggests that Luce died before he could finish the book, and that the bulk of it must be attributed to Helie de Boron.

My close study of the prose romance certainly bears this out. Although it would be impossible to pinpoint the exact place where Luce left the work and Helie took over, there are, I believe, certain indications.[2] Luce's aim was clearly to write a story based to a large extent on the *Tristan* legend. Most, if not all, the key adventures of the two lovers can be found in the early part of the romance up to the point where Tristan, having married Iseut of the White Hands, is none the less drawn back to Cornwall to see Iseut the Queen. Thereafter the story is no longer linked to events that take place in the *Tristan* poems, and once Tristan sets out for Great Britain, there is hardly anything to remind one of the traditional tale. A deluge of Arthurian episodes and characters submerges the elements of the primitive legend. We are now faced with an author whose attitude is entirely different, who is concerned with Tristan above all as forming part of the Arthurian world. This is no longer a story about Tristan and Iseut, but a Round Table romance in which Tristan plays a part, albeit an important one. So little interested is Helie in the lovers' problems that he even forgets all about Tristan's wife, Iseut of the White Hands, and after Tristan has left for Great Britain she never appears in the story again.

Although it is clear that the prose romance as it has come down to us today has been modified and progressively expanded

---

[1] *E*, 756, *V*[3], and *Gh*.

[2] I examine this question in greater detail in the 'Introduction' to vol. iii of my critical edition, pp. xxv–xxviii; see also below, note to p. 213 and second note to p. 228.

by subsequent redactors, it is my belief that the original *Prose Tristan* was already the work of two men; a situation very similar to that of the *Romance of the Rose*, begun by one author who wrote a compact first section, and continued by another who had very different ideas, added all sorts of extraneous matter, and is responsible for the greater part of the *Roman de la Rose*. It is therefore the early parts of the *Prose Tristan* which will be of interest to those who want to read about the love of Tristan and Iseut.

Originality

The overall theme of the prose romance as it was conceived by Luce is that of the traditional legend: the irresistible, uncontrollable passion which leads the two lovers irrevocably to their death. The main thread of the traditional story has been preserved, namely the adulterous love of Tristan, nephew of King Mark of Cornwall, with the King's wife, Iseut the Blonde. The most famous episodes are barely modified: the fight with the Morholt; the notched sword; the love potion; the marriage of Tristan to Iseut of the White Hands. Even the secondary characters can be found unchanged: Gorvenal and Brangain; the Morholt; Kahedin and Dinas, the Seneschal. And yet within this framework innumerable and vital modifications can be observed which bear witness to the originality and creative activity of the author.

It has to be said straightaway that the prose romance is not, like the poems, primarily the story of the love of Tristan and Iseut, but rather a detailed biographical romance about Tristan. The book begins with a lengthy account of the hero's remote ancestors, making him the descendant of Bron, the brother-in-law of Joseph of Arimathea. Equally novel is the description of Tristan's premature birth in a wood where his mother was looking for her missing husband, King Meliadus, and where she dies in labour. We are given a detailed account of Tristan's childhood, and we follow him, year by year, through his adolescence. We read about his first apprenticeship in matters of love with the young Belide, daughter of the King of Gaul, and with the wife of the knight Segurades, before he actually drinks the philtre. In the poems, one is very aware that the love potion was at the same time a draught of death; there the lovers do not long survive the havoc it wreaks in their lives, and both are very young when they die. This is by no means the case in the *Prose Tristan* where, if one follows the chronology of the endless adventures that befall our hero, he is undoubtedly middle-aged by the time he dies. The circumstances of his death are also totally different in the prose romance, for here it is Mark himself who finally kills his nephew in a fit of jealousy; and Iseut does not expire on her lover's body of a broken heart, but is squeezed to death by Tristan in one last powerful embrace.

Some of the characters are inventions of the prose author, such as the figure of Tristan's stepmother. King Meliadus waited seven years after the death of his wife before he remarried, but unfortunately his second wife was an evil woman. She began to hate Tristan because she wanted her own baby-boy to succeed to the throne, and tried on two occasions to poison him. The theme of the wicked stepmother is of course a common one in folklore, but it is used here effectively to enhance the sense of threat and danger which hangs over Tristan's life, and has done from the moment he was born. King Meliadus's two unscrupulous relatives who appear at Tristan's birth are clearly introduced into the story for the same reason. Riding through the forest, they come upon the new-born baby lying beside his dead mother and want to kill him in order to inherit the kingdom; as so often later on, Tristan is saved only by the skin of his teeth. The character of Palamedes is another creation on the part of the prose author. He is a knight of exceeding prowess, generosity and intelligence, and moreover a Saracen, a fact which, no doubt wisely, he keeps to himself. As soon as he sets eyes on Iseut in Ireland he falls passionately and hopelessly in love with her. Although he realizes when Tristan defeats him at the second tournament in Ireland that he can now no longer hope to win Iseut's love, his feelings for her do not diminish. When she mocks him for his folly in loving her although he knew for certain that she did not love him at all, he replies: 'My lady, the fact that you don't love me won't stop me from loving you. The more you hate me, the more I shall love you! As God is my witness, even if I had the power to tear my heart away from you, I wouldn't do so, since I derive more happiness, it seems to me, from loving you all my life without having any other reward than if I loved someone else and had all I wanted' (see below, p. 115). His steadfast, unfaltering love for Iseut, from whom he never receives the slightest encouragement, makes him a very sympathetic figure, and the theme of the rivalry between these two superior knights adds another dimension to the love story of Tristan and Iseut.

A new element is also introduced by the episode of Tristan's madness. A message from Iseut had brought Tristan and his brother-in-law Kahedin to Cornwall. One day our hero finds a surprisingly affectionate letter which the Queen had addressed to Kahedin, and takes this as proof of her infidelity. Distraught, he rides off into the forest where for eight days he weeps and laments; on the ninth day he goes out of his mind.

The theme of Tristan's jealousy is not without parallel in the legend. In Thomas's poem we saw the exiled Tristan succumb momentarily to doubts and suspicions about Iseut, and we also witness a disagreement between them which drives Tristan for a while to complete despair. As for his madness, there can be no doubt that the germ of this is already present in the traditional story. In both poems of the *Folie Tristan* the hero's longing is such that it very nearly drives him insane, and this probably gives him the idea of going to see Iseut in Cornwall disguised as a fool. To make himself look more convincing, he shaves off his hair, tears his clothes and scratches his face, all actions of which we find an echo in the *Prose Tristan* (see below, pp. 214, 286). But there is one fundamental difference: in the poems Tristan was playing the fool and pretending to be mad; in the prose romance he *is* mad. Here his jealousy is violent and prolonged, for he is absolutely convinced of Iseut's infidelity. He rushes wildly into the forest, thinking that he had lost his beloved for ever, and this thought deprives him of his reason. Iseut, hearing the false news of Tristan's death, also wants to die, and tries to take her life. For the first time, we see a complete rift between the lovers; and although the misunderstanding is eventually resolved and Tristan is restored to health, the episode leaves us with a presentiment that things will not be the same again for a long time to come. It is as though the prose author wanted to develop the full potential of certain sentiments and ideas which he found in embryo in the traditional legend, and he has certainly made the most of the dramatic possibilities of Tristan's frenzy.

The 'Arthurianization'

Many of the changes are no doubt due to the influence of the *Prose Lancelot*. Composed in the early part of the thirteenth century before the *Prose Tristan*, this work enjoyed an extraordinary popularity, and it is clear that our author borrowed many features from it. This can be seen already in the opening chapters, for Lancelot's genealogy too is linked with the first guardians of the Holy Grail. It is not surprising therefore to see this Arthurian hero play an important role in our romance, as also Queen Guinevere and many of the famous Round Table knights, such as Gawain, Kay, Hestor, Mordret, etc. A kind of parallel is established between the two pairs of lovers. Tristan's prowess and worth are often compared with that of Lancelot, and many of the characters can be seen arguing as to which is the better knight. Similarly Queen Iseut's beauty and intelligence are discussed with reference to her counterpart in Great Britain.

Whereas the Arthurian influence is not very pronounced in the early parts of the *Prose Tristan*, it becomes more and more important as the story progresses. It is no longer sufficient that Tristan's exploits should be admired by knights-errant in Cornwall and Great Britain; it is now essential that his fame should become known at King Arthur's court itself, and eventually Tristan even becomes a companion of the Round Table and takes part in the Quest of the Holy Grail. The infiltration of the Arthurian world into the Celtic legend, already apparent in the poems of Beroul and Thomas,[1] is here complete. Not only are many of the themes and characters of the *Prose Lancelot* incorporated into the *Prose Tristan*; in the later sections one finds whole episodes which have been transposed. The love of Tristan and Iseut is not forgotten, but it forms part of a wider universe where chivalry and the conquest of glory seem more important than love.

Realism

It is perhaps by considering the prose romance in relation to the traditional legend that one can best appreciate our author's tal-

---

[1] Beroul: lines 3249 *et seq.* (Arthur's part in the episode of the ambiguous oath); Thomas: Fragment Sneyd[1], lines 662 *et seq.* (the story of the giant and the beards).

ents. If one may describe Beroul as a born story-teller and Thomas as an astute psychologist, one could well define Luce as a realist. Some of the changes he has introduced are clearly designed to make the story more convincing, more true to life. The dragon episode is a good example. In the prose romance it is not this grisly monster belching smoke and flames from its jaws that Tristan has to fight in order to win the Irish king's daughter Iseut; here this reward is granted to him because he agreed to fight a legal battle to defend the King who had been wrongfully accused of murder. The same regard for verisimilitude can be observed in the prose author's treatment of the episode in the legend often referred to as 'the return from the forest'. The fact that the lovers decide of their own free will to leave the forest and go back to Mark's court, even to separate, presents quite a problem to the story-tellers, for how can one reconcile this voluntary parting with their overpowering passion? Would they really ever have agreed to part when they could not even bear to be without seeing each other for a single day? Different authors have dealt with the situation with varying degrees of success, the abatement of the philtre being no doubt the way Beroul and Eilhart chose to explain the lovers' behaviour; but no one dealt with it more realistically than Luce. In the prose romance Tristan and Iseut quite simply make no such decision at all: one day while King Mark is riding through the forest with a large company of knights, four shepherds tell him where the lovers are hiding. He makes his way there and has no difficulty in abducting Iseut since Tristan and Governal are out hunting. The lovers' separation is therefore brought about totally against their will— quite a neat and satisfactory solution of the problem.

The prose author's attitude to the love of Tristan and Iseut is also more down to earth, and this reflects on his conception of these two characters. We have already seen that Iseut is not the only woman in Tristan's life (see above, p. xix). His first amorous adventure takes place in Gaul where the young princess, Belide, becomes infatuated with him, throws her arms round his neck and kisses his mouth and his eyes. Admittedly Tristan does not respond, which is hardly surprising seeing that he is not yet thirteen years old! More significant is our hero's relationship in Cornwall with the newly married wife of the knight Segurades.

During his first stay in Ireland Tristan had fallen in love with
Iseut, but on his return to Cornwall he was so struck with this
lady's beauty 'that he no longer thought of Iseut the Blonde. He
put Iseut out of his mind and forgot all about her on account of
this lady' (see below, p. 56). It was Segurades's wife who initiated
him into the pleasures of physical love, though his nocturnal
delight was all too soon cut short by the unexpected appearance
of Segurades. Our hero does not cut a very noble figure here as
he hastily dresses and hurries away, all the more so when we see
him severely wounded by the outraged husband who had followed him. The same comment could be made about the manner
in which Tristan falls in love. With him it is not a spontaneous
reaction springing from genuine and praiseworthy feelings, but
rather a somewhat questionable sentiment inspired by rivalry and
pride: 'Tristan had often looked at Iseut and she pleased him very
much, but not in a way which made him fall in love with her.
However, when he saw that Palamedes was so infatuated with
Iseut that he said he would die if he did not have her, Tristan for
his part said that Palamedes would certainly never have her if he
could help it' (see below, p. 46). The situation is very similar in
the case of Segurades's wife, for King Mark had conceived a great
passion for this lady and would have done anything to possess
her, but this in no way stopped our hero from making advances
to her; quite the contrary! Tristan's behaviour here may appear
unworthy, but by no means devoid of psychological truth.

Iseut's feelings are also described very realistically. There can
be no doubt that she loves Tristan with depth and total commit-
ment. And yet one notices in her a certain unwillingness to
sacrifice everything for her love. She wants Tristan unremittingly
and she is well aware of the dangers of this relationship; but she
also enjoys her social position and the pleasures of court life, and
she has no wish to forego either. Twice Tristan asks her to go
away with him, warning her that if King Mark found out he
would have them both killed. Twice Iseut refuses:

We've carried on our relationship as wisely as we could in such a way
that no one has noticed it, and, God willing, we could go on doing so
for a long time. But if we were now to go off as you've suggested, our
guilty love would be known by everyone. . . . In my opinion it would
therefore be better for us to . . . continue to live as pleasurable a life as

we've done up till now. And if it ever came about that people began to talk and we could no longer live this life in King Mark's court, then there would still be time enough for us to make other plans (see below, p. 124).

As Queen of Cornwall she has perhaps more to lose than Tristan. Be that as it may, soon after that the lovers are caught red-handed and have to escape to the forest. And although Tristan offers her a life of love and comfort in a beautiful and secluded house in the woods, Iseut still regrets that they 'would see no ladies and no knights, no people and no entertainments' (see below, p. 165). All this is no doubt far removed from the primitive *Tristan* legend, but no less true to life for that.

The Lays

Another interesting feature of the *Prose Tristan* is the inclusion in the prose text of some twenty poetic compositions (not including the riddles one finds in the opening section on Tristan's ancestry). Many of these are referred to as 'lays' (see third note to p. 191) and are sung to the accompaniment of a harp by one of the characters in the story or by a harpist. The most complete musical source is a manuscript in the Vienna National Library (MS 2542) which contains seventeen of these lays with musical notation. A few poems are introduced as 'letters' and are handed to the person in order to be read without being sung. It would seem that the intercalation of these lyrical pieces was an afterthought, for although Tristan can be seen playing the harp already on his initial journey to Ireland, the first lay does not occur until page 229 of this translation, and thereafter they become more and more frequent. The inclusion of long musical compositions in a prose romance was not common at this time (nothing of the sort can be found in the *Prose Lancelot*), though the practice becomes more popular in later works.

The form of these lays is varied. All are written in lines of eight syllables, but some are arranged as monorhyming quatrains, while others are non-strophic and consist of a single extended stanza written usually in octosyllabic rhyming couplets. They also vary in length: the shortest comprises nine lines, the longest thirty-four stanzas.

Love is the subject-matter of the vast majority of the lays, and many of them tell of love's torments leading to death. If the themes dealt with may seem somewhat banal and add nothing new to what we have already been told in the prose narrative, the repetition in poetic form does give us a heightened awareness of the characters' intentions, feelings and thoughts. In this respect the technique is quite a good idea, though its execution leaves much to be desired. In spite of a certain care in the choice of the rhymes, one has the impression that these compositions were the work of an author who wanted to try his hand at writing poetry rather than that of a true poet. Amongst the more interesting of these poems are the two 'Mortal Lays' of Tristan and Iseut, and the interchange between Iseut and Kahedin. As these are also the first four poems to occur, they have been included in full in this book, rendered into English octosyllabic rhyming couplets.

Tristan composes his 'Mortal Lay' when he laments, distraught, in the forest thinking that Iseut had abandoned him (see below, pp. 229 *et seq.*). He blames in turn Iseut and Amor, the god of love, describes his physical and mental torments, and announces his imminent death. The reiteration of Tristan's suffering in lyrical form creates an impression of crescendo which precedes the hero's madness. Iseut's lay (see below, pp. 258 *et seq.*), although it is not given a name, is also a kind of mortal lay, for after having heard the false news of Tristan's death, she does not wish to survive him. And yet her song of death is very different. Tristan, believing himself to have been betrayed by Iseut, holds her responsible for his fate. Iseut's intention to commit suicide is her own free choice, since she sees it as a means of joining her beloved. Successively she recalls Tristan's exploits, the life they led together in the Forest of Morroiz and their past happiness. Without him she sees no meaning in life and decides to kill herself with his sword. Iseut's lay has a much clearer and more coherent plan than Tristan's, and this corresponds to her character in the *Prose Tristan*.

The interchange between Kahedin and Iseut is very much shorter, twenty-eight and thirty-two lines respectively. Kahedin, having previously written Iseut a letter where he unsuccessfully asks for her love, returns to Brittany in the throes of despair. Here he makes one final plea, and composes a lay in which he asks Amor to intercede in his favour (see below, p. 276). He sends a harpist to Cornwall and instructs him to sing these verses to her.

Iseut's reply (see below, p. 279), which she sends back with the same harpist, is the more notable of the two pieces, giving us a further insight into her character and her attitude to life. Her tone is most unsympathetic, and she makes it quite clear to Kahedin that she has no room for anyone who persists along a path which leads nowhere: it is nothing but an act of folly.

> If he should die, none should regret
> His death; he chose it on his own.
> For such a man one should not moan.

Although Iseut no doubt intends in this way to bring Kahedin to his senses once and for all, these verses betray an almost cruel streak in her, which is of course also apparent when she sends Brangain to her death (see below, p. 97).

Form and Expression

What further enhances the reader's pleasure is the diversity of tone and of form which one finds in this work. We have mentioned the numerous lyrical lays interspersed in the prose narrative; equally unusual is the presence of a number of personal letters, most of them written by the female characters, all dealing with love, and all in varying degrees rhetorical in style. This is particularly true of what one might call the 'Arthurian correspondence', namely Iseut's letter complaining to Queen Guinevere about Tristan's marriage and asking her advice, followed by Guinevere's reply (see below, pp. 184–5 and 188–90); and, as a kind of sequel, an interchange between Tristan and Lancelot.[1] This correspondence of course links the *Tristan* story with the *Prose Lancelot*; no such personal letters however are to be found in that romance.

Other examples of the author's predilection for rhetoric are the long love laments of the hero and heroine and various other characters scattered throughout the romance, such as the Cornish people's expression of grief at the arrival of the Morholt (see below, p. 30), Tristan's eloquent declaration of love (see below, p. 165), as well as his long farewell speech as he lies on his

---

[1] These two excessively long letters, where the author seems to have been carried away by his epistolary enthusiasm, are included in the story of the *Vallet a la Cote Mautailliee*, in which they really have no place; see fourth note to p. 191.

deathbed (see below, pp. 317 *et seq.*). Side by side with these flowery passages, there are many examples of skilful and natural dialogue. The verbal exchanges are often quite animated, especially when two characters are at loggerheads, as for example King Meliadus and his second wife whom he suspects of trying to poison him (see below, pp. 14–15). The short, spirited expostulations, so full of irony and venom, that we find in the conversations between Mark and Iseut, are very evocative and true to life (see particularly, pp. 131, 139–40, and 247). Equally sarcastic is the Morholt's reply when he hears that the young Tristan is to fight a duel against him: 'Indeed!' said the Morholt, 'I think he'll regret this undertaking. Today he was made a new knight, and tomorrow he'll be made to meet a new death!' (see below, p. 35).

Irony is closely associated with humour, and if, as we would expect, the tone of this tragic tale is often solemn and serious, at other times the author's sense of the ridiculous effectively lightens the tension. He is well aware that excessive emotion can lead to comic situations, as when the love-sick Belide throws herself frantically round the twelve-year-old Tristan's neck; she holds on to him in spite of his struggles as he tries desperately to extricate himself from the embrace of the princess, who shrieks so loudly that the whole palace is alerted (see below, pp. 23 *et seq.*). Another occasion is the scene where Tristan boldly rushes into the midst of twenty knights who are waiting for him outside the room where he had been sleeping with Iseut. He strikes one, splitting his head down to his teeth. 'Alas, I'm done for!' cried the knight as he fell. 'When the others heard these words, they were so dismayed that they thought they were all done for, and many of them even dropped their swords, they were so frightened.' Meanwhile our hero jumps out of the window and escapes (see below, p. 146).

At other times the humour springs from the author's mockery of convention. One thinks particularly of his portrayal of the venerable institution of marriage in the episode where King Mark has received the gift of a drinking horn which has the magic power of revealing adultery. From amongst a hundred ladies gathered in the King's hall, only four could drink from the horn without spilling the contents all over themselves: only four were faithful wives! (See below, pp. 138 *et seq.*). Equally ridiculous is the picture of the courtly lover Palamedes sitting in front of the tower where Iseut was sheltering, absorbed in his thoughts of love for her. Tristan rides up challenging him to a duel. So loud is his call to battle that all the people inside the tower hear it and rush to the windows and battlements to watch. But Palamedes himself has heard nothing, and sits in their midst quite unawares! (See below, p. 121).

Dramatic irony is also in evidence in our text. If only the numerous messengers who were combing the forest for Tristan could have found him and explained the truth to him, the misunderstanding between the two lovers would have been resolved. Alas, they never succeed, not even Fergus who had promised to return to the spot where Tristan was sitting that very night with Iseut's message; but then he reveals our hero's whereabouts to a maiden who so irritates Tristan that he rushes off blindly to escape her and is lost in the forest (see below, pp. 221 *et seq.*).

All in all the prose romance presents us with a very varied and original version of the *Tristan* legend. The author has not hesitated to introduce quite bold changes when the traditional story struck him as unsatisfactory. These are for the most part in accordance with the trend of the early thirteenth century which was towards greater realism. Thus he rejects most of the elements of Celtic myth and magic, so popular in the second half of the twelfth century. On the other hand, he adds a supernatural touch by the inclusion of the prophet Merlin, clearly the influence of the *Prose Lancelot*, which accounts also, of course, for the participation of so many knights of the Round Table. He has sacrificed much of the complexity, mystery and poetry of the primitive legend, and substituted for it a more rational approach to life and to people. The three main protagonists—Mark, Tristan, Iseut— emerge from the story with a different character, but though different, they are on the whole true to life. There is no doubt that the author has reworked his material in an imaginative way, and that much careful planning, logical thought and creative activity have gone into his interpretation of the *Tristan* story.

In conclusion, it is worth stressing that the *Prose Tristan* enjoyed a tremendous popularity and was one of the most widely read works in medieval France. It was indeed in the prose version rather than in poetic form that the *Tristan* legend was known in the Middle Ages. The scarcity of the surviving manuscripts of the Old French *Tristan* poems suggests that after the twelfth century there was little demand for them to be copied. This may have been due to a reaction of the public against the inherently anti-social and immoral nature of the lovers' passion, a reaction which was perhaps set in motion by Chrétien de Troyes in his romance *Cligés*, often described as an 'anti-Tristan'. As we have seen, in the *Prose Tristan* this passion is very much toned down, and Iseut does not cease to stress the importance of maintaining their position at court and their place in society. In later parts, when Tristan becomes a Knight of the Round Table, her love is seen to inspire him to great deeds rather than to destroy him.

Whatever the reason for its success, the *Prose Tristan* had a considerable influence on European culture, even after the Middle Ages. Not only have we discovered over eighty manuscripts and fragments of the romance, but eight early printed editions were undertaken in France between 1489 and 1533, showing that its popularity did not diminish in the Renaissance. The work was also translated into various other languages. In 1485 Caxton printed Sir Thomas Malory's *Morte d'Arthur*, Books VIII to XII of which are an adaptation of the *Prose Tristan*. Our romance is the main source of two Italian prose compilations, *Tavola Ritonda o l'istoria di Tristano*, dating from the beginning of the fourteenth century, and *Il Tristano Riccardiano*, thought to be slightly earlier. We also have a Spanish prose compilation, *Don Tristán de Leonois*, composed in the fifteenth century. There is even a Serbo-Russian derivative of the *Prose Tristan*, difficult to date, which has survived in a Russian manuscript of the late sixteenth century. The success of our romance continued until the publication in 1835 of the *Tristan* poems by Francisque Michel, an event which for quite a while switched the attention of European scholars and readers away from the prose romance to the poetic versions of the story. I hope that the present translation will help to redress the balance, and convince an even wider public of the interest of the *Prose Tristan*.

SELECT BIBLIOGRAPHY

Editions and Translations

BEROUL

Text: *The Romance of Tristran by Beroul: A Poem of the Twelfth Century* ed. A. Ewert (Oxford: Blackwell, 1939, repr. 1977).

Translation: A. Fedrick, *The Romance of Tristan by Beroul and the Tale of Tristan's Madness* (Penguin Classics, 1970).

Norris J. Lacy, *The Romance of Tristan*, ed. and trans. (New York: Garland, 1989).

Stewart Gregory, *The Romance of Tristan by Beroul*, ed. and trans. (Amsterdam, 1992).

EILHART

Text: Eilhart von Oberg, *Tristrant*, ed. D. Buschinger (Göppingen, 1976).

Translation: This edition includes a translation into modern French; there is no English translation.

FOLIE DE BERNE

Text: *La Folie Tristan de Berne*, ed. E. Hoepffner (Paris, 1934; 2nd edn. revised and corrected, Paris, 1949).

Translation: A. Fedrick, *The Tale of Tristan's Madness*, second part of trans. of Beroul (see above).

FOLIE D'OXFORD

Text: *La Folie Tristan d'Oxford*, ed. E. Hoepffner (Paris, 1938; 2nd ed. revised and corrected, Paris, 1963).

Translation: No English translation; translated into modern French by J. C. Payen, *Tristan et Yseut* (Paris, 1974), 265–97.

GOTTFRIED VON STRASSBURG

Text: *Tristan und Isold*, ed. F. Ranke (Berlin, 1961).

Translation: A. T. Hatto, *Gottfried von Strassburg 'Tristan'* (Penguin Classics, 1960; repr. with revisions, 1967). Trans. into English prose.

Prose Tristan

Text: *Le Roman de Tristan en prose*, critical edn. by Renée L.
               Curtis, vol. i (Munich, 1963), vol. ii (Leyden, 1976), vol. iii
               (Cambridge, 1985); vols. i and ii reissued Cambridge, 1985.

Translation: None, apart from the present work.

Sir Tristrem

Text: 'Sir Tristrem', critical edn. by R. W. Kelton (Ph.D. thesis,
               Ohio State Univ., 1974).

              Sir Tristrem, ed. G. P. McNeill (Edinburgh, 1886; repr.
              New York: Johnson Reprint Corp., 1966).

Thomas

Text: Thomas, *Les Fragments du Roman de Tristan, poème du XII*
              siècle, ed. B. H. Wind (Textes Littéraires Français, 1960).

Translation: A translation into English prose appears at the end of A. T.
              Hatto's translation of Gottfried (see above).

              Stewart Gregory, *Tristan*, ed. and trans. (New York: Gar-
              land, 1991).

Tristan als Mönch

Text: *Tristan als Mönch*, ed. B. C. Bushey (Göppingen, 1974).
Translation: None.

Tristrams Saga

Text: *Tristrams Saga og Ísoddar*, ed. B. Vilhjálmsson (Reykjavík,
              1949).

Translation: P. Schach, *The Saga of Tristram and Isönd* (Lincoln: Univ.
              of Nebraska Press, 1973).

Books

There have been very few full-scale books written about the *Prose Tristan*, and none in English. For a list of the many articles written on this work, see my critical edition.

BAUMGARTNER, E., *Le 'Tristan en prose': Essai d'interprétation d'un roman médiéval* (Geneva, 1975).

—— *La harpe et l'epee: Tradition et renouvellement dans le Tristan en prose* (Paris, 1990).

CURTIS, R. L., *Tristan Studies* (Munich, 1969).

FOTITCH, T., and STEINER, R., *Les Lais du Roman de Tristan en prose* (Munich, 1974).

LÖSETH, E., *Le Roman en prose de Tristan: Analyse critique d'après les manuscrits de Paris* (Paris, 1890; repr. New York: Burt Franklin, 1970).

THE ROMANCE OF
TRISTAN

PROLOGUE

I HAVE read and re-read the great Latin Book many a time, the very one which clearly tells the story of the Holy Grail, and I am amazed that no worthy man has undertaken to translate it from Latin into French, for it would be something that rich and poor alike would enjoy to hear; provided of course they wished to listen and harken to the pleasant story of the memorable adventures which actually took place in Great Britain during the reign of King Arthur and before, as the story of the Holy Grail relates and testifies.

But seeing that no one has dared to undertake this task, because it would be a too arduous and grievous thing to embark upon— for the tale is extremely long and full of marvels—I, Luce, knight and lord of Gat Castle near Salisbury, being a knight of amorous and joyful disposition,* have taken it upon myself to translate* a part of this story; not that my French is altogether fluent, since I was born in England, and my language and vocabulary are therefore closer to English than to French. But my wish and my intention is to translate the story into French to the best of my ability, in such a way as to reveal the whole truth without indulging in any falsehood; and I shall make known what the Latin Book tells about the story of Tristan, who was the most sovereign knight ever to have lived in the kingdom of Great Britain either before or after King Arthur, except only for the great knight Lancelot of the Lake. And the Latin text of the Grail story clearly narrates that at the time of King Arthur there were only three brave knights who deserve to be honoured for their chivalry: Galahad, Lancelot, and Tristan; it is these three that the Book mentions most of all, and praises and extols. And because I know full well that it was the truth, I wish to begin my romance at this point and tell the story of Sir Tristan as follows.

I

TRISTAN'S BIRTH

THE kings of Cornwall succeeded each other in direct line until a king came to the throne who was called Felix. He was a cunning and evil man, who held noblemen in such contempt that in the end he was condemned in the principal church of Norholt.*

This king named Felix had two sons and four daughters. One of the sons was baptized Mark because he was born on Tuesday* and in the month of March. In the course of time King Felix died and so did his wife, but as he lay on his death-bed he had his son Mark crowned King of Cornwall. The Cornish people were very pleased to have him as their lord.

Soon after his coronation, King Mark successfully negotiated the marriage of the eldest of his sisters, Elyabel, with Meliadus, King of Leonois,* a brave knight and a righteous and just man. This Elyabel was extraordinarily beautiful, and King Meliadus loved her more than he loved himself or anyone else. Both were very unhappy that God did not bless them with the birth of an heir. What more shall I tell you? They were married for a long time before the Queen at last became pregnant; and when the people of Leonois heard of it, they were delighted.

One day King Meliadus went hunting with a large company of men. In the course of the hunt he encountered a young lady* from that region, very beautiful, and so much in love with him that she could feel no love for any other man. The lady was riding through the forest searching for King Meliadus here and there, for she was eager to talk to him; and while she was looking she saw that the King had dismounted in front of a fountain because of a knight who was lying there dead. Seeing him, she rode over in that direction, and when she had come up to him, she wished him good day, and he returned her greeting. Then she spoke to him as follows:

'King,' she said, 'I've heard much good about you. If I believed that you were as valiant as people say, I would this very night show you one of the most remarkable adventures you have ever seen, provided you had the courage to follow me.'

The King, who was very daring and very keen to brave remarkable adventures whatever might befall him, replied:

'I'd like to see it very much.'

'And I'll take you there,' she said.

The King promptly mounted his horse.

'Let's go! I'll follow you.'

The young lady set off, turning aside from the main road and the highway. After she had gone some distance and ridden like this until nightfall, it was not long before they came to a tower which was high up on a rock. The young lady made straight for the tower, followed by the King, and there they dismounted. The inhabitants welcomed them with great joy, for the tower belonged to the lady. She asked the King to take off his sword, and he did so. Then she led him to one of her rooms, which was beautiful and elegant and had been devised with great skill. As soon as he was inside, his heart and his will changed so completely that he could remember no one in the world except the lady he saw in front of him. And you should know that he was so bewitched that he did not recall his wife nor his land nor anything on earth apart from the one who was holding him captive.

In this way, just as I am describing it to you, the King remained with the lady, so totally in her power that he had forgotten himself and everyone else. When his men saw that he was not coming back, they rode everywhere looking for him, until they were all quite exhausted; but no amount of riding resulted in their hearing or discovering any news about him. They returned to their lodgings so sorrowful and unhappy that they did not know what to do about the matter, nor what to believe, except that some of them thought that the King had been treacherously murdered.

Queen Elyabel loved her husband more than any lady could love her lord; and when she saw that he was delaying so long, and that his men had lost him in the woods and could not find out anything about him, she said to one of her maidens that she would look for him herself, and go so secretly that none of her household would know, if she could help it. She did what she said, for she set out next morning, taking a young girl with her. Then she made her way into the forest and began to search for him here and there; and while she was thus seeking him, she

happened to encounter the prophet Merlin who was coming
down from a rock and walking through the woods all alone.
Seeing the Queen, he went up to her and greeted her. The
Queen, who took him to be a forester, readily returned his
greeting, and asked him with much grief and sorrow:

'Tell me, forester, can you give me some information or news
about my lord, King Meliadus, who is lost in this forest, we don't
know by what misadventure.'

'My lady,' replied Merlin, 'the things one has lost, one never
recovers thereafter. But this one will yet be recovered.'

'Ah! dear friend,' exclaimed the Queen, 'please tell me if you
know any news about him, and if he is alive.'

'My lady,' he said, 'I can tell you truly that he is fit and well,
and more comfortable than some people would like. But one
thing I will reveal to you: you'll never see him again.'

When he had spoken these words, he turned away so swiftly
that the Queen did not know what had become of him. And she
immediately began to lament on hearing the news which Merlin
had told her, and her distress became so great and so intense that
she was unable to ride any further, but dismounted in between
two trees, in a very wild and strange place. She wept and wailed
and wrung her hands and lamented and cursed the hour she was
born, since she had been unfortunate enough to lose her husband
in this way. The Queen was so beside herself with grief and
anguish that it brought on her labour; and her pregnancy was
already far advanced, so that she was quite near her term.

When the pains started, she told her maiden, who wept for
pity, and said:

'What! my lady, couldn't you ride as far as the city?'

'No, I can't,' said the Queen. 'This is where I have to wait for
the hour of my delivery. May it please Our Lord to send it to me
soon!'

Then she began to cry out aloud, and to call on God and the
Virgin Mary. She was in such agony and torment that she
thought she was going to die. When the young girl saw the extent
of her suffering and could do nothing to help her, she was so
upset that she almost died herself.

All that day and the whole of the night the Queen was in
labour. At dawn next morning she gave birth to a son, as it

pleased Our Lord. Her labour had been so difficult that she felt sure she was going to die. She said to the maiden who was holding her baby:

'Show me my child.'

The girl did as she was asked. The Queen took him in her arms and saw that he was the most beautiful being on earth, given his age.

'My son,' said the Queen, 'I've longed to see you. Now, by the grace of God, I see that you are the most beautiful baby which to my knowledge any woman ever bore. But your beauty will not bring me much joy, for the labour pains I've suffered will cause my death. I was sad when I came here and sad when I gave birth, and the first happiness I felt since I gave birth has turned into sadness and sorrow. And since you came into this world in sadness, you shall be called after your first adventure; and because of my sadness and the sadness of your birth you shall bear the name of Tristan.* God grant that you may spend your life in greater joy and greater good fortune than you had at your birth!'

When she had spoken these words, she kissed her baby; and instantly her soul left her body, and she died in such torment and such grief as I have described. These were the circumstances of Tristan's birth, the brave and handsome knight who was later to suffer pain and anguish for love of my lady Iseut. In such sorrow was Tristan born, whose story I shall relate to you; it is so beautiful and so pleasing that it should be heard by all noblemen in love, and by all men of high rank.

As soon as the maiden saw her lady dead, she was beside herself with grief; she wailed and shrieked at the top of her voice so that the forest resounded with it far and wide. While she was lamenting thus, two knights from Leonois happened to come that way; they were closely related to King Meliadus, and were riding through the forest looking for the King. When they found their lady dead and saw the baby lying on the ground covered with the Queen's cloak, they dismounted, and one of them said to the other:

'This lady is dead, and the King is lost; we need have no fear that he'll come back. If this baby were now to die, the kingdom would be ours by rightful inheritance, for we're closer in line than anyone else. Let's kill it, and the land will be ours!'

'Ah, have mercy, for the Lord's sake!' cried the maiden. 'Don't kill the child, but give it to me, and I promise you here and now, as I am a true Christian, that I shall take it to such a place that you will never hear of it again. And you have good reason to do this for the love of God and for pity's sake; certainly, if you killed this baby now, it would be the most treacherous and unworthy act in the world.'

The maiden pleaded so much with the knights that they agreed to let the baby live on condition that she swore then and there to take it to such a place that they would never hear of it again. They picked up the Queen, dead as she was, and carried her to the city. There they showed her to the people, saying that they had found her dead like that in the forest. The maidens, who were well aware that the Queen had been pregnant when she left and now saw her delivered of the baby, declared that she had died in childbirth.

'You must hand the baby over to us, dead or alive!'

They replied that they knew nothing about this, and had seen nothing. And the worthy men of the land said:

'My lords, you must hand over the heir born to this lady.'

And the maidens added:

'Either these two knights have taken the heir, or the young girl who accompanied the Queen has got him.'

While they were talking like this, Merlin appeared amongst them, and said:

'These two knights deserve to be put to death. Detain them, and I shall reveal to you how disloyal they are, and what they've done.'

Then he began to relate how they wanted to kill the baby in order to have the land, but let it live at the young girl's entreaties. Merlin told them all the words that had been spoken, and when the two knights heard them repeated word for word, they were so astounded that they did not know what to say, except that they admitted the truth of the matter as it had taken place. They were instantly seized and put in prison; and everyone there declared that they would never be freed until the baby was recovered fit and well.

Merlin then said to the barons of Leonois:

'I'll tell you how you can have your lord back. You'll go into that forest straight to the Rock of the Cornishwoman. There you'll find King Meliadus so bewitched that he doesn't remember you or anyone else: he's forgotten you and forsaken you all. This is due to the young lady who owns the place, who loves him so greatly that she loves no one else as much. Seize her and force her to break the spell, so that the King is restored to his rightful mind. Then put her to death, for otherwise she'll bewitch him all over again, just as she has done now.'

The people there asked Merlin:

'Sir, who are you who've given us all this information?'

'I'm a stranger,' he replied. 'Never mind about me, but do as I tell you, for your own sake, not for mine.'

And they said they would do so. They were none the less very eager to know who he was. But that was impossible, since he wanted to conceal his identity from them.

When the barons had set out towards the tower which Merlin had told them about with a large company of men both armed and unarmed, Merlin said to those who had remained behind:

'Rejoice, for your lord will be back here tomorrow morning.'

Then Merlin called a youth who was staying there, a very intelligent and worthy young man; he was born in the Kingdom of Gaul and was of noble birth, but having caused the death of one of his brothers, he had taken flight across the sea for fear of being killed. He was such a handsome and worthy young man, and so noble in many ways that he was loved by all who knew him except by those who were filled with envy; and he was called Gorvenal. Merlin, who knew him better than anyone else there, said to him when he had called him:

'Friend,' he said, 'if I thought you would look after the heir to the throne of Leonois loyally—the very one whom the two imprisoned knights are being asked to hand back—in such a way that no harm would come to him in his youth through negligence on your part, I would entrust him to you. And let me tell you that if you look after him loyally, it will be to your advantage; and the time will yet come when for nothing in the world would you not have wanted to look after him and be his tutor,* for such will be his grace on earth that you'll be amazed at his beauty and his worth.'

Hearing these words, Gorvenal replied:

'I don't know who you are, but whoever you may be, if you were to entrust the child to me, I'd protect him from all his enemies to the best of my ability, and he need fear no ill from which I could shield him.'

'In that case I'll entrust him to you,' said Merlin. 'Make sure you look after him loyally.'

Merlin now takes Gorvenal to the Fountain of Infertility—so-called because any woman drinking of it would become sterile—and shows him an inscription on a marble stone prophesying the fame and glory of three knights: Galahad, Lancelot, and Tristan. Then they go to find the young girl who has the baby, and Merlin orders her to take it back to the city of Albine, to which King Meliadus had already returned. Merlin reveals his identity to the King, and predicts a glorious future for his son; he asks him to entrust the child to Gorvenal. The maiden tells King Meliadus that she has had the baby christened, and that he has been given the name of Tristan, as his mother had requested. The sight of his son helps to alleviate the grief the King feels at his wife's death. He engages a wet-nurse to suckle the child and nurture him as required.

The very day of Tristan's birth, messengers from Ireland arrive in Cornwall to ask for their tribute.* Mark gives it to them in the most cowardly fashion, despite the bitter condemnation of his young brother Pernehan, whom, to avenge himself, he kills a week later in front of the Fountain of the Lion while they are out hunting. [§§ 222–43 of vol. i]

II

TRISTAN'S CHILDHOOD

THE story now relates that King Meliadus did not remarry for a long while after the death of Queen Elyabel. When he felt the urge to take a wife, he married the daughter of King Hoel of Brittany. She was extremely beautiful, but also very malicious, pleasure-seeking and fickle, more than was seemly. She was unfaithful to her husband in the very first year of her marriage.

Tristan was by now already seven years old, and so comely that every lady who saw him declared him to be the fairest creature on earth. Why should I describe his looks to you at great length? In a nutshell: he was in every way so beautiful that there was no young boy in the whole world at this time who could match his beauty, except Lancelot of the Lake. These two, beyond a doubt, surpassed all others in beauty; and they were so chivalrous that all worthy men should hear about their acts of prowess.

When Tristan's stepmother saw him grow up into such a fine young boy, loved by all, she did not know what to say or do, because she herself had a child by her husband which was now one year old, and she was sure Tristan would be so brave that he would never let his brother rule, but would disinherit him. For this reason she would have liked nothing better than to find a way to cause Tristan's death, if ever she had the opportunity; though she did not see how she could achieve this except by using poison. She thought no further, but decided to poison him, for that was something which no one would be likely to notice. While she was plotting this, certain that she would succeed—and she had already prepared the poison in a silver vessel and placed it at the head of a bed, and was waiting only for Tristan to go into this room—it so happened that a maiden went in there carrying the little prince in her arms. It was very hot, and the baby started crying with thirst. None of the nurses was there at the time; they were asleep in the bedrooms.

When the maiden saw that the baby was fretting so because he was hot and thirsty, she began to walk round in the hope of finding some water to give him. And as she was searching here and there, she chanced upon the silver vessel which contained the poison; and I can tell you that it was so well prepared and so clear that you would have taken it for fresh water, pure and cold. The young girl took some and gave it to the baby to drink; and as soon as he had drunk it, he fainted, writhing in her arms, and instantly his soul left his body.

The girl, seeing this, cried out at the top of her voice: 'Help! help! woe is me!' Everyone came running up to find out what had happened. As soon as they caught sight of the dead baby, the clamour and uproar which broke out was such that even a thunderbolt from heaven would have gone unnoticed. They seized the maiden and said she would be put to death; she deserved no better seeing that she had in this way killed a tiny creature which should inspire tenderness in everyone.

While this commotion and outcry was going on as I have described, the Queen appeared in their midst. When she saw her baby dead, the being in the world that she loved the most, she fell backwards in a swoon. They lifted her up, and when she came round, she addressed the young girl:

'Maiden,' she said, 'what harm have I done you that you've killed my baby?'

The girl, who did not know how else to justify herself, replied:

'My lady, it wasn't I who killed him, but whoever put the poison here. It was done with evil intent, and it's my misfortune that I'm being blamed for it. Now do what you will with me!'

The maiden was seized and brought before the King, who was very distressed by this incident which had already been related to him. And when she had come before him, and he had enquired how it had all come about, he said to her:

'You are not responsible for this death, but the person who prepared the poison. And I can tell you that it was prepared not so much for this baby as for someone else.'

The King had the maiden freed and said that she would not be put to death for this misadventure: she had not caused the calamity, it was another's doing. Gorvenal, who was very shrewd and perspicacious, addressed the King, saying:

'My lord, I'm sure this treachery was planned in order to kill you or Tristan, and that either a lady or a maiden committed it.

If you're wise, you'll take care of yourself, for I shall certainly take care of Tristan who is in my charge, so help me God.'

The King saw and realized that what Gorvenal had said was true, and he knew that the poison had been prepared for one or other of them. He mentioned it to a friend of his and asked him what he could do about it: he very much wanted to know who was reponsible for this act. His friend answered:

'That won't be very easy to discover. But since the plan failed and neither you nor Tristan have come to any harm, all you can do now is to be on your guard, for you may be sure that the person who is plotting the death of one or other of you is near at hand.'

The King said that he would do his best to have himself guarded, and then he fell silent, and said no more about it. However, he was more apprehensive than he was wont to be, not knowing whom he should guard against.

The Queen wept for her son who had lost his life in this way and by her own doing. She was so grief-stricken that she wished she were dead. She said to herself that now she was well and truly shamed, since she had killed her own son and had failed to do what she had planned. She was very upset and distressed about the whole matter; and when she saw Tristan coming and going in front of her and she remembered her baby, all her grief and all her anger were directed against him. It was his fault, so it seemed to her, that she had lost her child; it was his fault that she was so unhappy. But she would avenge herself, if she could, somehow or other. In this way, and for the reason I have described, the Queen of Leonois was filled with such wrath and such hatred for Tristan that she said she would rather face death and ruin than not make him die in pain. She therefore tried as hard as she could to bring about his death.

Gorvenal, who was very shrewd and quick to notice things, was so wary of the Queen that he realized she hated Tristan with all her heart, and it occurred to him that he was the one for whom she had prepared the poison. He therefore drew Tristan to one side and said to him:

'Tristan, I order you not to go near your lady more than you have to, and not to eat or drink anything that I haven't given you with my own hands. If she tries to offer you something to drink, beware of taking it. What more shall I tell you? Do everything else she bids you, but don't accept food or drink; take that only from me.'

And the boy promised him not to disobey his command in any way.

Thus Gorvenal cautioned the boy who was in his charge, and Tristan paid heed to what he said. But the Queen, who knew nothing of all this, made every effort to find an opportunity of putting Tristan to death. And I should tell you that she had the poison ready so that she could give some of it to Tristan as soon as she had the chance, provided he would drink it.

Tristan was by now eight years old, so beautiful and so sensible that he surpassed all other children. The King, his father, derived greater joy from him than from anything else, and he loved the boy more than himself or any other person.

One day the King was alone in his room except for his son Tristan. It was hot, and the King was very thirsty and asked for a drink.

'Tristan,' he said, 'go and fetch me something to quench my thirst.'

The boy went over to a window, and the first thing he found was the silver vessel filled with the poison. He did not notice anything wrong, but poured some into a cup, and gave it to his father to drink. Just as the King had taken the cup, the Queen happened to come into the room; and, seeing the vessel which Tristan was holding, she cried out:

'Ah, my lord, don't drink that, or you'll be dead!'

As soon as the King heard these words, he drew back his hand, and said:

'Lady, what is it, then?'

She did not dare to say it was poison because the King would immediately accuse her of wanting to kill him.

'My lord,' she said, 'this drink is not good for you.'

'And why do you keep it here, then?' he asked.

She did not know how to answer that. This straightaway made the King think that she had planned it all to bring about his death, so he said:

'Either you drink it, or I shall kill you!'

And she answered:

'In that case you can kill me, for I have no intention of drinking it.'

'No?' he asked. 'Then I shall put you to death, but not in the way you intended to make me die.'

The King summoned his barons and told them what had happened. When the Queen heard herself accused of this misdeed and this misadventure, she was most dismayed, and said, since there was nothing else she could say:

'My lord, I didn't prepare it for you.'

'And who was it for, then?' he asked. 'I must know.'

The Queen, seeing herself in such a predicament, begged him for mercy.

'That will avail you nothing,' said the King, 'I must know.'

The Queen began to weep when she found herself so hard pressed that she was being forced to admit exactly how she had acted. And the King ran towards one of his swords which was lying on top of a bed and, drawing it from the scabbard, he made straight for the Queen, full of anger and ill-will, and said that she had come to her death if she did not reveal the truth about the matter. She was in dread and terror of dying, since she knew the King to be very strong-willed, so she did not dare to conceal the facts from him any longer, but confessed everything openly, saying that she had done it to kill Tristan.

'By my faith,' he said, 'you've acted wrongly! You deserve to die, and if all my barons agree that you should die, you'll be put to death: as God is my witness, you will not be spared from this judgment. Tristan has done nothing to you which could justify your seeking his death.'

The King then handed her over to those who were in his presence, and they put her in safe custody until such a time as she would be freed by judgment or condemned to death, for that, so it seems to me, was her predicament. And those to whom she had been entrusted took her away.

Thereupon King Meliadus sent for the wisest men in his court and told them all the facts. He made them swear on holy relics* that they would pass a rightful judgment; 'and you may be sure that if you fail to pass a rightful judgment I shall have you all slain.' They took counsel together, and then replied briefly, saying that she deserved to die. And the King replied that therefore she would die: in no way would she be spared from the judgment they had made. When the ladies there heard that the sentence had been passed and that the Queen could not escape from death, they were exceedingly distressed and began to lament bitterly amongst themselves.

Tristan was in the palace at the time, and seeing so many people grieving, he asked what it was all about; and they told him. As soon as he heard that the Queen was to die on account of this, he said no more to any of them, but went straight to the King, knelt down and asked his father to grant him a favour.* It never occurred to the King that he would ask what he did, for in that case he would certainly not have granted it, and so he said:

'Ask, my son, and you shall have it; you are the being I love most in the world, and I wouldn't refuse you anything. I would put my own life at risk to save yours, if I could do so.'

Then Tristan addressed his father, not at all like a timid child, and said:

'My lord, many thanks for the favour you've granted me. And do you know what it is? It's that you no longer feel any ill-will towards my lady the Queen because of what you see has happened, and that she'll be acquitted of the judgment which you and your councillors have made against her.'

The King was quite astounded when he heard these words; he did not think that the child had said this of his own accord, but rather that he had been advised to do so. Also he had no wish whatever to see the Queen escape punishment for this deed, because there was nothing in the world that King Meliadus hated as much as murder and treachery. Then he spoke and said:

'I'll grant you the favour you requested, since I promised it to you. But I want you to tell me who advised you to ask this.'

And the boy replied:

'My lord, I assure you that I had no counsel other than what I felt to be right and reasonable, which led me to believe that I shouldn't let my lady die when I could save her.'

The King replied:

'My son, your words show loyalty, and yet she acted disloyally and treacherously by attempting to murder you. She has been more fortunate than she deserved.'

In this way Tristan's stepmother was saved from death, and by Tristan himself whom she had tried her hardest to kill. And you should know that this kind and noble deed, inspired by Tristan's reason and good sense, was praised by all the wise men of Leonois. And they all said that he could not fail to be a worthy man, if God granted him a long life. The Queen continued to live in harmony and peace with her lord, but I can tell you that never thereafter did he love her as much as he had done before, nor did he trust her.

Not long after this incident the King went hunting in a wood, and he had with him a large company of knights and noble men. Tristan was there and Gorvenal, who was loath to leave him at any time. Although Tristan was still very young, Gorvenal had taken him so that he would get accustomed to the woods and to hunting; and he had made him wear full hunting dress.

While the King was riding along with his men, two fully armed knights appeared in their midst. Seeing the company, they asked which one was King Meliadus, and he was pointed out to them.

'And where is Tristan, his son?' they enquired.

Gorvenal, always on his guard, leapt forward and said:

'He isn't here; we left him in the city. What do you want of him?'

They did not answer, but went up to the King, saying:

'King Meliadus, we feel great enmity towards you. You haven't deserved it, but you will, or a man from your lineage, for without fail we shall be shamed and dishonoured either by you or by someone from your lineage, and all Cornwall will tremble with fear. And since this is certain to happen unless we can prevent it, we don't know whom to hold responsible except you, and we shall avenge ourselves as best we can, namely on you.'

Thereupon they put their hands on their swords and fell upon the King and killed him before any of his men could come to his aid; but they both paid for it with their life. They were vassals of the Count of Norholt and belonged to the most powerful family in Cornwall. They had been told by a Cornish prophetess that the heirs of Norholt would be killed by King Meliadus or by a man from his lineage, and had come to Leonois as a result, more on the advice of King Mark than for any other reason, because King Mark feared no one else as much as Tristan. But it happened

just as the prophetess had predicted, for Tristan later slew the
Count of Norholt with his own hand and destroyed all that
lineage, and then had the city razed to the ground so that not a
stone remained standing.* However, the story now stops talking
about this matter, and returns to the death of King Meliadus.

The barons of Leonois were so distressed to see their lord dead
that they did not know what to say. When they did speak, they
said that no knight had ever been as badly protected as he had
been, and they all affirmed that it was their heedlessness and their
stupidity which had led to his death. The grief and the outcry
began on all sides. Tristan wept, and so did Gorvenal, and all
those who were there. For a long while they lamented; then they
cut down some trees to make a bier suitable for the horses to
carry* and placed the King's body on it, and in this way brought
him back to the city which was nearby. The people of Leonois
grieved and wept bitterly for their lord; and when they had
lamented for a sufficient length of time, they buried the body
with great honour as befitted the burial of a king at that time.

King Mark, who was still in Cornwall, was all alone in his palace
one day, lost in thought. At that moment a dwarf passed in front
of him who was a soothsayer; he had lived in Great Britain where
Merlin had taught him a great deal about these things. The fact
that he was a dwarf did not stop him from being of noble birth,
for he was King Hoel's son; but because he was a dwarf and so
small, the King had banished him from his court, since he was
ashamed to have him in his company. King Mark, seeing that he
was wise, resourceful and trustworthy had retained him in his
service. This dwarf knew so much about the occult and about
things to come that no one apart from Merlin understood more
about it. Seeing King Mark so deep in thought, he stopped and
said, as though in anger:

'Think, King Mark; think carefully! Tristan, your nephew, the
fair, the brave, the paragon of all children, sends you word that
he will one day give you cause to think, in sadness and in sorrow.
As a result of his deeds you will yet call yourself a miserable and
wretched king.'

When King Mark heard these words, he stopped thinking and
said:

'He'll never do me the great harm you describe, for I shall forestall him. I'd have him killed rather than live in fear of his disloyalty.'

'That would be a great pity because his chivalry will be a source of inspiration to the whole world.'

'Truly?' asked the King. 'Will he be such a valiant knight?'

'Yes, indeed,' replied the dwarf.

'In that case,' said the King, 'I won't do anything which will give him cause to be afraid of me. But if you hadn't told me this, it would have gone ill with him before long.'

That was where the matter was left at that point.

Gorvenal, who had remained all this while in Leonois, was so often in the Queen's company that he realized she was intent on bringing about Tristan's death because she thought she would inherit the country if he were to die. He was worried and frightened that she would kill Tristan, and therefore called him one day and said:

'Dear child, your stepmother hates you so much that I don't know at what point she'll treacherously kill you by some means or other; and she would have done so already if it weren't for her fear of me. Let's act wisely and go to King Faramon's court in Gaul. There you'll learn how to serve and how to behave at court, and how a high-born and noble man should conduct himself. And when it is God's will that you receive the order of knighthood, and you have achieved so much that your great prowess will be renowned throughout the world, if you then felt like returning to the Kingdom of Leonois, you wouldn't find any man there who would be bold enough to oppose your wishes.'

Thereupon the boy replied and said:

'Master, I'm ready to go with you wherever you want. No one has ever shown me compassion or love except you,* and for that reason I wouldn't part from you for anything in the world.'

'Let's leave tomorrow morning, then,' said Gorvenal.

And Tristan instantly agreed. [§§ 244–61 of vol. i]

III

TRISTAN SERVES IN GAUL

THAT night Gorvenal made his preparations for the journey as best he could, and took as much gold and silver as possible. Next morning a little before daybreak, they mounted their horses. What more shall I tell you? They rode on until they arrived in France,* without anyone to accompany them. As they came near to where King Faramon resided, Gorvenal forbade Tristan to divulge where he came from, who was his father or anything about his lineage; if someone asked him where he was from, he must answer that he was a foreign youth.

'Dear master,' said Tristan, 'that's good advice. You may be sure that I won't disobey your instructions.'

When they had reached King Faramon's court and the King saw the tutor and the child, he made them very welcome and invited them to stay, saying that it would give him great pleasure.

Thus Tristan remained at the court of King Faramon of Gaul. He grew up into such a fine youth that everyone was amazed. He was so good at playing chess and backgammon that nobody was able to teach him a single thing. Within a very short while his skill at fencing was such that he could not be beaten by anyone. He excelled at riding, and indeed whatever he undertook he did so well that there was no youth to equal him. At the age of twelve he was so brave and so good-looking and so successful at everything he did that all who saw him were full of admiration. There was not a lady nor a damsel who would not have been overjoyed if Tristan had granted her his love. He served King Faramon so satisfactorily in every way that the King preferred Tristan's service to anyone else's who was around him, and he loved and esteemed Tristan more than all the other young boys at his court. No one there had the slightest idea who he was; they knew him by sight but nobody except for Gorvenal had any knowledge of his lineage.

King Faramon had a very beautiful daughter; she was an extremely intelligent, charming and attractive young girl, praised for her beauty above all the other maidens in Gaul. She watched

Tristan coming and going, and as a result fell so deeply in love with him that she did not know how to deal with the situation; she loved Tristan with all her heart, more than she had ever loved anyone, even herself. She did not know what to say or do about her feelings because he was still a child who had no knowledge of such things, nor would have unless he was initiated. She thought very hard, but her thoughts came to nothing that pleased her, since she did not succeed in restraining her love: she was quite unable to tear it from her heart. And if she revealed to Tristan that she felt such a great and inordinate passion for him, he would think she was mad, and would not dare to do anything about it even if he wanted to, for he would be too afraid of the King.

Thus she pondered and speculated, more unhappy than anyone else could be. When she realized that she was not able to solve the problem, she decided to open her heart to Gorvenal; and she told him unreservedly that she felt such an extraordinary passion for Tristan that she loved no other person in the world as much.

'Now see to it that I can have him,' she said. 'If you don't bring it about, I shall make sure that he will suffer for it, and I myself shall suffer for it too.'

When Gorvenal heard these words, he was so dismayed that he did not know what to do, for he saw that she ardently desired Tristan, who was still so young and innocent that harm could come of it, both to one and to the other. Even if there was nothing between them, many people would soon think there had been. He replied to the young girl as best he could, saying:

'Damsel, I'm very grateful that you have deigned to disclose your innermost feelings to me. I shall do my utmost to bring your love to fruition; I don't think Tristan will stand in the way. And if he were to refuse because he has never been in love, seeing that at his age he has not yet any knowledge of such things, none the less I think I could persuade him to agree to it.'

The young girl thanked him very much for this promise.

Gorvenal was dismayed when he left the King's daughter, as he did not really know what he could do about this matter. He greatly feared the King, and with good reason, since he knew him to be so strong-willed and resolute that if he were to

discover this affair he would be so displeased, he would shame
him as well as his daughter and Tristan.

That same day the Morholt* of Ireland arrives in Gaul with many men;
he is one of the most famous knights in the world at this time. King
Faramon loves him very much, and they have sworn allegiance to each
other. While Tristan is serving at table, the Morholt is very struck by his
noble bearing, and asks who he is; but no one can tell the Morholt
anything about him except his name. At this moment the King's fool
comes in and predicts that the Morholt will die at Tristan's hand. The
Morholt bursts out laughing, but King Faramon warns him that the fool's
predictions always come true: a year ago a young girl had arrived
carrying a sword, and the fool had told her that she would die by that
very sword. The girl too had laughed, but the same week a knight had
struck her dead with it and then killed himself. However, the Morholt is
not worried and pays no attention to this warning, though it turns out
to be the truth. Gorvenal however is uneasy in case the Morholt harms
Tristan in some way.

That evening Gorvenal said to his charge, Tristan:

'What are you going to do, Tristan? The King's daughter is so
infatuated with you that she says she'll kill herself if you don't
give in to her wishes and become her lover. Now tell me what
you want to do, for she has instructed me to ask you.'

The boy replied with great sense, saying:

'Sir, if the maiden loves me in a seemly fashion, in accordance
with her own good and her honour, I shall love her with all my
heart; but if she loves me foolishly, let her keep her folly: I shall
never be a party to her foolishness. I would be disloyal if I were
to bring shame and dishonour on her father while he shows me
such kindness in his court without even knowing who I am.'

When Gorvenal heard the boy's reply, he wondered how he
could speak so sensibly at that age, since he was not yet thirteen
years old. And so to test him further, he went on:

'What! Sir Tristan, are you refusing the love of a maiden as
beautiful as the one I mentioned to you, who could have you
slain if she wanted, or let you live if it pleased her?'

And the child answered yet again:

'Sir, she may be beautiful, but her beauty shouldn't make me
do anything, if I were wise, which the King could consider

treacherous in any way whatever. And it would be treachery, so it seems to me, if I were to agree to his shame while he treats me with such kindness. Even if I desired the maiden as foolishly as you say she desires me, and you knew about it, you should do your utmost to dissuade me.'

They said no more about it at that point. The following day the young girl came back to Gorvenal and asked him how Tristan had reacted; and he told her the whole truth without concealing a thing.

'What, sir!' she cried, 'he's refused me? Well, that was wrong of him. He'll regret it!'

With that she left Gorvenal; she felt more upset than anyone else could be, cursing the hour she was born. And when she had returned to her room, she grieved as silently as she could, determined that nobody should notice it.

One day shortly after this incident she was sitting in a room lost in thought, unable to forget her love for Tristan; nor did she really want to forget it provided she could have what she desired. The room was rather dark, and while she was sitting there thinking, Sir Tristan happened to come in, intending to pass through into a small meadow. He did not see the young girl, though she could see him clearly. As soon as he was inside, she leapt forward and threw her arms round him, kissing his mouth and his eyes. When he saw her, he was greatly dismayed and wanted to push her away from him; but in vain, for he was not yet strong enough and she kept hold of him. Tristan was terrified in case someone came in and saw them and suspected the worst. For that reason he tried to extricate himself from her grasp, intending to turn away; but the girl who was distraught and almost mad with anguish let out such a piercing, awesome shriek that the knights in the palace heard it clearly, and so did the King, but he had no idea it was his daughter.

The knights hurried to the scene and found the girl still holding Tristan. When she saw them, she was scared that the King would kill her if he knew what had happened, so she cried out to those whom she saw coming:

'Help! help! my lords. Look at Tristan who wants to dishonour me.'

'Truly,' they said, 'he'll be punished for it, in the name of the Lord.'

They seized him instantly and brought him before the King, and told him the whole story as they thought it had happened. The King was greatly distressed and looked at Tristan proudly, saying:

'Are you such that you bring about my shame when all the while I have honoured you? You deserve to die.'

And he ordered him to be put in prison, and they carried out his command.

When Gorvenal who was in his lodgings heard this news, he was very upset. He called himself wretched and miserable, and said he would be heart-broken and nothing would ever again bring him joy if Tristan were to die as a result of this misadventure. He did not know what to do, for he could not think of any way at all to free him. Nevertheless, he went to the court, where he found many people who insulted him on account of Tristan, saying he had brought him up badly; 'had he been honourable as we thought, he wouldn't have shamed the King in this manner.' Gorvenal did not answer them, but went straight to King Faramon and begged him for the Lord's sake to listen to what he had to say.

'Speak!' said the the King.

'My lord, by your grace, I don't want to speak in front of everyone, but rather in private, and I swear that good will come of it to you and to the whole kingdom.'

The King went into a room followed by Gorvenal. Once in there, the latter began to tell him all he knew about the maiden and the effect of Tristan's beauty on her.

'I assure you,' he said, 'that things are not as you believe them to be. Your daughter loves Tristan more than anyone else in the world, whereas he only loves her on account of you.'

The King was very wise, and when he heard the extraordinary story which Gorvenal was telling him, he thought there might be some truth in it; however, he decided to verify his testimony before he let the matter drop. He said:

'I have heard what you've told me. You may be sure that I shall make every effort to establish the whole truth of this affair by tomorrow evening. If it's as you said, Tristan will be freed; if it's otherwise, he'll be put to death without delay.'

Thereupon Gorvenal left the King, who did not forget his promise. He sent for his daughter and said to her:

'Dear daughter, aren't you pleased with the way I've dealt with Tristan on your account? Since he's been caught in the act, I shall cause him such shame and dishonour that you will be well avenged.'

The young girl did not dare to say what she thought, but answered in a subdued voice:

'My lord, it is just that everyone should pay for his folly.'

And the King replied:

'He will suffer whatever death you condemn him to: the judgment shall be yours.'

And the girl immediately thought that if the judgment were hers, then he would not die at all, however much she would be blamed for it. The King said no more at that point, but he realized well enough that she did not hate Tristan as much as was believed.

Next morning after daybreak* the King called his daughter to come before him in one of his rooms. Then he ordered Tristan to be taken out of prison, as well as a youth related to the maiden who had treacherously killed a knight that very week; he had been jailed by the King and was condemned to die. This youth was the girl's first cousin. When he had been released and brought before the King, the latter rose, took hold of a large sword and, drawing it, said to his daughter:

'You see in front of you two youths who deserve to die. One of them is related to you, since he's your first cousin; the other is not related to you at all. But although they have both been justly condemned to death, I give you the choice of saving whichever one of them you prefer. Take the one you would like to have, and I shall have the other. The one you choose shall be acquitted; the one you leave me has reached the point where I shall cut off his head with this very sword, and no ransom will redeem him. It's your choice: you can do as you please.'

When the young girl heard these words, she did not know what to say, for she thought the King would be angry with her if she did not acquit her cousin; but if she let Tristan die, the being in the world she loved the most, she was lost. The King, seeing her hesitate, realized that she loved Tristan; none the less, in order to bring further pressure to bear on her, he repeated:

'Daughter, hurry up and choose the one you want. If you take too long, you may find you'll have neither one nor the other.'

The young girl was very afraid of her father and did not dare to say what she thought. After a moment the King repeated:

'Daughter make up your mind quickly!'

She was so upset and so scared that she said:

'I would rather my cousin Meliant was acquitted.'

'Then I want Tristan to die,' said the King.

He lifted his sword and pretended he was going to cut off Tristan's head. Seeing this, the girl rushed up to him like a madwoman, quite distraught, for in no way did she want Tristan to die, and cried out in her anguish:

'By God, father, I made the wrong decision!' she said. 'I take back my choice. If you please, I'll have Tristan on my side, and you have Meliant.'

The King began to smile, and replied:

'It's too late now! You shall have the one you chose, and I shall have the one you left me. Tristan can't escape death.'

The King lifted his sword a second time, and pretended that he was going to cut off his head, though he had no intention of doing so. The girl immediately sprang forward, saying:

'Father, don't kill him; kill me! Let him live and put me to death instead.'

'That's quite out of the question,' said the King. 'He will have to die.'

'In that case give me the sword,' she requested, 'so that I can kill him. I'd rather he died at my hands than at someone else's.'

The King gave her the sword, and when she held it, she stepped back, and said:

'Father, either you spare Tristan, or I shall kill myself with my own hands here and now, as God is my witness.'

The King then asked her:

'Why do you want to kill yourself? Do you love Tristan so much?'

'Yes,' she replied, 'more than myself. If you kill him, I shall kill myself; if you let him live, I shall live.'

Thereupon the King answered:

'Daughter, then let it be according to your choice: since you want Tristan, you shall have him. Take him on your side, and I'll take Meliant on mine. Put down the sword; you don't need to fear me any longer, nor does Tristan. His tutor, Gorvenal, told me the truth. I was a fool not to believe him!'

She put down the sword, and the King turned to Tristan:

'You are free. No one will call you to account for this affair as far as I am concerned.'

Tristan thanked him greatly, and then he thanked the maiden for having saved him from the predicament she had got him into. Thereupon he left the room and returned to his lodgings where he found Gorvenal who had not stopped lamenting, so dismayed was he and so frightened for Tristan: he never thought he would have him back. But when he saw him face to face, he was delighted and overjoyed. He asked him how he had been freed, and Tristan related the whole truth to him, and told him that he would never have been spared at that point if it had not been for the maiden; and he described how it happened.

'Dear son, seeing that God has saved you from such peril, and you left the King in this manner with his blessing, I don't think it would be advisable for you to stay at his court any longer. Since you were unwilling to satisfy the young girl's desires, I'm sure that harm will come of it in one way or another. For this reason I'd like us to leave Gaul and go to another country.'

'Where would it be best for us to go, sir?' asked Tristan. 'Have you thought of anywhere?'

'We'll go to the court of your uncle, King Mark, in Cornwall. There you'll be able to serve amongst the other young boys without being recognized. You've grown and developed so much since you left Leonois, thank God, that no one who knew you then would know you now; and so you could stay there like any other foreign youth without being recognized as Tristan. And when you've served your uncle for as long as you like, and the time is ripe and you are of the age to receive the order of knighthood, either your uncle or another will knight you, as you please.'

Tristan agreed to this proposal.

Tristan takes leave of King Faramon, who tries in vain to persuade him to stay. At the King's request he divulges that he is the son of King Meliadus, and Faramon reproaches him for not having told him earlier.*

Tristan and Gorvenal cross the Channel to Cornwall and ride to
Glevedin, the castle where King Mark is presently residing. They are
overtaken by a squire who presents Tristan with a beautiful hunting dog
and a letter from King Faramon's daughter, Belide, in which she reiterates her love for him and affirms that she will kill herself with the very
sword her father had used to threaten Tristan. She prays to God that
before he dies he too will know the havoc passion can cause in the
human heart. The squire confirms that Belide has indeed committed
suicide, and Tristan is very distressed to hear it. The squire asks to stay
with Tristan, who consents provided he does not try to find out more
about him than he knows already. He was later to become a famous
knight and a companion of the Round Table; but during the Quest of
the Holy Grail Tristan himself accidentally kills him. [§§ 262–84 of vol. i]

IV

TRISTAN SERVES IN CORNWALL: THE MORHOLT

ACCOMPANIED by Gorvenal and the squire, Tristan presented himself to King Mark and offered him his service. The King asked who he was.

'My lord,' he answered, 'I've come to your court from a faraway land to serve you. If this is agreeable to you and meets with your approval, I shall remain.'

'I shall be pleased if you stay,' the King replied, 'for you strike me as a young man of noble birth.'

And so Tristan remained with his uncle. The King did not know who he was, but took him to be a foreign youth; he learnt soon enough that his name was Tristan, and it would not have been long before he found out that he was his nephew if Tristan had not taken care to conceal his identity.

Within a short while Tristan did so well in his uncle's service that there was not a young boy in the whole court who was esteemed a jot compared to him. If Tristan went into the woods he was praised for his hunting skills more than any of his companions. Whatever he served at, he was acclaimed above all his peers, so much so that when the King went to disport himself, whether on the river or in the woods, he always wanted Tristan to accompany him. Tristan was ready to meet any challenge; he undertook nothing which he did not bring to fruition, and so wisely that no one could find fault with him. And because everything he did was crowned with success, the young men in King Mark's household were so envious of Tristan that they did not know what to do, except that they were overcome with distress and vexation, for all of them were passed over since his arrival.

Tristan remained at his uncle's court for so long that he grew up to be a young boy of sixteen. At that age he was so brave, so deserving and so sensible that everyone marvelled at him, great and small alike. There was not a knight in Mark's court who was as nimble as Tristan or as strong, and this had been proved many a time. Gorvenal was overjoyed to see that the child he had brought up had grown into such a fine young man, and he felt it would not be long now before he was knighted. And once he was a knight, Gorvenal had such hopes for him, he was sure he could not fail to achieve great fame, if God protected him from misfortune in his knighthood.

About this time at the beginning of May it so happened that an Irish ship arrived in Cornwall. The Morholt, the dauntless knight, was in command of it, and he had come to ask for the tribute which the Cornish people owed the Irish at that period. He had many valiant knights in his company who had come with him from Ireland; and also some from the Kingdom of Logres,* from King Arthur's court, all of them brave and bold. And there was one from there who was very young called Gaheriet whom the Morholt had kept with him on account of his prowess. At that point King Arthur was only just beginning his reign; the good king had not been crowned for long.

When the Cornish people heard that the Irish had come for the tribute which so often already had been asked for and so often granted, they began to lament far and wide; they were so upset that they felt they would rather be dead than alive. The ladies and the knights began to mourn for their sons and their daughters, saying:

'Children, alas that you were ever conceived and born! Alas that you were ever nurtured since you are destined to be taken to Ireland in bondage and slavery. Earth, why did you not open up and swallow our children! It would have been better for us and more honourable if they had all been buried or engulfed in the bowels of the earth, or if wild beasts had devoured them rather than that the Irish should take them away; for this tribute is a source of eternal anguish and shame for us, and an eternal reproach. Treacherous and cruel sea, why were you so treacherous and cruel to us? Why were you so hostile that you brought our mortal enemies to our shore? Ah! god of the winds, all this year you have not been as still as you are now, but blew over the seas and created such storms that we said the god of the winds was angry; and he blew with such violence that it was amazing to see. Now, to our sorrow and misfortune, you are calm and still. Your peace brings us all our woes; your enmity all our blessings.'

In this manner the Cornish people grieved and lamented. Great was the suffering that could be seen at King Mark's court. The ladies wailed so loudly that even a thunderbolt from heaven would have gone unnoticed. King Mark himself was so upset that he was at a loss what to say.

Tristan who was elsewhere at the time and who did not know the cause of their affliction, asked a knight who was sitting beside him and who was a friend of his:

'Tell me, what is this grief all about?'

And the knight replied:

'Tristan, this Morholt the King is talking about is the brother of the Queen of Ireland and one of the best knights in the world. The Queen of Ireland has sent him here because of his prowess, for if by some chance one of the Cornish knights wanted to prove by a duel that Cornwall does not owe the tribute they're demanding, the Morholt would immediately be ready to show that they do owe it by fighting against the knight who dared to take up arms to challenge him.'

'And if it came about,' said Tristan, 'that some knight could defeat the Morholt, what would happen then?'

'By my faith,' replied the knight, 'then Cornwall would be freed from paying the tribute they're demanding.'

'In God's name,' said Tristan, 'then they can free themselves quite easily!'

'No, they can't,' he answered. 'There isn't a knight in the whole of Cornwall who would dare to take up arms against the Morholt, however brave he might be, for he would prefer to remain in bondage all his days.'

'How extraordinary!' exclaimed Tristan. 'As God is my witness, I never saw nor heard about knights more faint-hearted or more cowardly than the Cornish! I would rather die here and now, and I would win more honour if I died in battle against the Morholt than if I lived but was bound to him in servitude.'

'They aren't all as brave as you are,' replied the knight.

Tristan went to find Gorvenal and said to him:

'Master, what shall I do? The Cornish people are shamed for evermore, since they haven't enough courage to take up arms to fight the Morholt. I don't know why I should hide it from you, sir; I tell you openly that if I were a knight, nothing would stop me from fighting the Morholt to contest this tribute. And should it please God that I win, all my lineage would be honoured, and I would be more esteemed all my life. What do you think about this matter, sir? Here I can find out and prove whether I shall ever be a knight of great valour; and to be sure, if I am not destined to be a man of valour, I would rather be killed by the Morholt who is such a brave knight and so renowned for his chivalry. It would be better to die in honour than to live in bondage and servitude with the cowardly knights of Cornwall.'

Gorvenal, who loved Tristan more than anyone else in the world, replied:

'Dear son, your words are noble, and the exploit you speak of pleases me greatly. However, I'm very worried by the fact that the Morholt is of such prowess that I don't know his equal either here or elsewhere. He is a strong and sturdy knight, and you are but a young child; he is experienced in the art of fighting, whereas you've scarcely learnt anything about it. You should consider all this before you engage in such an adventure. It would be a tragedy if you were to die at your age, for you cannot fail to do great things if you live.'

'This is the test, sir,' he replied. 'If I fail in this undertaking, don't ever have any hopes for me again. But one thing gives me confidence, namely that my father was one of the best knights in the world, and since he was such a brave knight, his blood will prove itself in me.'

When Gorvenal heard Tristan's words he was amazed at his great sense, and he replied full of tears:

'Dear son, then you must do as you will.'

'Many thanks, sir,' said Tristan.

He left Gorvenal without delay and came before the King who was full of sorrow and sadness, for he had consulted his knights to find out if any of them would be willing to contest the tribute which Cornwall owed. But each one of them had replied to the King that he would not be prepared to take up arms against the Morholt in view of the kind of knight he was: they would rather pay the tribute just as their parents had paid it.

While the King was brooding thus because of his knights' refusal to come to his aid, Tristan appeared before him; he was not wearing his cloak, and was so handsome, so noble and so well-formed in every way that it would have been difficult to find a fairer youth. When he had come up to the King, he knelt down before him and said:

'My lord, I have served you as well and as devotedly as I could, and the reward I ask for my service is that you make me a knight either today or tomorrow. I have waited so long to be a knight that the majority of the people in your court are beginning to talk about it.'

The King replied:

'Tristan,' he said, 'you're very handsome, and in view of your prowess and your service you have certainly deserved to be knighted as you request; and I shall do so, since you ask it. But I would have done so with much more pomp and ceremony were it not for this calamity which has befallen us in Cornwall.'

'My lord,' said Tristan, 'don't be dismayed. Trust in God and He will save you from this disaster as from all others. And many thanks for agreeing to make me a knight at such short notice.'

The King raised him from his knees and handed him over to Dinas, his seneschal, and asked him to prepare Tristan and to procure for him whatever he needed, 'for I want to knight him tomorrow'. Tristan was delighted to hear this.

That night Tristan kept vigil in a church dedicated to Our Lady, and the following morning around daybreak King Mark knighted him as honourably as possible. All those who saw Tristan said they had never looked upon a more handsome knight in Cornwall.

While they were celebrating as joyfully as they could, given their unhappiness, four knights came in who were messengers from the Morholt, wise men and eloquent. Seeing the King, they said without greeting him:

'King Mark, we have been sent by the Morholt, the best knight in the world, for the tribute which the Cornish people owe the Irish. Make the necessary arrangements with your men so that this tribute is paid within a week; if not, we challenge you on his behalf, and you may be sure that if you anger him, you will end up without a single plot of land, and the whole of Cornwall will be destroyed.'

When King Mark heard these words, he was so dismayed that he did not know what to say; such was his disarray that he remained silent. Thereupon Tristan sprang forward and said:

'My lords, messengers from Ireland, who demand the tribute from Cornwall, you can go and tell the Morholt that if our ancestors in their foolishness paid the tribute to the King of Ireland, we, who by the grace of God are wiser and more judicious than they were, hereby inform the Morholt that the tribute will not be paid by us from now on. If he declares that we owe it to him, I'm ready to take up arms to prove that the Cornish people are free and not liable to make this payment. If I kill him, we are acquitted; if he kills me, we will pay it.'

The messengers then answered, saying:

'King Mark, is it with your consent that this knight has spoken thus?'

The King replied:

'To be sure, I never told him to say what he did, but since it is his wish to take up the fight for the freedom of Cornwall, I shall put my trust in God's will in defiance of the ill-will of the people of Ireland.'

And Tristan said:

'Now you can go and tell the Morholt that if he wants to have the tribute, he will have to come and fight for it!'

'Who are you,' the messengers asked, 'who want to undertake this battle?'

'I'm a knight from foreign parts. My name is Tristan. I've served King Mark so long that, by the grace of God, he knighted me today.'

'And from what lineage are you?' they enquired.

'Why do you want to know that?' Tristan retorted.

'Because the Morholt would only undertake to fight this battle against a man as nobly born as he is; otherwise it would seem dishonourable to him.'

'Then you can tell the Morholt', said Tristan, 'that the question of my noble birth won't prove an obstacle, for if he is the son of a king, so am I. King Meliadus of Leonois was my father; King Mark, who is in front of you, is my uncle. I've concealed my identity in his court for as long as I could, but since I have to reveal it, I do so now. This much you can tell your lord from me: if he wants peace, he shall have it; if he wants a battle, he can have that too.'

And they said they would deliver this message.

Thereupon they left King Mark and rode back to the port and told the Morholt the news they had brought him from the court. He was amazed and asked:

'Who is this knight who wants to do battle with me?'

They told him he was called Tristan and was King Mark's nephew and the son of King Meliadus of Leonois.

'He was only knighted today, but we doubt whether God has ever created a man as handsome as he is. He undertook the battle of his own accord, without the advice of anyone.'

'Indeed!' said the Morholt, 'I think he'll regret this undertaking. Today he was made a new knight, and tomorrow he'll be made to meet a new death! But tell me, did you determine where the battle is to take place?'

'No,' they replied, 'there was never any mention of that.'

'Then you'll have to return to court,' continued the Morholt, 'and settle where it's to be.'

And they said they were quite willing to go.

'But make sure to fix the battle for tomorrow. I don't want it delayed any longer.'

And they promised to see to it. Gaheriet said he would go with them to Mark's court 'so that I can have a look at this knight they've talked about so much'.

They got on their horses and rode back to the court; and when they had dismounted, they asked the King where he wanted this battle to take place. The King replied:

'I want it to be on an island which is known in this country as St Samson's Isle.* Let the two knights fight the battle there, and let it be on horseback; and when they are on the island face to face, all alone, then let the two of them settle this dispute by combat, as we have decided and established.'

The messengers readily concurred, and the battle was agreed upon in this way by both parties. Then they left the court; the King remained among his men, and the messengers returned to the Morholt.

Gaheriet, having had ample time to take a good look at Tristan, could not help exclaiming:

'Upon my word, if he doesn't turn out to be a brave and valiant knight, it would be the greatest wonder in the world, for he's the most handsome knight I've ever seen given his age! Certainly, he cannot fail to be a worthy man, provided he lives for long. I wish this battle between Tristan and the Morholt could be called off. It would be a tragedy if the Morholt were to kill him, and if Tristan killed the Morholt it would be equally disastrous for all knights-errant.'

This is how Gaheriet spoke about Tristan, though as yet he only knew him by sight. The messengers returned to the Morholt and told him the arrangements they had made, and that the battle was to take place on St Samson's Isle. He declared himself satisfied, and then turned to Gaheriet:

'What did you think of Tristan? Did you see him?'

'Yes, I did,' Gaheriet replied, 'I saw him very clearly, and I can tell you there is no man in the world I admire more, given his age and his appearance: and, so help me God, if you were willing to do something for me, I wish you would abandon this battle and find some way of making peace between you and the Cornish people.'

The Morholt replied that there was no way in which he would consent to make peace, for he was sure he would overcome Tristan easily. No more was said about the battle at that stage.

All night long the Cornish people prayed to God that He would save Tristan and give him the strength and the power to free the Kingdom of Cornwall from bondage. Tristan kept vigil nearly all night in a church dedicated to Our Lady; but before the night was out he lay down to get some sleep so that he would be nimbler and stronger when it came to the battle. Shortly before dawn he rose and went to hear mass, armed with his hauberk* and mail leggings,* and then he returned to the palace. His uncle came up to him in tears, and said:

'Dear nephew, fair youth, the most handsome of all young men, why did you conceal your identity from me for so long? Had I known you as well as I know you now, I'd never have granted you this battle. I would rather Cornwall remained for ever in servitude, because if you were now to die, I'd never have joy, and we'd be worse off than we were before.'

'My lord,' said Tristan, 'Have no fear! If it please the Lord, He won't forget us at this point. Pray to God that He sustain me, and I believe that your honour will be enhanced.'

And the King replied, weeping:

'Tristan, may God pay regard to my wishes and to the needs of Cornwall.'

While the King was weeping thus, he heard that the Morholt had already entered his boat and was making for the island. Tristan instantly asked for his helmet, and they brought it to him, fine and strong, and laced it on his head. The King himself lent a hand, being very eager to serve him. When Tristan was armed, he went to his horse, mounted and rode as far as the boat. Then he went inside, took hold of the rudder and steered himself to the island; once there, he removed his horse and all his armour. Then he pushed the boat into the water so that within minutes it had moved quite a distance away from the shore.

The Morholt was amazed to see this, and coming up to Tristan, asked him:

'Tell me,' he said, 'why did you push your vessel away from the shore?'

'I'll tell you,' Tristan answered. 'If you kill me, you'll go back in your boat and return to your men. If I kill you, I'll do likewise. And if we make peace, we'll both enter your boat and go where we've decided.'

'You're an intelligent youth,' said the Morholt. 'In view of the good sense you seem to have, I wouldn't want to kill you if I could help it, for one day you could be a man of great valour. On account of this I want you to know that if you are prepared to abandon the battle which you so rashly and foolishly undertook, I'll put aside my ill-will and retain you with me and make you my companion.'

To which Tristan replied:

'I would be prepared to abandon the battle if you were willing to renounce your claim to the tribute which you're asking the Cornish people to pay; otherwise I would not do so.'

'No?' the Morholt asked. 'Then I call you to battle.'

'And I'm ready,' Tristan said. 'That is what I came here for.'

Thereupon they charge at each other and are knocked to the ground. Both are badly hurt, but Tristan has been wounded by the Morholt's poisoned lance. Then they pull out their swords, and the fight begins in earnest. Each one soon realizes that he is faced with an opponent of exceptional prowess, and as the blood begins to flow freely, both men become increasingly dismayed as well as exhausted. But they know they must not slacken, for it is a fight to the death. The longer the battle lasts, the more worried the Morholt grows, since he cannot fail to notice that his adversary is quicker and more resilient. In the end Tristan, seeing the Morholt weaken, makes a supreme effort and deals him such a mighty blow that he cleaves his helmet and cuts into his brain; and as he withdraws the sword, a piece of the blade remains stuck in the Morholt's head. The latter, wounded to death, flees. The Cornish people who have been watching from afar, run to their boats and bring the victorious Tristan back to the mainland.

When they were back on firm ground and the King saw his nephew, he ran up to him with outstretched arms and kissed him more than a hundred times, asking him how he felt.

'My lord,' he said, 'I'm wounded, but I trust in Our Lord that I shall recover.'

The King took him to the church to render thanks unto God for this honour which He had granted him. Then he returned to the palace amidst such joy and merriment that never had greater been heard. Tristan took to his bed as soon as he was back in his uncle's court, for the pain and anguish he felt from his poisoned wound deprived him of all desire for play and laughter. The doctors came to see him; they put herbs on it and plasters of various kinds, and took such trouble and made such efforts to cure him that he recovered from all his wounds except the one where the poison was. That one did not heal at all, but only seemed to worsen, because the remedies they used had an adverse effect and made him more ill. They never examined the wound closely enough to notice the poison. Tristan, who felt very poorly, bemoaned his fate. He grew daily weaker. He became thin and ugly as a result of his great suffering. The wound swelled up and gave out such an unpleasant odour that nobody could bear it near him on account of the stench. Only Gorvenal remained, weeping and lamenting for the young man in his charge, whose condition, under his very eyes, had deteriorated so much that no one seeing him before would have recognized him now. Lord! how anguished the King felt and how often he wept! The worthy men of Cornwall did likewise, and said to Tristan:

'Ah, Tristan! you're going to die in agony and pain because of what has made us happy. The joy you have given us has brought about your affliction.'

One day Tristan was lying in his bed, so thin, so pale and so ill that everyone who saw him felt pity for him. A lady was by his bedside who was weeping very tenderly. When she had looked at him for some time, she said amidst her tears:

'Tristan, I'm very surprised that you haven't long ago done something, and taken some other advice than you've had in this country. All you do here is to languish and grow more ill from day to day. You can't seem to die and you can't seem to live. I know that if I were in your place, since you can't recover in this land, I'd have myself transported to another where perchance I'd find some cure.'

'Lady,' he said, 'how could I manage that? I couldn't ride and I'm not fit enough to be carried on a litter.'*

'Then I don't know what advice to give you,' she replied. 'May God help you to find a solution.'

The lady said no more. Tristan immediately had himself carried to a window facing the sea and began to look at it; and he could see quite a distance. Suddenly he had an idea, and he called Gorvenal and said to him:

'Master, please go and ask my uncle, the King, to come and see me.'

'Willingly,' replied Gorvenal.

He went to the King and said:

'My lord, Tristan would like you to come and speak to him.'

The King went at once and asked Tristan:

'Dear nephew, what is it you want?'

'My lord,' he answered, 'I beg you to grant me a favour in view of the loyalty you owe me, and I assure you that it will cost you little.'

Thereupon the King replied, weeping:

'Indeed, dear nephew, I would grant it to you even if it were to cost me much! Believe me, there is nothing I wouldn't do for you.'

Then Tristan answered and said:

'Uncle, I've been very ill ever since the day I fought the Morholt of Ireland for the freedom of Cornwall. I've borne such pain and suffering that no young man ever endured so much. Why should I remark upon it? It's evident enough! But despite this suffering I would be quite satisfied if only I could find a cure for my illness. But as I can't find it and don't seem to be able to live or to die, I must go to another land in the hope that God will give me guidance and help me to recover there, since I can't do so in this country.'

'Dear nephew,' said the King, 'how could you travel to another country? You're too ill to ride, or go on foot or even to be carried.'

'Uncle,' he replied, 'I'll tell you how. You will have a boat made for me, fine and swift, with a little sail which I can raise and lower at my will. Let it be covered with a silk canopy to protect me from the rain, the heat and the wind. I want my bed to be fitted in there, and I shall take with me my harp and my rote* and my other instruments so that I can play sometimes and console myself. When everything has been prepared according to my wishes, I want you to have me carried into it along with enough food to sustain me on the sea for a while. Then have the boat pushed away from the shore, and once I'm all alone on the ocean, if it please God that I die, then I shall be happy to die, for I have languished a long time. And if I come to a foreign land where I can find someone to cure me, and it so happens that I recover, then I shall immediately return to Cornwall. Let it be done in this way, that is how I want it. And I entreat you, for God's sake, not to delay in this matter. I shall feel no joy until I'm on the sea as I've described.'

When the King heard these words, he began to weep for pity, saying:

'Dear nephew, do you really want to leave me like that?'

'Indeed,' Tristan replied, 'it cannot be otherwise.'

'And what about Gorvenal?' he asked. 'If you were to take him with you, he'd be a great comfort to you at this point.'

'At this point,' said Tristan, 'I want no company except that of God. But if I die, I leave my land to Gorvenal. He comes from such a noble lineage that he could well be a king once he has received the order of knighthood; and he would have been a knight long ago had it not been for me.'

The King, seeing that he could not do otherwise, had the boat fitted as Tristan had requested, and equipped with all the things he had asked for. And when everything was ready, Tristan was carried there and placed inside, ailing and sick as he was. The

Cornish people displayed such sorrow at this parting as was never seen before. King Mark wept tenderly, and so did Gorvenal and Tristan's squire. When Tristan saw their grief, he wanted to delay no longer, and for this reason he put out to sea. He had raised his sail, which was small but very beautiful, and in no time at all he was so far away from the shore that he could see neither his uncle, nor his friends, nor any of those who were in such distress at his departure. [§§ 285–309 of vol. i]

V

FIRST VOYAGE TO IRELAND: DISCOVERY

THUS Tristan in his misfortune sailed over the seas with great difficulty. No young man ever suffered so many trials and tribulations. The wind bore him across the ocean, and his good luck was such that his boat did not sink, but rode the waves night and day just as a large ship would have done. However, it did not go as fast or as straight, for Tristan lowered the little sail whenever he was in doubt.

After about two weeks or more it so happened that he arrived one day in Ireland, and landed near a very beautiful castle called Hosedoc; and in this castle lived King Anguin of Ireland, husband of the queen who had been the Morholt's sister. With them was their daughter Iseut the Blonde, the most beautiful young girl alive and also one of the most intelligent. She was remarkably knowledgeable about cures and medicines, and knew the strength and effectiveness of all the herbs. There was no injury in the world so strange and no wound so unusual which she was not sure she could deal with successfully and heal. She was not yet fourteen years old.

When Tristan had reached the port and he saw the land which was quite unknown to him, his spirits rose a little on account of the pleasant aspect of the new country, and because God and good fortune had saved him from the perils of the sea. Then he took up his harp and began to tune it so that the large chords synchronized with the small ones in complete harmony. And when he had tuned it correctly, because it had such a sweet and pleasing tone, he began to play so melodiously that anyone hearing it would have listened with pleasure.

The King was standing by the window, and when the sound of the harp floated up to him and the beautiful notes which Tristan played, he found the music most enjoyable and delightful to hear. Then he noticed the boat, so richly equipped that it seemed like magic to him, and he pointed it out to the Queen who marvelled at it.

'My lord,' she said, 'let's go and see what it is!'

The King made his way down from the tower and did not permit anyone to accompany him except the Queen. When they reached the shore where Tristan was in his boat, trying to cheer himself up in his sick state by playing the harp, the King stopped to listen; and they remained there until Tristan had finished the last note and put his harp aside. Then he began to lament bitterly, for he felt the anguish of death upon him.

The King approached and greeted him, and Tristan returned his greeting very respectfully and courteously, and asked him the name of the country where he had arrived.

'What!' the King exclaimed. 'Don't you know where you are?'

'No, my lord,' Tristan replied. 'I've never been in this country before, and that's why I asked you its name.'

'Let me tell you, then,' said the King, 'that it's Ireland.'

When Tristan heard him mention Ireland, he was more uneasy than he had been before, because he knew very well that if he were recognized, he would be put to death on account of the Morholt whom he had killed. The King asked him:

'Where do you come from?'

'My lord,' said Tristan, 'I come from the Kingdom of Leonois from near the city of Albine. Such has been my misfortune that I've arrived here stricken by an illness for which I can find no cure. It's causing me so much suffering and anguish that if I had the choice, I'd rather have been dead long ago. But it doesn't please Our Lord that I should die just yet; much to my dismay, for death would be preferable to languishing like this in torment and misery.'

Hearing him speak thus the King felt great pity for him, since his pallor showed clearly that he was more often in pain and discomfort than was good for him. Then he asked him:

'Are you a knight?'

'Yes, my lord,' Tristan replied.

'In that case don't worry,' said the King. 'Since you're a knight, your wound will be cured, if there is a cure for it. I have a daughter who to my knowledge has more experience in such matters than any man or woman in this kingdom, and I'm sure she'll attend to it for the love of God and for pity's sake.'

And Tristan thanked him very much.

The King returned to his palace, and so did the Queen. And as soon as he was back, he ordered his men to go and fetch the ailing knight who was lying in the boat down at the shore, and carry him up to a room and put him there to rest. They did as he asked, carrying Tristan as gently as they could, and laid him down in a very beautiful and costly room. The King immediately sent for his daughter Iseut, and when she had come he begged her to take care of the foreign knight who was very ill and do her best to heal him quickly. And she promised to do all she could. She went straight to Tristan, and when she had examined his wound, she applied such herbs as she thought would be beneficial to him. He moaned and sighed deeply, for his pain and his anguish were great. The young girl who did not straightaway notice the poison comforted him and told him not to worry; she was sure she would soon have him hale and hearty with God's help.

'Ah, Lord!' he exclaimed, 'when will that be? If I had health, I wouldn't ask God for anything else.'

Tristan was in this room for ten whole days, and each day the young girl took care of him and dressed his wound as she saw fit. But his condition only grew worse from day to day.

Iseut was greatly dismayed when she saw this, and cursed her sense and her knowledge, saying openly that she knew nothing about what she thought she knew better than any woman in the world. When she had cursed and maligned herself for quite a while, she had another look at the wound; and after she had examined it closely, it suddenly struck her that the wound might be poisoned, and this was why it had not healed. If it was a question of poison, she could cure him of it easily enough; otherwise she wanted to have nothing more to do with it, for it would be a waste of time; if there was poison, in that case she would deal with it.

Then she had Tristan carried out into the sun so that she could see more clearly. And when she had taken a good look, she said to him:

'Now I understand what prevented you from recovering for so long. The lance-head* which wounded you was poisoned. All those who tried to heal you were deceived, since they failed to notice the poison. Now that by the grace of God I've seen it, rest assured that I'll cure you with His help.'

Tristan was extremely pleased to hear this, and said that he hoped God would grant her the power. The young girl sought and procured what she felt would be most effective for drawing out the poison. And when she had extracted it, she did her best to bring him back to health. Once on the road to recovery, Tristan began to feel better and to regain his good looks and his strength. She took such pains and nursed him so devotedly that before two months had passed he was as fit and well as he had ever been, though he was not yet as sturdy or as handsome as before. And then it occurred to him that he should return to Cornwall as soon as possible, for if he were recognized in Ireland, he would suffer a painful death on account of the Morholt whom he had killed.

About this time three knights from Arthur's court arrive in Ireland: Gaheriet, Kay the Seneschal, and Bademagu; they have come, as also many other foreign knights, to take part in a tournament to be held in front of the Castle in the Moors, and are very honourably received by King Anguin. Fortunately Gaheriet does not recognize Tristan because his illness has so greatly changed him, but the latter is terrified.*
The King sets out to watch the tournament accompanied by Tristan who is not yet strong enough to take part. They meet Gawain, King Arthur's nephew, with his squire Hebes the Renowned who is Belide's one-time messenger, and who asks to be knighted by Tristan; the latter agrees, but enjoins him not to reveal his identity.
The victor of the tournament is an unknown knight wearing a black shield and two swords, a sign of his readiness to fight against two opponents: he is Palamedes the Saracen. Nobody knows he is not a Christian; he has eleven brothers, and his father Esclabor is also a knight of great valour. The King of the Hundred Knights proclaims a new tournament to take place in ten days' time. King Anguin follows Palamedes and begs him to stay at his court whilst he is in Ireland; Palamedes is happy to accept, and they make their way back to the castle.

That evening Palamedes was served and honoured by everyone at court more than he could have wished. The following day Iseut waited at table with many young girls to keep her company. She was so beautiful and so becoming in every way that when Palamedes saw her he was quite overwhelmed, and said to himself that she was the most beautiful being he had ever beheld. He completely lost his heart to her; she pleased and attracted him so much that there was nothing in the world he would not have done to possess her, even abandon his faith, though that was the one thing he would have been most unwilling to do. None the less, he would have done it in order to have Iseut, if that were possible.

Palamedes gazed at her so much that Tristan noticed it and realized from his behaviour that he loved her with all his heart. Before that Tristan had often looked at Iseut and she pleased him very much, but not in a way which made him fall in love with her. However, when he saw that Palamedes was so infatuated with Iseut that he said he would die if he did not have her, Tristan for his part said that Palamedes would certainly never have her if he could help it. Palamedes might be a dauntless knight, but there were others equally brave in the world. He himself, once he had completely recovered, would prove himself as valiant in one day as Palamedes had done a short while ago.

Thus pride and arrogance took hold of Tristan for love of my lady Iseut. He eyed Palamedes with anger because he felt he would be a hindrance and an obstacle to him in his love. Palamedes who was very observant had not been there four days before he realized that Tristan loved her and hated him mortally for her sake. This did not endear him to Palamedes who began to feel such a deadly hatred for Tristan that he hated no one else as much, for, seeing that he was such a handsome knight and so well formed in every way, it seemed to him that he was stealing Iseut's love from him and that she was head over heels in love with Tristan.

Thus Tristan conceived a mortal hatred for Palamedes, and Palamedes for Tristan. Iseut knew nothing about all this and never noticed it; she did not suspect that either of them loved her, since she had never herself thought about love, nor was she thinking of it now. She had with her a young girl who was a virgin and of noble birth; she was very perceptive, not because she was advanced in years but because she was highly intelligent. She began to take note of the two knights, and it was not long before she saw and realized that they both loved Iseut with all their heart and hated each other mortally as a result. She told Iseut jokingly that the two knights loved her in this way, to which she replied:

'Well, I can't stop them, but it doesn't affect me. They'll find they've wasted their efforts, for it means nothing to me at the present time.'

The young girl was called Brangain. When she heard Iseut's reply, she said to her, laughing:

'Suppose you were to grant your love to one of them, which one would you prefer: Palamedes or our knight?'

And Iseut answered:

'If it came to the point where I'd have to make a choice, I think I'd prefer Palamedes on account of his prowess. But if our knight were equally brave and valiant, and as noble as he appears to be, one should in preference choose him because, once cured, he would undoubtedly be the most handsome knight in the world.'

Tristan who was lying in this very room, seemingly asleep, had heard every word the maidens had said. They went off to another room without having noticed him. When they had gone he jumped out of bed and made his way into a small meadow, where he began to think very hard. After he had pondered a long time, he said to himself that he would never succeed in his love unless he could break Palamedes's pride, and that could only be done with great difficulty and a lot of hard fighting, for he knew well that Palamedes was the best knight he had ever seen. He decided in the end that he would have to shame Palamedes, or Palamedes him. That was as far as his thoughts went.

King Anguin sets off to watch the second tournament, and Tristan pretends to feel too weak to go with him. He follows in secret, however, clad in the white armour which Brangain had lent him, and accompanied by her two young brothers, Perynin and Mathael. When he belatedly arrives at the scene, the black knight had already done wonders. Tristan, guessing him to be Palamedes, joins the opposing side, and charges at him so fiercely with his lance that he knocks him and his horse to the ground. Soon everyone realizes that this white knight is far superior to the black one, and it is not long before he is acclaimed the victor of the tournament. Palamedes turns away in great shame, but Tristan follows and challenges him to a duel for the love of Iseut; this alerts Palamedes as to his opponent's identity. They draw their swords, but Tristan is speedier, and, full of anger, deals Palamedes such a mighty blow on his helmet that it sends him reeling to the ground, so stunned that he does not know if it is night or day. Tristan bothers with him no further, but rides off delighted with his success.

A young girl he meets asks him who won the tournament, and after a moment's hesitation he informs her it was the most beautiful maiden in the world, much to her surprise. He refuses to tell her his name, but agrees to take off his helmet so that she can see his face. She had come from Great Britain to look for the knight who had conquered the Dolorous Guard* (Lancelot), and, until undeceived, she thought it was Tristan because of the close resemblance of the two knights.

On leaving him she meets Palamedes, overwhelmed with grief. When she assures him that the White Knight is not a member of Arthur's household, his despair redoubles, for, having been the bearer of two swords, he is now not allowed to wear any arms at all for one year and one day. He rides off in anguish, having thrown his entire armour to the ground.

The young girl next meets Gawain who is also looking for the knight who conquered the Dolorous Guard and believes him to be the White Knight. When she corrects him, he decides to stay in Ireland no longer, and they both set out for Great Britain together.

Tristan returns to King Anguin's castle. Brangain has been waiting for him and immediately asks him for news of the tournament. He does not admit his success, though his swollen face soon makes it apparent to everyone that he has been fighting fiercely. Three days later King Anguin comes back in the company of many foreign knights, including Gaheriet, Brandeliz and Yvain. There is much talk about the knight with the white armour, and many of them think he may well be the unknown victor of the Dolorous Guard. Hearing this conversation, Brangain begins to suspect that the knight they are talking about is none other than Tristan, and her enquiries confirm the truth of this.

That day Brangain spoke to King Anguin:

'My lord,' she said, 'are you very eager to know who the knight with the white armour is, the one who won the tournament?'

'Indeed I am,' he replied.

'Well, don't be dismayed,' she said. 'I think I can shortly clear up the mystery to your satisfaction.'

'Nothing would please me more,' he answered.

Next morning as the day was dawning Brangain said to the King:

'My lord, if you please, come with me to a room in which there is something I want to show you.'

The King said he was quite ready to follow her, and she led the way to a room where she had placed the shield Tristan had worn at the tournament.

'My lord,' she asked, 'did you see this at the assembly?'

'Yes,' the King replied, 'the brave knight wore it the other day at the tournament. By God! if you know something about him, tell me!'

'My lord,' she answered, 'since you're so eager to find out, I won't conceal it from you any longer: he's the knight you found in the boat at the shore in such a weak and sickly state, as you well know, the one who's stayed here so long.'

The King was amazed to hear this, for he did not and could not believe that the knight was of such great valour. Nevertheless, because he remained in some doubt, he said to Brangain:

'How do you know?'

And she told him.

'Upon my word!' he exclaimed, 'now I do believe you.'

'If you don't believe me,' she said, 'ask my two brothers who were his squires at the tournament.'

And the King sent for them and asked them if it was the truth.

'My lord,' they answered, 'there's no doubt about it. He is definitely the one.'

The King, who was very happy to hear this, went to find Tristan and said to him:

'Sir Knight, I have a complaint to make to you about yourself, namely that you have now stayed at my court for quite a while without ever making yourself known to me. For the love of God, please tell me your name and what lineage you are from.'

When Tristan heard these words, he was afraid of being recognized, as he knew well that he was living amongst the very people who felt the most deadly hatred for him and that he would not have a chance of surviving in their midst. He therefore replied as politely as he could, saying:

'My lord, you have done so much for me that you're the man I'm most indebted to in the world, and I would readily acquit myself of this debt, so help me God, if you were in need and I was in a position to assist you.'

'I'm not asking you to acquit yourself of any debt other than to tell me your name,' the King replied.

'My lord,' he said, 'there's no way in which I would tell you my name at this point.'

'Since you don't want to reveal it,' the King retorted, 'at least tell me if the other day at the tournament you wore the white armour which Brangain gave you.'

'My lord,' he said, 'I did indeed wear it. I'm very upset that you've found out.'

'In God's name,' the King exclaimed, 'you shouldn't be upset at being known! It's greatly to your honour. And because of the prowess you displayed, I offer myself to you and all I possess.'

Tristan thanked him warmly.

In this way Tristan's prowess became known in the Kingdom of Ireland, and henceforth he was served and honoured by the King and by all his people. There was not a lady or maiden at the King's court who would not have loved Tristan willingly if she had thought he might be interested, with the exception of the beautiful Iseut. She paid no attention to such things, for she was an innocent young girl who had been brought up strictly. She neither hated him, nor did she love him, though there were quite a number of young girls at court who thought she did. The King himself would have been only too pleased if they had loved each other and if Tristan had taken her for his wife: he was sure she could not make a better marriage. But there was nothing the King desired so much as to know his name. However, as Tristan wanted to conceal his identity, he refrained from asking him for fear of making him angry.

One day it so happened that Tristan was having a bath* in one of the Queen's rooms, and the Queen herself had come to serve him, as well as Iseut and many other young girls who were joyful and merry on account of Tristan. There was also in the room a youth related to the King, and while the others were serving Tristan in this way, he was looking round and chanced upon Tristan's sword which he found lying on a bed. It was the very sword with which he had killed the Morholt, and it still had the piece missing which had remained in the Morholt's head. The youth looked at the sword, and it seemed so costly to him and so well made that he did not think there could be another one like it in the world. In order to see it more clearly he drew it from its scabbard and instantly noticed the notched blade. He was very surprised, and began to examine it more closely; and while he was doing so, the Queen happened to come over to him. The sight of the sword set her thinking, and she asked the youth:

'Whose sword is this?'

And he told her the truth.

'Indeed!' she exclaimed. 'Then for God's sake bring it into that room over there for me.'

'Willingly, my lady,' the youth replied.

Once in there the Queen took out of a casket of hers a silken cloth in which she had wrapped the piece from Tristan's sword that had been discovered in the Morholt's head. The Queen herself had found it and had kept it with great care for love of him. She took this fragment out of the casket, and when she had fitted it to the blade of the sword, she immediately realized that it had come from there and that they had been one and the same.

'Ah, God!' she exclaimed, 'now I've found my brother's murderer. This knight here is Tristan, and he only concealed his identity from us for so long because he was afraid we would put him to death if we knew who he was. He's the one who killed the Morholt; it's he who shamed and humiliated us, and he will pay for it.'

Then the Queen seized hold of the sword, mad with rage, and went off to the room where she had left Tristan, who knew nothing of all this; and once she was in there, she cried out at the top of her voice:

'Ah! Tristan, nephew of King Mark of Cornwall, there's no point in trying to conceal your name: it's all up with you. You killed my brother the Morholt with this sword, and with this sword you will have to die at my hands.'

And she rushed forward, intending to strike him as he lay quite naked in the bath. Tristan did not move a muscle, nor did he show any sign of fear. A squire, seeing the Queen's wrath and fury, leapt up to her and said:

'Ah! my lady, don't kill the best knight in the world like this in your own court. At all events, it's not for you, a lady, to avenge this misdeed, but let the King deal with it, and I'm sure he will see that your honour is upheld better than you would.'

In spite of all the squire said, the Queen did not curb her anger, but still wanted to attack Tristan. However, the squire restrained her by force and did not let her do it.

Thereupon an extraordinary uproar broke out in the room, for the Queen kept crying:

'Iseut, dear daughter, what are you going to do? This is Tristan who killed your uncle.'

Hearing the noise, King Anguin came in and was amazed to see the Queen holding a naked sword in her hand.

'My lady,' he said, 'what is making you so angry?'

'Ah, my lord,' she answered, 'I can't bear it. We've found the disloyal traitor who killed my brother the Morholt in Cornwall. It's Tristan whom you see here in front of you and who has concealed himself for so long amongst us. Either I shall kill him, or you kill him. This is the sword he used to kill my brother; by this same sword I want him to die.'

The King who was very wise and prudent replied:

'My lady, now do be quiet and restrain your anger and leave this vengeance to me. I assure you that I'll deal with it in such a way that nobody will be able to blame me.'

'My lord,' she answered, 'many thanks. You've taken a weight off my mind.'

'Now hand me this sword,' he said. 'It's not right for a lady to be holding a sword in this manner.'

And she gave it to him.

'Now I want you to leave,' he said; and she did so.

The King then turned to Tristan, saying:

'Tell me, are you Tristan who killed the Morholt?'

And Tristan replied:

'My lord, there's no point in concealing it: I am indeed Tristan. If I killed the Morholt, no one should blame me, for I had no choice.'

'You'll die,' said the King, 'if I so wish.'

'That's true, my lord,' replied Tristan. 'I can see it only too well.'

'To be sure, I don't know what to do!' the King exclaimed. 'If I let you go free, some people will blame me. And if I were to kill you, it would be a grave misdeed because you are such a valiant knight.'

'My lord,' said Tristan, 'it's up to you whether you kill me or let me live.'

'Now put your clothes on,' said the King, 'and come to the great hall.'

Thereupon he went out of the room, leaving three squires with Tristan.

When he had dressed himself, Tristan made his way to the hall where he found many noble men. He became quite bashful and appeared even more handsome as a result. They all gazed at him, and said that in their opinion God had never created a more handsome man; even if he were not such a brave knight it would be a crime to make him die for someone who could not be brought back by any means. The King also looked at him, and knowing him to be a knight of such great valour, he put aside all his anger. The Queen for her part cried out:

'King, avenge me of this traitor who killed my brother the Morholt. If you don't take vengeance now, you'll never have such a good opportunity.'

The King loved his wife very much and did not know what to do. If he put Tristan to death, it did not seem to him that this loss could be repaired on account of Tristan's great prowess. He thought the matter over very carefully, and when he had pondered for a while, he said in the hearing of all:

'Tristan, you've done me a great wrong and caused me grievous harm. The Morholt's death is a loss of such magnitude that nothing would deter me from having you killed if it were not for two considerations: one, that I would be committing a grave misdeed on account of your prowess, for certainly I've never seen any knight who could surpass you; two, that I brought you to my court when you were at the point of death and restored you to health. And having once delivered you from death, if I were now to put you to death, it would be the greatest villainy in the world. For these two reasons which I've given you, you can leave my land freely without being stopped. But I want you to know one thing: if you ever come back here again and I find out about it, you may be sure that I'll cause you bodily harm if it's in my power. That is why I want you to leave and be gone from my country as soon as possible, for the mere sight of you offends me.'

When Tristan heard these words, he thanked the King very much and took his leave from all those present. The King gave him arms and a horse, and Brangain gave him her two brothers to serve him, and wept very tenderly at his departure. However, she did so as secretly as she could, because she was very frightened of being found out by the Queen, Iseut's mother, who was full of wrath and indignation that Tristan was going off scot-free; more than anything else she wanted him brought to justice. Iseut was not too worried by it, nor were the other ladies at court; they all said it was better that Tristan should leave the country freely than that he should be punished for the sake of someone who could never be brought back.

Tristan and the two squires made their way to the port and waited until the wind was right for them to set out. And when they had embarked and put to sea, the wind was so favourable and so strong that in no time at all they arrived in Cornwall. [§§ 310–54 of vol. i]

VI

TRISTAN'S CLASH WITH MARK

WHEN Tristan landed in Cornwall and recognized the country and the region where he had once had so much honour and joy, he thanked the Lord with all his heart and said that he had fared well in this voyage by the grace of God. Tristan and the two squires rested for a while on the beach, and then mounted and rode along the sea-shore and across the country asking for news of King Mark. They found out eventually that he was resident in Tintagel, a strong castle, well situated and facing the sea. Tristan, who was very eager to see his uncle and all the other barons, rode in that direction with his two squires until he arrived at court. And when they saw him fit and well, there was such great rejoicing, you would have thought God himself had descended amongst them. The King was delighted and so were all the others; they embraced him and welcomed him with the greatest possible joy. But the one who was happiest of all was Gorvenal.

The King asked Tristan how he had fared, and he told them how chance and good fortune had borne him to Ireland, and how King Anguin had found him and had ordered him to be taken to his court because he felt sorry for him, and then asked his daughter to cure him, Iseut the Blonde, who knew more about cures and medicines than all the maidens in the world; she had healed him. After this he told them how beautiful she was, more than any young girl he had ever seen; how he was recognized by the notch in his sword and how the Queen threatened him with death from which the King saved him, and then sent him away from Ireland quite honourably. But he did not tell them how well he had done at the tournament, nor how he had defeated Palamedes, the brave knight. The King was very pleased to hear this account, and so was everyone else.

Tristan remained with his uncle, lord and master over all things in Cornwall no less than the King himself. He was loved and respected by every man and woman, and because of his valour the barons stood much more in fear and dread of the King than they used to.

There lived in the Kingdom of Cornwall a lady who was the daughter of a noble count. She was so beautiful that there was no lady or maiden in the country who could match her. What more shall I tell you? She was the loveliest being in the whole of Cornwall. She was newly wed; a knight from the Kingdom of Logres had married her for her beauty. King Mark himself loved her so passionately that there was nothing he would not do to possess her, if that were possible. The lady often stayed at the court, for her manor was near Tintagel; and the King resided there more frequently than anywhere else.

One day this lady I am telling you about came to stay at King Mark's court, where she was very well received by the King himself who loved her with all his heart. When she arrived there Tristan began to look at her. He found her very attractive, which was not surprising for he saw clearly that she was the most beautiful woman he had ever beheld, except for Iseut the Blonde. Because of her loveliness he took great pleasure in gazing at her; but all the same he did so as discreetly as he could, since he wanted at all costs to avoid his uncle noticing it so as not to bring trouble on himself. The lady for her part looked at Tristan, and found him so handsome and so pleasing in every way that she said to herself that she had never seen a knight to equal him. She fell so ardently in love with Tristan and he pleased and captivated her so much that she would have considered herself fortunate if she could have made him her lover. She had already learnt who he was and knew quite a lot about his valour and his prowess.

In this way the lady loved Tristan as fervently as I have described, and yet she had never seen him before. And Tristan loved her so much that he no longer thought of Iseut the Blonde. He put Iseut out of his mind and forgot all about her on account of this lady, and she forgot everybody else on account of him. Each looked at the other fixedly, and by dint of looking the one perceived clearly enough what was in the other's heart and mind. Tristan saw and knew quite well that she was thinking of him; she realized the same about Tristan, and both were very happy and joyful about this affair.

One evening as darkness was beginning to fall the lady took leave of the King and returned to her manor with her retinue. As she was leaving she said to Tristan:

'Sir Knight, I am yours.'

And he replied:

'Dear lady, many thanks for deigning to say so, and I would have you know that I consider myself your knight.'

Thereupon they parted, and nothing else was said at that point. The lady went back to her manor, but she could not forget Tristan, nor Tristan her. When she realized that she was quite unable to overcome her desire for him,* she called a dwarf of hers whom she trusted implicitly, and revealed her feelings to him, saying:

'I want you to go to Tintagel and find Tristan, King Mark's nephew. You will convey my greetings to him and tell him not to let anything stop him from coming to see me as soon as the night sets in. You yourself will take him to the Fountain of the Pine outside.'

'My lady,' he said, 'I am at your command.'

'Make sure,' she went on, 'that he comes wearing all his armour; it's always better to be armed than unarmed, for one never knows what might happen.'

'I shall certainly tell him, my lady,' he replied.

The dwarf took leave of the lady and before long arrived in Tintagel. As soon as he saw Tristan, he drew him to one side away from the others and gave him the lady's message. Tristan was very happy at this news and said how grateful he was to her.

'Since she's sent me this message I'm prepared to do whatever she wishes.'

'Then wait till nightfall,' said the dwarf, 'when we can leave together. If you were to go now, someone might see you and suspect the truth.'

'I'll wait as long as you like,' he answered. 'You remain here, but I'm going out for a little while.'

Tristan went to his lodgings and secretly ordered his squires to have his armour ready so that he could take it whenever he wished.

'Sir,' they said, 'at your command.'

King Mark who was in his palace and had seen the dwarf talking to Tristan in private, and knew very well that he was the messenger of the lady he loved, immediately guessed what it was all about, and realized that the lady desired Tristan. He was very angry at this, for he had already sought her love on many prior occasions, but she, far from complying with his wishes, had totally rejected him. When he saw that she was prepared to give herself to someone who was not nearly as deserving as he was, he said to himself that truly women were wretched and inferior beings who always chose the worst and refused the best. This is what the King thought, for he believed he was far more worthy than Tristan in every way, both as regards his chivalry and his prowess, and for that reason he was certain that Tristan would not be able to get the better of him.

When the King had pondered for a long while, he rose from amidst his barons and went off to one of his own rooms, and then sent for the dwarf, ordering everyone else to go. Once the two of them were alone together, the King asked him:

'That conversation you had with my nephew Tristan, what was it about? I want to know!'

'Ah! have pity on me, my lord,' said the dwarf, 'I can't tell you that! It would be disloyal and treacherous of me to reveal what I ought to conceal. Don't insist on knowing, my lord: I assure you it has nothing to do with you and it can't cause you any harm.'

'All the same,' retorted the King, 'I want to know what it was. Either you tell me, or I'll kill you here and now.'

The dwarf, who was terrified of being slain, replied in great dismay:

'Ah! my lord, I'll tell you the truth rather than have you kill me. But I beg you for the love of God and for pity's sake to keep it secret.'

'I promise you,' said the King, 'that I won't mention it in any place where it could get you into trouble.'

Thereupon the dwarf told him what his lady's message to Tristan had been, and how Tristan was to come to her that very evening after nightfall. When the King heard this he was much more angry than he showed, for he considered it an indignity and an outrage on her part to have refused him and then given herself and her love to Tristan, who was still only an ignorant young boy, a youth without reason or moderation.

'I know of a nobleman of great importance and great authority,' he said, 'as high-born and as powerful as Tristan, and more valiant; he sought the lady's love, but to no avail, for however often he asked her, she always spurned him. And since she's refused a noble man and given her love to a boy, it seems to me that she should be punished and put to death.'

'Ah! my lord,' exclaimed the dwarf, 'you shouldn't blame my lady! One always sees that a queen loves a poor knight who is neither as handsome nor as brave as her husband, and that a rich king loves an impoverished lady who is neither as beautiful nor as worthy as the queen. Love doesn't choose in accordance with what is right but with what it wants; the only reason it follows is the pursuit of its inclination.'

Hearing this, the King answered him and said:

'Dwarf, that's what happened to me. I, a noble and powerful man, as you well know, have loved your lady, and still do, and have many a time asked her for her love, but she never wanted to listen. And since I see that she's rejected me for someone inferior, I'll make her recognize her folly by destroying her and her lineage for what she's done.'

The dwarf loved his lady very much, and when he heard these words he became quite frightened and dismayed; he knew the King to be a cruel man who might well carry out this threat. He began to ponder, for it seemed preferable to him, if it could be arranged, that King Mark should somehow or other take Tristan's place: his lady would thereby be saved, and it would be to Tristan's advantage as well, seeing that, since the King loved her, he must needs hate his nephew and might even cause him some harm. The King asked him what he was thinking, and he told him the whole truth. When King Mark heard that the dwarf was prepared to back him rather than Tristan, he was delighted and said:

'You could easily arrange it, if you were willing, in such a way that I can have your lady without her noticing it at all. And when I've been with her once, she'll accept me readily enough after that.'

'I'd be only too happy for you to have her if it were possible,' said the dwarf. 'But I'm not sure what to do about Tristan. After having given him the message I told you, I know he would kill me if he found out that I was deceiving him.'

'Don't worry about that,' replied the King. 'I know what we'll do. I'll leave here as soon as it grows dark, fully armed, with only one squire, and wait for you at the Thornbush Ford near your lady's manor. You will bring Tristan along, and if I don't make such an assault on him that he'll have no desire whatever to go any further, I don't want to wear arms ever again nor a crown. And when we're rid of him, then we can ride on; I'll go to your lady in place of Tristan in such a way that she'll never notice it. If you do that for me I promise you it will be to your advantage.'

'My lord,' said the dwarf, 'I'm quite prepared to do it. But how do you know that you can rid yourself of Tristan so easily? He's reputed to be such a valiant knight! That's why you shouldn't put your life at risk in a situation like this.'

'What!' exclaimed the King. 'Are you saying he is a better knight than I am? So help me God, if Tristan and I were face to face in single combat, I'm quite certain I could defeat him by force of arms in less than an hour. So don't be afraid for me! I assure you I'll make him withdraw from this undertaking in shame.'

'Let's do it like that, then, my lord,' replied the dwarf.

And the King agreed.

That was the end of their deliberation. The dwarf left the King's room and went to find Tristan who received him very cordially and said:

'I'm ready to start out whenever you wish.'

But the dwarf replied that it was not yet time.

That evening as it was growing dusk the King said to one of his most trusty squires:

'Prepare my armour and my horse. I want to ride out as soon as it's dark, and I want you to come with me. But take care not to mention it to a single man or woman, because I don't want anyone to know.'

The squire promised to do as he asked.

That evening when darkness had fallen, King Mark retired to his room, pretending he was unwell and wanted to rest, and he asked for the palace to be cleared so that there would be no noise. His orders were carried out. The King entered his room, took his armour and went into a garden, and from there on to a plain. Here he mounted his horse, and the squire mounted his, carrying the King's lance and shield, though not his helmet, as the King was already wearing this.

Thus they rode on until they came to the Thornbush Ford. The King stopped as soon as he got there and said to the squire:

'We must rest here a little while and wait for the knight on account of whom I came to this place.'

When the squire heard these words, he guessed that the King was planning some misdeed and some wickedness, for he knew his lord to be extremely cruel and treacherous. The King dismounted and the squire did likewise, and they waited there for Tristan to come; but the squire did not know this. While they were waiting and the moon had already risen, bright and clear, causing them some discomfort, Tristan came riding slowly with the dwarf. As soon as the King caught sight of them, he went to his horse and mounted; then he took his shield and his lance and put on all his armour. The squire asked him what he intended to do.

'Can you see this knight approaching?' the King asked.

'Yes, my lord,' he answered, 'I can see him clearly.'

'That knight,' said the King, 'is the man I hate most in the world. It's on account of him that I came here, and I want you to know that I'll never be happy until I've defeated him in combat.'

'Ah! my lord,' exclaimed the squire, 'that's not a very wise course of action. Since he's in your land, you should send another to deal with this matter on your behalf. If by chance you were to meet with some mishap here, the whole kingdom would be shamed and disgraced, and you yourself would be humiliated and greatly dishonoured.'

'Don't worry about that,' said the King. 'If it please God, none of that will happen.'

Thereupon he cried out to Tristan:

'Sir Knight, defend yourself against me, for I'll kill you if I can!'

Tristan was greatly dismayed to hear these words and to see the knight intent on attacking him. He did not know what to do except to fight, since he could not extricate himself from the situation in any other way. For that reason he charged forward as swiftly as his horse would go, and the King did likewise. They struck each other so fiercely that their hauberks tore and the sharp lance-heads cut into their bare flesh. Fortunately for them the lances shattered to pieces, so that the heads remained lodged in their bodies, more deeply in one case than in the other. The King was badly wounded in his left shoulder; Tristan's injury was not nearly so grave. The King flew off his horse with such force that he was severely bruised and battered, and as he fell to the ground he uttered a loud groan in the manner of someone who was seriously hurt. When Tristan saw the blow he had dealt him, he looked at the King no longer, but turned away, saying to the dwarf:

'Let's go. This knight won't cause us any more trouble!'

When the squire saw his lord lying on the ground, he dismounted and went up to him and started to wail as loudly as he could, for he was convinced that the King was dead. King Mark lay in this state a long time before he regained consciousness, and could not say a word for a considerable while after that. Then he groaned loudly and said to the squire:

'Bring me my horse and I'll mount, and let's leave this place. If it's turned out badly for me here, never mind. I'll avenge myself so well another time that the knight who struck this blow will regret it.'

The King mounted his horse in great anguish and great pain; he was so badly injured and so bruised that if he had not been such a powerful man he would not have been able to ride in that condition. The squire, fearing that his lord was fatally wounded, had not stopped lamenting, and asked him how he felt.

'Considering what's happened to me,' said the King, 'I'm quite well, thank God. But if the lance which struck me had penetrated a little more deeply, I would have been dead without any doubt.'

Talking thus they rode along till they reached Tintagel. They dismounted in the garden and from there went on inside. Then the King was overcome with weakness, for he had lost so much blood that it was a wonder how he could keep upright. He had himself disarmed, after which he hurried into his bedroom and sent for the doctor who came without delay. When he had removed the lance-head and examined the wound inside and out, he could not help remarking:

'My lord, you've been badly hurt. But, by the grace of God, you're fortunate in that it's not a fatal injury.'

'And do you think you can cure me?' asked the King.

'Yes, I do, my lord,' the doctor replied, 'with God's help.'

'Then I'm not concerned about what's happened to me,' said the King. 'But make quite sure, as you value your life, not to reveal this to anyone in the world. I shall stay in this room until I'm cured, and I want my men to be told that I have some other illness.'

And the doctor assured him that he would see to it.

Thus the King remained in great distress and sorely wounded. And Tristan rode on with the dwarf until he came to the lady's manor. But first he had disarmed himself and bandaged his wound as best he could, for he was very fearful of losing too much blood. The dwarf had helped him to take off his hauberk and put it on again. They stopped when they reached the spot where the lady had told the dwarf to bring Tristan.

'Wait for me here, Tristan,' said the dwarf. 'I'll go and find out from my lady whether she intends to come out here or wants you to join her in there.'

'Go quickly,' Tristan told him.

The dwarf went to his lady and found that she had already gone to bed and was about to sleep, since a large part of the night had by this time passed. As soon as she saw him she asked him softly:

'Where is Tristan? Have you brought him?'

'Yes, my lady,' he answered, 'he's outside in the orchard and awaits your command.'

'Go to him quickly', she said, 'and tell him to come here.'

'Willingly, my lady,' he replied.

The dwarf went to fetch Tristan, and the lady sent away the maidens who served her, for she wanted to make quite sure that they did not know what was going on. Thereupon Tristan came in, fully armed as he was. He greeted the lady, took off his armour and undressed himself, and lay down beside her. They speedily extinguished the candles and had great pleasure and delight; but unfortunately while they were together thus, Tristan's wound burst open and began to bleed. He was so hot that he did not pay attention to it nor realize he was bleeding, and the lady did not notice anything either, but took the moist blood to be perspiration.

They enjoyed themselves greatly and talked together of many things. In the midst of their happiness the dwarf burst in and said to his lady:

'My lady, hurry! Get up quickly and send away Tristan. My lord is down below and will soon come up here.'

The lady was most alarmed at this news, being very afraid of her husband.

'Quick, Tristan,' she said, 'get up and take your arms and go! If my lord finds you here, you will be killed and I shall be shamed.'

Tristan was not very pleased to hear this, since he had no wish to part from the lady so soon. He dressed and got ready, took his armour and went to where he had left his horse; then he mounted and set off towards Tintagel, happy and joyful at what had taken place between them, but grieved at having been forced to leave in such haste.

The knight who was the lady's husband disarmed himself and went straight up to the lady's bedroom; a young girl led the way carrying a burning torch. When he came to the bed and saw the sheets stained crimson with the fresh and new blood,* he was stunned, and so was the lady, for she instantly realized that this blood must have come from Tristan. She considered herself stupid for not having been more heedful and taken note of it.

'Ah! lady,' said the knight, 'where has this blood come from?'

Not knowing what to reply, she said in great dismay:

'Ah! sir, it came from my nose which didn't stop bleeding all night.'

'Lady,' he replied, 'it's no use lying! That blood came from someone other than you. Tell me who it was, or I'll kill you, so help me God, this instant.'

The lady was so frightened that she could not think what to say, for she saw clearly that there was no point in dissimulation. He put his hand on his sword, and drawing it, naked, from the scabbard, he said in anger:

'Either you tell me who was in bed with you, or I shall kill you this instant, as God is my witness!'

When she saw that she had no alternative, since all the while he was holding the naked sword and threatening to kill her if she did not tell him what he wanted to know, she answered:

'Sir, it was Tristan, King Mark's nephew, and this blood which you see here is his.'

'And how long ago did he leave?'

'Sir, he can't have gone very far yet.'

The knight was exceedingly distressed to hear this, as he loved the lady very much. He began to think hard, and when he had pondered for quite a while he said:

'Lady, I never loved anyone as much as you, and you have brought this shame upon me.'

That was all he said. Then he asked for his armour, and as soon as it had been fetched, he armed himself and went into the courtyard. There he mounted his horse, took his shield and his lance, and departed all alone; he did not want anyone to accompany him. When he had reached the highway, it was not long before he saw in the moonlight the hoof-marks of Tristan's horse, for the latter was riding along slowly, lost in thoughts about his adventure with the lady. The knight rode on till he reached Tristan, and cried out as soon as he caught sight of him:

'Turn back! You've dishonoured me, but I'll make you pay for it dearly if I can.'

At these words Tristan looked round, and seeing the knight approach with his lance outstretched, he turned the head of his horse towards him, drew his sword and covered his breast with his shield. The knight, who was very strong, gave him such a blow that he pierced his shield and hauberk and thrust a large part of the lance-head into his body; and if the lance had not broken into pieces, he would undoubtedly have killed him. At this onslaught, Tristan gathered all his strength and struck him so fiercely with his sword on top of the helmet that he made him feel the blade in his head. The blow was mighty and struck in anger, and if it had gone straight, he would certainly have slain him; but the sword went askew, and that saved his life.

Tristan, feeling that he was injured, said to the knight in wrath and indignation:

'Sir Knight, you've wounded me, but you haven't gained much thereby, for I think you're on the point of death!'

The Knight made no answer to what Tristan said, nor had he the power to do so. And Tristan rode straight back to Tintagel, badly wounded and hurt, and made his way to his lodgings; he had already lost a lot of blood. When his squires saw him in this state, they wanted to start lamenting, but he said to them:

'I order you to be quiet, as you value your life. There's nothing wrong with me.'

'Ah! Tristan,' exclaimed Gorvenal, 'I've looked after you badly. If I were as wise as many people say, I would never have allowed you to go there without me. I should be blamed for this mishap more than you, because I should have taken care of you.'

'Sir,' replied Tristan, 'don't be dismayed. I assure you I have no wound or injury which won't heal soon.'

The doctors were sent for without delay, as quietly as possible, since Tristan did not want his uncle to know anything about it. As soon as they arrived, they examined his wounds thoroughly and found the last one more serious than the first; however they assured him that he would not die as a result. Gorvenal, who had been very worried about him, was greatly relieved.

Tristan remained in bed suffering great pain, for he had been badly wounded. He wanted his men to keep it as secret as they could; if anyone asked about him they pretended he had some other malady. King Mark also enquired, and they told him Tristan was ill, but that they did not know what was wrong with him. When the King heard this, he thought it was as a result of the wound he inflicted on him at their encounter by the Thornbush Ford, and this made him think even more highly of himself than before. And to show that he was stronger than Tristan, he decided that he would not remain in bed any longer; he got up, dressed, and called the squire who had accompanied him.

'I have some news for you,' he said. 'Tristan is laid up as a result of the wound I gave him when we jousted together at the Thornbush Ford. You thought that I'd had the worst of it by far, but that's not so, as you can see quite clearly: Tristan is confined to his bed, and I'm up and about.'

The squire was quite amazed at this, for he thought it was the truth, judging by the evidence the King had given him.

'Let's go and see Tristan,' said the King, 'and we'll find out how he is.'

'Willingly, my lord,' replied the squire.

As soon as the King was able to ride, he mounted his horse and went to see Tristan who was gravely ill; he had lost so much blood that it was a miracle he had survived. The King asked him what was wrong with him, and Tristan, seeing that he could not conceal it, answered:

'My lord, why should I hide it from you? I had the misfortune to be wounded, but I don't know who did it, so help me God.'

'My dear nephew,' said the King, 'now you can see that there are knights as brave as you in this country. You almost died as a result of your folly, and it would have been a pity if that had happened, for you could still be a knight of great valour.'

'My lord,' he answered, 'I'm not dead yet, by the grace of God, and I'll recover well enough. But you may be sure that this blow I've received will be dearly paid for.'

When the King heard this threat, he was convinced it was aimed at him, and that Tristan was well aware that it was he who had wounded him in this way. Now he could no longer doubt that he was a brave knight; none the less, the King did not fear him as greatly as he did before they had jousted together, for he reckoned that Tristan had not fared much better than he at that encounter.

'Tell me,' said the King, 'will you be able to find out who did this to you?'

'My lord,' he answered, 'if I don't know at present, it won't be long before I do; and you may be sure that I'll avenge myself one day even if I haven't done so already.'

King Mark really believed that this was directed at him, and he wanted to rid himself of Tristan in some way, but he did not say what was in his mind.

After the King had been with Tristan for a long while, he took his leave and departed, and Tristan remained, very distressed and angry. However, those who were taking care of him saw to it that within a short time he was able to ride and wear arms. When the King found that Tristan was cured, and as handsome and strong as ever, he was very frightened; he was sure Tristan hated him, but he did not know what to do about it.

Shortly afterwards at Christmas-time the King invites all his knights and ladies to court, including the beautiful lady he loves and her husband called Segurades, the same who later fights with Gawain for the Lady of Roestoc* whom Segurades forcibly wants to marry.

A knight-errant called Blioberis arrives and asks the King for a favour, namely to be allowed to take away the lady of his choice. The King agrees, whereupon Blioberis chooses the wife of Segurades. The latter follows and attacks Blioberis, but is badly wounded. Tristan does not dare to go in pursuit for fear of King Mark.

Two knights-errant are seen passing nearby, and Mark expresses a wish to speak to them. Audret, Tristan's first cousin, offers to bring them back to court; he has just been knighted, and is so envious of Tristan that he hates him bitterly. A beautiful young maiden appears asking for Tristan, and when he comes forward, she publically reviles him. He rides after her to find out the reason, and Gorvenal goes with him. They come upon Audret in a very sorry plight; he has tried to force the two knights, Sagremor the Reckless and Dodinel the Wild, to go back with him to Mark's court, and Sagremor has knocked him off his horse. Tristan offers to avenge his cousin, and badly wounds both knights. Sagremor is distraught when he learns that he has been defeated by a knight from Cornwall, and, throwing down his arms, declares he will never fight again till he hears that he is not the only one of the Round Table companions to have been vanquished by a Cornish knight.

Tristan rides on in pursuit of the maiden, and at dusk he sees her entering a castle in the company of Blioberis and a lady whom he recognizes as Segurades's wife; he now realizes that it was she who had sent the girl to insult him. He spends the night nearby at the house of a widow, whose son remembers him as the victor of the Irish tournament; but Tristan denies it, for he always conceals his knightly deeds. Next morning he challenges Blioberis to a duel. They fight fiercely for a long time, each inflicting serious wounds on the other, but each determined to fight to the death.

When they had kept up the first assault for as long as they could, and had reduced each other to such a state that they were forced to rest in order to recover their strength and their breath, they stood back a little way from each other. Blioberis, a very wise and valiant knight, was eager to come out of this battle honourably, for although he was full of courage, he none the less feared the prowess he had seen Tristan display. He therefore said to him after they had rested a little while:

'Sir, we've fought together long enough for me to realize that you're the best knight I've ever come across. However, don't let my praise go to your head; you may be certain you won't get off any more lightly on account of it. You for your part are well aware that I can hold my own, and in case I win this battle I would like you to tell me your name so that I would know whom to boast about; and similarly I shall tell you mine in order that, if you kill me, you'll know whom you have killed.'

Thereupon Tristan answered him saying:

'My name is Tristan.'

'Tristan,' said Blioberis, 'are you King Mark's nephew?'

'Yes, indeed,' he replied.

'Truly?' said Blioberis. 'Then in God's name this battle is over, for I won't fight against you any longer. I've heard many people speak of you so highly that even if I had defeated you, I would have declared myself vanquished. And, so help me God, on account of the prowess I've found in you, I relinquish this battle in your favour and surrender myself to you, if you like.'

'Ah! sir,' exclaimed Tristan, 'I can't accept this honour: I haven't deserved it. But since you wish this battle to cease, I'm quite agreeable.'

When Gorvenal saw that the fight was over, he stretched out his hands towards the heavens; never had he been so afraid for Tristan as now. Tristan then said to Blioberis:

'You must hand over this lady; I came here for no other reason.'

'Sir Tristan,' said Blioberis, 'that's quite out of the question. We might as well resume the battle, for you know perfectly well that I have a rightful claim to the lady. But now listen to what I'll do for love of you: I'll put the lady here between us, and the one to whom she gives herself, let him take her.'

'No one could ask you for more than that!' exclaimed Tristan.

And that is what they did. They took the lady and placed her between them, and said to her:

'Lady, this battle has been fought for you. Now go to whichever one of us pleases you most, and that will be the end of our quarrel.'

'Many thanks,' she replied, 'for allowing me to settle this dispute.'

Then she turned to Tristan, and said to him:

'Tristan, I loved you very much. But when I found that you were so craven and so cowardly that you let me be carried off from your uncle's court by a single knight, you may be sure that I shall never love you again.'

Thereupon she walked over to Blioberis.

When Tristan saw that she had thus rejected him in favour of Blioberis, he was so upset that he had never been more grieved about anything that happened to him, because without any doubt his love for her was very great. He turned away, so distressed and sorrowful that he was unable to utter a syllable; he went to his horse and mounted without saying another word to the lady, and returned to court in grief and anger.

The King had already learnt from some of his men how Tristan had dealt with the two knights-errant, and this exploit as well as others he had been told about made him very frightened that Tristan would one day dispossess him of all his land; and that was something he wanted to think about very carefully.

Once Tristan had returned to court, the King called him and said in the presence of many noble men:

'Tristan, dear nephew, I have heard things about you which I find it very difficult to believe. And because I want to be certain, I bid you and beg of you, by the faith you owe me, that you'll swear on holy relics to tell me the truth about what I'm going to ask you; and rest assured that it will bring you greater honour than it will me, and that you won't be shamed by telling me.'

Tristan was very afraid of his uncle, as he was well aware that the King hated him mortally; and Gorvenal himself had pointed it out to him. He therefore did not dare to refuse his uncle's request in front of so many noble men as were present. For that reason he replied:

'My lord, I'm prepared to tell you what you want to know since it won't bring me dishonour, for on that condition I'm willing to speak.'

'Then swear it,' said the King.

And he swore in accordance with what the King had promised him.

'Now I beg you,' continued the King, 'to tell me all the knightly deeds you've ever done from the time I first knighted you.'

And Tristan replied in some distress:

'Since you want to know, I'll tell you, but I assure you I'd much rather not.'

Then he began to relate the deeds of valour he had done in Ireland and elsewhere, and there is no doubt that his account gave great pleasure to many worthy men. When he had finished, he said to his uncle:

'My lord, now you've heard the story of my life, and you may be certain I've concealed nothing that I should have told you. But you could have refrained from making it all known, if you'd wanted.'

'Dear nephew,' said the King, 'I wouldn't have missed this story for anything! Now I know you to be such that you can't fail to be one of the best knights in the world, if God grants you a long life. And for that reason I have more faith in you now, and shall have, than I did in the past.'

The barons said:

'My lord, henceforth Cornwall need not be dismayed. As long as Tristan is with us, fit and healthy, there's no reason to fear any man in the world.'

The King replied:

'May God grant him health and prowess and renown!'

He said nothing else about the matter at that point, and did not divulge to any man what was in his heart, but he felt much more uneasy than before because now his fear of Tristan was greater than ever. For that reason he wondered what he could do, for there was nothing in the world he would have liked better than to put Tristan to death, provided he could do it in such a way that Tristan would not suspect anything. He was well aware that if he were to banish him from his court, he would inevitably incur his ill-will, and that was a sure way of bringing trouble upon himself; and were he to keep Tristan with him, he was such a valiant knight and so loved by one and another that if a quarrel broke out between them, he could not escape from being shamed by Tristan in the end. He was at a loss what to do; it seemed to him he would not go unscathed whichever way he turned. And when he had thought for a long while, more worried than anyone else could be, he had an idea which pleased him greatly, for he reckoned he had found a means of ridding himself of Tristan, and if Tristan were to die as a result, he did not care: he preferred to see him dead rather than alive.

Shortly after this time the King was sitting amongst his barons and they were impressing upon him the desirability of his marrying. Tristan himself, who was there, declared:

'My lord, my lord, it would please me greatly if you were to take a wife, for the whole Kingdom of Cornwall would gain thereby.'

And the King replied:

'Tristan, if it pleases you, then I shall have a wife: you are the only one who can bring her to me.'

'My lord,' said Tristan, 'since I am the one who can bring her to you, you shall have her; I assure you I would rather die than not do so.'

'And how can I be sure of that?' asked the King.

Tristan stretched out his hands towards a chapel and swore that with the help of God and the saints he would do his utmost. The King answered:

'Many thanks. You have said enough, and I'm satisfied. I'll tell you now who is the one I'm asking for. You know well, and you yourself have often said so and advised me, that if I were to take a wife, I should take one whose beauty could give me pleasure and delight. As far as beauty is concerned, you have praised only one woman, but that one you have praised as more beautiful than all other women in the world. She is the one I want, and she is the one I shall have, if I have any at all. And do you know whom I'm talking about? It's Iseut the Blonde, the daughter of the King of Ireland. She is the one you must bring me, and I love her more than all the other ladies or maidens I have ever heard about. Now start out at once, and take with you as many men from my court as you want; and make sure you don't rest until I have her in my possession as you have promised me.'

When Tristan heard these words, he immediately realized that his uncle, the King, was sending him to Ireland more for his death than for any other reason. But whatever might come of it, he agreed to do what he had promised. And to cover up the truth, the King continued:

'Tristan, dear nephew, are you doing this for me willingly?'

'My lord,' he answered, 'rest assured that I would rather die than not bring her to you.'

'Many thanks, dear nephew,' said the King. 'Then get ready, and take as many men from my court as you like. Make sure that you fulfil this task successfully, for I shall never be happy till you've come back and I see Iseut the Blonde in my court.'

Tristan, as the true story relates, would gladly have extricated himself from this situation if he could, but he had taken his oath in the presence of so many noble men that there could be no question of retracting. He therefore said no more, and yet he knew he was being sent to Ireland to die, because his uncle, the King, was well aware that nowhere else in the world was he hated as mortally on account of the Morholt whom he had killed. And since the King was sending him there, it was quite clear to him that it was not for his good but for his misfortune. Well, come what may, he was prepared to take the risk.

Then he chose up to sixty knights, all young men, the best he could find, and all of very noble lineage. They were so upset at being chosen that they would rather King Mark had stripped them of all their land than sent them to Ireland; there they would be shamed if they were recognized, for no men were hated so mortally in Ireland as were the Cornish people. However, whether they liked it or not, they equipped themselves with arms and all they needed. The ship was ready and they embarked. Tristan took Gorvenal with him; he did not want to leave him behind. Gorvenal wept for Tristan and said to him:

'Now you can see clearly how your uncle loves you! He has hatched this plot to bring about your death, that's certain. His aim is less to have the maiden than to rid himself of you and make you die.'

'Don't be too dismayed, sir,' said Tristan. 'If my uncle hates me now, I shall accomplish so much by my strength that he'll end up loving me; nor will his heart be so cruel that I won't vanquish it if I can. And let him not worry about the maiden: I'll see to it that he shall have her.'

'May God grant it!' said Gorvenal. [§§ 354–99 of vol. i]

VII

SECOND VOYAGE TO IRELAND: THE PHILTRE

THUS Tristan put to sea with his companions in a very costly and beautiful ship; he enjoyed and amused himself and comforted his fellows. But they were so frightened that they did not know what to say when they remembered Ireland where they were hated so mortally and where they knew they were certain to die. However, Tristan comforted and reassured them so much, promising them joy and honour from this exploit, that they became more cheerful; such was their faith in his prowess and nobility that they felt only good could come to them wherever he was, and this hope kept them joyous and happy.

While they were sailing thus it so happened that a violent and terrible storm blew up over the sea, and the waves became so turbulent that everyone thought they were going to die. The sailors were frightened and dismayed, for they saw clearly that the wind was totally against them. 'Oh God,' prayed Tristan, 'help us and save us from death', and all the others cried out in like manner. When the sailors realized that neither their skill nor their efforts were of any avail, they gave themselves up to the winds and let the ship go wherever the winds blew it. They no longer knew what to do except to ask God for mercy. The storm raged in this way for one night and one day; and the wind had been so strong and so fierce that when it began to drop and the sea became still and calm, they found themselves the next day in Great Britain, one English league* away from a very wealthy city called Camelot, the richest and most beautiful which was at that time in Great Britain. King Arthur liked to reside there because it was such a fine city and well endowed with all things a nobleman might need. However he was not in residence when they landed there; he was staying in the city of Carduel in Wales* with a large company of noble men.

When Tristan saw that they were aground he asked his sailors:

'My good men, do you know where we've landed?'

'Yes, sir,' they answered, 'we do. We're in Great Britain, King Arthur's country. Here we need have no fear or anxiety.'

'Since we've come to a safe place,' said Tristan, 'and we've suffered more discomfort than was good for us, I suggest we go ashore and rest for a little while.'

The sailors did as he had proposed, for they went on shore without delay and pitched as many as six very costly and beautiful tents on a meadow. The knights placed their shields outside in order to make it known that they were strangers, and they also had their armour brought out of the ship.

Two knights appear, Marganor and Hestor, who recently met outside Camelot and are not well acquainted with each other. Hestor, a young man who has not been a knight for more than a month, is Lancelot's brother, though neither of them knows of this relationship.* Noticing the shields placed outside the tents, they take this as an invitation to joust. A knight from Leonois sees them getting ready and warns Tristan, who is delighted, and straightaway puts on his armour. He jousts first with Marganor and then with Hestor, and knocks them both to the ground. The latter wants to continue the fight with his sword, but Tristan, seeing no cause for a battle between them, refuses, much to Hestor's annoyance. He is even more irate when he hears that he has been beaten by a Cornish knight, and, discarding his armour and his horse, he goes off on foot. Tristan and his companions find his behaviour highly amusing.

Next morning around daybreak, while the Cornish knights were enjoying themselves by the seashore as I have described, it so happened that a ship arrived at the very spot where they had landed. And if anyone were to ask me whose ship it was and who was inside it, I would say that it came from Ireland and that inside it was King Anguin of Ireland and many other knights. When they had come ashore and they saw the tents of those from Cornwall, they went over towards them to find out who they were. King Anguin himself rode up, mounted on a big charger, and asked them where they had come from. They replied:

'We are from Cornwall.'

'From Cornwall?' asked the King. 'And what adventure has brought you here?'

They told him that a storm at sea had brought them but that they would leave as soon as the wind was favourable; that was all they were waiting for.

When the King heard mention of Cornwall he immediately remembered Tristan, and asked:

'King Mark's nephew, Tristan, is he in this company?'

'Yes,' they replied, 'he is sleeping in one of these tents. But you, who ask us this, who are you?'

'I'm an Irish knight who would very much like to speak to him,' he answered, 'and I think he would be equally pleased to speak to me.'

'What is your name?' they enquired, 'so that we can tell him.'

'My name is Anguin', he said. 'As soon as he hears my name, I'm sure he'll remember me. For the love of God, make him come and speak to me.'

They did as he asked, never thinking he was the King of Ireland, since he did not as a rule come to the Kingdom of Logres.

As soon as Tristan heard the name of Anguin, he recalled the King of Ireland, and, leaping out of bed, he asked where he was.

'Sir,' they answered, 'he's outside waiting to speak to you. We don't know what he wants.'

Tristan hurried out of the tent when he heard this, and, seeing the King, he ran towards him with outstretched arms, and the King did likewise, and they greeted each other with great joy and pleasure.

'Tristan,' said the King, 'I'm so glad I've found you at this point, for I need your help more than I ever did before.'

'My lord,' replied Tristan, 'say no more. It was not long ago that you delivered me from death; and since you saved my life, you have the right to ask me to risk my life. And I assure you and promise you as a knight that there is nothing in the world I would not do for you to the best of my ability unless I saw clearly that it would bring me great shame.'

'Many thanks', said the King. 'Now I'll tell you why I came here. You will remember that at the time when you left, tournaments were often held in Ireland, and many foreign knights came to joust from the kingdoms of Logres, Wales and France. A short while after you had gone, a tournament was proclaimed outside the very same castle where you defeated the brave knight Palamedes. It so happened that four knights from the lineage of King Ban took part in that tournament which was held after your departure, and they did so well that they were declared the victors; and they fully deserved it, for they showed themselves to be very valiant. After the tournament I begged these four knights to come and stay with me at the very castle where you yourself lived for so long, and they accepted. And when they had come to my court together with many noble men, it happened, I don't know by what misadventure, that one of the four knights was killed there; that I can't deny. But, as God is my witness, it was neither by me nor at my instigation; on the contrary, I was so distressed that I would rather have lost the best castle I own than have this happen.

'When the three knights who had come with him saw this, they were most upset, but realizing the weakness of their position, they did not dare to call me to account. However, one of them, called Blanor, the brother of Blioberis, said in the hearing of all:

"King Anguin, you have shamed us by killing our brother like this in your court. This treachery was committed in an underhand fashion, but I shall uncover the truth! And do you know how? I shall make you admit it with your own lips at King Arthur's court, for there you'll have to fight with me, face to face, and there, God willing, I shall make you acknowledge yourself beaten in the presence of many noble men. And I want you to know that no treason has been committed in your kingdom for many a year which will be shown up as clearly as this one will be. I'll prove you to be disloyal and treacherous, I promise you, at the very same court I told you."

'As a result of this mishap which took place in the way I described to you, all the foreign knights left my court, and were so troubled by the death of this knight that they no longer wanted to stay in Ireland. A short while ago I received a letter from Logres in the name of King Arthur asking me to come to Camelot as I valued my life, ready to defend myself against the charge of treachery which Blanor had made against me; and if I didn't come, I could be sure of being ruined and disinherited for evermore, myself and my heirs. That was what the letter said, and I didn't dare to disobey this command, for I'm certain King Arthur would destroy me in the end. That is why I've come here, dismayed and frightened because I can't find anyone prepared to fight this battle against Blanor who is reputed to be an exceedingly valiant knight; and I know well that I couldn't hold out against him, since he's a better knight than I am. That's what worries me; if I were as good a knight as he, I wouldn't hesitate to take up arms against him. For that reason I would like to ask you to undertake this battle against Blanor; and to make you feel more confident, I shall swear to you that my cause is just and loyal, and that I am not guilty of this deed.'

When Tristan heard these words, he was very glad and joyful: it seemed to him that this was his opportunity of making the King grant him Iseut and give her to him in such a way that he could fulfil his obligation. He therefore replied:

'My lord, you have done much for me, and I for my part will agree to do this for you on condition that you'll grant me a favour after I've brought it to a successful conclusion.'

And the King acquiesced. Tristan then called all the men from Ireland and Cornwall who were there and told them what had been agreed by the two of them, namely that he would undertake the battle, and that after the battle the King would grant him any favour he would ask.

'Is that true?' asked Gorvenal.

'Yes, it is', replied the King.

Then the rejoicing began, for the Irish were delighted when they heard that Tristan had taken the battle upon himself: it appeared to them that this dispute had already been honourably settled. They thanked Our Lord for their good fortune, and for letting them come upon Tristan in the nick of time. And when they were all together, Tristan said to them:

'I beg you, my lords, as you value your honour and mine, not to reveal my name nor divulge who is fighting this battle for you. And when you take me to the court, I want to be armed in such a way that no one can see me clearly.'

They promised him to do all he asked.

In the midst of their rejoicing a young girl appears carrying a split shield, which, she says, will only rejoin when a noble lady gives herself to a valiant knight; but she refuses to disclose their names. She is on her way to King Arthur's court in Carduel, and tells them that King Carados Shortarm and the King of Scotland are in Camelot to make sure that the dispute between the Irish King and Blanor is settled justly; the latter has already arrived at court accompanied by many famous knights from the lineage of King Ban.

This young girl has been sent to King Arthur's court by the Lady of the Lake who has brought up Lancelot. She has learnt a great deal about magic from Merlin, but in the end she caused his death* by means of the enchantment he had taught her. The shield is destined for Guinevere to show her that the Lady of the Lake knows all about her relationship with Lancelot; the shield does indeed rejoin* after their first night together. For the moment, however, Lancelot is in the kingdom of Sorelois with Galehot, son of the Giantess and lord of the Distant Isles; he loves Lancelot so much that he dies when he thinks he has lost him.*

Shortly after the maiden's departure she reappears, distraught, for a knight, Breuz the Pitiless, has brutally snatched the shield from her. Tristan retrieves it by knocking him down, and sends him to Gawain who hates him mortally for his cruelty to ladies.

Next morning King Anguin and Tristan set out for Camelot with a large company of noble men. The pledges are handed to the two kings, who had been appointed as judges, and the duel between Tristan and Blanor is ready to start in a field outside the city, watched by a huge crowd. The two knights charge at each other with great force and are both knocked to the ground. Then the swordplay begins. The battle is fierce and arduous; both are badly wounded, but neither will give in. After a long time they are forced to rest, and Tristan, at Blanor's request, names himself. Then they resume the combat, threatening each other with death; in the end Blanor falls backwards from loss of blood, and asks his adversary to cut off his head. But Tristan, too generous, appeals to the two judges to make peace between the lineage of Ban and the King of Ireland, and they agree, whereupon Tristan rides off as quickly as he can. King Anguin wants to follow him, and in order to avoid a lengthy argument, consents to reveal the victor's name. That is how Tristan's strength and prowess, as well as his generosity, became known at Arthur's court.

In this part the story relates that when Tristan had left Blanor and returned to the tents which had been pitched by the sea-shore, his companions, who saw him arrive, came up to him and helped him dismount and asked him how he felt.

'Fine,' he said, 'by the grace of God, for I've cleared the King of the treachery with which he was charged.'

And they raised their hands towards the heavens and praised Our Lord.

'Sir,' they said, 'you're severely wounded.'

'That may well be so,' he replied, 'but I'm not too anxious or afraid of having a fatal injury.'

They all said they were delighted to hear it, and took off his armour and made him as comfortable as they could. Thereupon the King rode up with the large company of Cornish and Irish knights who had gone with him to court. As soon as he saw Tristan, he ran towards him with outstretched arms and embraced him many a time, and said:

'Tristan, you have done so much for me that I am yours; and you have fully deserved it by the wielding of your sword. But, for God's sake, tell me whether you can be cured, for I know well that you're seriously wounded and have suffered much.'

Tristan told him that he was not worried about any of his wounds provided he had a good doctor and time to relax and rest.

'You can rest now', said the King, 'and we'll find you a good doctor.'

They looked after Tristan as best they could. They had his wounds and injuries examined, and he was cared for by the King's own physician, a very knowledgeable man.

Tristan then said to the King:

'My lord, you remember the agreement which we made.'

'I do indeed', replied the King. 'I know that I must grant you whatever you ask, if it is in my power to grant it, since you have acquitted yourself well of the promise you made me in the presence of those of Ireland and Cornwall.'

'Thank you very much, my lord,' said Tristan, 'for acknowledging it. Now I beg you to tell me where you want to go when you leave here.'

'Indeed,' said the King, 'I'm not going to leave you before you've fully recovered, but then I shall put to sea and return to Ireland as quickly as possible. And, if you please, I would like you to come with me out of friendship and goodwill, and all your companions as well.'

'Is that really your wish, my lord?' Tristan asked.

'As God is my witness,' replied the King, 'I greatly desire it.'

'Then I accept,' said Tristan, 'since it pleases you.'

In this way they both agreed. And Tristan straightaway asked the sailors if the winds were favourable for a journey to Ireland, and they replied:

'Yes, sir, very favourable, thank God. We're only waiting for the King's command and yours, for we are ready.'

'Then I for my part don't want to delay matters,' said Tristan. 'I'm not so badly wounded that I can't stand the swell of the sea.'

King Anguin was happy to hear this, since he was eager to be back in Ireland. Both the Irish and the Cornish put to sea, having a joyful and pleasant time together; they used to be mortal enemies but as a result of this adventure which God had sent them they made up their differences and became good friends, wishing each other well. They crossed the sea without rancour, sorrow or anger, and God let them have winds which were favourable to them.

When they reached Ireland, they landed in front of the castle where the Queen was staying with her beautiful daughter Iseut. The Queen welcomed the King with great joy when she saw him safe and sound, for her heart had been filled with fear at the thought of King Ban's lineage.

'Lady, lady,' he said, 'are you happy that I've returned in good health?'

'Very happy indeed, my lord,' she replied, 'and so I should be.'

'Lady,' he went on, 'you have no one but Tristan here to thank for my return. I assure you, without him I would never have come back to Ireland, because the knight who accused me of treachery was exceedingly brave. I would have been shamed without any doubt if I had fought against him. But Tristan in his generosity and kindness, remembering the goodwill we showed him in Ireland, took up the battle for me against Blanor to clear me of this charge. Such was the pain he bore on the day of the battle that if his valour and his prowess were not as great as you know, he would have been dishonoured and slain, and I would have been disgraced and ruined for all time. And since he has brought us this happiness and joy, and freed us from grief and from shame, and he has endured much suffering for us as is clearly apparent, let us think of serving and honouring him as much as we can now that we have him with us in Ireland, and let us try to repay him to the best of our ability for the great kindness he has shown us.'

When the King had finished speaking, all those who heard his words cried out aloud:

'King, we're all prepared to do his command in view of what you've told us. It's only right after what he's done that the Kingdom of Cornwall should be on good terms with Ireland, and that Ireland should be on good terms with Cornwall.'

Tristan and all his companions were received in Ireland with great joy and honour. Tristan stayed at the King's court happy and of good cheer, and remained there until he was healed of all his wounds and injuries and fully recovered so that he was as agile and as fit as he had ever been.

Then he realized that he had stayed in Ireland long enough, in the company of the fair Iseut who had completely changed his heart, for her beauty, which was much talked about and envied by many, often filled him with conflicting emotions. On the one hand, he thought that it would be better if he were to take Iseut for himself rather than hand her over to his uncle; she was the most beautiful and most desirable young girl in the world and he loved her with all his heart, and it was clear to him that if he did not take her at this point, he would have lost her for evermore, and for that reason he wanted to keep her for himself. On the other hand, when he had thought about it for some time, he said to himself that he had promised and pledged Iseut to his uncle in the presence of many noble men, and if after that he did not hand her over to him, no one would hear of it who would not consider him base and disloyal. It would be preferable to safeguard his loyalty without Iseut than to have her in his possession according to his wishes and to be condemned as disloyal. And so in the end he decided that as a reward for his services he would request the hand of Iseut for his uncle, King Mark, and not for himself.

One day the King got up and went to his palace where many people had gathered. All Tristan's companions were there, because he had sent for them and told them he would that very day ask for the favour which King Anguin had promised to grant them when it was agreed that Tristan would fight his battle for him. Tristan rose and came before the King and said in the hearing of all the barons:

'My lord, you owe me a favour, as you know full well.'

'Indeed, that's true', said the King. 'Tell me what it is, and I'm quite prepared to grant it to you, provided it's something I'm able to give you.'

'Many thanks, my lord,' said Tristan. 'I ask you then for the hand of your daughter Iseut, and I should tell you that I'm not asking for myself but for my uncle, King Mark, who wants to crown her Queen of Cornwall. I should add that all of us here left Cornwall for no other purpose, and we only came to Ireland to win Iseut the Blonde. With God's help we were fortunate enough to encounter you when we did, as you well know, and consequently we say that we have won Iseut.'

Thereupon the King replied:

'Tristan, what you say is true. You have indeed won Iseut, and paid for her dearly, and for that reason I give her to you gladly so that you can take her as your wife, if you wish; and if you can't, because you are bound to King Mark to hand her over to him, that too pleases me greatly, for he's such a worthy and wise man that my daughter couldn't make a better marriage, so it seems to me. Therefore I'm quite willing to let you take her wherever you wish; I believe you to be such a loyal and noble knight that I'm sure you would do nothing with her which could be held against you.'

Then the King sent for his daughter, so beautiful and so pleasing in every way that at this time there was no young lady or maiden in the world who could match her. When she appeared before her father, accompanied by many young girls and ladies—even her mother, the Queen, had come with her who as yet had no idea why she had been summoned to court—the King took her by the right hand, and said in the hearing of all those who were present:

'Sir Tristan, in whose name are you asking for the hand of Iseut?'

'My lord,' Tristan answered, 'I'm asking for her hand in the name of my uncle, King Mark, who wants to marry her and crown her Queen of Cornwall.'

'Are you speaking thus in good faith?'

'My lord,' he replied, 'I speak as a knight.'

Then he began to relate how King Mark had sent him to fetch Iseut, and how he had left Cornwall in such a way that he could never return there if he did not bring her back as he had promised.

'You have told me enough,' said the King. 'I grant you Iseut for King Mark. Take her: I give you possession of her. May God in his mercy bring it to pass that they spend their lives together in joy and happiness and good fortune.'

'So be it,' replied Tristan.

Thereupon he accepted Iseut on behalf of his uncle, King Mark.

Then they began to rejoice and to celebrate with such fervour that you would have thought God himself had descended amongst them. The Irish were so happy and joyous that it seemed to them they had never experienced greater joy, for the war and the grievous discord which for so long had existed between them and the Cornish had caused them much damage; and the Cornish were overjoyed because instead of the shame and disgrace they expected to suffer, they found only honour and good fortune, and it had gone so well with them that they had achieved all they had set out to do, so that they would be held in high esteem when they returned to Cornwall. Great was the joy and the merriment on both sides; everyone rejoiced, rich and poor alike.

That night while King Anguin was lying asleep beside the Queen, he had an extraordinary dream. It seemed to him that he could see his daughter in a hall which was filled with an amazing number of people; everyone showed her great honour and made much of her and placed a golden crown on her head, and then kissed her feet as a sign of subjection. While they were venerating her in this fashion, Tristan appeared in their midst, sad and sorrowful and seemingly very angry. As soon as he saw her, he hastened over towards her, removed the crown from her head and flung it to the ground with such violence that it shattered into more than a hundred pieces. Then he seized hold of Iseut and took off all her clothes, except for her undergarment, and led her out of the palace. And all the people cried after him: 'See the disloyalty of Tristan! See the disloyalty of Tristan!' He never replied a word, but continued to lead her away; and she was so distressed that no one could have seen her without exclaiming: 'God, what a misfortune for Iseut!' King Mark himself accused Tristan of treachery and disloyalty.

King Anguin who saw all this in his dream was so upset and uneasy as he slept that he woke up and said to himself:

'Ah! God, that was an unpleasant dream, and full of hidden meaning.'

He took it so to heart that for the rest of the night he was unable to sleep, but kept thinking of his dream until dawn. The following day he related it to a wise man and begged him to reveal the dream's significance to him if he could. The man replied:

'King, I don't know what you'll say, but there's no doubt that your daughter will be shamed if you give her to Tristan. She will suffer more pain and torment than any noble maiden ever suffered if Tristan takes her away to Cornwall. The lots I have cast predict it, and it will happen as I tell you.'

The King replied:

'What can I do about it? I've promised her to Tristan; I'll have to let him take her away. I would be acting disloyally if I didn't keep this pledge. I love my daughter very much, and so I should, but I should not love her to such an extent that I would act disloyally for her sake, particularly towards a knight as brave as Tristan who has done so much for me, as you well know. Let God's will be done, for, by my faith, I won't refuse Tristan the favour I have granted him.'

Those were the King's words, and he kept to what he had said.

When Tristan had equipped himself for his journey and was ready to put to sea with his companions in order to return to Cornwall, the King gave him his daughter Iseut and many young girls to keep her company. Iseut left Ireland so well provided for with clothes and beautiful jewellery and other fine belongings that her wealthy background was very apparent. The King wept at his daughter's departure and so did the Queen; and when the ship was about to sail, the Queen called Brangain and Gorvenal, and said to them:

'I have here a silver vessel filled with a magic potion. Once King Mark is lying beside Iseut the very first night that they will sleep together, give some of this drink to King Mark and then afterwards to Iseut. And when they've drunk it, throw away the remainder, and take great care that no one else drinks any of it, since it could have grievous consequences. This draught is a love philtre. As soon as the King has drunk it and then my daughter, they will love each other so ardently that no one in the world will be able to cause discord or anger between them. I've brewed the philtre for the two of them; make sure no other person partakes of it.'

They promised her to do as she asked, and put it in their ship.

Then they left the shore, for the sailors had prepared everything they needed. The weather was fine, the air pure, the sea still and calm, and the wind according to their wishes, making them move off as soon as the sails had been raised. Those on the ship were joyful and merry; they played and chatted. Iseut amused herself with Tristan, and they talked together of many things. Tristan had no wrongful thoughts; if he loved and cherished Iseut, it was on account of his uncle, whom he would not have harmed under any circumstances while he was in his present frame of mind.

They remained at sea for three days, happy and joyous at the fine weather which God had sent them. On the third day round about noon Tristan was playing chess with Iseut. It was extremely hot; Tristan was only wearing a light silken tunic, and Iseut was dressed in a green silk garment. Tristan, who was feeling the heat, asked Gorvenal and Brangain for a drink, and it so happened that they chanced upon the love potion, without however noticing what it was; there were so many other silver vessels standing around that they were deceived at that point. Gorvenal picked up the vessel without looking at it, and Brangain took the gold goblet and brought it to Tristan. Gorvenal poured it out and Brangain handed it to him; and Tristan who was hot and thirsty drank it all up thinking it was good wine. And indeed so it was, but it contained much else besides wine of which he was quite unaware. When he had finished it, he asked them to give some to Iseut, which they did, and she drank it.

Ah! God, what a draught! What distress it caused them thereafter! Now they have drunk it; now they are in the grip of the suffering which will never leave them while their soul is in their body. Now they have embarked on the path on which they will have to endure anguish and torment all their life. God, what sorrow! They have drunk their destruction and their death. The draught was very enjoyable, but no joy* was ever so dearly bought as this one. Their hearts changed and became completely transformed. As soon as they had drunk it, the one looked at the other and both of them were quite taken aback. Now their thoughts were very different from before. Tristan was thinking of Iseut, and Iseut of Tristan. King Mark was entirely forgotten. Tristan asked for nothing other than the love of Iseut.

While this was going on in their minds, they wondered where these thoughts had so suddenly come from; prior to that they would not have entertained the idea of such wickedness for anything in the world. Now they were so aroused by it that nothing on earth would have stopped Tristan from loving Iseut, or Iseut Tristan. They were so totally united in feeling about this that they had no intention of changing their mind. The fact that Tristan loved Iseut did not worry him at all, nor did he think it should worry him, for she was so beautiful and so pleasing in every way that he knew well he could not have given his heart to a lovelier or worthier being. The fact that Iseut loved Tristan made her happy and joyful, and she felt that she could not under any circumstances have fallen in love with anyone more desirable; it seemed to her that he was the bravest and best-looking knight in the world. He was very handsome and she was very beautiful; he was high-born and she was of noble lineage; it was only right that they should come together.* Let King Mark never be mentioned again. She loved Tristan more than she would have done the richest king in the world. King Mark could find himself another wife, for she wanted Tristan.

Iseut was very pensive and kept thinking of Tristan. She looked at Tristan and Tristan looked at her; and they gazed at each other in this way for so long that the one realized what was in the other's heart and mind. Tristan knew that Iseut loved him with all her might; Iseut knew that Tristan loved her. She was overjoyed, and he was so pleased that he felt himself to be the happiest knight ever to have lived, now that he was loved by the most beautiful maiden in the world.

When they had drunk the love potion as I have just described, Gorvenal looked at the vessel and recognized it, and became quite alarmed. He drew back a little, looking at it a while longer, and then he knew for certain that it was the philtre. He was so upset that he wished he were dead, for now he realized that Tristan loved Iseut and Iseut loved Tristan. He and Brangain would be held responsible, and it was only right that they should bear the blame; it was not the fault of Tristan and Iseut who knew nothing of the drink.

As soon as he had returned to the cabin he said to Brangain:

'Brangain, we're in trouble. We've done a terrible thing. Our mistake will be the ruin of Tristan and Iseut, unless God intervenes.'

'How?' she asked. 'Tell me what this is all about.'

And he showed her the vessel which contained the philtre.

'This is what we've given them to drink! We've betrayed them cruelly. Now they can't help loving each other. We've acted wrongly.'

When Brangain heard these words and she saw that he was telling her the truth, she replied weeping:

'We've committed a misdeed. Great harm is bound to come of it. They will pay for our foolishness.'

'I don't know what will come of it,' said Gorvenal, 'but we'll have to wait and see what happens.'

Gorvenal and Brangain were very distressed and grieved by what their blunder had brought about. They both wept and lamented bitterly, but they did so as quietly as they could, for they did not want anyone to notice.

These two were upset, but those who had drunk the philtre had no misgivings; they were only intent on each other. Tristan looked at Iseut's noble bearing and it so roused and inflamed him that he desired nothing other than Iseut, and Iseut desired only Tristan. They were of one mind on this matter. It was all decided; there was no point in concealing it. Tristan revealed his thoughts to Iseut and said that he loved her with all his heart, and she told him openly:

'Tristan, I'm happy and delighted that you love me, for I also love no one else in the world but you, nor shall I as long as I live; and I tell you truly, I don't know how this has come about.'

What more shall I tell you? As soon as Tristan realized that Iseut shared his desires, there was nothing to hinder them, since they were all alone in the cabin, and did not have to worry about chance-comers nor to be afraid of anyone. He did with her what he wanted so that she lost her virginity.

This is how it happened that Tristan conceived such a passionate love for Iseut that never thereafter could he tear his heart away from her, nor did he love or sleep with any other woman. This passion which the philtre instilled in him caused him such great pain and anguish that no knight before or after was ever tormented by love as much as he was. He is to be greatly pitied because of this misadventure, it seems to me, for he was so valiant that in King Arthur's time there were few better knights in the world.

Gorvenal then spoke to Brangain and said to her:

'Brangain, what do you think about the fair Tristan* and about Iseut?'

'I think', said Brangain, 'and I'm sure I'm right, that they've slept together. There's no doubt that Iseut is no longer a virgin; I saw them lying side by side. We'll be shamed when King Mark finds out that Iseut is not as she should be. He'll put her to death, and us as well, who should have taken care of her. Now see what we can do about it.'

'Don't worry,' said Gorvenal. 'Since it's our fault and due to our carelessness, we must act so wisely that it won't be known or noticed, and that no harm will come to them and no dishonour to us.'

'And how can we manage that?' asked Brangain.

'Leave it to me,' said Gorvenal. 'I'll see to it well enough. Rest assured that we'll never be blamed for it.'

'May God grant it by his mercy,' said Brangain.

Tristan, who knew nothing of all these deliberations, led a happy and joyful life; he had his pleasure with Iseut and did what he most desired. He asked for no other paradise, nor did Iseut. Each one felt an all-embracing love for the other, and their love grew and became so powerful that they did not know how they could do without one another. Thus they sailed towards Cornwall by the shortest route the sailors knew; and they would have come there much sooner than they did had they not been diverted by a misadventure which I shall describe to you.

A tempest takes their ship to the Distant Isles, which are ruled by Galehot. Much to their consternation they arrive in front of the Castle of Tears, well known for its evil customs. Six men appear and order them to come up to the castle. Tristan would have preferred to stay in the ship and defend himself, but since his companions disagree, he leaves the choice to Iseut, who opts to go to the castle. With the exception of the sailors, therefore, they all go up, and are taken to a large meadow with rooms to one side and surrounded by strong walls; they realize they are prisoners. The following day six knights inform them that they will never regain their liberty unless they have in their company a knight of exceptional strength and a lady of exceeding beauty, and Tristan immediately tells them that they have.

The custom of the Castle of Tears was established at the time of Joseph of Arimathea by a pagan giant called Dialetes who, in order to stamp out the Christian faith which had been promulgated in the Distant Isles by Joseph's missionaries, killed his twelve converted sons, and beheaded the missionaries and all those who refused to revert to the pagan faith. Then he had a castle built on the Giant's Isle at the very spot where the missionaries had landed; and he ordered that all strangers who arrived at their shore as the missionaries had done should be imprisoned in that castle which should be named Castle of Tears to symbolize the tears they would shed. He himself went to live in the Castle of the Giant's Rock, on top of the rock where his sons had been buried, in the company of the most beautiful lady of the Distant Isles; and in order that the strongest knight and the fairest lady should always reign in these isles, he established that if any knight defeated the lord, he must kill him and take his place; and if any lady arrived who was more beautiful than the ruling lady, the latter must be ousted and put to death.

At the time of Tristan's arrival, the lord is Brunor, Galehot's father, and he lives with a very beautiful giantess. It was to escape this custom that Galehot had gone away to conquer other lands, until he became one of the most powerful princes in the world. Tristan fights against Brunor; the battle is fierce and long, but in the end Brunor falls down dead of exhaustion. Since Iseut has been declared more beautiful than the giantess, Tristan is forced against his will to kill the latter. Thus Tristan and Iseut remain lord and lady of the Distant Isles, but they are not allowed to leave.

Brunor's daughter Delice embarks with her father's body and the head of her mother in search of her brother Galehot; he is riding from one country to another looking for Lancelot who has been carried off by Morgan Le Fay. One day the brother and sister meet at the entrance of the Kingdom of Sorelois, and decide to make their way to an abbey to bury their parents. That evening they arrive at the Castle of the Enchantress where they find the King of the Hundred Knights, who is one of Galehot's vassals. Galehot orders him to go to the Giant's Isle with five hundred men in order to abolish once and for all the evil custom of the Castle of Tears, while he himself will fight a duel against Tristan to avenge his parents' death. He leaves his sister at the castle and sets out, after having first buried his parents at a nearby abbey. He has to force the frightened sailors to take him to the Giant's Isle.

They arrive at the Castle of Tears, and Galehot, incognito, declares himself ready to fight Tristan. Fifteen knights take him to the Castle of the Giant's Rock where, for the last three months, Tristan and Iseut have been leading a joyous life, forgetful of the rest of the world. Gorvenal and Tristan are afraid that the unknown knight may be Lancelot, and are therefore relieved to find out just before the duel that he is Galehot. After a long battle Galehot is on the point of being defeated when the King of the Hundred Knights, who in the meantime has destroyed the Castle of Tears and vanquished the inhabitants of the island, arrives with two hundred knights. He wants to kill Tristan, but Galehot spares our hero and forgives him for his parents' death. After they have both recovered from their wounds, Tristan declares that he has to return to Cornwall. Galehot accompanies Tristan to the sea-shore, and Tristan sets sail with his company. Galehot then writes a letter to Queen Guinevere telling her of the liberation of the Giant's Isle, and affirms that there are only two knights and two ladies in the world: Lancelot and Tristan; Guinevere and Iseut; they are unequalled in chivalry and in beauty. [§§ 399–482, end of vol. i and beginning of vol. ii]

VIII

THE WEDDING OF MARK AND ISEUT

THE story now relates that when Tristan had left Galehot, he and his companions were fortunate in that the wind was just right; indeed, it was so favourable that in less than five days they arrived in Tintagel in Cornwall. At that point King Mark was in residence there with a large company of knights. He heard the news of Tristan's arrival as he was in the midst of his barons, and the man who told him said:

'My lord, Tristan has landed with his companions, and believe it or not, he's brought you Iseut the Blonde, daughter of King Anguin of Ireland.'

When King Mark heard this, he was furious, for he had hoped never to see Tristan again; there was no one in the world he feared as much, and for that reason he hated him bitterly. King Mark was very upset by this news, but he pretended to be pleased, so that nobody there would notice. He said to those who were with him:

'Go and meet my nephew. He has certainly carried out what I asked him to do. I wonder how he managed it!'

Then they all went to meet Tristan and received him with great honour. But when they saw Iseut's beauty, they said that they had never in their life seen such a beautiful woman: 'Tristan has done well to win a lady as lovely as this one.' King Mark kissed his nephew, and yet he hated him more than anyone in the world; and then he kissed the other companions.

When they had dismounted and come to the King's palace, Tristan took Iseut by the hand and went up to the King and said:

'Uncle, here is the daughter of the King of Ireland. You asked me for her in this palace, and in this palace I give her to you. I have fulfilled my promise before all the barons in your court. And you should know that it caused me more hardship than I expected to have.'

The King received the maiden with great pleasure and thanked him warmly for this gift, and said:

'Tristan, you have carried out your mission so successfully that the whole world should applaud you; and I myself praise and esteem you, and shall do so for the rest of my life, and so will all the Cornish people.'

That is how Tristan won Iseut the Blonde and liberated her from the Giant's Isle and handed her over to his uncle King Mark. Many people were jealous when they learnt of the trials he had undergone to win her, and how he had brought her back as a result of his strength and prowess.

King Mark who had never seen anyone to equal her in beauty, fell so passionately in love with her that he realized clearly he could not do without her for long. He therefore said that he did not want the wedding to be delayed. He proclaimed throughout his land that everyone should come to Tintagel at a certain date, great and small, rich and poor, for on that day he wanted to marry Iseut and crown her Queen of Cornwall; she was so beautiful that it was only right for her to wear a crown.

What more shall I tell you? The wedding-day drew near, and the barons assembled in Tintagel. Then Tristan spoke to Gorvenal and said:

'Gorvenal, what can we do? You know well, and I don't want to hide it from you, how things are between me and Iseut; and the fault lies not so much with me as with you and Brangain who by your carelessness gave me the love philtre, which caused Iseut to lose her virginity. What shall we do when we hand her to my uncle and he finds out that she isn't a virgin? He'll kill her instantly, and he'll blame us for not having taken better care of her. And I tell you, I love her so much that if I saw her put to death for any misdeed whatever, I would kill my uncle and myself. After the death of my beloved I wouldn't want to live a single day.'

In the course of this conversation Brangain happened to come in, and they disclosed their worries to her. And Brangain said:

'So help me God, I don't know what we can do about it. But tell me if you have thought of something which might save the situation.'

'Brangain,' said Gorvenal, 'I'll tell you how you can help to protect Iseut. You will see her to bed, as is your duty, and the candles will be extinguished. When King Mark is ready to lie down, we'll put you in the bed, and Iseut will slip out. And after King Mark has had his pleasure with you, you will withdraw and

Iseut will take your place. Once King Mark has found you to be a virgin, the candles will be relit, and he'll see Iseut beside him and think he has taken her. In this way Iseut will be saved, for he'll be convinced she was the one he had deflowered. That is how we'll have to do it if we want to save Queen Iseut.'

And Brangain replied:

'I'm prepared to do it, since there's no other way. But if the King recognizes me, he'll have me put to death.'

'Don't worry,' said Gorvenal. 'So help me God, Tristan and I will see to it that you'll come to no harm and Iseut will be saved.'

'And I shall take the risk,' replied Brangain, 'even if I were to die as a result.'

All four of them agreed to this plan, and devised how best to carry it out.

What more shall I tell you? The wedding-day arrived and all the people rejoiced and made merry. Tristan was there, so handsome and so spirited that everybody looked at him. Iseut was there, so beautiful and so pleasing in every way, so gentle, so unaffected, so radiant that everyone marvelled at her beauty and her noble bearing. All the ladies and knights gazed at Iseut. And then they looked at Tristan, who was beside her. If the one was beautiful, the other was even more so; and many people re- marked when they had looked at them for a while that it was a wonder Tristan had handed Iseut over to his uncle; they were more suited to one another both as regards their beauty and their age, and if God had allowed them to be joined together, it would have been the most wonderful wedding which one could ever have seen in any land. This is what most people said. But it was to no avail, for it was quite out of the question: King Mark took Iseut as his wife in accordance with the law of the Holy Church, and afterwards bestowed upon her all the land of Cornwall.

Then the King and Iseut, both wearing their crowns, returned from the church. Everyone in the country rejoiced. The festivi- ties were so extensive and so widespread that there was no one, great or small, young or old, who did not make merry and spend the day in revelry.

But the night was drawing near when Iseut had to sleep with King Mark. She was much more upset about it than anyone would have thought, for she could not forget Tristan whom she loved with all her heart. She said to herself that she would rather have remained in the Giant's Isle where she could do as she wished with her beloved, than have come to Cornwall in order to be with King Mark. When night had fallen, dark and black, Iseut lay down in the bed which had been prepared for her, and King Mark joined her soon afterwards. There was no one in the room except Tristan and Gorvenal. Once the King had taken off his clothes and his shoes and had lain down in the bed beside Iseut, Tristan extinguished the candles, so that neither could see the other. The King asked Tristan why he had done this.

'Uncle,' said Tristan, 'it's the custom in Ireland that when a noble man lies with a virgin, the candles are extinguished so that the maiden is less bashful and more likely to find pleasure with her lord; and this is a very courtly way to behave. Her mother beseeched me to keep up the custom, and I've done it for her sake.'

'You've done well,' said King Mark.

While they were talking thus, Iseut slipped out of the bed and Brangain entered in her place. The King took her and had his pleasure with her, and found her to be a virgin. And when he had enjoyed himself as much as he wanted, he drew back a little from her. Brangain immediately slipped out, and Iseut returned to the bed. Brangain dressed herself and got ready and left the room, and went back to where the other maidens were, so that no one would notice what had taken place.

Next morning King Mark got up shortly after daybreak, and when he was dressed and properly attired he went into the hall. As soon as he saw Tristan, he said in the presence of all his barons:

'Tristan, dear nephew, now I clearly see and recognize your loyalty! You have taken good care of Iseut. In gratitude for this service I shall make you my chamberlain,* and bestow upon you after my death the Kingdom of Cornwall.'

Tristan knelt down and thanked him warmly. And when the Cornish people heard that the King had made Tristan his heir, most of them were delighted, and they all cried out with one voice:

'King, you've done well, for you should indeed cherish and honour Tristan. There is no doubt that he has fully deserved this mark of esteem.'

Then the jubilation began in the court so great that I cannot describe any greater to you. The wedding of Iseut the Blonde and their lord was celebrated by the Cornish people with exceeding joy and gaiety. King Mark truly believed that Iseut had been a virgin because he had found Brangain to be so; nor would it ever have entered his mind that they would dare to make such a change-over. He had his pleasure and delight with Iseut; he found her so beautiful that he completely lost his heart to her to such an extent that he loved neither himself nor anyone else as much. She on the other hand did not love him as she should have done, for the philtre she had drunk had estranged her from her husband and impelled her towards Tristan. It was Tristan she loved with all her heart, Tristan she could not do without, Tristan she thought about the whole time; and however loving she was to King Mark in bed and out of it, this was only because she was afraid he would detect her love for Tristan. And she knew well that if he discovered it, he would have them both killed. For that reason she concealed her feelings as best she could. [§§ 483–6 of vol. ii]

IX

BRANGAIN AND THE SERFS

WHEN Iseut had led this life for at least half a year without hearing her love mentioned or talked about, it seemed to her that she could go on living like this for ever and have her heart's desire whenever she wanted, if only she was not betrayed by Brangain who knew the whole truth. This made Iseut very apprehensive, even more so because she noticed that King Mark seemed to find greater pleasure in being with Brangain than with any other young girl, and she might well end up telling him everything. This possibility made her so frightened that she did not know what to say, except that Brangain must be put to death. If she were rid of her, then she would be sure that no one would ever talk about the matter, for only Brangain and Gorvenal knew anything about it.

After she had thought for a long time, she called two of her serfs* into a room and said to them:

'I want you to do something for me which I shall tell you, and it must be done so secretly that no one in the world will know anything about it except the two of you and myself.'

'My lady,' they replied, 'at your command. Tell us what it is, for we're prepared to do what you want.'

'Many thanks,' she said. 'You may be sure that I'll make it worth your while. Now I'll tell you what it is. You know well that I brought Brangain with me to this country and have always held her in high esteem. She paid no regard whatever to the honour I showed her, but has acted so wrongly as to sleep with my lord, King Mark, who now treats me with much less respect than he used to and greatly hates me. You must avenge me for this shame, and I'll tell you how. I shall send her with you to a forest on an errand; she herself will know well what it is. And when you've taken her right into the forest, kill her instantly with your own swords. Don't have pity on her whatever happens!'

And the serfs replied:

'My lady, at your command. If you hear a word of this henceforth, then have us put to death.'

There was no reason for delay. Iseut sent for Brangain and said to her:

'Go into the forest for me and pick me some of the herbs which I've described to you, and make sure you come back soon.'

'Willingly, my lady,' she replied. 'And who's coming with me?'

'These two young men will take you,' she answered.

'May God protect me, my lady,' said Brangain, who suspected nothing of all this.

And because the two serfs came from her own country, she trusted them as much as she would have done her two brothers.

Brangain mounted her horse and went on her way. When she had come to the forest, the two serfs made for what they thought was the densest and least inhabited part.

'Young men,' said Brangain, 'this is not the right direction. We're going into the thick of the forest where we could easily lose our way. Let's turn back!'

'Don't worry,' they replied, 'we're going the right way.'

They went on till they came to a valley full of rocks where few people lived, for there were many wild beasts which were fierce and dangerous, and the spot was very remote. When they had got there, one of the young men said to the other:

'Let's do what we came for! What else are we waiting for?'

Then they put their hands on their swords. Seeing this, Brangain was so terrified that she was quite dumbfounded. One of the youths said to her:

'Brangain, what wrong have you done my lady Iseut? She's sent us here to kill you. Tell us what you've done to her, so help you God!'

She replied weeping and very frightened:

'As the Lord is my witness,' she said, 'I've never done her any wrong which should make her hate me.'

'That can't be true!' exclaimed the serfs. 'If you hadn't done her some harm, she wouldn't have ordered us to kill you.'

Thereupon Brangain replied, saying:

'What! young men, have I reached the point where I must die, and can't escape from it?'

'Yes,' they replied, 'without fail. You'll never see another hour.'

At this Brangain began to weep bitterly, as one who saw death staring her in the face. And when she spoke, she said:

'Now you can kill me when you want to. May Jesus Christ have mercy on my soul! But you can be sure that if my lady had remembered a kind deed which I once did her, she would not want to put me to death but rather to cherish me.'

'And what kind deed was that?' asked the serfs.

'I don't mind telling you,' said Brangain, 'so that you can remind her of it after my death, and, so help me God, if she has any nobility in her, she will regret it, more perhaps than she realizes now. The kind deed I did was that when she left her father's house in Ireland together with a noble maiden whom she had taken with her, she had in her possession a lily* which brought her great honour, and the maiden I mentioned had one as well. In her excitement Iseut lost her flower, with the result that when she came before her lord King Mark and had to present the flower to him, she was unable to do so, since she no longer had it. The maiden, who had taken better care of her flower, lent it to Iseut, and in this way Iseut was saved: if the King had found her without a flower, it would have gone ill with her. This kindness which the maiden did to help Iseut is making me die, as far as I can see. As God is my witness, I don't believe there's any other reason.'

Then she started weeping bitterly again, for she saw them holding their naked swords.

'Ah! young men,' she entreated them, 'for the love of God, I beg you, let me escape, unhappy wretch that I am, and I'll swear to you here and now by all I hold sacred that I'll go away to some place where Iseut will never hear me spoken of, and neither will you.'

Brangain lamented and wept so much that the two serfs had pity on her, and each one said that as far as he was concerned, under no circumstances would he kill her with his own hands. Instead they decided to tie her to a tree; should the wild beasts devour her, that was not their concern. If she died, let her die, they did not care what happened to her provided they never heard her mentioned again. They did what they had decided: they took Brangain and tied her to a tree with a bow-string, her hands behind her back, in such a way that she would not be able to escape unless someone freed her. Then they remounted without delay; but in order to have some proof that they had put her to death, they killed a greyhound bitch which they had brought with them, and they both stained their swords with its blood; and one of them cut off its tongue and put it in his bag.

Then they returned to Queen Iseut and said to her:

'My lady, we've carried out your command concerning Brangain. You'll never hear her mentioned again: you may rest assured that we've killed her.'

And one of them pulled the greyhound's tongue out of his bag, and said:

'Here is the proof.'

'Show me your swords!' she said, and they showed them to her.

When she had seen this evidence, she really thought they had carried out her orders. Then she asked them to tell her how Brangain had behaved at her death and what she had said. They told her that she had lamented bitterly, and reported the words she had spoken about the lily.

'Did she say anything else when she was about to die?' asked the Queen.

'No, my lady,' they answered, 'except that she earnestly commended her soul to Our Lord.'

When the Queen heard this, she instantly realized Brangain's nobility, and she was so distressed at having ordered her to be killed that she would have given whatever she possessed for it not to have happened. She called herself a miserable wretch, and said she was the most worthless woman alive, since she had caused the death of the maiden who had honoured her more than any other in the world. Then she said to the serfs:

'I repent of this death. I have acted very wrongly! But seeing that it can't be undone, I want you to bring me her body in whatever state you find it as quickly as you can.'

After this conversation the serfs left the court and went straight back to where they had abandoned Brangain. But before they got there it grew pitch-dark, which caused them great discomfort and hindered them from doing what their lady had asked. However, here the story stops talking about them, and returns to

Brangain in order to relate what happened to her when they left her tied to the tree as already described.

After the serfs had parted from Brangain and gone some distance, leaving her bound to a tree, the maiden, who was very young and frightened, realizing that she could not move without somebody's help, began to wail loudly and bitterly, for she saw that she was in danger and knew that the serfs had gone away; she let out such a shriek that the whole forest resounded with it. While she was lamenting thus, a knight in full armour happened to come that way as he was riding all alone through the forest. When he heard her cries he turned his horse in that direction, for he knew straightaway that it was a maiden in need of help. And before he had gone far, he found in a thicket the horse on which Brangain had come; and it had such costly equipment that it was evident it belonged to a wealthy lady. He took the palfrey* and led it beside him as best he could, and rode on in one direction and another until he came upon Brangain bound to a tree as the two serfs had left her. He dismounted when he saw her, and she immediately cried out to him:

'Ah! noble knight, free me!'

And he replied:

'Don't worry, maiden, you're freed.'

He attached the horses to a tree, removed his shield and his lance, and went over to Brangain and untied her. Then he asked her who she was; he had not recognized her, although he had seen her prior to that.

'Sir,' said Brangain, 'I'm a maiden from a foreign land who as a result of misfortune and adversity—not that I've deserved it, to my knowledge—have been placed in peril of my life, as you can see. But thank God you've rescued me.'

'What is your name?' he asked.

And she named herself. He was quite taken aback, and looked at her; and when he had examined her for a long time, he said:

'What! Are you really Brangain?'

'Yes, indeed,' she answered, 'I really am.'

'Upon my word!' he exclaimed, 'then I'm one of the happiest knights in the world, since God has granted me the honour of rescuing you from misadventure. As the Lord is my witness,

you're one of the maidens I love most in the world for the sake
of my lady Iseut who brought you to this country.'

And she thanked him warmly for the kindness he had shown
her. The knight then said:

'Maiden, let's mount and ride off. I'm ready to take you
wherever you want to go.'

'Sir,' she replied, 'I'm very grateful to you. I'd like you to take
me somewhere other than the city of Norholt, for that's one
place I don't want to go to.'

'As you wish,' he said. 'I'll take you wherever you want to go.'

'Near here', she continued, 'is an abbey of nuns. If I could get
there, I would enter it and remain inside all the rest of my life for
the salvation of my soul.'

'What?' asked the knight. 'Does that mean my lady Iseut is
angry with you?'

'Yes, indeed,' she said, 'but, so help me God, I've done
nothing to deserve it. She's probably been led to believe some
lies which have poisoned her against me, and which would have
caused my death if God had not brought you here so quickly.'

Talking thus they rode all that evening till they came to a
mountain which was part of the forest, where there was a very
wealthy and beautiful abbey of nuns in which many noble ladies
lived. This abbey originated from a royal abbey in Gaul, the very
one which had been built for King Ban of Benoïc who died there
long ago. When the ladies saw the knight and the maiden, they
received them gladly and greatly honoured them. They did not
recognize Brangain when they saw her, though they realized
clearly enough that she was of noble birth. They asked her who
she was, but she did not want to tell them anything except that she
was a sad and sorrowful maiden. The serving men there hastened
to disarm the knight, and as soon as he was relieved of his armour
so that Brangain was able to see him clearly, she knew at once
it was Palamedes, the brave knight, the one who so loved my
lady Iseut.

'Ah! sir,' she exclaimed, 'now I know who you are! I'm so glad
to see you! I saw you formerly in Ireland when you won the
tournament held at the Castle in the Moors.'

'Maiden,' he said, 'you may well be right. But if I was greatly
honoured at that point, shortly afterwards I suffered shame and

dishonour at the other tournament which was held in front of the same castle.'

She made no answer to that.

Palamedes stayed in the abbey that night without telling anyone there who Brangain was, though he was asked by many. Very early next morning as he was about to ride off, Brangain begged him for the Lord's sake not to speak about her to anyone, man or woman.

'I want to take the veil in this abbey as quietly as possible in such a way that no one knows I'm here or who I am. If I find the rules of the religious order too rigorous, I'll manage somehow to get back to Ireland, the land where I was born.'

And he replied:

'I assure you that I shall never speak about you unless I'm forced to do so.'

Thereupon he departed, fully armed as he had come; Brangain remained and he went off. Now the story stops talking about him and returns to the two serfs who were looking for Brangain in the forest.

In this part the story relates that the two serfs rode all night but were quite unable to find the spot where they had abandoned Brangain. The following day they recognized the path they had previously taken, and went straight to the valley where they had left Brangain as I have described. They searched here and there until they came to the very tree to which Brangain had been tied. When they did not find her there either dead or alive, they called themselves unhappy and wretched, for they really thought that wild beasts had devoured her and had eaten her up flesh and bones. They looked for her high and low, far and wide, but they had no hope of finding her, since she was not there. When they had gone on searching for so long that they were quite exhausted, they said to each other: 'What can we do?' Finally one of them suggested:

'Let's go back and tell my lady that we can't find Brangain, neither flesh nor bones, and she will believe us soon enough because of the vicious beasts which live in this forest.'

In the end they agreed to do this, and returned to their lady and told her that wild beasts had devoured Brangain, for they could find neither flesh nor bones. She was so upset that she nearly went out of her mind with grief. She retired into one of her rooms and said she would never again be happy after she had so unjustifiably put to death the maiden who had done more for her and who loved her more than anyone else in the world. Queen Iseut was very distressed about Brangain; no one could console her or stop her from grieving day and night.

Shortly after this it happened that King Mark went hunting in a forest near Norholt. Queen Iseut followed him with a large group of ladies and maidens to amuse herself, as the King had ordered. Palamedes was so madly in love with her that he had left the Kingdom of Logres for good and the company of his father and brothers; and when he heard that the Queen was coming to enjoy herself in the woods, he was sure she would go to the spring which was called the Giant's Fountain; she had been there many times already, for it was more beautiful and agreeable than any other fountain in Cornwall. Palamedes went there as quickly as he could; and because he wanted to remain unseen and at the same time to be able to observe the Queen freely, he dismounted in a thickly wooded copse, laid down his shield and lance in there, and fastened his horse nearby. Then he went close to the fountain and hid himself in a thicket. He had not waited long before he saw the arrival of some ladies and maidens who dismounted in front of the fountain. The Queen herself dismounted there: she was so beautiful and so attractive in every way that Palamedes said to himself that she really was the most beautiful lady that any man could hope to see. She was the lady of ladies; it was to his misfortune that he ever set eyes on her beauty, for since he was unable to have even a part of what he wanted, there was no way in which he could escape from dying of it in the end.

While Palamedes was hiding in the thicket as I have described, it so happened that the Queen went towards the spot where he was concealed all by herself. She was still very upset about Brangain, but no one in her company knew the reason for her grief. When she was quite near the place where Palamedes was hidden without her knowing it, she uttered a loud moan and said in great distress:

'Ah! Brangain, how unhappy I am about you! As long as I remember my cruelty towards you I shall feel no joy, but shall be sad and sorrowful all my days. If I can't find some comfort somewhere, my suffering for you will cause my death.'

And while she was saying this, the tears were running down her face. Palamedes, who realized clearly from her words that all this grief was for Brangain, could not stop himself from saying in order to console her somewhat:

'My lady, don't be so terribly distressed! By the faith I owe you, I'll bring you back Brangain within three days.'

The Queen looked round and saw him concealed in the thicket; and because she thought he was hiding there in fear of someone, she did not ask him anything about himself, but answered very softly:

'If you bring me back Brangain fit and well, I shall grant you any request that you might make.'

'My lady,' he said, 'remember your promise well. If you keep your side of the bargain, I shall never ask for anything else in the world.'

'You may be sure', she replied, 'that I shall keep my promise, provided you bring me back Brangain in the way you have pledged.'

'My lady,' he said, 'many thanks. I ask for no more than you have said.'

Thereupon the Queen left him and went back to her company very much happier than she had been, for she felt sure after what the knight had said to her that Brangain was still alive; and if that were so, she would be overjoyed. The Queen stayed at the fountain for as long as she liked, and when she had returned to the city, she instantly called the two serfs and said to them:

'I order you as you value your life to tell me the truth about what I shall ask you.'

'My lady,' they replied, 'ask by all means. You may be sure that we won't lie to you in any way, if it's something we know about.'

'Then tell me whether you killed Brangain or whether you let her go free,' she said. 'Tell me the whole truth, if you want to allay my anxiety. I've learnt news about her which has made me very happy, if only it could be true.'

When the two serfs heard this, they did not dare to conceal the truth from her any longer, but told her everything as it had happened.

'Is that really what took place?' she asked.

'Yes indeed, my lady,' they answered.

'May God be thanked for the tidings!' said the Queen. 'Since you left her alive, the man who spoke to me must really know something about her.'

The Queen was delighted at this news of Brangain and could not wait for her to come, for since she had proved so clearly that even when in peril of death she had revealed nothing about her relationship with Tristan, she could trust her implicitly from now on and need not hesitate to confide in her.

As soon as Palamedes, who had remained in the thicket, saw that the Queen had departed with all her company, he leapt out of his hiding-place and went to where he had concealed his horse and his armour; then he mounted and proceeded by the shortest route he knew towards the abbey in which he had left Brangain. He rode on, hardly stopping anywhere, until he reached the place where Brangain was. She received him with as much pleasure as she could, but she was so distressed at having lost her lady's love that she could find no comfort.

'Maiden,' he said, 'how have you fared since I left you?'

'Not very well, sir,' she replied. 'I shall never have any joy in this country as long as I stay here, given the ill-feeling my lady has for me. Perhaps if I were far away from her in Ireland where I was born, I might find it easier to forget my sorrow than I would do here, where there is no one to comfort me.'

'Now don't be so upset, Brangain,' said Palamedes, 'for I bring you good news.'

'What is it? Tell me!'

And he began to relate all that the Queen had said and promised him.

'Consequently there's no reason for us to stay here,' he said. 'Let's mount our horses and make our way to the court. My lady is so exceedingly eager to see you that I know well she'll never be happy until she has you with her.'

When Brangain heard this, she was so delighted that she let herself fall at his feet and wanted to kiss them; but he would not allow it and quickly lifted her up.

'Let's mount without any further delay,' he said, 'and go to court; I know you'll be very welcome there.'

They did as he said. The palfrey which Brangain had brought was still there. Palamedes himself put on the saddle and got it ready as best he could. When they had taken their leave of the ladies in the abbey, they departed and rode on until they reached the court. The King was sitting at table, and he had a large number of people with him. The Queen was eating in her own room with many ladies and maidens. And Palamedes, who had found out where the Queen was, dismounted in the middle of the courtyard, put down his shield and his lance, and, taking Brangain by the hand, he went from room to room, without entering the hall in which the King was sitting, until he came to the one where he found the Queen in the company of many ladies and maidens. Palamedes went straight up to the Queen and greeted her as best he could, though not as well as he would have wished, for he was so overwhelmed by his love and so timorous that he hardly dared to look at her. And when he could speak, he said:

'My lady, I bring you your maiden Brangain. I have fulfilled my promise to you. Take her! Now I beg you as my lady and as the most beautiful being which God ever created to keep your part of the agreement. As you know well, you promised to grant me any request I might make after I had brought you back Brangain.'

The Queen, who was overjoyed that he had returned Brangain to her, and who had no idea what he intended to ask, replied:

'I did indeed make that promise to you, and I'm still prepared to honour it.'

'Many thanks, my lady,' he replied. 'I shall now go and see King Mark.'

And she said:

'Go by all means, since that is your wish.' [§§ 487–95 of vol. ii]

X

ISEUT'S ABDUCTION

PALAMEDES went to find King Mark, armed as he was, and when he came before him he greeted him, and the King returned his greeting.

'King Mark,' he said, 'I'm a foreign knight from the Kingdom of Logres. I've spent some time at the court of Arthur, the good king. I'm a knight-errant seeking the adventures and marvels to be found in the world. I've searched for so long that, by the grace of God, I came upon an adventure in this country which enabled me to serve my lady the Queen, your wife, according to her wishes, so much so that she promised me as queen to grant me any favour I might ask. However, since you have more jurisdiction over her affairs than she has herself, I would like you to take this pledge upon yourself, if you were willing, in such a way that you would be bound to grant me any favour I might ask just as she is bound to do so.'

King Mark enquired whether the Queen was bound to this knight in the way he had described, and she came forward and said:

'Yes, indeed, my lord, I have pledged to give him whatever he requests.'

When the King heard this, he said to Palamedes:

'Sir Knight, now you can ask for anything you like. Since the Queen bears witness to your claim, I promise you as king that you shall have whatever you ask for.'

'Many thanks, my lord,' he replied. 'In that case give me my lady the Queen who is here. There's no one in the world I love as much, and I've stayed in this country because of her for over a year. But now, by the grace of God, I've been fortunate enough to win everything I desired in one go.'

When the King heard these words, he was so taken aback that he did not know what to reply, and so were all the others. And when the King could speak, he said:

'Ah! Sir Knight, make some other request, I beg you, for if you carry off the Queen in this way, you will have shamed me and I shall never be happy again.'

'Ah! my lord,' said Palamedes, 'it's no use asking me that! I am more concerned with *my* happiness than with yours! I was desperate and hopeless for love of Iseut; I loved her beyond measure, and yet I had little chance of attaining her. But since with God's help I have rightfully won her, I wouldn't give her back to you, as God is my witness, for all the Kingdom of Logres. I'm more content with Iseut than I would be with the whole of King Arthur's realm, and it would be better for me to be a poor knight with Iseut, it seems to me, than to possess the whole world without her.'

The King who saw and knew that he could not break his promise without being considered base, dishonourable and ignoble, particularly as he had made it before so many worthy men, replied:

'Sir Knight, since you are not willing to listen to my entreaty and still insist on taking her away, I grant her to you in order to honour the agreement I've made with you. But I want you to know that if she is taken from you after you've received her, I'm not to blame.'

'No, that's true,' said Palamedes, 'provided I lose her according to the custom which is adhered to by knights-errant.'

'And what custom is that?' asked the King.

'I'll tell you gladly,' he replied. 'Once I'm in possession of the Queen and have departed from here, if a knight were to come after me either from this court or from another who in single combat could win her from me and bring her back, in that case I would have no complaint against you. But you won't have her back in any other way.'

'I agree to that,' said the King, 'Now receive her and take her away; I give her to you in the hope that you may be as unlucky as I was when I granted you the favour you asked for.'

After these words without more delay the King ordered the Queen's palfrey to be brought, and when his command was carried out, he said, weeping:

'Lady, mount and go with this knight who has deceived and shamed me; and you likewise have brought about my shame as well as your own misfortune.'

The Queen who was so upset that no one could be more so, and who saw clearly that there was no question of remaining,

mounted in the courtyard below. The King forbade anyone to
escort her, and they refrained from doing so, since they heard that
the King did not wish it. Palamedes mounted instantly and took
his arms and led the Queen away through the city without
finding a single person who dared to stop him in any way, for
they greatly feared King Mark. The King was so distressed that
he wished he were dead, and so were all the other knights, ladies
and maidens who were there.

Tristan was not at court at the time, but had gone hunting that
morning in the woods with a great company of knights and
youths. Gorvenal had remained at court and had seen Palamedes
ride off with the Queen. He was so grieved that he did not know
what to say.

'Ah! Tristan,' he exclaimed, 'your absence from court has
caused us great harm, and Cornwall will be shamed and dishonoured by it for evermore. At this point the prowess of the
Cornish knights is clearly apparent who let their lady be abducted before their very eyes, and not a single one dares to take
up arms and go after Palamedes to save her! Ah! to be sure,
Tristan, valiant knight, you should be greatly honoured and
esteemed, for if you were here all alone and there were three of
him who is carrying off my lady, you would pursue them and do
your utmost to rescue her, that's how bold and brave I know you
to be.'

This is what Gorvenal said in front of all the Cornish barons,
and yet there was not one who had the courage to take up his
shield, because they were sure that the knight who had abducted
their lady was of great valour. The King had already found out
that it was Palamedes, one of the best knights in the world, and
he was at a loss what to say, since he knew the Cornish knights
to be so faint-hearted and cowardly than none of them would risk
putting himself in danger. He himself would have taken up arms
and gone to fight Palamedes if he could or should have done so;
but it was neither possible nor honourable for him to do this, for
what he had given he could not himself rightfully take away
again. Then he regretted Tristan, saying:

'Tristan, dear nephew, valiant knight, braver and bolder than
any I have ever seen, why are you so late in coming back? Your
delay will make me die of grief. Today I lost the being I love

most in the world, and I shall be totally shamed by it, and the whole of Cornwall will be dishonoured.'

While the King is lamenting thus, a knight from the Kingdom of Benoïc called Lanbeguet hears of Iseut's abduction. He has been badly wounded by Audret and another Cornish knight, and the King, impressed by his courage, is having him looked after at his court. The Queen herself has taken great trouble to cure him, and he is on the road to recovery, but still after almost three weeks far from well. When he hears the news, he is determined to rescue the Queen, despite the warnings of those who are tending him. He forces them to arm him, and rides after Palamedes. The King however has no illusions about his strength, and declares that unless Tristan takes on Palamedes, Queen Iseut is lost.

Lanbeguet, a dauntless knight, nephew of Farien, was one-time tutor to Boort of Gaunes, Lancelot's cousin. The Latin Book relates a very noble deed of his: when King Claudas was threatening to destroy the city of Gaunes unless Lanbeguet, whom he hates, was handed over to him, and the citizens refuse, Lanbeguet offers himself up to Claudas of his own accord in order to save the city. The King is so struck by his boldness that he has mercy on him.

Before long Lanbeguet catches up with Palamedes, who is trying in vain to console the weeping Queen. Hearing himself challenged, Palamedes thinks the knight is Tristan, and charges at him with his lance. They both unhorse each other, and then continue the battle with their swords. Unfortunately for Lanbeguet, all his wounds burst open, and soon the ground is stained scarlet with his blood. Palamedes draws back and asks his name; and hearing he is not Tristan, he declares himself ready to spare his life. Lanbeguet wants to go on fighting, but he is too weak and falls down backwards in a faint.

When Palamedes saw this, he sheathed his sword, went back to his horse and mounted. He expected to find my lady Iseut nearby where he had left her, but she was not to be seen anywhere, for she had plunged into the forest quite a while back, and was hastening towards a river called Orinsce which ran through the forest in many places. She was trying to reach this stream with the intention of drowning herself, since she preferred to die, of whatever death it might be, rather than lose Tristan whom she loved with all her heart, and remain in the hands of Palamedes. That is why she was making for the river as speedily as she could, and it did not take her long to reach it. But before she had quite got there, it happened that she encountered a Cornish knight who was going to court with a maiden. When they saw the Queen, they failed to recognize her, not having met her often, but in view of her fine apparel they thought that she must be of high standing. They were very surprised that she was so frightened, and therefore went up to her and asked her what was wrong.

'What's wrong!' she exclaimed. 'I have so much grief and vexation that I want to drown myself in this river, for I would rather die than go with a knight who is carrying me off by force. I know that he's following me and is near at hand.'

The knight who could see that she was so distressed that she wanted to jump into the river and drown herself, seized her horse by the bridle, and said:

'Ah! lady, I beg you, don't be so dismayed. I can think of a much better way out.'

'Tell me what it is,' she said.

'Lady,' he replied, 'near here there's a very beautiful and very fine tower. If you were inside, you wouldn't need to be frightened of the two best knights in the world were they to attack you. Come inside quickly, and I assure you that you'll have no cause to fear any man in this land, with the exception of King Mark and his nephew Tristan; against these two I certainly wouldn't dare to protect you, for they are my liege lords.'*

When the Queen heard the knight say this, she turned towards him with clasped hands and said:

'Quick, lead me to that tower, for the love of God! If you can take me to a safe place and keep me there, you will be better off for the rest of your life: I would have you know that I am Iseut, the Queen of Cornwall.'

Hearing these words, the knight looked at his lady and recognized her, and said:

'Come quickly, my lady! Once we've crossed this river, we needn't be afraid of anyone coming after us.'

The Queen straightaway plunged into the water, and as she was well mounted, she had soon passed across.

What more shall I tell you? They rode on till they came to a very beautiful tower well situated in the midst of a marsh.* As soon as she had reached the tower and was inside, she said:

'Shut the door! Never was a lady so fortunate after having suffered such adversity in the presence of so many noble men. If only Tristan knew about this misadventure, nothing of all that has happened would matter to me. But I'm so worried about the anguish he'll feel when he hears about it that I'm very frightened he will kill himself.'

'Ah! my lady,' said the knight, 'don't worry about that. We're so near Norholt that I hope to be able to tell him the truth this very night.'

'I wish he knew it already,' said the Queen, 'for the sooner he knows, the sooner he will come here to rescue me.'

'I'll go once I've taken my arms,' said the knight.

Thus Queen Iseut of Cornwall was fortunate enough to be helped to safety when she thought she was completely lost. The knight at once took his arms and mounted his horse, and the Queen said to him:

'I beg you not to tell any living soul about this adventure except Tristan, but I do want him to know about it and about how I was rescued.'

The knight assured her that he would gladly carry out this message, and thereupon went on his way. But he had not gone very far when he met Palamedes who was so distressed that he wished he were dead. When Palamedes saw the knight, he said to him:

'Sir Knight, so help you God, have you seen my lady Iseut? Tell me if you know anything about her.'

The knight who was not at all afraid of him, since he had little idea of his great prowess, replied:

'I know very well where she is. Are you the one who abducted her?'

'Yes, indeed,' said Palamedes.

'Then you should know,' said the knight, 'that you've lost her, and you've lost her through me, for I've put her in that tower until such a time as Sir Tristan arrives. There she is and there she'll stay; she's in no danger from you or anyone else as long as she wants to remain there.'

'Indeed!' said Palamedes. 'You've deprived me of my life and my joy. As God is my witness, you've done me a great wrong, and you'll pay for it!'

And without more ado he put his hand on his sword and attacked the knight who did his best to defend himself; but Palamedes went at him with such wrath and ill-will on account of my lady Iseut, and struck him such a fierce blow with his sharp sword right through the middle of his helmet that he split it down to his teeth. The blow was mighty and struck in anger, and as he withdrew his sword, the knight fell to the ground, for he was already dead. Seeing this, Palamedes replaced his sword in the scabbard, and then said:

'You've done me so much harm that the whole world could not make up for it, and you've paid for it dearly; but I've gained nothing thereby, since your misfortune is of no benefit to me.'

Then he left him lying on the ground, and made his way to the tower. When he found the door locked and realized he could not get in, he called himself a miserable wretch and said that now he had completely lost the being he most loved in the world.

Queen Iseut was at one of the windows of the tower, and when she saw Palamedes outside, mounted on his horse, she said:

'Sir Knight, now you can wait as long as you like! You deceived me by a ruse, but I escaped from you by my good sense, and, God willing, I shall never fall into your hands again.'

Hearing the Queen speak in this way, he raised his head and looked at her as best he could, and said:

'My lady, since you're no longer in my power, I shall suffer it as one who is the most unhappy and unfortunate man who ever wore arms. And God has shown me clearly at this point that I'm more ill-fated than anyone else. But since you command me to wait, I shall wait in order to see if God and Fortune are willing to reward the hapless knight with a bit of luck.'

'Upon my word!' said Queen Iseut, 'if you value your life, I don't advise you to wait here any longer. Should Tristan, the brave knight, chance to come this way and find you, the whole world wouldn't protect you from being killed by him.'

'My lady,' replied Palamedes, 'whatever you might say, I shall never go away from this door as long as I know you to be inside. If Tristan comes and attacks me because of you, and kills me, I shall die gladly; it would be a great honour to die for your sake. It matters little to me whether I die for you or live through you.'

Thereupon the Queen replied, saying:

'May God forsake me if I ever saw a more foolish knight than you, or a more senseless one, to love me like this when you know for certain that I don't love you at all.'

'My lady, the fact that you don't love me won't stop me from loving you. The more you hate me, the more I shall love you! As God is my witness, even if I had the power to tear my heart away from you, I wouldn't do so, since I derive more happiness, it seems to me, from loving you all my life without having any other reward than if I loved someone else and had all I wanted.'

Hearing the knight's folly, the Queen left the window, for she realized that she would not rid herself of him whatever she said.

Once Palamedes was no longer able to see her, he dismounted from his horse, took off its bridle and let it graze; then he hung his shield on a tree and straightaway went to sit down in front of the door of the tower because he did not want anyone to come out or go in without his intervention. When the Queen saw herself besieged in this way, she smiled to herself and said that without any doubt he was the most genuinely foolish knight she had ever seen. Those inside the tower asked her who he was.

'Upon my word,' she replied, 'he's a very brave knight and of great prowess, but however strong or valiant he may be, he'll never succeed in having me in his power again as he did today.'

'Don't worry, my lady,' said those who were with her. 'By the grace of God, you are rid of him.'

'That's true,' said the Queen. 'The Lord be praised for having freed me in this way.'

This is how the Queen spoke about Palamedes, and she prayed to God that He would send Tristan, for once he was there, she need have no fear. But now the story stops talking about Palamedes and Iseut, and returns to King Mark and his company, and to his nephew Tristan.

At this point the story relates that when the Queen had left the court as I have described, King Mark remained, so upset and so disconsolate that he felt he would never be happy again; and there was such consternation amongst those in his company that they did not dare to raise their heads. In this way they stayed there all day long without anyone saying a word. In the evening Tristan returned from hunting joyful and contented. When he

came to court and found them all so downcast and so pensive that
nobody addressed a word to him, he was quite taken aback,
accustomed as he was to being welcomed very warmly whenever
he arrived there. He went up to his uncle, holding his head high,
and greeted him, and the King returned his greeting very mourn-
fully.

'My lord,' said Tristan, 'please tell me how it is that you and
everyone here are so dejected, and yet when I left your court this
morning you were all joyful and merry.'

'Nephew,' replied the King, 'that's the way of the world; one
moment we're happy, and the next we're sorrowful. True
enough, when you left us this morning we were joyful and
merry, but since then an incident occurred which made us all
unhappy, for we shall be dishonoured as a result of it, and the
whole of Cornwall will be shamed.'

Then he told him how he had lost Queen Iseut and how a
knight had abducted her, 'and there was not a knight in my court
who dared to take up his arms.'

When Tristan heard these words, he was so distressed that his
face grew flushed with anger, and he said:

'Uncle, don't worry! If the Cornish people have failed you at
this point, here is Tristan who won't fail you. I would rather lose
my life than that you should lose Iseut. But tell me the name of
the knight and what arms he is wearing.'

And the King told him.

'Ah!' exclaimed Tristan, 'he's the best knight I ever encountered. But his prowess will serve him nothing; even if he were
a still better knight than he is, he would have to give me back
my lady Iseut. Her loss is not something I would take lightly.
I'd put up with any other loss, but this one I wouldn't accept
under any circumstances.'

Then he asked for his armour. And the King leapt forward, saying:

'What do you want to do? You can see that it's night and
pitch-black; you wouldn't know where to go if you were outside
there now. I order you to wait until tomorrow. Then you can go
after the knight, and may God grant you the strength to acquit
yourself so well that it will be to your honour and to ours.'

Tristan, who loved Iseut more than did the King himself, said
that he would not wait in any way whatever, and the King

insisted that he would. Then he ordered him categorically to stay. When Tristan saw that he was forced to remain, he replied, saying:

'Uncle, you do wrong and it makes me very angry!'

Then he went off to a room and locked himself in; and all night long he did not cease to grieve and to lament, cursing the King and all the Cornish knights. He grieved bitterly, but as quietly as he could, for he did not want it to be noticed.

At dawn next morning he left the room, ate a little, and then took his arms and mounted his horse; he did not wish anyone to accompany him except Gorvenal. Then he left the city and rode until he came to the spot where Lanbeguet had fought with Palamedes. He found Lanbeguet still lying there quite stunned, for he had lost so much blood that he did not know whether he was dead or alive. He had remained lying on the ground on his shield, with his helmet still on his head, having lacked the strength to take it off; and his sword lay beside him. When Tristan saw the knight, he immediately recognized him by his arms; and indeed, he had been told by those at his uncle's court that Lanbeguet had gone after the Queen to rescue her. For that reason he rode up to him and dismounted, greatly fearing for his life because he saw the ground around him all covered with blood. Tristan gave him a little nudge without saying anything, and when he saw him move, he asked him:

'Sir Lanbeguet, how do you feel?'

'Who are you who ask me this?' said Lanbeguet.

'I'm Tristan, your friend,' he replied. 'I'm very distressed by your misfortune, so help me God. Tell me, for heaven's sake, if you think you can recover.'

'I would recover all right if I could rest,' said Lanbeguet, 'and had someone with me who knew how to take care of my wounds. But since chance has brought you here, I beg you for God's sake to assist me by looking for my horse which ran away into this forest. I don't think it's very far away. If I were on horseback, I could at least return somehow or other.'

'I shall gladly do that for you, God willing,' said Tristan.

He mounted and rode in one direction and another until he found the horse beside a fountain. He took it and brought it back to Lanbeguet who mounted as best he could.

'Tell me', said Tristan, 'which way did the knight go who is abducting my lady Iseut?'

'He went in that direction, sir,' he answered.

And Lanbeguet showed him the way, and as soon as he had done so, he set off. Tristan advised him to ride as slowly as he could until he reached Norholt. Thereupon the knight left Tristan and made his way towards King Mark's court. He rode with great difficulty until he reached it, and he told the people there that he had spoken to Tristan who was going in pursuit of Palamedes.

'Ah! God,' said the King, 'may it please you to save my nephew and help him to bring this adventure to a successful conclusion in a way which will be to the honour of all the Cornish people.'

Tristan continued on his way and rode on until he came to the river which the Queen had crossed. As soon as he had reached the other side, he looked and saw the knight whom Palamedes had struck dead lying in front of him, the one who had gone to fetch Tristan to save the Queen. When Tristan saw the knight struck down like that, he drew back a little, quite dismayed, and said:

'Ah! Gorvenal, Palamedes has come this way. Upon my soul, this is one of his blows! There isn't a knight in Cornwall who could have dealt such a blow. Whoever wants to fight a man like that certainly has to take exceeding care.'

'Truly,' said Gorvenal, 'Palamedes deserves to be greatly praised and esteemed.'

'You're right, sir,' said Tristan. 'So help me God, if he weren't such a threat to me in my relationship with the lady I most love, I would feel more friendship for him than for any man I know. However, that's out of the question at present, for he has caused me too much pain and vexation by taking away what is dearest to my heart. But who could this knight be who's lying here?'

'I don't know, for sure,' said Gorvenal.

Then they continued on their way and soon found two roads, one which led into the forest and the other over a plain; and the tower where Iseut was staying was clearly visible.

'Master,' said Tristan, 'here are two roads. Since I don't know which one Palamedes took, you'll follow this one and I'll take the other; and we'll meet at the Scarlet Cross* at midday tomorrow. You know well where the Cross is. If you get to it before I do, you can wait for me there, and I'll do the same if I'm there before you. You may be sure that if I'm not at the Cross in time, the reason for the delay will be Palamedes. As you go along your road, ask everywhere you come to for news of him; and if you find out anything, you'll let me know when we meet at the Cross.'

Gorvenal said he would willingly carry out all he asked, since it was his wish, but he was very unhappy that they were parting company.

Then each one embarked on his route: Tristan took the highroad which led into the forest, and Gorvenal went in the direction of the tower. And when he was quite near to it, he saw Palamedes sitting under a tree, so lost in thought that he hardly knew where he was; and anyone who saw him like that would have been amazed. As Gorvenal approached the tower and noticed the shield hanging from the tree, he immediately suspected that it was Palamedes whom they were seeking; however, not being sure because shields were often quite similar, he instantly went over to him to find out the truth. And when he had reached Palamedes and saw that he did not move, he thought that he must be asleep, so he called out and said to him:

'Wake up, Sir Knight, and tell me what I want to know!'

Palamedes was in such a profound reverie that he did not hear his words, for his heart and his soul were so absorbed with Iseut that he was unable to understand, hear or see a thing, any more than if he were a stone. And Gorvenal called a second time, but again he did not hear him, since his attention was focused on higher things.

'Upon my word!' exclaimed Gorvenal, 'this is one of the greatest marvels ever to be seen. Here is a knight who neither hears, nor sees, nor understands! This isn't Palamedes whom we're seeking. I must find out something about him and discover who he is.'

Then he bent down from his horse towards him and took him by the helmet and gave it a good tug. And Palamedes came to at once just as if he had been asleep, and opened his eyes. And when he saw himself confronted by the man who had roused him from his meditation and realized he was not a knight, he said:

'You've done me a great injury by depriving me of the sweet-est thoughts I've ever had. If you were a knight, you would pay for it with your life, so help me God. But because you're a squire, I excuse you; I wouldn't lay hands on you under any circum-stances. But now let me be, and go away, and I shall see if I can recapture the pleasurable thoughts I had before.'

'In God's name,' said Gorvenal, 'I won't go away like that! If you please, you will first tell me your name.'

'My name', he replied, 'is Palamedes. Now for God's sake, go away! You're taking from me what the whole world couldn't give me back.'

'Tell me,' continued Gorvenal, 'have you any news about my lady Iseut?'

'Yes,' replied Palamedes, 'she's inside that tower, and it's on account of her that I'm sitting here, so that she can't come out without my intercepting her, for if God and Fortune were kind enough to let her fall into my hands again as was the case not long ago, I would never ask for any other happiness on earth.'

'Well, it's not very sensible of you to stay in this place,' said Gorvenal. 'If King Mark's nephew, Tristan, were to find you here, it would go ill with you.'

And when he had said this, he left him and went off in the direction where he thought he would be most likely to find Tristan. He rode on until he came to the path which Tristan had taken, and he was going along at great speed when he encountered a knight and a young girl who were on their way to the court; and the knight was unarmed except for his sword. Gorvenal asked them whether they had seen Tristan, and they replied:

'He's going along ahead of us, all alone. You'll find him in a meadow nearby.'

Gorvenal was very happy to hear this and spurred his horse and rode so quickly that he reached Tristan in the very place which the knight and the maiden had indicated. As soon as he saw him, he cried out loud enough for him to hear:

'Return, sir! Return.'

At these words Tristan looked round, and when he caught sight of Gorvenal he turned back, for he knew well that he had brought him news of Palamedes. As soon as Gorvenal had come up to him, he said:

'Master, what news are you bringing me?'

'Tristan,' he replied, 'we've been lucky! I've found both Palamedes and my lady Iseut.'

And he told him in what manner.

Tristan stretched out his hands towards the heavens when he
heard these words and exclaimed:

'Lord God, grant that our love may not be debased by any
living man!'

And then he said:

'Master, let's go. I can't wait to see the man who wants
to deprive me of my love. I'll show him what Iseut's lover can
do!'

They continued on their way until they reached the tower
where the Queen had taken refuge. Palamedes was still sitting in
front of the door beneath a tree, no less absorbed in his thoughts
than he had been before. As soon as Tristan saw him and came
close to him, he cried out:

'Get up! Get up, Palamedes! Take your arms! Protect yourself
against me!'

The moment the Queen who was inside heard Tristan challenging Palamedes so loudly, she immediately recognized his
voice, and went to the window of the tower. And when she saw
Tristan, she called out:

'Ah! Praise be to God!'

All the people in the tower ran to the windows and the
battlements to watch the duel between the two knights who
were so famous. Palamedes, being lost in thought, had not heard
Tristan call out to him. Gorvenal dismounted, took him by the
helmet, and pulled it towards himself. Palamedes was jolted out
of his reverie and said to Gorvenal:

'Base and wicked squire, what do you want from me? This is
the second time you've interrupted my thoughts, and your behaviour is boorish.'

'Palamedes,' said Gorvenal, 'your thinking won't do you any
good. Here is Tristan who's challenging you to fight.'

When Palamedes heard this, he thought no more, but made for
his horse which was standing fully equipped in front of him,
mounted as quickly as he could and took up his shield and his
lance. Once ready, he said to Tristan:

'Tristan, it's very wrong of you to deprive me of my love. I had a fair chance of success in Ireland when you robbed me of it. Now you want to rob me of it by killing me. I won my lady Iseut and brought her away from King Mark's court, and here you are intending to take her from me. I won't have it!'

'Ah! Palamedes,' said Tristan, 'how could you be so foolish as to set foot in Cornwall when you knew that I was there? And then you abduct my uncle's wife! Did you really think you could keep her? You'll regret your action, because I'll do all in my power to make you pay for it by your death.'

Thereupon they instantly put their hands on their swords and attacked one another without saying another word; they struck each other such mighty blows on the helmet that sparks flew up, and the one hurt the other as much as he could. So great was their strength that each damaged the other's helmet and impaired the shield and hauberk; and before the first attack was over, even the fitter and the stronger of the two was reduced to such a state that he was in dire need of a doctor, for each one had wounds both great and small. When Queen Iseut saw this battle which had been undertaken for her sake, she was so frightened for Tristan, her beloved, that she did not know what to say, because the unexpected often happened, and if Palamedes had a bit of luck, he might just as soon kill Tristan as Tristan him. Queen Iseut watched the battle in sorrow and distress, and she was more upset watching it than many others would have been. She trembled all over with fear when she saw the mighty blows which Palamedes gave Tristan whom he did not consider as his friend, and it seemed to her that she was receiving them all herself. For this reason she left the tower, unable to bear the battle any longer. As soon as Gorvenal saw her coming he went towards her and said:

'Ah! noble Queen Iseut, for the love of God and for pity's sake, stop this duel if you have the power to do so. Should either of these two knights die, it would be a terrible misfortune, for they are without fail the two best knights I have ever seen.'

'I shall stop it, if I can,' she replied. 'I'm very upset and annoyed that it's gone on for so long.'

Thereupon Iseut went towards them full of anger and said:

'Tristan, stop fighting until I've spoken to you, and Palamedes likewise!'

'My lady,' they answered, 'at your command.'

Then they drew back a little from each other, and the Queen turned to Palamedes, saying:

'Palamedes, you've given me to understand that you love me?'

'My lady,' he replied, 'I truly love you more than any other woman; indeed, I love you more than myself and the whole world. You alone do I love, and you alone shall I love in such a way that my heart will never experience joy and good fortune or sink into sadness and grief except through you.'

'Since you love me so much,' said the Queen, 'it seems to me that you should not refuse to do anything I might command you.'

'Nor would I, my lady, I assure you,' he answered. 'You could not order me to do anything which I would not carry out unquestioningly, however much it might harm me.'

'We'll see,' she said. 'I now give you a command, and if you don't obey it, don't ever expect me to wish you well.'

'My lady,' he said, 'tell me what it is, and you may be sure that I shall do it, even if I could see clearly that it would cause my death.'

'I command you', she said, 'to withdraw from the battle, mount your horse, and go off to King Arthur's court by the straightest route you know. You will convey my greetings to Queen Guinevere whom I have heard greatly praised for her beauty and her courtliness, and say that I hope God will grant her joy in her love, and that I have given my heart to someone equally noble. Tell her from me that there are only two ladies and two knights in the world: she is one of the ladies and I am the other; her beloved is one of the knights and mine is the other. And if mine had been in Great Britain as long as hers, I would have no hesitation in saying he was his equal in beauty, courtliness, prowess and noble birth. And I would like her to know that if I could bring it about that she and I and our two lovers were to meet face to face, I would have a judgment passed on her beauty and mine, and on the strength and valour of our two knights. This is the message I want you to give her. And when you have carried out this errand, I command you by the love you feel for me that you never come to any place where you know me to be unless I'm in the Kingdom of Logres.'

Palamedes replied, weeping:

'My lady, at your command. Now I see clearly that you've driven me away from you with great cunning. Certainly I shall never go to any place where I know you to be unless you come to the Kingdom of Logres. But this much I beg you as my lady before I part from you that you never give your heart to anyone less worthy than I am.'

'Palamedes,' she replied, 'may I never feel joy again if I forsake my first love.'

Thereupon Palamedes departed, badly wounded, for Tristan had injured him grievously in this battle; and Tristan himself did not feel so fit that he was not in greater need of resting than of fighting. Then they went into the tower and disarmed Tristan, and Iseut examined his wounds and injuries, and did all she could for him. And they decided to remain there the rest of the day.

The following day after they had eaten, Tristan said to Iseut:

'My lady, what shall we do? You know well how things are between us. I can't do without you and you can't do without me, and if King Mark, who doesn't feel too kindly disposed towards me, were to find out, he would shame both me and you. For that reason it would be better for us to go away together at this point to the Kingdom of Logres where we could both lead a joyous life with one another, either at King Arthur's court or elsewhere. Then we wouldn't need to fear King Mark or the Cornish people.

Thereupon the Queen replied and said:

'Tristan, you know well by what ill-luck and misadventure it came about that you and I fell in love with each other. We've carried on our relationship as wisely as we could in such a way that no one has noticed it, and, God willing, we could go on doing so for a long time. But if we were now to go off as you've suggested, our guilty love would be known by everyone, and you would be accused of betraying your uncle and I would be decried as a disloyal and adulterous queen. In my opinion it would therefore be better for us to go back to King Mark at this stage and continue to live as pleasurable a life as we've done up till now. And if it ever came about that people began to talk and we could no longer live this life in King Mark's court, then there would still be time enough for us to make other plans.'

'Is that how you want it, my lady?' asked Tristan.

'Yes, it is,' she answered. 'I don't think we can do any better at this point.'

'Well, let's do it like that, then,' said Tristan. 'But my uncle is so malicious that if he finds out about our love, I'm afraid that we'll never again have such a good opportunity of leaving the Kingdom of Cornwall as we have now.'

'Yes we will,' she replied. 'Don't worry about it.'

That was the end of their conversation. Tristan stayed there for two days, and had his pleasure with the Queen as much as he wanted. The people in the tower asked everywhere for news of their lord, but these two could not give them any information.

When they had remained there for as long as they liked, they set out and made their way straight back to Norholt. As soon as they arrived at court, Tristan went into the presence of his uncle, armed as he was, and said to him:

'Uncle, here is the Queen. You gave her away very lightly, and I've won her back with great difficulty. Another time take better care of her if you are concerned about your own honour and that of all Cornwall.'

The King thanked Tristan for this kindness, and said that whatever else he might do, he would never again put his wife at risk. The Cornish people were very happy and joyful to have their lady back, and they said amongst themselves that Tristan had proved himself in so many adventures that they had just cause to consider him the best knight they had ever seen in Cornwall. They all spoke a lot about him and sang his praises, even those who were very envious of him. But whoever might be pleased at his prowess, King Mark was most unhappy about it, for on account of the valour he saw in Tristan and the natural grace he had, the King was very frightened of him, and terrified that he would dispossess him of Cornwall in the end; and that was why he would have liked to find a pretext for killing him or for banishing him from his land. [§§ 495–512 of vol. ii]

XI

CAPTURE OF THE LOVERS

SHORTLY after Iseut had been rescued from the hands of
Palamedes, it happened one day that Tristan was standing by a
window in the palace and was chatting with the Queen in the
sight of everyone.

'My lady,' he said, 'how did you know that Queen Guinevere
had a lover, and how did you dare to send her the message which
you asked Palamedes to give her?'

'I'll tell you, Tristan,' she replied. 'Actually, it was Love's
torment and ardour which made me do it, for it causes many a
wise man and woman to do many foolish things. Tristan,' she
went on, 'the truth is that I love you so ardently that if I were
given a free choice tomorrow to have the whole world or you, I
would reject the whole world in order to take you; and since my
love for you is so great, there is, in my opinion, not a knight
anywhere who could equal you in strength or beauty. Therefore
when it happened that a young girl came here from the Kingdom
of Logres, I welcomed her very warmly and asked her to tell me
some news of King Arthur's court and Queen Guinevere, and I
pressed her until she did so. She spoke very highly of King Arthur
and said that he was undoubtedly the best prince in Christendom.
Then the conversation turned to Queen Guinevere; I asked her
how the Queen was conducting her life, and the young girl told
me that she was conducting her life in a very courtly manner, for
she loved a knight who resided at her palace. When I heard this
I said that the Queen was acting very basely, since she was
married to the most worthy prince in the world and then shamed
him for the sake of a simple knight. Thereupon the maiden
answered me saying: "Certainly, no one should reproach her for
this, because she could well claim that she had given her heart to
the handsomest knight who ever wore armour in the Kingdom
of Logres. No lady should be so bold as to blame her for her love;
all of them should keep silent about their relationships except the
Queen, since she alone has bestowed her love on a superior being
and all the others on an inferior one." I was very angry at her

words, as I didn't think, and still don't, that there is anyone to equal you in the world, either as regards your beauty or your prowess, and therefore I don't believe that Queen Guinevere's lover is as handsome or as brave as you are. And I went further than that: I instantly showed you to the maiden and asked her what she thought of you. She replied that you might well be as handsome as the knight she had been talking about, but that your chivalry could not be compared to his, for there was no knight to equal him on earth. This made me indignant and I replied and said: "Please the Lord that they could both meet face to face! If they were fighting against each other in single combat, so help me God, I don't think that Tristan would have the worst of it!" "My lady," said the young girl, "that's quite impossible; the one I'm talking about is the most proven knight in the world, and Tristan is as yet quite unknown." That is what the maiden said to me, and because of her words I sent the message you heard to Queen Guinevere. Now we'll have to wait and see what comes of it.'

Tristan began to smile at this, and yet it troubled him, so he said.

One day not long after this conversation Tristan was in the King's bedroom all alone with the Queen. Audret, who hated Tristan bitterly, had watched him many a time until he had clearly perceived that he and the Queen were having an illicit relationship and that this relationship brought dishonour to King Mark. He therefore went to the King and said to him:

'My lord, I have something remarkable to tell you. You are harbouring in your court the man who day and night is shaming you by consorting with the Queen, and since you put up with this, you are the most base and the most ignoble king in the world.'

The King was very angry to hear this and said:

'Who is the one who is shaming me in this way?'

'My lord,' said Audret, 'it's Tristan, your nephew. I've kept his shameful behaviour from you as long as I could, but since I see that he doesn't want to alter his ways, I'm informing you of it in order to keep the oath by which I am bound to you.'

'And how can I be more certain about this?' asked the King.

'My lord,' Audret replied, 'if you go to your room without delay you'll be able to see their lawless conduct.'

'Indeed!' said the King, 'then in God's name I shall find out what's going on shortly.'

Thereupon he ran towards a sword which was hanging by a window in front of him, unsheathed it, and said to those who were around him:

'Come with me!'

'Willingly, my lord,' they answered. 'Go wherever you wish.'

Then the King went towards the bedroom, his sword drawn. Gorvenal who caught sight of him said to Tristan:

'Here comes King Mark, a naked sword in his hand. He's out to harm you. Make sure that you aren't caught.'

'Master,' said Tristan, 'don't worry. The King will never be so foolish as to attack me without just cause; he's well aware that I know how to defend myself.'

Then he drew away from the Queen.

As soon as the King had entered the room, he said loudly enough for all to hear:

'Vassal, you have shamed me by consorting with the being I loved most in the world. I herewith defy you and then I shall shame you.'

Thereupon he took two large steps forward and wanted to strike his nephew on top of his head. But Tristan leapt sideways, thus making the King miss him, and then went over towards a bed where the King's own sword was lying, drew it from the scabbard, and lastly took hold of a cloak which he wrapped round his arm. When he had done this, he said to the King:

'Uncle, you're committing villainy and treason by wanting to kill me in your court without any reason. I don't know what more to say: since you want to cause my death, I could be accused of lacking courage if I didn't defend myself. Henceforth be on your guard against me, for, by my faith, I shall not spare you.'

When the King heard these words, he said to those who were with him:

'Seize this traitor and take care he doesn't escape you, otherwise I would never be happy again.'

Tristan then said:

'Uncle, don't make your men die! If they move, so help me God, every single one of them will be killed. But you who call me a traitor, come and prove it here and now if you have the courage.'

King Mark feared Tristan more than anyone else in the world, and when he saw that not one of his men was prepared to move, whatever he said, he was so dismayed that he did not know how to reply. And Tristan, in order to frighten the King, thrust forward his naked sword towards him, and the King, seeing it coming, was too cowardly to wait for it, since he knew full well that the whole world would not protect him from death if Tristan could reach him; and for that reason he fled from the room. But Tristan who was very agile struck him so fiercely with the flat part of the blade on his bare head that the King flew to the ground and lay there full length, thinking he had received a mortal blow. Tristan stood over him and said:

'King Mark, now I could easily kill you if I wanted and if I considered your treachery. But I won't do it, for I wouldn't gain any honour or renown thereby.'

And when those who were there saw this blow, they were all intent on fleeing rather than on assisting the King.

Tristan went towards Iseut and said to her:

'My lady, come away with me. You may be certain that if you stay here, the King will punish you on account of me.'

'Don't worry,' she replied. 'I assure you that he loves me so greatly that he couldn't bring himself to harm me. But now go from here, and I shall do my best to reconcile you with the King.'

'I'm very much afraid for you,' said Tristan.

'Don't be afraid for me,' she replied, 'but go, I beg of you.'

'My lady,' he said, 'at your command.'

Thereupon Tristan went back to his quarters with Gorvenal, and found four knights there who were his companions. When they learnt what had happened, they were all dumbfounded. And these four companions who were in his lodgings came not from Cornwall but from other lands, and had lived for a long time in the Kingdom of Logres and at Arthur's court. One of them was called Lanbeguet; the other Nicoraut the Poor; the third Fergus* who was descended on his father's side from peasants but was of noble lineage on his mother's side, and undoubtedly a brave knight and a good-looking young man; and the name of the fourth was Driant of the Isle. These four knights had stayed in

Cornwall for love of Tristan. When they heard the news which Tristan himself told them, they said:

'What do you want to do about it? We're prepared to stand by you and, if need be, die with you.'

Tristan replied:

'Please God you won't die on my account. There is no reason, nor have I deserved it. But I'll tell you what we'll do. Let's take our arms and go into that forest out there. King Mark will never dare to leave his court as long as he knows that this is where we are, nor will any of his household, and for that reason he'll have to make peace with us according to our wishes.'

'In God's name,' said Gorvenal, 'that's the best plan of action I can see.'

And the others readily agreed. As soon as they were armed, they mounted their horses and set out, and went through the city into the forest; once there, they lodged in the house of a forester who loved Tristan a great deal more than King Mark.

The King had remained amongst his men,* and when he recovered from his shock and realized he had been struck with the flat part of the sword-blade, he rose to his feet very ashamed at having been thus humiliated, and for nothing. Then he cried out to his men:

'To arms! If Tristan escapes us in this way, we'll be dishonoured for evermore.'

He himself ordered his armour to be fetched and this was done. When the others realized that they were obliged to arm themselves, they did so, but very reluctantly, for they feared Tristan more than anyone in the world. The King mounted and with him no less than a hundred men on horseback, all of them armed. When they came to Tristan's lodgings and found neither Tristan nor any of his companions, the King was so angry that he did not know what to say. He asked in what direction they had gone, towards the forest or the sea, and he was told that they had taken the road to the forest.

'Ah! God,' exclaimed the King, 'we've lost Tristan! Now he's more of a threat to us than I thought, since we'll never be able to leave this city without his charging out at us.'

The King was furious that Tristan had escaped him like this. He returned to his palace and had himself disarmed, and then went to find the Queen and said to her:

'Lady, you have shamed me! You deserve to be put to death.'

The Queen replied and said:

'My lord, you could say better than that, if you wished. I assure you that I've never done you any wrong which would warrant my death. And in order that you may have greater faith in my words, I am ready and prepared to do whatever you should decide.'

'Lady,' he replied, 'your defence is worthless. I'm well aware of how things are, and I want you to know that before I've finished with you, you'll have no further desire for Tristan's company.'

'My lord,' she said, 'Tristan's company can't do me any harm. You ought not to blame me for enjoying his company in all innocence, since you know well that he has done more for me than any knight in the world, if only that he rescued me from the hands of Palamedes, the brave knight, who was carrying me off to a foreign land to your shame and dishonour without there being a single knight here bold enough to take up his arms; it was Tristan who fought against him and rescued me by force. And once he had me thus completely in his power, if he had loved me unlawfully, he could at that point have taken me to the Kingdom of Leonois or wherever else he wished and he wouldn't have let the thought of you stop him. And since he brought me back here and returned me to you of his own free will, as you saw, you should never suspect him of ill-conduct, whatever malicious gossip you were told about him.'

'Lady, lady, you know how to talk your way out of anything! But all these words will avail you nothing. You'll pay for Tristan's love, so help me God!'

'That may be so, my lord,' she replied.

The King said no more at that point, but he was greatly upset that Tristan had escaped him in this way, for he very much wanted to put him to death if he could. However, for the moment he was at such a disadvantage that he was more afraid of him than ever.

Next morning at about nine o'clock,* as the King was sitting at table amongst his barons, a knight came in wearing a hauberk, mail leggings and a sword; he was mortally wounded right through his body by a lance which stuck out in front and behind.

He carried in a helmet the head of a knight who had been quite recently killed. The knight who was bringing the head came from Cornwall and was related to King Mark. As soon as he had come in and seen the King, he said to him:

'King Mark, your nephew Tristan greets you as one should greet one's mortal foe. He has just wounded me, as you can see, and he has killed my brother whose head he sends you as a token of deadly enmity. And he also wants me to tell you that he will do the same to you as he has done to my brother if he can get hold of you outside the gates of this city.'

And no sooner had he said these words than he fell off his horse as one who was in the throes of death. When King Mark saw this, he was very frightened, much more so than usual, and ordered the knight to be removed from his presence; and this was done. And the knight actually died in the arms of those who were carrying him away.

King Mark retired to his room in great distress, and sent for Audret. As soon as they were alone there together, the King said:

'Audret, what can we do about Tristan? He's such a valiant knight that he is to be greatly feared. I wish I could find a way of bringing about his death.'

'My lord,' replied Audret, 'if I thought that you'd take my advice, I'd tell you how you could catch him in such a way that his treachery would be apparent, and even those who loved him best would condemn him to death. And I shall see to it that he is seized when he's in a situation where he can't defend himself so that you can have him killed without delay.'

'Upon my soul!' exclaimed the King, 'I'd be prepared to give up the best city in Cornwall if we could manage that.'

'In God's name,' said Audret, 'I shall do it, since you've given me leave; and if I don't hand him over to you bound and captive, you can slay me. Now I'll tell you how it can be accomplished.'

'Tell me, then,' said the King, 'for I wish it were already done.'

'You will send Tristan a letter,' said Audret, 'and in it you will write that you are asking him, your dear nephew, to pardon you for the wrong you've done him. He can come back to court in complete safety: you are prepared to forget all the discord which existed between you and him, and he may be sure that you will make full amends, as he himself designates and determines, for all the harm you've caused him. When he sees the letter and the worthy man who will deliver it on your behalf, or some maiden, he'll be quite ready to return; and I assure you that once he's back at court, I shall do all in my power to hand him over to you bound and captive as I've promised you.'

'And I agree', said the King, 'and leave it all in your hands.'

Then King Mark went into the great hall and summoned all his barons, and said to them:

'My lords, it was wrong of me to drive away my nephew Tristan from my court: no good will come of it. No one will ever be afraid of us; it was only on account of him that the whole of Cornwall was held in awe. And since I see that we can't do without his strength, I beg all of you who are here to bring it about that peace will be made between him and me. I shall make amends according to your judgment for all the wrong he says I've done him.'

When the Cornish barons heard what the King had said, they were overjoyed, because they really thought he had spoken sincerely and in good faith, and they all replied with one voice:

'Ah, King Mark, may God bless you! You had placed us in a desperate and shameful situation by incurring Tristan's ill-will, for we never dared to leave here as long as we knew him to be our enemy. But since you have had this change of heart, praise be to God who has brought it about. We fully agree to your proposal, and the whole of Cornwall will benefit by it. King Mark,' continued the barons, 'send him a letter, sealed with your seal, and he will come back instantly.'

'And who shall take him the letter?' asked the King.

'Brangain,' they replied, 'Iseut's lady-in-waiting. Tristan will believe her more readily than he would any of us.'

'Then let it be done in this way,' said the King, 'since you wish it.'

The letter was written and Brangain was immediately sent for. When she had come, the King gave her the letter and ordered her to take it to Tristan on his behalf and to look for him until she found him. Brangain took the letter and went off to her lady, and told her about the errand on which she had been sent.

'But what do you think, my lady, of this hatred which has so quickly been appeased?'

'Indeed,' said the Queen, 'I'll tell you what I think of it. I'm sure the Cornish people want this peace not for love of Tristan but for fear of him. As for King Mark, I know his treachery well enough to be aware that he's doing this more for Tristan's ill than for his good; so that if Tristan comes to court, he'll have to be more careful than ever not to behave imprudently, for I'm convinced that King Mark hates him mortally. And since you'll soon be with him, give my love both to him and to all his companions, and you can tell them from me that everyone at King Mark's court has been terrified.'

Brangain said that she would willingly deliver this message. Thereupon she left the Queen and mounted her horse and set out in the company of two maidens and two squires.

Once Brangain had departed from court, she rode on until she reached the forest and found Tristan and his company who were on the look-out for adventures. When Tristan saw her coming, he was so happy and joyful that he was at a loss what to say; he knew well that she would not be coming to find him if she were not bringing good news. He pointed her out to his companions and said to them:

'Look, there's Brangain! You may be sure that our peace is made.'

And then he said to Brangain:

'Welcome! How is my lady Iseut?'

'Very well, sir,' she replied. 'She sends you her heartfelt greetings, and to your companions as well. Your uncle, King Mark, asked me to come and give you this letter.'

Tristan took it and broke the seal, and saw that the King greeted him as his dear nephew and wrote saying that he asked him for mercy and forgiveness in respect of the dissension which had been between them, and that he was prepared to make amends for all the wrong he had done him in accordance with the decision and judgment of all the Cornish people; he could come back to court in complete safety, for the King wanted nothing in the world as much as his return.

When Tristan's companions heard what was in the letter, they said:

'Thank God, our peace is made! Now all we have to do is go to court. Whoever wants the discord between you and your uncle to continue, doesn't care about you at all.'

Thereupon Gorvenal spoke and said:

'So help me God, King Mark is a man of such cunning, I think he's only doing this out of malice.'

And Brangain instantly told them the message which Iseut had sent to Tristan concerning King Mark.

'Have no fear!' said Tristan. 'Let's go back! As God is my witness, I'm quite sure that my uncle, King Mark, would not be so stupid as to attack me whatever the circumstances.'

Then they mounted their horses and returned to the city. And I can assure you that they were as warmly welcomed by everyone as if they were all first cousins. The King greeted Tristan with such a show of pleasure that no one would have suspected him of harbouring thoughts of deceit and disloyalty towards Tristan unless he knew about the treachery he had planned. Tristan's position was as powerful as before, indeed more so than ever. But Audret, who was filled with deadly anger and envy, did everything he could to bring about his downfall.

There were in the city as many as thirty knights who were all related to the two brothers whom Tristan had killed in the forest. They would readily have avenged their death, had they dared, but they lacked the courage, for they feared Tristan more than God himself. Audret approached these kinsmen and revealed King Mark's wishes to them and how Tristan was committing adultery with the King's wife; and he told them that if they could catch Tristan with the Queen, the King would be more grateful to them than if they were to give him a city. The knights then replied and said:

'Audret, we aren't so intimate with the Queen that we could go and see her whenever we liked. But you who have influence over her could easily arrange it if you wished.'

'And if I did arrange it,' Audret said, 'would you be brave enough to seize Tristan?'

'Yes,' they replied. 'If you give us the opportunity and he escapes us, may King Mark put us to death.'

'Then I promise you', he replied, 'that I'll give you the opportunity to bring this matter to a successful conclusion.'

And they promised him that they would do all they had pledged. Thereupon their deliberations ended, since they had come to a mutual agreement.

One day after this conversation it happened that King Mark was in a meadow not far from the sea, no more than four bowshots away from Tintagel. The King had ordered tents and pavilions to be erected on account of the great heat, and everyone who was there with him was having a very pleasant time. At that point many knights from Cornwall and from other lands were staying at his court, and a lot of them came there just to see Tristan, whose remarkable fame had spread far and wide. The day I am talking about was the Tuesday after the Feast of St John,* and King Mark and the Queen had left the pavilions and were enjoying themselves amongst a large company of knights, ladies and maidens. And while they were thus intent on their pleasure and amusement, two knights came towards them, fully armed and mounted on fine and richly apparelled horses; and they had emerged from a forest which was nearby. Their armour showed clearly that they had received many blows, for it was very damaged, though their horses did not seem too tired. They rode slowly towards the pavilions, their lances lowered. As soon as King Mark saw them he said to those who were with him:

'Look, here come two knights-errant. Let them approach, and we'll hear what they have to say.'

And he withdrew to his pavilion, and so did many others out of respect for him. Queen Iseut was playing chess with Tristan at the time, and a lot of noble men were watching the game. The two unknown knights went up to the King and greeted him, and he returned their greeting very courteously, asking them to dismount.

'Many thanks, my lord,' they replied, 'but we won't dismount just now, as we have much to do elsewhere. However, we'd very much like to take a look at Queen Iseut: we've travelled many a day to see her beauty.'

'By all means,' said the King, 'you can see the Queen in front of this pavilion where she's playing chess with Tristan.'

They made no reply, but went straight there, and came up as quietly as they could to where the two were playing, still on horseback. The Queen was very engrossed in the game because she saw clearly that Tristan had the advantage over her. Tristan was less absorbed, for he was well aware that he had won, but he did pay attention in so far as he knew the Queen was a bit annoyed at losing; and she was a remarkably good chess player. The two unknown knights who, as I have told you, had ridden up to them while they were playing, began to look at the Queen very intently.

The two knights, Lamorat and Driant, sons of King Pellinor, begin a heated argument as to whether Iseut is more beautiful than the Queen of Orcanie, and Iseut rebukes them for their lack of courtesy. Lamorat does not want to leave before having jousted with the Cornish knights, and he sends a maiden to King Mark to challenge him. Mark orders two of his knights to take up the challenge, but both are speedily knocked off their horses. The King tells his men to arm themselves in order to avenge the two, and more than forty obey his command. Driant is dismayed, but Lamorat reassures him, and indeed before long they have unhorsed so many of the Cornish knights that the rest return to their tents and refuse to joust. King Mark then orders his nephew to arm himself; Tristan protests that the two knights are by now too tired, but the King insists and Tristan has to obey, declaring however that he would go unaided. Two blows suffice for our hero to knock both Driant and Lamorat to the ground. The latter in particular is mortified and calls on Tristan to fight him with the sword, but Tristan declines in spite of Lamorat's furious insults.

The two brothers make their way to Logres, where one day they come across a knight accompanied by a squire and a maiden who is carrying a very beautiful ivory horn. The knight reveals to Lamorat that a lady has sent him to King Arthur's court with this horn from which no woman can drink who has been unfaithful to her husband without the contents spilling all over her. The knight is unwilling to divulge the lady's name, but after Lamorat has defeated him in combat he is forced not only to disclose that the lady was Morgan le Fay but also to agree that he would present this magic horn* to King Mark instead, with the message that it was being sent to his court out of ill-will towards Tristan by the knight whom he had refused to fight outside the pavilions.

Lamorat and Driant take the road to King Arthur's court, whereas the knight and his company make their way to Cornwall. They arrive in Tintagel on the day of St Mary Magdalene,* and the knight delivers the horn to King Mark. The King, upon being told of the magical properties of the horn, is delighted; Tristan however is exceedingly angry at this act of hostility on the part of Lamorat, and very upset at the threat it poses to Queen Iseut.

The King noticed very clearly that Tristan was angry, and this made him happy and joyful. He asked the knight:

'How can I test the marvel that you've told me about?'

'I'll tell you how soon enough,' said the knight. 'Order all the ladies in your court to come to this great hall, rich and poor alike, even the Queen herself. Once they're here, have the horn filled with wine. No lady who has dishonoured her husband and taken a lover outside her marriage will be able to drink from this horn without spilling the wine all over herself; but the one who has been faithful can drink from it safely, for the wine will never overflow.'

'Upon my word!' exclaimed the King, 'this test is the finest I've ever heard about, and we'll do it just as you've described.'

Once the King had been told about the matter and agreed to it, the news began to spread that a knight had come to court with these tidings. The Queen enquired whether it was true, and they assured her it was. She grew very alarmed and upset, knowing full well that she had been unfaithful to the King many a time for love of Tristan. She was very uneasy, and racked her brains to see what she could do about it; but the great confidence she had in Tristan gave her hope. Whilst she was pondering thus, a knight entered who said to the Queen:

'My lady, the King has sent for you, and commands you to appear before him together with all the ladies and all the maidens who are here with you. Make sure that none of them remains behind, as the King wants you to see a marvel which has been brought to court.'

The Queen replied and said:

'I am ready.'

She ordered the tables to be removed, and told all the ladies and maidens that they must come with her to the great hall. The Queen went first and all her company followed; and there was not a knight in the hall who did not rise to his feet as she came in, with the exception of the King.

Tristan who was very distressed said to his companions:

'We've got a fight on our hands, it seems to me, for King Mark is intent on shaming Queen Iseut, and I couldn't suffer this under any circumstances whatever. If it comes to a confrontation, don't be dismayed, but each one of you defend your life, and let's try, if we can, to bring away the Queen. Meanwhile let's make sure our armour is in order, so that we find it ready if we should need it.'

And his companions said that they were prepared to stand by him and, if need be, die with him. Then they sent their squires to their quarters to have their arms ready in case they should require them.

King Mark ordered the horn to be filled with wine, and this was done; when it was full he ordered it to be taken to the Queen. She looked at it and asked where it had come from.

'Lady,' said the King, 'never mind that, but drink, and we'll see what happens.'

'My lord,' she replied, 'saving your grace I won't do that until I know what it is. It may be a magic horn made in order to upset the noble ladies who haven't acted in accordance with the wishes of all the enchanters and enchantresses of Great Britain. Indeed, I'm sure that it came from Great Britain, which is full of enchantments, and that it was sent to you with the intention of creating discord between you and me or between other good people in Cornwall.'

'Lady, lady,' said the King, 'your excuses will avail you nothing! Do what I command you, and we shall soon see your disloyalty.'

'I don't know what you'll see', she answered, 'but I'll do what you say.'

And as she intended to drink, a large part of the wine spilt all over her, so that she was quite soaked by it. As soon as the youth who had given her the horn saw this, he ran up to the Queen and took the horn out of her hands and gave it to another lady who was sitting beside her. The King was extremely angry and said to the Queen:

'Lady, this will never do! Now your disloyalty is apparent! You deserve to die. The law is such that a lady who is unfaithful to her husband should be put to death and burnt.'

'That may be so', said the Queen, 'provided she has been proved guilty.'

'You have been proved guilty clearly enough,' replied the King.

'Certainly, my lord,' said the Queen, 'if you want to put me to death on the testimony of this horn which has been made by enchantment, then your felony and your disloyalty and your cruelty will be much more evident than my infidelity. There isn't a knight in the whole of your court who could call me to account for what you've accused me of whom I wouldn't, in my defence, cause to be slain or defeated in front of you in less than a day.'

'Lady,' he replied, 'you have at your disposal such a champion that there isn't a knight in all Cornwall who would dare to take up arms against him.'

'My lord,' she said, 'I don't know whom you are referring to or why you say this, but I feel myself so innocent of the charge you've made against me that I wouldn't hesitate to ask a knight to defend me in judicial combat against anyone who would accuse me of it.'

'Lady, lady,' said the King, 'I know well how things are. You've said enough; we'll see what happens.'

As he spoke these words, he was watching the lady who sat beside the Queen and who was already quite wet, for she had spilt a great deal of the wine.

'My lord, my lord,' said the Queen, 'it seems to me that if the testimony of this horn leads to death, I won't be the only one to die! This lady is just as guilty as I am, if guilt comes into it.'

The King replied:

'Both of you have deserved to die. Let's watch the others and we'll witness the fidelity of the Cornish ladies!'

What shall I tell you? All the ladies present, of which there were at least a hundred or more, tried to drink from the horn, but only four managed it without spilling the wine all over themselves. The King declared that these four were blameless, but that all the rest were faithless and wicked, and should rightfully be put to death; and he asked for judgment to be passed on them. But the Cornish barons who loved their wives as much as themselves and who had no wish at all to see them die, especially as they did not believe this proof to be valid, said to the King:

'My lord, my lord, you can put to death whom you wish, but whatever you do to the Queen who is yours, we shall keep our wives. God forbid that we should have them killed for such a poor reason as this one seems!'

'No?' asked the King. 'You see clearly that they've shamed you, and yet you don't dare to take vengeance!'

'My lord,' they replied, 'saving your grace, we don't see or know this at all. Because you feel ill-will towards the Queen, that is not how we feel towards our wives.'

The King was quite pleased to hear this, for though he might have said what he did to chastise the Queen, he would not have wanted her to die without seeing her guilt more clearly than he had done. Then he spoke and said:

'In truth, my lords, since each of you wants to acquit his wife of this offence, I for my part shall acquit mine; and seeing that you consider this test to be invalid, I shall consider it invalid too: it would be more to my honour if it were false than if it were true.'

And all those who were there cried out:

'Many thanks, oh King, many thanks!'

Thus the Queen was acquitted of this misdeed, as well as all the other Cornish ladies.

Meanwhile Audret was still trying to find a way of catching Tristan together with Queen Iseut. He therefore had some very sharp scythes made, and one evening placed them beside Iseut's bed, thinking that if Tristan came there, he would be very likely to maim himself. The Queen was lying in her bed in an upstairs room, and Tristan and Audret were guarding her. Tristan never for a moment thought that Audret would be so bold as to try and catch him. King Mark was not feeling very well at the time and was sleeping in another room some distance away. When Tristan saw that Audret had fallen asleep, he rose and went to the Queen's bed where he came up against the scythes, one of which injured him so badly that it gave him a large and deep wound in his leg which bled copiously. Tristan however paid no heed to this, being eager and impatient to have his pleasure, and he lay down beside the Queen. But they had not been together long before she felt that the sheets were wet, and she knew well that it was not due to water or perspiration. Consequently she was quite taken aback and wondered what could have caused this. She quietly told Tristan about it, and he immediately realized what it was, and informed the Queen.

'Ah! dear beloved,' she exclaimed, 'we've been trapped. Go back to your bed as silently as you can, and I'll think of a plan whereby neither you nor I shall incur any blame.'

'Well, we'll see!' said Tristan. 'If you can bring that about, we're saved, otherwise there's no way that we won't be found out.'

Thereupon Tristan went back to his bed so softly that Audret did not hear anything. And when he had reached it, he bandaged his wound tightly to stop the bleeding.

The Queen got out of bed and deliberately knocked herself against the scythes so that she was severely wounded. Then she plunged back into her bed and cried out as loudly as she could:

'Help! help! Brangain, come quickly, I'm hurt!'

The maidens, hearing her cries, hastened there as speedily as they could with candles and torches, and when they found the scythes, they said:

'We've been betrayed! These scythes were placed here after we went to bed. Sir Tristan, come forward! Either you or Audret left them there in order to kill my lady. A curse on King Mark if he doesn't put you to death!'

Audret swore for all he was worth that he knew nothing about it, and so did Tristan.

The King turned up when he heard the commotion, and finding the Queen wounded, he asked:

'Lady, who gave you this wound?'

'Either Tristan or Audret who put these scythes here,' she replied. 'They did it to kill me. I beg of you, avenge me for this misdeed.'

The King pretended to be very angry, and said he must know who had planned this treachery. Tristan replied:

'My lord, if you were to say that one of us was responsible, I for my part can vouch for it that I knew nothing about it and that the scythes weren't placed there at my behest, and I shall prove that it was Audret who did it. And if he were willing to defend himself, I would either cause him to die or admit himself vanquished by tomorrow afternoon.'*

When the King saw that things had reached the point where Tristan wanted to fight with Audret, he said to him:

'Tristan, it would not be proper for enmity to exist between the two of you: you are first cousins and both my nephews. Even though it was a wicked deed, I don't want you to say any more about it at present; the matter can never be so well concealed that I won't find out who was responsible.'

And Tristan said he was quite happy to comply with the King's wishes.

In this way King Mark covered up the truth about the scythes which Audret had treacherously planted to trap Tristan. The Queen was ill for a long while as a result of this wound which she had given herself. Audret saw clearly that Tristan had also been injured by the scythes and that the Queen had saved him through her quick wit. He told the King about it, who observed Tristan until he found out it was true. Then he conceived a mortal hatred for Tristan, though he made a great show of loving him. However, he left Audret in no doubt that there was nothing for which he would be more grateful to him than if he could catch Tristan with Queen Iseut.

'And you may rest assured', said the King, 'that if he were caught in the act, I would not spare him, even if I would gain the Kingdom of Logres by doing so.'

'I'll tell you how you should proceed,' said Audret. 'You will forbid Tristan to enter the Queen's bedroom at night, whereupon I shall instantly do all I can to seize and capture him, and hand him over to you.'

The King did as Audret had advised; indeed, he acted even more judiciously, for in the hearing of all his household he forbade that anyone should be so bold as to enter the Queen's bedroom at night, unless it was a lady or a maiden. And whosoever entered there would be put to death, even if it were his nephew Tristan himself.

Tristan was furious when he heard this, realizing as he did that the King had given these orders because of him, and he did not know what to say about it. The Queen was so angry that she found it difficult to restrain her wrath. Tristan, uneasy as he was, never for a moment curbed his love, and said to the Queen that he would not let any ban imposed by the King stop him from coming to her.

'Dear beloved,' said the Queen, 'naturally I want you to come, but I'm so afraid of your being caught that I don't know what to suggest. If I were sure of your safety, I wouldn't be concerned about myself, for I know the King wouldn't dare to kill me: he is well aware that he wouldn't live very long if he had killed me because of you; therefore, do be careful, beloved.'

Tristan declared that he could not stop himself from coming to her.

'I'm not worried about your coming,' she said, 'provided that it doesn't turn out ill for you.'

'Don't let it trouble you, my lady,' he replied.

They said no more at that point.

Audret sent word to those who hated Tristan mortally that they should all prepare their armour and be ready that night. And they told him that they were all ready; he could send his messenger whenever he liked.

There was at court a young girl from Cornwall who was called Bessille; she had fallen in love with Tristan and had asked him for his love. But because he did not respond to her and had in fact called her a foolish maiden, she now hated him more than any other man. She had recently met Audret and was very much in love with him, and he with her. And because she loathed Tristan, when it came about that the King forbade any man to enter the Queen's bedroom at night, she said to Audret:

'Audret, do you know what you can do? Since Tristan will not be sleeping in the room, and the door leading to it from the palace will be locked, I can tell you how he'll get in. Do you see that room there which is facing the garden? That's the way he'll come without any doubt: he'll climb up that tree to the window and then go to the Queen's bedroom; there is no other way.'

'You're right,' said Audret, 'and now that you've told me, I'll make sure that if he comes through there, he'll never get away, because I'll do all in my power to have him caught.'

'We'll see what you'll do,' said the maiden. 'If he escapes you, you'll be dishonoured for evermore; and the King himself will feel ill-will towards you.'

Thus it was that on the very evening of his conversation with Bessille, Audret placed twenty fully armed knights, who all hated Tristan mortally, in the room facing the garden, the one through which Tristan would have to pass, since there was no other way he could come. Audret himself stayed there with them. Then the other knights asked him:

'Audret, how are we going to set about this?'

'Very easily,' he replied. 'As soon as you see Tristan approaching, don't say a word, but allow him to go into the Queen's bedroom unimpeded. And when he's inside and in bed with the Queen, he may well fall asleep, in which case a maiden who is in there will alert us. Let's wait here in silence: we'll see him coming, but he won't see us. One thing is certain, if we don't succeed at this point, we'll never have such a good opportunity again.'

And they replied:

'Don't worry, Audret. Rest assured, he can't escape us.'

While they were talking thus, the moon had already risen, which greatly hindered Tristan, for if it had not been so light, he would already have got there some time ago. He remained in the garden, hiding amongst the trees in order not to be seen; he was armed only with his sword, since it would have been difficult for him to put on and take off his hauberk, and the clinking of the chain-mail might have been heard. After he had waited for a long time under the trees, he decided that everyone indoors must be asleep, and climbed up a tree with great agility; from the tree he jumped over to the window which was open, and from the window into the room. All those inside saw him clearly; unfortunately for him he did not see a single one, but passed through them all into another room, and from this room he went into the Queen's bedroom and towards her bed where he found her fast asleep. He woke her up, and she roused herself with difficulty, for she had been sleeping soundly. When she saw that it was Tristan, her beloved, she received him with great pleasure, and welcomed him as joyfully and gladly as she knew how. King Mark was not sleeping in the bedroom that night, but was deliberately pretending to be ill in order to see if Tristan could be caught.

Whilst Tristan was in bed with the Queen, and those outside were waiting until they thought the two would have fallen asleep, Brangain suddenly appeared at the bedside as silently as she could and said to Tristan:

'Get up, Tristan! get up! You've come in here very foolishly. Out there in that room facing the garden more than twenty fully armed knights are lying in wait to pounce on you. If you stay here any longer, you will be seized and shamed, and so will the Queen.'

As soon as Tristan heard these words, he jumped out of bed, dressed in great haste, threw a cloak over his arm and asked Brangain in a whisper:

'Where are those who are lying in wait for me?'

'They're in that room facing the garden,' she replied.

'Upon my word!' he exclaimed. 'I can see what they're up to! But they'll regret it before long, if I have anything to do with it.'

'Ah! beloved,' cried the Queen, 'you will die unless God protects you. You will never escape alive, and I shall be lost if you die.'

'My lady,' answered Tristan, 'never fear. I shall get away without any difficulty in spite of them.'

Thereupon he left the Queen's room and went into the other one. When he reached the room where they were still waiting, intent on attacking him, he caught sight of one of them by the light of the moon and immediately rushed in amongst them, saying:

'You're done for, you bastards! You came here seeking to harm me, but the tables are turned now. Here is Tristan who will bring sorrow on you!'*

And he struck one of the knights so fiercely that in spite of his helmet Tristan split his head down to his teeth. The knight who felt himself mortally wounded staggered, and as he fell, he let out an anguished cry and said:

'Alas, I'm done for!'

When the others heard these words, they were so dismayed that they thought they were all done for, and many of them even dropped their swords, they were so frightened. Tristan turned towards another who was making for the window and hit him so hard that he cut off his entire left shoulder. And the knight fell to the ground, crying:

'Alas, I'm done for!'

Tristan, who could not see what was going on around him and who was afraid that someone might strike him from behind, went to the window and leapt out on to the garden lawn. Fortunately for him, he was not hurt or wounded by this jump, even though the window was more than twenty feet from the ground.

Once Tristan had freed himself from his enemies, he returned to his quarters happy and joyful, and told his companions how the twenty knights had lain in wait for him and how he had escaped from amongst them all.

'As God is my witness,' he said, 'if it had been broad daylight at that point, not a single one of them would have got away, for I would have killed them all. Never have there been such bad knights as the Cornish. And if God lets me live, I will yet make them pay very dearly for trying to keep me away from my beloved.'

'Ah! Tristan,' said Gorvenal, 'I'm very anxious about you and very much afraid that your love will cost you dear. It was a great misfortune and a great sorrow for us to have been so deceived as to the philtre!'

'Don't worry, sir,' said Tristan. 'It won't make any difference, so help me God: those who are most eager to bring about my downfall are the very ones who will die the soonest, if I catch them at the right moment.'

Tristan's companions were delighted and overjoyed at his escape. But in King Mark's palace those who had lost their friends wept and lamented. A great and extraordinary commotion broke out: candles and torches appeared from all sides; knights, ladies and maidens came along and the King himself arrived, convinced that Tristan had been caught. However, when he was in their midst and he heard their grief and saw the men lying on the ground and perceived the great blows which Tristan had given them, he could not refrain from saying:

'These are not blows dealt by a child. Ah! Tristan, dear nephew, what misfortune has been your lot! If you hadn't betrayed me, I know of no man on earth whose worth could have equalled yours. Queen Iseut, may you burn in hell! It's your fault that I've lost him, and I'm shamed by it, but rest assured that I'll shame him, and as a result all Cornwall will be full of sorrow.'

And when he had spoken these words, he went back to the room where he had been sleeping and began to grieve most bitterly, lamenting and regretting Tristan's prowess. After he had lamented for a long while, he sent for Audret, and when he had come, the King asked him:

'Audret, how could you let Tristan escape? You knew he was completely unarmed, and you were all in full armour!'

'Indeed, my lord,' he answered, 'it's small wonder that he escaped, for no one could match his prowess.'

'That's no excuse,' said the King. 'Since you undertook to capture him, it's up to you to hand him over to me captive.'

Audret replied that he would do his best, but that he was more afraid of him than before, because now he knew well that Tristan was not a man to be trifled with, and that nobody could ever catch him if he was on his guard. Audret left the King and made his way back to where they were still grieving, and had the two dead men taken away and carried to their quarters.

The King continued to lament for a long time, and then went to the Queen's room and said:

'Lady, I won't have it! You're doing your utmost to bring about my shame and my misfortune by robbing me of my nephew Tristan. May your beauty be cursed! I tell you, you'll pay for it with your life, and so will Tristan, the best knight in the world; and his loss will be a greater tragedy than yours, for after his death I don't think there will remain in the world a knight as brave as he is.'

The King spoke these words to the Queen in exceeding anger; and the Queen, seeing his fury, was so terrified of him that she did not dare to say a thing. And the King returned to his room, sorrowful and upset.

At dawn the following morning, he ordered that the Queen should be put in his tower in some place where she would find it impossible to see Tristan, and Tristan her; and his command was carried out. When Iseut found herself imprisoned, she was so distressed that she wished she were dead. Tristan who was quite fearless made his way to court that day just before dinner. The King saw his nephew, but ignored him and went off with the other knights. Tristan secretly asked where Queen Iseut was, and they told him that the King had imprisoned her in his tower in such a place where no one could speak to her except at his command. Tristan was so upset by this news that he called himself an unhappy wretch and said that he would never again feel any joy, since he had lost his lady in this way. Not wanting to remain at court, he went back to his quarters, and once in his room, he began to lament so bitterly that no one could have heard it without being filled with pity for him.

'Alas,' he said, 'what can I do? Now that I have lost my lady, my beloved, there's no hope for me, I'm finished. Ah! treacherous and cruel Love, you have subjected me to your rule and you keep me in great sorrow and great pain while others feel joy and happiness, so that I pay for their pleasure and their good fortune.'

Tristan was full of grief and anger and cursed the hour that he was born. He stopped eating and drinking, and no longer went to court as he used to: since he could not see Queen Iseut, his lady, he was not interested in any of the others. He did nothing but look at the tower where his lady was imprisoned. As long as it was daylight he kept gazing at it, with the result that he forgot all about food and drink. As soon as darkness fell, he started to grieve so bitterly that no one could comfort him. What more shall I tell you? His condition deteriorated from day to day. He became so thin that all those who were around him said that this was a malady from which he would never recover.

King Mark did not know that Tristan was so ill, but upon hearing the news he went to see him and found him even more ailing than he had been told. When he saw him looking so pale and wan, and remembered how handsome he used to be, he could not stop himself from bursting into tears. After he had wept for a long time, he said in great distress:

'Tristan, you sealed your fate when you fell in love! You will die as a result, I can see it clearly, for no help will come to you from where you hope to find it. You will die in pain and suffering, and it will be the greatest tragedy which to my knowledge ever happened in Cornwall. I know well that there has not been a knight here as brave as you are since Cornwall became converted to Christianity, of that I am quite certain. And because you are going to die in Cornwall as a consequence of your folly, Cornwall will be honoured by the fact that your body will remain here. But the loss is immeasurable, and I myself will lose more by it than anyone else.'

Tristan, who could not conceal what was in his mind, replied:

'My lord, you say that I cannot fail to die of love, and you claim that this is a great disaster on account of my prowess. If I was indeed a valiant knight and at the same time so completely overcome by love that I am having to die of it, that is after all not such a rare phenomenon. Absalom the Fair, King David's son, who was extremely handsome, also died of love; Samson the Strong was deceived by it most treacherously; so was Solomon the Wise and Achilles the Greek, the brave knight who in his time was more illustrious than I am. Merlin himself died of it, even though he knew more than anyone else in the world. And since so many noble men have died of love, I, whose worth is nothing compared to theirs, should not be unduly pitied, rather should it be considered as a mark of honour that I shall be their companion in this misadventure.'

When the King heard these words, he was so distressed that he did not know what to say. And Tristan continued:

'Uncle, if I die in Cornwall, Cornwall will not be able to boast that my body has remained there. I don't love this country enough. Only one person keeps me in Cornwall, and if she were not here, I myself would not have remained.'

'That may well be,' said the King. 'But where do you want your body to be carried, if you die?'

'I want it to be taken to the Kingdom of Logres', he replied, 'and placed in King Arthur's court right in front of the Round Table, for that is undoubtedly where all the best knights in the world are to be found. Since I can't go there in my lifetime, I want to go there after my death. Once the Round Table companions, who have heard so much about me, see my body in front of them, they cannot fail to honour it and put it in some worthy resting-place. And if this is done, I ask for no other honour in this world nor for any earthly thing except only one which I cannot now attain.'

When Tristan had said these words, he fell backwards on his bed as if he were dead. But after a while he spoke again:

'Tristan, why were you ever conceived and born in order to live on this earth in pain and torment? The only day on which you ever experienced good fortune was when you killed the Morholt of Ireland. It would have been better for you to have died then and there in the act of freeing Cornwall from the dolorous servitude to which she was subjected, for then at least your suffering would have been over and done with which you cannot end either in your life or by your death. Ah! wretched and cruel death, why don't you come to see the unhappy and sorrowful Tristan who cannot terminate his sad existence for all his misery and anguish!'

The King was so moved by Tristan's words that tears ran from his eyes; and because he could not bear to hear any more, he departed with his company. He went back to his palace in great distress, and said that he was shamed since he had lost his nephew for so poor a reason.

If Tristan was suffering anguish because of Iseut, Iseut for her part was so unhappy that she hardly ate or drank anything at all.

And when she was given to understand that Tristan was definitely dying, she called herself wretched and miserable, and declared that if he died she would kill herself with her own two hands. Then she said to Brangain:

'Brangain, what are we going to do?'

'I don't know, my lady,' she replied, 'so help me God. Tristan is paying for your love very dearly, since he is dying for it; and I know that is so, for I saw the King weeping about it just now in the palace.'

'Is it really true then that my beloved is dying?' she asked.

'It's definitely true, my lady,' she replied. 'There can be no doubt about it. It's a terrible tragedy.'

The Queen wept bitterly at this news, and thought about it and pondered, and then said to Brangain:

'Brangain, now we shall see what you're prepared to do for my sake and for the good of Tristan. I've conceived a plan whereby you can bring Tristan here without it being noticed.'

'Then tell me, my lady,' Brangain answered. 'I'm ready to do it even if I were to die as a result.'

'In that case I'll tell you,' said the Queen. 'As soon as night falls, you will go straight to Tristan and greet him on my behalf, and make him put on a woman's dress and bring him here like that. If anyone asks you about him, you will boldly say that Tristan is a messenger-girl who has been sent to me from Ireland.'

'That's a good idea, my lady,' Brangain declared.

'You can do this quite safely,' said Iseut, 'and Tristan can stay here two or three days.'

This is how the Queen wanted it done, and Brangain said she would do it without fail. That evening as darkness fell she went to Tristan's lodgings as quietly as she could. She had gone there many a time already without bringing him any news which might have cheered him, but now when she told him that Iseut wanted him to come to her and in what manner, he was so overjoyed and so happy that he jumped out of bed as though he had not been ill at all, and kissed and embraced Brangain, saying:

'Ah! God, will the hour never come when I can see my lady Iseut?'

'Yes,' she replied, 'you will definitely see her tonight.'

And without further delay she sent for the dress of a young girl and gave it to Tristan; no one was there who knew about it except Gorvenal. He it was who attired Tristan and handed him over to Brangain, and said to her:

'Whatever you do, take good care of Tristan for me. I'm entrusting him to you safe and sound, apart from his indisposition, and that is how I expect him back.'

And she said she would do her utmost.

Thereupon Tristan set out, dressed in woman's clothing, but wearing his sword under his cloak to be on the safe side. He passed right in front of King Mark and the other knights without being intercepted by any of them. The King recognized Brangain well enough, but he did not know Tristan on account of his dress. Brangain continued on her way and Tristan followed her, and they kept going until they reached the tower. The porter who was guarding the door made no attempt to stop them, thinking they were young girls, and so they went straight to the room where Iseut was waiting for Tristan. When she saw Brangain entering and Tristan coming after her, she recognized him at once by his build, and she let them approach; and she had already asked all the ladies and maidens to leave the room some time before. Then Tristan and Iseut were so overjoyed and so happy that it would be impossible ever to see anyone more so. Tristan stayed there for three days, during which time he had his pleasure with his lady, and she also with him.

On the fourth day he happened to be sleeping in a dimly lit room where the Queen thought she had safely hidden him when Bessille, Audret's girl-friend, found him there. She had opened the door quite softly, and was looking for one of the Queen's cloaks, the very one with which Tristan was covered. Seeing him asleep, she was afraid that if he woke up and recognized her, his dislike of her would make him kill her. She therefore turned back and closed the door as quietly as she could so that Tristan would not hear it, and she thought to herself that since he had got in there, he would never leave again without being captured.

Then she came to Audret and said to him:

'Dear friend, I'm bringing you amazing news. Believe it or not, but Tristan is hidden up there in a room where I found him just now fast asleep.'

'Really?' Audret asked. 'Well, keep it to yourself, and don't let anyone suspect that you know. Upon my word, he's gone in there so foolishly that he will never get away without being shamed!'

And she promised not to breathe a word about it to anyone.

'Now we shall see what you'll do!' she said.

Audret went straight to the knights who hated Tristan and told them the news; and they were delighted and joyful, and said they were ready to go and seize him.

'As soon as it's dark,' he told them, 'conceal yourselves fully armed at the foot of the tower by the porch,* and when I see that the opportunity presents itself, I'll send for you.'

'That's fine,' they said.

That evening as darkness fell Audret joined the porters who were completely under his control, for the King had told them to obey any order that Audret might give them. He said to Bessille:

'Let me know the moment that Tristan is in bed with the Queen.'

'Don't worry,' she replied. 'I'll put you in a position where you can catch him so that he won't have a chance of escaping you.'

'We'll see,' he said. 'I leave it to you.'

'You can rely on me,' she answered.

Thus the plan was devised to catch Tristan with the Queen.

When it was quite dark, the knights who were coming to seize Tristan concealed themselves by the porch at the foot of the tower; and they were well armed with helmets, hauberks and trusty swords. As soon as Audret saw them, he placed them inside the doors as quietly as possible, for he did not want anyone but the porters to notice; and there were twenty-two of them in all. At that moment the vicious maiden appeared and said to Audret:

'You can come up safely now! The Queen has fallen asleep, and Tristan with her.'

'Indeed?' he said. 'Well, if he escapes us now, it would have to be by a miracle!'

Then he called to the knights whom he had asked to come:

'We can go now. Tristan is asleep.'

Thereupon they went up the steps so silently that none of the ladies heard them. When they entered the Queen's bedroom, they carried in many candles, but they did this as covertly as they could. Then they approached the bed where they found Tristan sleeping beside the Queen in his undershirt and breeches; and both of them were so sound asleep that even the light did not wake them up, as Fortune who was adverse to them at this point decreed. One of the knights leapt forward and said to Audret:

'Do you want me to kill him? I can cut him to pieces with my sword before he wakes up!'

'No, I don't want you to do that,' Audret replied. 'The King has forbidden it. I would prefer us to catch him without hurting him at all and to hand him over to the King as he is, then he can take whatever vengeance he sees fit.'

They all agreed to this and instantly seized Tristan from all sides so that before he had woken up they held him so firmly that there was no way he could escape. And they said:

'Tristan, Tristan, your strength won't do you any good now! You've carried on for so long that at last you're caught. You can't fail to receive an ignominious death for this act. You will be shamed, and so will the Queen.'

When Tristan saw that he had been captured in such a base and treacherous fashion while he was asleep, he was so angry that he did not know what to do. And Audret, who hated him bitterly, said:

'Ah! Tristan, you're done for! King Mark will have you killed, and there's no way out.'

'I don't know what he will do,' said Tristan.

Then the vicious and malignant traitors took him and tied his hands, and the Queen's as well. Audret had the door of the room locked, and said that he did not want anyone to know about the matter yet, and that they would not move from there for the remainder of the night; but next morning as soon as King Mark had got up, he would take Tristan and Queen Iseut to him, and then the King could do what he liked with them. In this way they remained in the tower the rest of the night. The Queen wept and lamented bitterly, but Tristan never said a word.

At dawn next morning when King Mark had got up and gone to the great hall where many knights had already gathered both from his household and from outside, Audret appeared before the King and said to him:

'My lord, I bring you extraordinary news. We've captured the traitor who has so often caused you anger and shame by consorting with Queen Iseut.'

'What?' asked the King. 'You've caught Tristan?'

'Yes, indeed, my lord.'

'How did you catch him?' King Mark enquired. 'I want to know, so that these barons who are assembled here will also know.'

And Audret instantly told him in the presence of all how he had found and caught them both.

'In God's name,' said the King, 'my shame is evident, and if I don't take such cruel vengeance that everyone who hears it will speak of it after my death, then I never again wish to wear a crown. Have them brought here, and I shall see them.'

Tristan's four companions, Lanbeguet, Nicoraut, Driant of the Isle and Fergus, were in the hall when these words were spoken, and, hearing them, they gave no sign that they knew anything about the matter, but hurried out of the palace as quietly as they could and returned to their quarters. There they found Gorvenal and told him the news, and he expressed his distress and dismay. Together they deliberated what they could do about the situation, for they had no intention of letting Tristan die if they could rescue him; they would rather die with him. In the end they agreed to leave the city and to hide in a thicket about three bowshots away from the spot where all those who had been condemned to death were taken; and if Tristan was brought there to be killed, they would rescue him or die in the attempt. That was the plan they decided on, and they took their armour without delay and left their quarters; and Gorvenal went with them. On reaching the thicket which was high and dense, they dismounted, and reiterated that if Tristan came this way, they would rather die than not save him; that is what Tristan's companions affirmed.

King Mark was still in the great hall, and Tristan and Queen Iseut, both of them bound, were brought before him. And when he saw and beheld the beauty of one and the other, and remembered Tristan's prowess and bravery, and called to mind the great love he had for Iseut, he was so upset that he did not know what to say.

'Tristan,' he declared, 'you are very handsome and very chivalrous. I have loved and cherished you, as you well know. But
since it is clear that whilst I showed you honour, you sought my
shame, no one can blame me if I now bring about your shame
and your dishonour. Indeed, I shall cause you so much of one and
the other, seeing that you have been caught in such an act, that
you will never shame me again.'

Then he ordered a great and mighty fire to be lit close to the
sea-shore, and said that once it was ablaze, Tristan and Iseut
should both be thrown into it and burnt to death.

'Ah! my lord,' cried the Cornish barons, 'by your grace, have
mercy on the Queen! Don't let her die such a cruel death.
Avenge yourself in some other way.'

'How?' asked the King. 'Tell me that!'

'My lord,' they replied, 'hand her over to the lepers, and let
them do what they like with her. It will be worse for her to serve
them than to be burnt a hundred times. She has lived in honour
and in plenty; now she will have to suffer greater dishonour and
greater ignominy and greater privation than any other unhappy
wretch: this will be the most cruel vengeance a king ever took on
his wife.'

'Barons of Cornwall,' said the King, 'is that how you want it
to be?'

And the majority of them agreed to it because they realized
that it was what the King wanted; and yet there were many of
them who would have preferred to see Tristan pardoned for this
misdeed rather than be killed, for they knew well that he enhanced the honour of Cornwall more than all the other knights
who were there.

That was the end of the discussion. A huge fire had already
been lit near the sea-shore where the King had ordered it, and
this was very close to the thicket where the companions were
hidden. The King commanded that Tristan should be taken and
led to the fire and burnt without delay, and that the Queen
should be handed over to the lepers; and this order was given
more to Audret than to the others. And Audret said that he would
bring the matter to a successful conclusion, and gave Tristan,
bound as he was, to ten big and strong churls, and Iseut for her
part he gave to another ten, and then he left the palace. When

King Mark saw Tristan, the best knight in the world, being led away like that, and Iseut, the most beautiful lady he had ever seen, he rushed into his room and shut himself up in there, beside himself with grief, and said that he was the most worthless king ever to have worn a crown, since he had in this way caused the death of his nephew whose prowess had surpassed that of all the knights who had ever entered Cornwall. King Mark lamented bitterly and cursed all those who had ever advised him to have his nephew caught, for he would have preferred to have kept Iseut for himself rather than let the lepers take her. [§§ 513–45 of vol. ii]

XII

ESCAPE: THE FOREST OF MORROIZ

THE churls who were leading Tristan away took him right through the city. And as the people saw Tristan being led ignominiously to his death, they all cried out as if demented:

'Ah! Tristan, dear lord, knight of great valour, if King Mark had remembered the difficult and arduous duel you fought against the Morholt of Ireland for the freedom of Cornwall when all the cowardly Cornish knights left him in the lurch, you would not now be killed, but honoured and served as you should be, and the Cornish cowards who treacherously set this trap for you would be banished from court, and you would be lord. As for you, King Mark, who have authorized this death, you may well live to regret it, you may well one day find yourself in need, as you are bound to before you die.'

This is what the Cornish people said; and I should tell you that all this happened in the city of Norholt.

In this way Tristan was led along until he came to an old church by the sea-shore built long ago on a rock which had crumbled in many places; and huge breakers were beating against the foot of it. When Tristan found himself in front of the church, it seemed to him that if he could get inside, God would somehow come to his aid. Then his fear of death gave him such strength that he succeeded in breaking the rope with which he was bound; and as soon as he felt himself free, he seized hold of a sword which one of the churls was carrying and snatched it from him, and with it instantly struck one of the men so hard that he knocked him down dead. When the others witnessed this blow and realized that Tristan was in possession of a sword, they did not dare to wait for any further blows, but fled, some in one direction and some in another. Tristan, seeing himself thus freed from the churls who had caused him so much shame and humiliation, went towards the chapel which stood in front of him and leapt inside and made straight for a window looking out over the sea, at least eighty yards* above it. As soon as he saw the sea beneath him so deep that it was awesome to behold, he said to himself that now he no longer had anything to fear from the cowardly Cornish knights, for he would rather jump into the sea than be in their power; if he had to die, he preferred that the sea should cause his death rather than his enemies.

No sooner had he reached the window than Audret appeared, fully armed, and with him more than twenty others, who said to him:

'By God, Tristan, you won't escape that way; we'll see to it that you die.'

'If I die, you bastards,' he replied, 'it won't be through you! I'd rather perish in the sea than die at the hands of men as base and cowardly as you are.'

They instantly rushed at him, their naked swords outstretched; and Tristan, realizing that he could not hold out against them unarmed as he was, struck one of them so hard with his sword that he knocked him down dead, and then he jumped into the sea, still clasping his sword. When they saw this leap, they were all confounded, and said:

'That's the end of him! We needn't be in doubt any longer, for if everyone in Cornwall had jumped down there, not a single one would have survived.'

Then they turned away, saying that this leap should really be called 'Tristan's Leap'.

Audret left the chapel and mounted his horse, and his companions likewise mounted, and they went to a house of lepers and handed Queen Iseut over to them. These were evil men, full of baseness and cruelty, and they took the Queen saying that she would never escape them: they would subject her to more dishonour and unpleasantness than ever King Mark showed her honour; she would have shame and humiliation and poverty and abuse, and would be given little to eat if she did not earn her livelihood as they had to. When the Queen heard this, she cried out:

'Audret, I beseech you, for the love of God and for pity's sake, kill me with your sword rather than hand me over to such vile men! I absolve you of all blame, dear friend; however, if you don't want to do it, then give me your sword and I'll kill myself. To be sure, it will be more honourable for you and for all noble men if I die at my own hands than if I remain with these wretched people.'

'Lady, lady,' Audret said, 'you will have to endure the punish-ment that has been meted out to you. Tristan's love was your undoing!'

Hearing these words the Queen cursed the hour that she was born. The lepers took her and led her away, whereupon the others all departed, leaving the Queen behind.

But news travels fast, and Tristan's companions soon heard about it, for a maiden who was one of Queen Iseut's ladies-in-waiting and who had gone after her lady weeping and shrieking like a madwoman, saw her being handed over to the lepers. The maiden was in fear and trembling that she herself would be ill-treated on account of her lady, so she turned back and fled in the direction of the thicket. Gorvenal, who knew her well, saw her coming in full flight towards the thicket and went to meet her, saying in order to allay her fears:

'Ah! maiden, don't be frightened, you won't come to any harm!'

As soon as she recognized Gorvenal, she stopped and said:

'Ah! Gorvenal, I have bad news. My lady has been handed over to the lepers. Never before has any lady been so debased.'

'And have you any news about Tristan?' asked Gorvenal.

'No, I haven't,' said the young girl. 'But for God's sake, if you have the power, then help my lady Iseut and rescue her from those horrible men to whom she has been committed by the Cornish traitors.'

At these words Tristan's four companions came up, all of them armed and mounted, and when they heard the news about Iseut, they declared that she would be freed in no time since now they knew where she was. They said to Gorvenal: 'Mount!' and he did not delay but speedily mounted his horse. Then he rode straight to the house where the Queen was imprisoned, and entered and took her without finding anyone bold enough to stop him, and lifted her up in front of him and then returned with her to the thicket. They went right into it, and there found the four companions waiting for them. When they saw the Queen fit and well, they received her with great joy, and told her she was safe now and need not fear the ill-will of any man, not even King Mark. At these words she praised and blessed the Lord for granting her this good fortune. Then they asked her if she had any news about Tristan.

'Well,' she replied, 'all I know is that he entered a chapel and leapt into the sea from a rock so high that out of a hundred thousand men not a single one could survive such a jump.'

Hearing this, they began to lament most bitterly, and said that if Tristan was dead, they would never again feel any joy, for they loved him inordinately.

'In God's name,' said Gorvenal, 'since the brave knight is dead, it would be a good idea to try and recover his body by some means, so that we can take it to King Arthur's court and place it in front of the Round Table. He often expressed this wish during his lifetime, and it would be a very worthy act to carry out his request.'

And they said they would be very happy to do this if they could find his body.

'Then I'll tell you what you must do,' Gorvenal answered. 'Driant of the Isle and Lanbeguet, you will stay here to guard the Queen, and Fergus and Nicoraut will go to the chapel, and I'll go with them, and there we'll search until, God willing, we find Tristan's body.'

This plan met with their full approval: the two remained in the thicket with the Queen, and the other two set off towards the chapel.

Once they got there, they dismounted at the entrance and went straight to the window from which Tristan had jumped. And when they saw the height of the rock and the depth of the sea, they reaffirmed that Tristan must indeed be dead.

'But how can we recover his body? It would need a miracle for us to find it.'

After they had considered the leap for a long while, Fergus, who was very intrepid, said to Nicoraut:

'By my faith, this leap isn't as dangerous as we thought! The sea is so deep that were any man to jump from here who had great courage and great strength and who was a good swimmer, may God confound me if there wouldn't be a good chance of his surviving. Not that it isn't very frightening on account of the height of the rock!'

While they were talking thus, they saw Tristan sitting by a small boulder, clasping his naked sword; and he was hiding there until nightfall because he did not want to be seen by the Cornish people, unarmed and defenceless as he was.

'In God's name!' exclaimed Fergus to Nicoraut, 'I think I can see Tristan, fit and well.'

'I can see him too,' said Nicoraut. 'The Lord be praised for saving him! But how can we join him? There's no way that we could get to him, nor can he come to us unless he goes back into the sea.'

Then Fergus cried as loudly as he could:

'Sir Tristan, how can we get to you, or you to us?'

He looked over towards them, and when he recognized them, he was overjoyed, and pointed with his sword to indicate that they should go to the shore which was to the right of the rock. Then he went back into the sea, his sword in his hand, for he never let go of it. He reached the shore safely and sat down there beside a large boulder, waiting for his companions. It was not long before he saw them galloping up; and Gorvenal was with them, so happy at the news they had told him about Tristan that he would not have been as happy if he had been given half the world.

When they came to the shore and found Tristan there clasping his sword, they ran up to him with outstretched arms, kissing and embracing him, and he did likewise. They asked how he felt.

'Very well,' he replied. 'By the grace of God, I wasn't hurt or wounded by my fall, for I plunged straight into the sea.'

And they praised Our Lord who had safely delivered him from this peril.

'Have you any news of Iseut?' he asked.

'Yes,' they answered, 'you need have no fear on her account. We will give her back to you in no time, safe and sound.'

'Truly?' he asked. 'Then nothing that's happened to me matters. If you can give me back Iseut, all is well.'

Thereupon he mounted Gorvenal's horse, and Gorvenal mounted behind one of the two companions, and they rode straight back to where they had left Iseut; they found her in great distress and in great fear, for she truly believed that she had lost Tristan, her beloved. But when she saw him riding up hail and hearty, anyone who has ever loved will know the joy and happiness which filled her heart. Tristan dismounted as soon as he caught sight of Iseut, and she cried out at the top of her voice:

'Beloved, how are you feeling?' she asked. 'Are you all right?'

'Yes,' he said, 'thank God I am; and since I see you before me fit and well, and delivered from the hands of the disloyal Cornish traitors, nothing else I might see could have the power to harm me. And now that God has reunited us in this way, I never want us to part again whatever happens; from now on we'll spend our youth together in pleasure and delight.'

Whereupon she replied:

'Tristan, what is there to be said? I never wish to be separated from you again come what may. I would rather be with you wherever you want to live than without you and have half the world freely in my possession.'

Thus the two lovers were of one accord, and they both chatted together, happy and joyous that God had permitted them to be reunited unharmed, even though they had come very close to complete disaster.

Tristan then asked his companions:

'Do you know of any good dwelling-place where we could take shelter for the night?'

'Yes,' they replied, 'near here at the edge of this wood beside a rock there's a house belonging to a very worthy and very courtly knight. If we can go as far as that, we can't fail to be well looked after.'

'Yes, I know the house you're talking about,' said Tristan. 'We can get there quite easily.'

Then they mounted as best they could, for they did not at this point have as many mounts as they needed, and rode as far as the knight's abode; and he received them gladly. And when he recognized Tristan who had done him many a service and many a great kindness, and whom he knew to be one of the bravest knights in the world, and when he called this to mind, as well as the fact that Tristan had been in such great danger of death that very day and yet had escaped through his prowess, he ran up to him and said:

'Welcome, sir. I'm at your disposal and so is everything I own in this world; and you may be sure that, if it pleases you, I won't refrain from serving you for fear of the cowardly Cornish knights who treacherously wanted to put you to death.'

'Never mind them,' said Tristan. 'As God is my witness, those who tried to harm me will be sorry for it one day. I shall never leave the Forest of Morroiz until I've avenged myself on them. As for what you have promised me, I am most grateful.'

The companions stayed there that night, and the lord of the manor put at their disposal all he had in order to make them comfortable and to serve them; and he gave fine and beautiful garments to both Tristan and Iseut. Next morning he made sure before they left that each one had a horse. Tristan was very obliged to him for what he did at that point, and said that one day if he had the opportunity he would pay him back for his kindness. And you should know that this forest of which they were on the edge was called the Forest of Morroiz,* and it was the largest and most beautiful forest in the whole of Cornwall.

The knight escorted them a long way, and after having parted from them he turned back, whereas they took the main road into the forest. Sir Tristan, who rode in front, was deep in thought, and when he had pondered at length without saying a word, he called Queen Iseut and drew her to one side, saying:

'My lady, what shall we do? The fact is that you love me so passionately that you can't do without me, and I for my part can't do without you. If we go to the Kingdom of Logres amongst all the brave knights, I know that in spite of my great chivalry I shall be branded as a traitor because of my love for you; and you will be called a disloyal and wicked queen since you left your husband for Tristan's sake. Words will be addressed to you, and also to me, which may well give rise to such trouble that it will not be easy to redress. If on the other hand I go to Leonois, the land which is rightfully mine, and I take you with me, the whole world will blame me, and both the foolish and the wise will say that I am living with my uncle's wife in sin. I have spoken these words to you, my lady Iseut, so that we know what we're doing before we go to the Kingdom of Logres or to the land of Leonois.'

'You know more than I do,' she said. 'You decide what we should do, and I'll agree to it without question.'

'Then I shall tell you what I think,' said Tristan. 'The forest we're in is the most exquisite, the most enjoyable, the most pleasant in the world, and full of wild animals, more so than any forest I know of; and it's also very large. Further on in this forest, near a rock called the Wise Damsel's Rock, there is a house which is so elegant and so beautiful and surrounded by such pleasant fountains and orchards that if you were there at this moment, the delights of the place would make it seem to you like an earthly paradise. My lady, if we went to live in that house, you and I and Gorvenal and a young girl who would always be around to serve you, we would be so secluded there that no one would ever chance upon us who would reproach us with anything. There we could be together day and night; there we could have our pleasure and our delight and our joy, just as we would wish. And after we've stayed there for a year or two or as long as we like, God will send us some other counsel.'

'Ah! Tristan,' she replied, 'I can see what you mean! I know well that you love me with all your heart, and I too love you more than any lady ever loved a knight. But now tell me, if we were to remain in this forest in the way you describe, wouldn't we be deprived of the whole world? We would see no ladies and no knights, no people and no entertainments: we would have lost the world and the world would have lost us. What do you think about that?'

'My lady,' said Tristan, 'I'll tell you what I think about it. As long as I have you by my side and can take my pleasure with you, just the two of us, without anxiety or fear of anyone, what else do I need? I want no shield or armour except you; I want no lord or lady except you. I love you more than I love the whole world, for if the whole world were with us now, I would see only you, and I would love but you alone. And since by the grace of God I have you with me safe and sound, I want to leave the whole world for you, because you matter more to me than all the rest. And for that reason I want us to remain in this forest, provided you agree, in the very house I mentioned to you. I shall cherish you as I would the whole world if it were mine, and you likewise will cherish me.'

'And I agree,' she answered. 'Since that is what you want, I shall raise no objections.'

Then Tristan went to his companions and said to them:

'My lords, it's a fact that we've been comrades-in-arms for some time and that you've stayed in this country more for love of me than for any other reason. But now I feel the urge to go away with my lady Iseut to a place where you can't join us. We shall remain there for a while, and when we don't feel like staying there any longer, we'll go either to the Kingdom of Logres, if we want, or to my country, Leonois. However, I am deeply grateful to you for your companionship.'

'What, Sir Tristan?' asked the four companions. 'Have we got to part?'

'Yes,' he replied. 'I'm afraid that is how it has to be. You'll take the highway through the forest, and I shall take this other road.'

They were very upset about this parting and asked him:

'Sir Tristan, do you think that we might see you again at some time in the future?'

'I don't know, so help me God,' he replied. 'But in the event that you go to King Arthur's court, I beg you by the love you bear me that you convey my sincerest greetings to Sir Lancelot of the Lake, should you find him at court. I've heard so much good about him that he's the knight that I'd most like to see in the world, and towards whom I feel the greatest goodwill—I'm talking here of the knights I've never met. Also, give my regards to Lamorat of Wales; it's true he behaved rather badly towards me when he sent the horn to King Mark, but I don't bear him any grudge: he's a remarkably brave knight for one as young as he is.'

They promised to deliver this message, as they intended to go straight to King Arthur's court, if nothing delayed them. Then they ran up to Tristan and kissed him, and Tristan kissed them. That was the end of their conversation. The four companions set off along the main road through the forest, and Tristan went the other way along a narrow path in the company of Queen Iseut, Gorvenal and the maiden.

They continued on their way until they reached the dwelling which Tristan had described. It had no tower or strong-point, but was a house nestling at the foot of the rock, so beautiful and so costly that it was wondrous to behold. A Cornish youth had it built for a young girl he loved and had taken her there, and they had lived in the house together for a long time; and she was called the Wise Damsel because of her considerable knowledge of magic, with the result that when her parents came to look for the place where she was living and they were standing directly in front of the rock, they could see neither the spot nor the rock nor the house, for she had so enchanted them that she often spoke to them, and yet they could not see her. The youth was long since dead and so was the girl, and neither man nor woman lived in the house, because it was in the depth of the forest and in a very out-of-the-way spot.

When they arrived there, they dismounted and found the house so exquisite, so luxurious and so delightful that it seemed like magic.

'My lady, what do you think of this manor?' Tristan asked.

'Sir,' she replied, 'it's beautiful! The place pleases and delights me so much that I have no wish to leave as long as you want to stay.'

'It will be pleasant to live here. Look at these fine, fresh springs! And we can have venison every day. As for the other things we need, Gorvenal will go and fetch them for us from a castle which is nearby.'

'Then everything is all right,' she said.

And so Tristan remained in the great Forest of Morroiz with Iseut, and with Gorvenal and the maiden called Lamide who had come to Cornwall with Queen Iseut from Ireland.

One day Tristan asked Gorvenal:

'What shall I do about my charger Passebruel which King Mark has in his possession? If only I had my charger and my hound Hudenc, I wouldn't ask anything else of him.'

'I'll go to King Mark on your behalf', said Gorvenal, 'and tell him to send you your horse and your hound. I don't think he'll keep them after he's seen your messenger and heard your request.'

'Ah! Gorvenal, dear friend,' said Tristan, 'do go.'

And he said he would go without delay. He mounted his horse and set out, and rode on till he came to Norholt. He found King Mark amongst his men, very angry that Tristan and Iseut had escaped, for he had already been told everything that had happened. The King was extremely worried about it because he feared and dreaded that Tristan would do his utmost to harm him. And the Cornish people were very uneasy and frightened because they knew well that every single one of them would be put to a speedy death if they were seized and captured by Tristan, and this greatly alarmed them.

When Gorvenal came before the King, he said without greeting him:

'King Mark, Tristan, my lord, in whose service I am, as you well know, requests that you let him have his horse, Passebruel, and his hound, Hudenc. He is not asking for anything else that is yours, but these two things you must send him.'

And King Mark said that he was quite prepared to do this; 'even if Tristan were to ask me for something that is mine, I would let him have it.' He ordered the horse and the hound to be fetched, and gave them to Gorvenal. Then he asked him where his nephew Tristan was. And Gorvenal replied:

'You'll never find out any news about him from me, either good or bad.'

Thereupon he left without saying another word to the King, and rode back to where Tristan was waiting for him. When Tristan saw his horse and his hound, don't ask whether he was delighted; and the Queen too was very happy about it.

Now Tristan began to hunt. His main preoccupation and delight was to catch and kill wild animals. And once he had made his catch, he returned to Queen Iseut who welcomed him back with great pleasure. In this way Tristan enjoyed and amused himself: he hunted, he caught his prey and brought the venison back to my lady Iseut. His hunting in the forest and his pleasure with his lady filled his whole life. He left chivalry and all other joys for the sake of this delight. He no longer remembered King Mark nor King Arthur nor Lancelot of the Lake, nor indeed anybody at all, intent only on cherishing his lady and rejoicing in her company. And she herself had put the whole world out of her mind to such an extent that she thought only of Tristan.

Tristan caught as much venison as he liked, and because he wanted King Mark to remain ignorant of his whereabouts so that he would be unable to have him ambushed and treacherously seized, he taught and trained his hound Hudenc to hunt down his prey without barking, and took him to his quarry without allowing him to make a sound. The King knew full well that Tristan was in the Forest of Morroiz, but he did not know where, and for that reason he never rode through the forest without having with him at least twenty knights or more, for he greatly feared Tristan as did all the Cornish people.

One day King Mark was riding in the forest accompanied by many knights both armed and unarmed; and you may be sure that even though Iseut was not with him, he was no less desirous of seeing her than he had been in the past. Indeed, he loved her so much that he would willingly have given up half his kingdom if he could have had her back, provided he would never again lose possession of her. Whilst he was riding thus through the forest, he chanced upon four shepherds who were sitting by a fountain guarding their sheep.

'Dear youths,' said the King, 'can you give me some information about a knight who lives in this forest, I don't know where, but I think he often rides a sorrel horse?'

And the youths replied in all innocence:

'Ah! sir, you're asking about our lord King Mark's nephew?'

'That's right,' said the King. 'Can you tell me anything about him?'

'Yes, sir, we can,' they answered. 'He lives by a rock further on, in the Wise Damsel's house. He's often given us some food in recent months.'

'And how many people has he got with him?' asked King Mark.

'Sir,' they replied, 'he has a lady and a young girl and a squire, that's all.'

The King asked those who were in his company if they knew the house.

'We do indeed, my lord,' they answered. 'It's in a valley along there in a very out-of-the-way spot.'

'Since he has no one else with him,' said the King, 'there's nothing to stop us from going there.'

'That's true, my lord,' they replied, 'and here is the road which will take us straight to it.'

Thereupon the King set off in that direction, and they went on until they came to the house; and there were over sixty of them on horseback, some armed, others unarmed. And I should tell you that at the time when they came to the place neither Tristan nor Gorvenal were at home; Tristan had gone hunting in the forest early in the morning, and he had taken Gorvenal with him.

When King Mark reached the house, he made the majority of his men dismount and ordered them to go inside and bring out Iseut.

'And if Tristan tries to defend her, don't hesitate to kill him; show him no mercy at all.'

They dismounted and went in, and found Iseut playing chess with the young girl. At the sight of the knights coming at her so unexpectedly, and moreover fully armed, she did not feel exactly reassured. They seized her without more ado, and she cried out at the top of her voice:

'Sir Tristan! Help, help!'

'Lady, lady,' said those who were leading her away, 'your cries won't serve any purpose. Tristan can't help you at this stage.'

Then they seized hold of the young girl and handed them both over to King Mark. And when he saw Queen Iseut whom he loved so much and on whose account he had passed so many sleepless nights and brooded so much, and he realized that now he would have her in his possession according to his wishes, he said to those who were around him:

'Let's go! By the grace of God, we were very lucky to have accomplished so easily what we came here to do. Now Tristan can find himself another Iseut, for he's lost this one!'

Then King Mark set off again and returned straight to Norholt. As soon as they reached the city, he ordered the Queen to be imprisoned in his tower. He saw to it that she was dressed and apparelled as finely as was possible, and he served, honoured and flattered her as much as was in his power. But whatever he did was of no avail: had he given her the whole world and everything contained in it, she could have felt no joy or happiness as long as Tristan was not with her. The King realized this well enough, but he said nothing to her, not wanting to cause her greater distress than she had already. However, because it was his ardent desire that the Kingdom of Cornwall be rid of Tristan and that he should not live there or stay there ever again, the King had it proclaimed throughout every large city that each one should do his utmost to seek out Tristan, and whoever succeeded in catching his nephew dead or alive, the King would give him whichever city in Cornwall he would care to ask for; and he swore and promised this faithfully before the barons of his land.

When the proclamation had been issued as I have described, the Cornish people began to assemble, now twenty, now thirty, in all the places where they thought Tristan might be staying.

They knew for a fact that he only had Gorvenal in his company, and they felt they could safely attack him, since he would not be able to defend himself against twenty knights, or forty. Thus they went round looking for Tristan far and wide. He was well aware of it, and had he been fit, he would not have been afraid to engage in combat with them. But on the very day that my lady Iseut had been captured, as I have related, he happened to be sleeping by a hedge in the early evening,* and he was quite unarmed. Gorvenal was not with him at this point, for Tristan had left him in a valley with his horse, and had pursued his prey on foot across a mountain where a horse would have found it difficult to go; and there he had caught up with the animal and killed it. While Tristan was thus sleeping beside the bush, a youth appeared who was coming that way on foot, carrying only his bow and quiver* and a great quantity of arrows. Finding Tristan asleep, he began to look at him, and after he had examined him for a while he realized that it was Tristan, King Mark's nephew.

'Ah! God,' the youth exclaimed, 'what can I do? Here is Tristan who killed my father! I shall never again have such a good opportunity of avenging him as I have now, for I can kill Tristan before he wakes up, if I want to. But if I kill him in his sleep, I would be committing the greatest villainy and the greatest treachery in the world. It would be better to wake him, and as he wakens, pierce his body with two or three arrows.'

That is what the youth decided, and he thought no further, but drew back and cried out to Tristan as loudly as he could:

'Tristan, be on your guard, for I defy you!'

Tristan, who was always apprehensive and fearful of being caught unawares in some way, jumped to his feet, and as he did so, the youth shot a poisoned arrow into his left arm, so close to the bone that he almost injured it. Feeling himself thus wounded, Tristan took hold of his sword and rushed at the youth who let fly another arrow, intending to shoot it right through his body; but he missed, for Tristan leapt sideways, and seized hold of the youth by the right arm—not wanting to strike him with his sword as he was not a knight—and flung him away from himself and hurtled him against a rock with such violence that he dashed the youth's brains out, and instantly his soul parted from his body. Tristan drew out the arrow which had struck him, and thought the wound would heal of its own accord. However he had not gone very far when he realized that the arrow which had wounded him was poisoned, for he saw his arm swell up to remarkable proportions. He was not too worried by it in the knowledge that he would soon be back at his abode where he expected to find Iseut who knew more about such things than all the ladies in the world. When he joined Gorvenal, he told him about the youth who had wounded him with a poisoned arrow, and Gorvenal said to him:

'Sir, all you can do is to ride as quickly as possible to your dwelling. If you aren't cured of the poison soon, and it were to reach your heart, you would die on the spot.'

Tristan mounted his horse and so did Gorvenal, and they rode at great speed till they reached the house. It was already growing quite dark, and Tristan began to look round and saw the grass on one side trodden down and crushed by the horses which had ridden over it.

'Ah! Gorvenal,' cried Tristan, 'a lot of people have been here! I trust that God has saved us this day from disaster! I very much fear that King Mark has been to the house and that my lady Iseut has been taken from us.'

'Don't be dismayed,' said Gorvenal. 'That will never happen, please God.'

They dismounted in front of the house and called, but no one came to answer them, because no one was there.

'Ah!' said Tristan, 'I am lost! King Mark has taken away Iseut. I wish I could find someone who would kill me so as to put an end to my suffering more quickly, for after this misadventure I shall never be happy again.'

Then Gorvenal went indoors and Tristan did likewise, and when they failed to find Iseut, it was very clear to Gorvenal how unhappy and distressed Tristan felt, since he was right beside him. He comforted him as best he could, but no comfort was of any use: Tristan said that whatever happened he would never again feel joy, for he had now lost what he would not be able to recover by any means at all.

'As God is my witness,' he declared, 'I'd kill myself with my sword if it weren't for the fact that it would be considered sinful; and I truly deserve to die for having left my lady, my beloved, without protection. I have lost her, and I am lost as a result and undone.'

Tristan was very angry with himself and in great torment; as long as the night lasted he did not cease to grieve. Gorvenal, who was very upset, did his best to comfort him, but it was of no avail, for Tristan affirmed that the only person who could comfort him was Iseut.

Tristan spent that night in great sorrow. Next morning as the day dawned bright and clear, he saw that his arm was larger than his thigh, since the poison had spread all over it. Then he felt quite frightened, for he was in no doubt that unless he could find a remedy before long he was in danger of dying. Gorvenal was very alarmed and said to Tristan:

'If you don't receive help quickly, you are in peril of death.'

And Tristan replied:

'Now that Iseut is lost to me, I don't think anyone else can help me. Do you remember the wound which the Morholt of Ireland gave me and which made me languish for so long? No one could cure me of that until Iseut took charge of it. For this reason I tell you that we must find some means of informing her about my indisposition. She would know immediately how to deal with it, either on her own or with the help of someone else.'

'If you like,' said Gorvenal, 'I'm prepared to take the risk of going to Norholt, or to send someone else there, should that be preferable.'

'Go there quickly, by all means,' said Tristan, 'and I myself will come with you as far as the edge of the forest nearest to Norholt.'

Then they mounted their horses and rode as far as the outskirts of the city. There they met one of Iseut's ladies-in-waiting whom the Queen loved greatly; she had come from Ireland with her and was related to Brangain. She was very fond of Tristan, and Tristan of her. She was riding in the company of a squire who was her brother, and she was returning from a castle nearby where King Mark had sent her. When Tristan saw her coming, he recognized her and went over to greet her; and as soon as she caught sight of him she burst into tears. Tristan asked her for news of Iseut.

'She's shut up in that tower there in such a fashion that, believe it or not, no one can speak to her except two maidens who serve her and King Mark; and the maidens never move from there. That is how it's been decreed by the King, who doesn't want anyone to see her except himself.'

'Ah! God,' said Tristan, 'what can I do then? I'm wounded, as you can see. I know well that I would soon be cured if only I could have Iseut's help.'

'That you certainly won't be able to have,' said the young girl. 'It would be a waste of time to rely on it. But if you could get in touch with Brangain, I think she might be able to advise you in some way.'

'Ah! maiden,' said Tristan, 'how can I get hold of her?'

'I'll send her to you soon enough,' replied the young girl, 'if it's at all possible. Wait for me here!'

'Go quickly, then,' said Tristan, 'and tell Brangain to hurry, if she can.'

Thereupon the maiden departed and did not stop until she came to court and immediately gave Brangain Tristan's message; and since she loved him dearly, Brangain mounted her horse as soon as she could and set off without any company straight to where Tristan was waiting for her. They greeted each other with great joy and pleasure, though this was somewhat tempered by the fact that Tristan was so unwell and so upset about his loss of Iseut. When Brangain saw how ill Tristan was, she said to him:

'Sir, you're in dire straits and in real trouble if someone doesn't do something for you quickly. I have to tell you that I myself wouldn't know how to help you, nor would any living soul in this country, with the sole exception of Iseut; but there can be absolutely no question of your receiving any help from her: no one can even speak to my lady Iseut apart from King Mark and two maidens who don't move from there and constantly watch over her.'

'Oh! God,' said Tristan, 'what can I do, then? Am I going to die for such a poor reason?'

'No, please God,' replied Brangain, 'for I shall advise you what to do.'

'Tell me, then,' he begged her.

'You will take a boat near here,' she said, 'and cross over to Brittany. And when you've arrived, you'll go straight to King Hoel's court. The King has a daughter who is one of the most beautiful ladies in the world, and her name is Iseut. She knows so much about medicine that if you can get there, she'll cure you in no time, you may be sure of that. I've heard Queen Iseut praise her for her intelligence, her breeding and her beauty more than all the maidens in the world.'

When Tristan heard this and realized that if he went to Brittany he would find Iseut, the very name filled his heart with such joy that it seemed to him he was quite cured already.

'Brangain,' he said, 'you've been a great help to me at this point and in the past. Since you advise me to go to Brittany, I'll make my way to King Hoel's court and leave this country; and I commend you to Our Saviour. For the love of God and for pity's sake, as soon as you are able to speak to my lady Iseut, greet her on my behalf more than a hundred thousand times, and you can tell her from me that I am Tristan the wretched who will never have good fortune or joy except through her. From her alone I await my salvation and my safety; she alone will be my life for as long as she wishes, and when it pleases her, she will be my death.'

That was the end of their conversation. Brangain returned to the city, feeling so sorry for Tristan that she wept bitterly; and Tristan for his part set off towards the port as speedily as he could and boarded a ship with Gorvenal and his mounts. [§§ 546–59 of vol. ii]

Escalot, the Tower of Marvels   173

beautiful ladies in the world, and her name is Iseut. She knows so
much about medicine that if you get there, she'll cure you in
no time, you may be sure.' ... for ... your praise
her for her ... ... beauty more than
all the smiths ... to the world

XIII

ISEUT OF THE WHITE HANDS

WHAT shall I tell you? Our Lord sent them favourable winds, so
that before long they landed in Brittany in front of a castle which
in those days was known as Hansac. As soon as they had gone
ashore and taken their horses and Tristan's armour, they enquired
where they could find King Hoel; and they were told that he was
living in a city of his called Alinge. He was fortifying one of his
castles there against a neighbour who was waging war on him, a
wealthy count and an exceedingly dauntless knight, whose name
was Agrippa the Tall, for he was a remarkably tall man. Tristan
made straight for Alinge, and came upon King Hoel in front of the
gates of the city. He greeted the King without knowing who he was,
and the King returned his greeting. Seeing Tristan so thin and pale
and ashen that he looked like grim death, he asked him who he was.

'Sir,' he replied, 'I'm a foreign knight, very sick and ailing, and
I've come here because I've been told that King Hoel's daughter
would cure me, if anyone in the world could do so.'

The King looked at Tristan and saw that he was of powerful
build and so well formed in every respect that he was clearly a
man of great strength, if it were not for the fact that he seemed
to be very ill.

'I don't know who you are,' he said, 'but whoever you may be,
I shall instruct Iseut to take care of you and ask her to cure you.'

'Thank you, sir,' said Tristan.

The King turned back, and all those who were with him. And
when they had arrived at the main fortress, he sent for his
daughter and she came before him, so noble, so beautiful, and so
attractive in every way that nobody could find fault with any
aspect of her beauty.

'Dear daughter,' said the King, 'here is a foreign knight who is
very ill. I don't know who he is, but since he came to this
country because of his faith in you and his belief that you would
cure him by your skill, I beg you to do your utmost to bring
about his recovery even as you would if it were myself.'

'Willingly, my lord,' she replied.

The young girl took Tristan and led him away to her apartments, and looked at his arm. And as soon as she saw it uncovered, she said to him:

'This has poison in it! Please God, we'll cure you of it soon enough.'

'May God grant you the power,' he replied.

The young girl sought and procured what she considered would be most beneficial to him, and day after day she tended him until she saw and knew that he was on the mend, which greatly pleased her. And as he recovered, he looked more fit and more handsome every day, so much so that all were amazed at his good looks. Tristan for his part kept gazing at Iseut, for he found her very beautiful, and she pleased and attracted him greatly; and what was most instrumental in making him fall in love with her was the name Iseut, for it seemed to him that if he could have the company of this Iseut and his pleasure with her, he would never remember any other Iseut.

Such were Tristan's thoughts and that is how he planned to free himself of his love for Queen Iseut. He left one Iseut for the other, and believed he could forget his love for one by his love for the other. When he saw the bearing and countenance of this Iseut where one could find no flaw, it seemed to him there were many reasons why he ought to leave the other Iseut for this one, for his relationship with the other Iseut had been against God and against the law, since he should not rightfully have slept with his uncle's wife under any circumstances; moreover, there was no worthy man on earth who would not consider him treacherous and disloyal if he learnt the truth about what he had done. For that reason he decided it preferable, both with regard to his honour and his happiness, to leave Iseut of Cornwall and to take Iseut the daughter of King Hoel of Brittany. That is what he decided to do in the end; but he never gave any indication that the young girl meant anything to him.

Iseut, the noble maiden, who had no such thoughts, did her best day and night to make him recover. And when Tristan felt himself fit enough to wear armour, then he was happy and cheerful, then he was overjoyed and amused himself with everyone, then he was such that all who saw him said that if he was not a brave knight he really must hate his fine body. And in truth he was so handsome that Iseut herself, who was called Iseut of the White Hands, fell madly in love with him. She had never before thought of any man or fallen in love; now she loved so passionately that her heart and her thoughts were completely absorbed by Tristan, and she loved nobody else, nor was there anything she would not have done for him, even if she were sure that it would bring her great shame.

Iseut has a brother who is twenty-four years old called Kahedin, a very valiant knight who greatly helps his father in his war against Agrippa. One day King Hoel is defeated in battle and Kahedin is badly wounded. Knowing this, Agrippa lays siege to the city of Alinge with ten battalions of five hundred men in each; he advances on the town with two battalions and hides the rest in a wood nearby. King Hoel fears that all is lost without his son, but Gorvenal sings the praises of the knight he serves, and Hoel sends for him. Tristan has already decided to sally forth from the city against Agrippa even if he has to go alone. He calls Gorvenal and has himself armed. Gorvenal alerts the King who assembles his knights and organizes a sortie. Tristan is the first to go out, and is immediately attacked by Agrippa's nephew Alquin whom he kills. Tristan then rushes in among a troop of knights and does wonders before the King has even emerged from the city with his men. Then the battle begins in earnest, and Tristan performs such feats that he is taken for Lancelot. When one of King Hoel's relatives kills Count Agrippa, many of his men flee, and Hoel is victorious. Hearing Tristan praised, Iseut of the White Hands loves him more than ever. King Hoel asks him who he is and Tristan names himself; the King is amazed to hear that he has never been to King Arthur's court.

Kahedin had already recovered, and he honoured Tristan for his great chivalry as much as did his father. One day Tristan and Kahedin were riding together, and it happened that Tristan began to think so deeply about Queen Iseut that he did not know whether he was asleep or awake. Kahedin was well aware of it, but he said not a word and gave no sign that he noticed anything. Tristan went on thinking in this way for so long that he heaved a profound sigh and then said:

'Ah! fair Iseut, you have been my undoing!'

At this he fainted and fell from his horse to the ground, and then came to as though he had been asleep and was waking up. He felt deeply ashamed on account of Kahedin, who said to him:

'Sir, it's not very sensible to think too hard!'

'You're right, sir,' Tristan agreed, 'but when one's heart has taken control of one, it's not surprising if one strays at times.'

And Kahedin replied:

'Tristan, I see you are more pensive than I would wish, and if there's any man to whom you would reveal your thoughts, I beg you to confide in me, for there is nothing I wouldn't do to help you if I could, even were it to result in my death. Do tell me the name of the lady you're thinking about, for I'm sure it's a lady or a maiden.'

Thereupon Tristan replied:

'Kahedin, I'll tell you. I love Iseut so much that I think of her the whole time. I'm pining for her, as you can see, and were it not for Iseut, I wouldn't be in this country now, and if you were willing to give me Iseut, I would be very happy.'

When Kahedin heard these words, he was overjoyed, for he had no doubt that Tristan was talking about Iseut, his sister, since he knew nothing about any other Iseut; and he wished for nothing better than that Tristan would marry her: Tristan was so valiant that she would be making a very good match, and the honour of all Brittany would be enhanced.

'Tristan,' he said to him, 'why have you concealed it from me for so long? I assure you, if I'd thought that you wanted to have her, there would have been no need for you to suffer pain. I'll give her to you as soon as we get back to court.'

'Very many thanks,' said Tristan.

Thereupon they turned back and rode on until they reached the court. And when they had got there, Kahedin did not delay but told his father straightaway how Tristan loved Iseut. The King was very happy to hear it and said:

'Ah! dear Lord God, we're saved! Since Tristan will have Iseut, no man can ever again wage war on us. Dear son, not only will I give him Iseut, but myself as well, and you and Iseut and all Brittany in its entirety; and if the whole world belonged to me, I would give that to him also, for he is very worthy of having the whole world in his possession.'

Then the King immediately sent for his daughter Iseut and gave her to Tristan, and Tristan received her with great joy. And I can assure you that if the other Iseut loved him, this one loved him even more.

What shall I tell you? The wedding-day arrived. All the people of Brittany came there without exception, rich and poor alike, and there was much rejoicing and merriment. They spent the day in great jubilation. But the night was drawing near when Tristan had to sleep with Iseut. However, Queen Iseut of Cornwall forbade him to have intercourse with her. She did not forbid him such activities as embracing and kissing, but if the other act came into it, that would be the end of their love.*

What shall I tell you? When the night had come, Tristan lay down beside Iseut, who was so very beautiful that it is not surprising if he desired her. There was no one else in the room, and they lay in bed quite naked. The light in the bedroom was so bright that Tristan could see Iseut's beauty very clearly. She had white and tender breasts, lovely bright and laughing eyes, fine slender eyebrows and a clear, pure face. Tristan kissed and embraced her. But when he remembered Iseut of Cornwall, he could not bring himself to touch this one. Great was the battle of the two Iseuts. This Iseut was in front of him, the other was in Cornwall and knew absolutely nothing about the whole matter, and yet she forbade Tristan as he valued his life to go no further with this Iseut; since he was fit and well, let him come to Cornwall without delay, and on no account do anything which was blameworthy with this Iseut.

That is how Tristan remained with his wife: in the end he decided to go no further. Iseut, who did not know anything other than the joy of embracing, fell asleep in Tristan's arms, and Tristan did likewise. And when he woke up, he dressed and went to the palace; and as soon as the King saw him, he said:

'Tristan, in view of all you have done, you have deserved that the Kingdom of Brittany should be yours. Take it, for I invest you with it in the presence of all.'

Tristan thanked him very warmly. Gorvenal was delighted; he really believed that this Iseut would make him forget the other one, and thought that Tristan had slept with her.

In this way, Tristan stayed with Iseut. He embraced and kissed her, and Iseut asked for no more, since she knew nothing about it, but supposed that there was no other love-play between a man and a woman because Tristan had already been with her so long and had never sought any other pleasure. Iseut loved Tristan with all her heart, and Tristan loved her for her name and her beauty; and everybody was convinced that he had slept with her. Gorvenal thought so as well and was very pleased about it. But now the story stops talking about Tristan and Iseut of the White Hands and about all the people of Brittany, and returns to Iseut of Cornwall in order to relate what happened to her after King Mark had taken her away from Tristan. [§§ 560–8 of vol. ii]

XIV

TRISTAN'S RETURN TO CORNWALL WITH KAHEDIN

NOW the story relates that when King Mark had recovered Queen Iseut and put her back in his tower, the Queen, realizing that she had lost Tristan whom she loved more than anyone else in the world, was so distressed that she nearly went mad with grief. She wailed and lamented and cursed the hour that she was born more than a thousand times each day. She made herself so ill by weeping day and night that everyone there was astonished. King Mark was so upset about it that he did not know what to do. He treated her with indulgence in order to make her forget her sorrow, but if he had given her the whole world, she would have found no solace without Tristan. He was her life, he was her death; without him nothing on earth could alleviate her suffering, and never, so she said, would she have any comfort. That is how the Queen conducted herself; she spent her life grieving: without Tristan nothing on earth could alleviate her suffering. And Brangain, who loved her more than any other maiden, did her utmost to comfort her and often told her to have pity on herself, for she ought to know that Tristan could not hold out long before returning to Cornwall.

'And once he is back, you would find some means whereby you could see each other. Don't destroy yourself, but take heart.'

This is what Brangain kept saying to Iseut until she gradually left off grieving.

One day after the Queen had succeeded in overcoming her grief, telling herself that she would send for Tristan and somehow bring it about that they could be together however closely King Mark was guarding her, it happened, while she was planning this, that news came to Cornwall of Tristan's marriage to Iseut of the White Hands. King Mark was overjoyed at these tidings; now he was convinced that Tristan was never going to return to Cornwall, and he really thought he was rid of him for all time. When Queen Iseut heard the news she was so grief-stricken that she nearly went out of her mind. This news was like a death-blow to her. Now there was no one who could ever give her comfort; indeed, she declared she would kill herself. Then she sent for Brangain and said to her:

'Ah! Brangain, have you heard how Tristan whom I loved so much has betrayed me? Ah! Tristan, Tristan! how did you have the heart thus to betray the one who loved you more than herself? Ha! treacherous, false and disloyal Love, full of broken promises, you deal out a poor reward to those who serve you, and poorly have you rewarded my service at this point. And since I see clearly that all others derive joy and benefit from their love whereas I am so wretched that I have nothing but pain, I no longer ask anything else of God but that he should send me my death without delay.'

Brangain for her part was so distressed about this matter that she was at a loss what to do or say. She did not know how to assuage her lady's suffering. And the Queen, who was so unhappy that she almost killed herself, decided to send Queen Guinevere a letter, as well-written as she knew how, in which she would complain about Tristan who had so cruelly betrayed her. She would let her know everything that had happened, and she told herself that Queen Guinevere was bound to respond by giving her some comfort when she heard about the great distress she was suffering. She thought no further; that is what she decided to do. Not that she stopped grieving on account of her decision; but she concealed her feelings as best she could from King Mark whom she greatly feared. The King was well aware of her grief, but gave no sign, not wanting to torment her even further.

Queen Iseut spent that day as I have told you, and the night as well, and all the while she pondered on how best to write this letter, for Queen Guinevere was such a wise lady that she did not want to send her a letter which was not very well expressed. Next morning she got up quite early, not having had any sleep that night, and asked all the maidens to leave the room so that she could concentrate on her letter. She thought about it at great length until she composed it to her satisfaction and wrote it as I tell you to the best of her ability in her most polished style. Then she instantly called one of her maidens and said to her:

'Get ready! I want you to go to Great Britain to King Arthur's court. You will convey my greetings to Queen Guinevere and give her this letter on my behalf.'

'My lady,' she replied, 'since this is what you wish, I shall carry out your command.'

Thereupon the maiden prepared herself for the journey and left the court; she rode on until she came to the sea and embarked on a ship which took her to the Kingdom of Logres.* Once she had arrived there, she left the ship and mounted her palfrey and enquired as to the whereabouts of Queen Guinevere. She was told that the Queen was in Camelot, and there she found her in the company of many ladies and maidens. The young girl came before the Queen and knelt down in front of her, saying:

'My lady, Queen Iseut of Cornwall sends you her greetings, and this letter which she asked me to hand you.'

When Queen Guinevere heard what the maiden told her and learnt that she was in the service of Queen Iseut, she received her with great joy and said:

'Ah! maiden, for the love of God, how is Queen Iseut?'

'In truth, my lady,' replied the girl, 'she is not as well as I've seen her in the past.'

What shall I tell you? Queen Guinevere, who had a very good idea of what was wrong, made no comment, but took the letter from the maiden, withdrew to one side of the room, and broke the seal; she found it contained many words written with great eloquence as follows:

> To you, my lady Queen Guinevere, who surpass all mortal ladies on earth in kindness, beauty, worth, intelligence, court-liness and nobility, and who are undoubtedly the most fortu-nate lady living at the present time, I, Iseut, Queen of Cornwall, the most wretched being alive, send my greetings.
>
> My lady, because nowhere on earth do I see or know of any lady with as much intelligence or as much knowledge as you who are an inspiration to all the ladies in the world, and because a man or woman in need is most likely to receive counsel from him or from her who is full of innate wisdom, I, who am the most unhappy and the most disconsolate of all the ladies in the world, and the most helpless of all those needing help, wish to communicate my great distress to your superior intelligence in the hope of receiving some comfort from you.
>
> I make my complaint to you about the two most mortal enemies I have at present on earth: firstly, Tristan whom I

loved more than all of paradise, who has betrayed me so basely and so cruelly that he has destroyed me by his treachery. Secondly, I complain about Love to whom I had given my all: my heart and my body, my faith and my hope, and all my service, more than to God himself or to any man; and I have, so I say, been ill-rewarded for my service. My lady, I complain about Love and about Tristan as forcefully as I can, and declare that they have betrayed me basely and cruelly. And it is to you, dear lady, that I make this complaint because you are the one in the world who are most fortunate in all things, who are most lucky in your love according to your wishes and who have been most nobly and fully rewarded by Love for your service. What more shall I say, dear lady? You are completely in control of your love; you deal with it as it pleases you. For that reason I wish to communicate to you the great distress which Love makes me suffer and endure. And because I know of no lady in the whole world who has the power and the wisdom to counsel me except you, I beg you for the love of God that in your great nobility you will be gracious enough to deign for the Lord's sake to retain in your mind a small part of my suffering in such a way that I may receive some comfort through the grace of the wisdom which you possess.

That was the tenor of the letter which Queen Iseut had sent to Queen Guinevere.

When she had read the letter from beginning to end and then reread it word for word, and she became aware of the polished style and the fair words of Queen Iseut, she marvelled at her great intelligence and said to herself that she would have to think very hard in order to answer her wisely in accordance with the content of the letter she had sent her. Queen Guinevere was very distressed to realize that Iseut was so unhappy, and she would have liked to find some way of consoling her if she could and if she knew how to do it. What shall I tell you? Queen Guinevere pondered at length about this matter, and greatly honoured the maiden whom the Queen of Cornwall had sent her. She asked her many questions and enquired about the affairs of King Mark and Queen Iseut and anything else she wanted to know. In this way the young girl remained there for three whole days. During this time Queen Guinevere wrote the letter she wanted to send to Queen Iseut, and then gave it to the girl and told her to convey her warmest greetings to the Queen of Cornwall. Thereupon the maiden took leave of Queen Guinevere and left the court without any further delay. But now the story stops talking about the maiden and returns to Tristan.

In this part the story relates that one day after Tristan had already been married to Iseut of the White Hands a long time, it happened that he was out riding with Kahedin when he remembered that a year had passed since he had lost Queen Iseut of Cornwall. He was so deeply distressed that he wished he were dead, and he began to weep bitterly. As soon as Kahedin saw his tears, he realized that this grief came from the depths of his heart, and he could not stop himself from saying to him:

'Sir, by the being you love most in the world, tell me the reason why you are weeping in this way.'

'Kahedin,' replied Tristan, 'you have invoked me most solemnly! If you promise me in good faith that you will not reveal it to a living soul nor bear me any grudge, I shall tell you.'

And Kahedin promised this faithfully.

'Kahedin,' said Tristan, 'I love a lady who is in another country; exactly a year has passed since she was stolen from me.'

Then he began to tell him the truth about his love.

'And I would have you know that I can hand you back your sister still a virgin as she was when you gave her to me, for I love the other Iseut so much that nothing on earth would make me misbehave towards her.'

'Sir,' said Kahedin, 'I'm amazed at what you tell me, though I fully believe what you say. But, in the name of God, why do you love this lady so much? Is she more beautiful than other ladies?'

'There's no point in dwelling on her beauty,' replied Tristan. 'I can assure you there isn't a lady in the world who's as beautiful as she is or who has ever loved a knight as deeply or as greatly as she loves me.'

'Certainly,' said Kahedin, 'if she is so beautiful and loves you as much as you say, I shall never blame you for loving her. But now tell me, what do you intend to do to alleviate this suffering?'

'I'll tell you,' answered Tristan. 'I shall go to the country where she lives and take her away from there, and then I shall go with her to the Kingdom of Logres or of Leonois. In this way we shall spend our life in joy.'

'To be sure,' said Kahedin, 'that would be the best thing to do. And certainly, I advise you to keep to the one you can't do without, for it would be better to live with her in happiness than with my sister in misery. And if you wish, I'll come with you, partly to comfort you, and partly to see this lady.'

Tristan agreed. And I should tell you that Kahedin concealed this matter so well that no one ever knew about it. But now the story stops talking about Tristan and Kahedin, and returns to Lancelot of the Lake.

Upon leaving King Arthur's court in search of adventures, Lancelot meets the messenger-girl carrying Queen Guinevere's reply back to Iseut. They spend the night at the house of a widow who entertains Lancelot by telling him about the evil custom of the Felon Castle, whose ailing chatelaine can only be cured by the blood of a virgin princess; forty knights are therefore always in readiness to detain all young girls who pass there escorted by a knight-errant. Lancelot realizes that for once his help is of no avail, since this evil custom can only be abolished by a maiden.

While they are chatting, a knight from Brittany arrives, and Lancelot asks him for news of Tristan, making it quite clear that he feels great ill-will towards him; much to the surprise of the knight, who sings Tristan's praises, whilst regretting that the latter is not as fit or as carefree as he was in Cornwall. Lancelot suspects that Tristan is beginning to regret his marriage.

They all leave the widow's house next morning; Lancelot parts from the messenger-girl and asks her to convey his warmest greetings to Queen Iseut. When the Breton knight, who is called Supinabel, finds out that the knight he has been talking to is Lancelot, he is greatly dismayed, and decides to return to Brittany to warn Tristan. Our hero is very upset at Supinabel's news, and realizes upon reflection that Lancelot must hate him because he thinks that his marriage to Iseut of the White Hands has made him forget Iseut of Cornwall. But Lancelot is mistaken, for Tristan loves her more than ever. He has never consummated his marriage and pines for the Queen day and night. His wife suspects nothing, thinking it is for her that Tristan writes the poems and songs in which the name of Iseut constantly appears. King Hoel too is completely deceived: he naturally assumes that the marriage has been consummated, and when he questions his daughter, she assures him that no man could cherish his wife more, since the name of Iseut is always on Tristan's lips. The King is delighted, and loves Tristan more than his own son.

In this part the story relates that when the messenger-girl had parted from Lancelot as I have told you, she rode on day after day with such company as she had until she came to the sea. At this point the youth who had escorted her at Queen Guinevere's request took his leave of her. Then the maiden boarded a ship, and the wind was so favourable that they had not been on the sea for long when they landed in Cornwall. The young girl left the ship, mounted her horse, parted from the sailors, and did not stop riding until she arrived that very day at the place where her lady Queen Iseut was staying; and she came so secretly that King Mark never knew anything about it. As soon as the maiden had reached the court, she went to find her lady; and when the Queen saw her, she was overjoyed at her return and instantly had the room cleared so that she could speak to the maiden more privately. Once everybody had gone and there were only the two of them, the Queen who was very eager to know what news the young girl had brought immediately addressed her and said:

'Welcome, maiden. What tidings are you bringing me from Queen Guinevere, the noblest lady on earth?'

'Good ones, my lady,' replied the young girl. 'Queen Guin-evere greets you as the lady in the world who loves you most and who is most desirous of seeing you and most distressed about your sorrow and unhappiness, and sends you this letter.'

Then she drew the letter from her bosom and gave it to her.

As soon as Queen Iseut saw the emblem of the Queen she began to kiss the letter, and after looking at it for a long time, she opened it and found that it read as follows:

To you, my lady Iseut, Queen of Cornwall, who are so worthy, so fair and so gracious in all things, and who have no equal on earth in beauty, kindness and breeding; to you who surpass all ladies in loveliness, who are the model and the paragon of all the women at present in the world; fair lady about whose beauty I could speak all my life without being able to do it justice, I, Guinevere, Queen of the Kingdom of Logres, ready to enhance your glory, your renown and your honour in any way I can, send my greetings as to my lady, seeing that you deigned to make known to me your state and your predicament, as I remember and recall to memory every day; and all my life I shall recollect the beautifully worded complaint which you communicated to me in your letter. All this I recall and shall recall for the rest of my life. And when I bethink myself of the great nobility of your person, I cannot see that I have sufficient sense or knowledge to be able to answer you as wisely or as well as would be fitting to such a worthy and intelligent lady as I have found you to be.

Your complaint, so it seems to me, stems from love, and you say that love has betrayed you basely and cruelly in view of all your service. Your complaint is about love and about Tristan. And if I have understood it rightly, I shall answer you as best I can: from love, it appears to me, we cannot always expect to have joy, but we should know for certain that since love is a human condition, human conditions are as unstable as the Wheel of Fortune which leads men where it wishes, now to the top, now to the bottom, now to joy, now to misery. That is why many people say that love is a human condition as changeable as the wind. At this point in time when you find love cruel and treacherous, when love makes you live in the greatest possible sorrow and bitterness, at this very point you may be sure that there is absolutely no question but that this sorrow must needs cease and that joy will return in the end,* for we always see it happen that great unhappiness in love is followed by exceeding joy. For that reason, my lady, you should console yourself and take heart, and bethink yourself that after this suffering you will find joy.

As for your saying that I am so lucky in love and the most fortunate lady you know, I reply to you as best I can, which is not as wisely as I would wish: love, it seems to me, is just like the fickle master who for a long while treats his servant with great kindness, and then changes his mind and, rightly or wrongly, throws him down from the heights to the depths. All these reasons often make me feel afraid, for when I see how well love has treated me up to now and how happily I have lived till the present day, I think to myself that at some stage love is bound to cause my downfall. And when this happens,

who will be more unhappy than I? No man or woman;
because he who falls from the greatest height is the most badly
hurt. Thus I say, Iseut, that you and I are currently going along
different paths; that is my reply and that is my opinion, and it
should comfort you and make me apprehensive.

When Queen Iseut had read and reread the letter and looked
at it many times, this answer pleased her greatly and made her feel
much better; and she affirmed that the Queen of Logres was truly
one of the most discerning ladies in the world: she had consoled
her courteously and effectively at this stage. For the next forty
days after the maiden's return, there was not a single day when
the Queen did not look at the letter which Queen Guinevere had
sent her, and she derived great comfort from it. During this time
she began to feel much more happy. Then Queen Iseut decided
to despatch a messenger to Brittany and send a letter to Tristan
asking him to come to Cornwall without any delay. That would
show her clearly whether Tristan loved her as much as he used to
and as much as she loved him, for if he still loved her as much,
nothing would stop him from coming to Cornwall. And once
they were together, they would find a way of escaping from King
Mark's clutches. Queen Iseut, who was very eager to bring this
about and who longed to be able to see Tristan with all her heart,
wrote the letter as soon and as speedily as she could, and sent
Brangain to Brittany with it to give to Tristan who was very
unhappy. But now the story stops talking about Tristan and
Queen Iseut of Cornwall, and returns to Lamorat of Wales in
order to relate some of his adventures and deeds of chivalry.

Lamorat, after leaving the knight whom he has sent to King Arthur's
court with the magic horn, boards a ship to go to Great Britain. But a
storm smashes the boat against a rock; Lamorat is the only one to survive
the shipwreck, and finds himself at the extremity of Norgales in front of
the Giant's Rock in a country enclosed on all sides by rocks and by the
sea, called the Land of Servitude. The narrow entrance to this country is
guarded by a castle full of giants, and the lord, a giant named Nabon the
Black, holds everyone who arrives captive.
    Meanwhile Tristan has had a boat built for himself, ostensibly for his
pleasure, but actually for his return journey to Cornwall, since he could
no longer bear to be separated from Queen Iseut. His wife and brother-
in-law admire the boat, and while they are all three asleep in it, it crashes

against a rock and throws them ashore. They meet Segurades who tells them that they are henceforth prisoners, as he is, in the Land of Servitude.

Nabon has ordered all the inhabitants to come to Glait Castle in three days' time to celebrate the knighting of his son. They all set out on foot, since none of the captives is allowed a horse or armour, and spend the night in a chapel where they find the tomb of a Round Table knight, Mennon the Small, whom Nabon had put to death. Tristan swears to avenge him.

The celebration takes place on a plain where numerous tents have been pitched. The people from Logres are placed on one side, those from Norgales on the other, and in the middle are two quarterstaffs* and two shields, for Nabon wants to see which group is the best at fencing. Lamorat, the representative of Logres, beats his adversary and then defeats all the knights from Norgales chosen to avenge him. Nabon, eager to show his superiority, invites Lamorat to fence, and, having overpowered him, asks if there is another knight who dares to come forward. Tristan, a past-master at fencing, accepts the challenge and succeeds in killing him; thereupon the knights of Logres and Norgales join forces and put to death all Nabon's relatives.

Tristan and Lamorat refuse the lordship of the country, henceforth called the Land that Tristan Freed;* Segurades accepts it, on condition that he can absent himself when he wishes in order to go in search of adventures in the Kingdom of Logres. Tristan, Iseut of the White Hands and Kahedin return to Brittany where they are received with great joy by King Hoel. The Bretons compose a lay* about this adventure which is called 'Lay of the Land that Tristan Freed'.*

The story now relates that in the same week* in which Tristan revealed his love for Iseut to Kahedin, the two of them were riding one day along the sea-shore when they saw a young girl coming towards them accompanied by two squires. The maiden was very well appointed, and if anyone were to ask me who she was, I would answer that she was Brangain, sent to Tristan by Iseut; and she had had a very difficult journey. When Tristan saw her coming with her companions, he knew well that they were strangers and he waited for them to approach. Brangain was completely enveloped in her wimple. As soon as she saw Sir Tristan, she recognized him at once and cried out with great joy:

'Ah! Tristan, Tristan! The Lord be with you!'

'Maiden,' he replied, 'may God grant you good fortune! Who are you who know me so well?'

'If you please, sir,' she said, 'you'll find that out soon enough.'

Then she took off her wimple, and Tristan was overjoyed when he realized who she was. He embraced her in tears, and Brangain also wept, and then he immediately asked her how his lady was.

'Sir,' she replied, 'not very well. She's never had a moment's joy since she heard that you had married, nor will she until she sees you. Here is a letter she's sent you; read it. You may be sure that however happy Iseut of Brittany may be, your Iseut of Cornwall is full of woe.'

Tristan took the letter, and when he saw Iseut's seal, he burst into tears and began to kiss it. Then he opened the letter and started to read; and I should tell you that it was a long letter containing many words, and it ran as follows:

Beloved Tristan, you who have plunged me into sadness and sorrow, through whom I have lost my joy both day and night, because of whom I am dying, for whom I have given up myself and the whole world, since I cannot have you, nothing pleases me.

Beloved, who hold me in bondage and have so ensnared my heart that you have taken it with you to Brittany; beloved, who have my heart with you and know it for certain, how could you bring yourself to leave Iseut the Queen for Iseut the maiden? You have made a bad exchange, for you have replaced a true and proven lady by one whom you do not know at all. Beloved Tristan, this exchange kills me. It makes me suffer all the pain that a miserable wretch can suffer. Every day I curse the hour I was born more than a thousand times, since I love the one who does not love me. When I think of that, I begin to weep and to lament. There is nothing else I can do, and you may see this very clearly in my letter which is in part obliterated by my tears; and this token, if it please God and yourself, should make you have pity on Iseut of Cornwall, your dear beloved.

What more shall I say? Dearest Tristan, my heart is so shattered that I am unable to write the hundredth part of what I would want to express to you. And for that reason I beseech you who are my life and my death, my joy and my grief, to whom I cry for mercy more than a hundred thousand times, with my heart not merely with my lips, beloved, I entreat you, weeping and dying the most cruel death to which a queen was ever subjected, that as soon as you have read my letter which Brangain is bringing you in my stead, you will come to Cornwall to see Iseut the Queen. Don't be afraid of King Mark, for however closely he is guarding me, I shall find a means whereby we can be together. Beloved, don't hesitate to come; if you delay too long, let all loyal lovers know that Tristan's love brought Queen Iseut nothing but misfortune.

This was the content of the letter. And when Tristan had read it, he said to Kahedin:

'Let's leave! The only thing to do is to go to Cornwall.'

'Sir,' replied Kahedin, 'I'm quite prepared to do your command.'

Then they returned to the castle from which they had come. Sir Tristan had Brangain lodged in one of the King's rooms and ordered that she should be served and honoured more than himself, for she had done him many a service; he said that she had come from Leonois to bring him a letter asking him to return to his country, and that he wanted to take Kahedin with him. The King knew nothing about Tristan's affairs and had no suspicion that all was not as it should be, and when he heard the news that Tristan told him, he did not doubt but that it was the truth and willingly gave him permission to leave. Indeed, he said that Tristan should choose from his court all those he would most like to take with him and that he should conduct himself as was fitting to his station and do whatever was necessary in order to arrive back in his country with honour. Tristan replied that of all those in Brittany he wished to take with him only Kahedin; but he did want to take, as he loved his company dearly. The King said he had no objection; and for Tristan's sake he made sure that the maiden and the squires were served and honoured in every way possible. But no one could have welcomed Brangain with greater joy than Gorvenal as soon as he saw her. He asked her about Queen Iseut's state and condition and how she had fared since Tristan had left Cornwall, and Brangain told him the whole truth, whereupon he replied, pensive and sorrowful:

'Brangain,' he said, 'we should feel very guilty about this. All their unhappiness and grief is due to us and our foolishness. They are paying more dearly for our folly than we are ourselves; the fault is ours rather than theirs. They have suffered much anguish, and will suffer more, unless God determines otherwise.'

And he already knew that Tristan had never consummated his marriage.

Tristan prepared himself for the journey and set sail once he had said good-bye to his wife and to the King and the barons of Brittany. He took with him Kahedin of whom he was very fond, and Gorvenal and Brangain, and her two squires. He also took good and fine armour for himself and for Kahedin, but nobody else accompanied him except those I have mentioned; in their company he put to sea.

The first day they had fair winds, favourable and pleasant, but on the second the wind changed so drastically that they were all afraid they would die, for a storm suddenly blew up which was so violent and so frightening that each one of them could but lament, and even the sailors were terrified. Tristan, who could see death looming before him, was very dismayed; it was all a question of chance. Brangain wept bitterly, and the squires bewailed their fate.

'God!' said Kahedin, 'what can we do? We shall have to die here in great torment without having done any act of prowess.'

'Ah! Tristan,' said Gorvenal, 'here prowess will be of no avail; here we shall die if God does not save us.'

Tristan said as little as possible, since he was well aware that at this point no lament would serve him any purpose. The wind and the tempest buffeted them so mercilessly that they knew beyond a doubt that they were no longer on course for Cornwall.

After three days they land in Great Britain at the frontier between Norgales and Logres, near to the Forest of Darvances where Merlin had been buried alive by the Lady of the Lake. Tristan decides to go in search of Merlin's tomb with Kahedin. He tells the sailors to wait ten days for them; after that they should leave for Cornwall, and he would make his way there either by land or by sea, and meet them at the Castle of the Pass. The two companions spend the night with a hermit who informs them that King Arthur has been in this forest for three months, so lost that he is unable to find his way out; he also tells them that there are many adventures to be encountered at the Pine of the Three Damsels.

The following day the two companions come upon a knight clad in black armour sitting by a fountain. Kahedin challenges him to joust and is badly wounded. Tristan wants to avenge his friend's shame, but is unhorsed in his turn. Thereupon Tristan and the black knight attack each other with their swords. During a pause, Tristan learns that his adversary is Lamorat, and in order to test him, he threatens him with death as a punishment for having sent the magic horn to King Mark's court; and this makes Lamorat realize that he is Tristan. Since Lamorat shows no sign of dismay, our hero stops the battle; Lamorat declares himself vanquished, and the two knights embrace. Lamorat has already spent two months in the forest looking for King Arthur, and Tristan decides to join in the search. Kahedin is too badly wounded to accompany them, and they take him to the house of a forester nearby. Lamorat tells Tristan that the majority of the Round Table knights are in this forest seeking the King.

As they are about to rest by a fountain, a strange beast appears with the legs of a stag, the thighs and tail of a lion and the body of a leopard; it makes as much noise as twenty hounds. This is the Howling Beast. It jumps into the water to drink and then rushes off again with the two knights in hot pursuit. They encounter another knight also hunting this animal: he is the Knight of the Howling Beast. Lamorat attacks him, but is knocked off his horse, and Tristan suffers the same fate. The knight rides off, followed by Tristan and Lamorat. They part at a crossroads, and our hero instructs Lamorat to tell the knight, if he finds him, to come back to fight him at the same fountain, and they arrange to meet there in four days' time.

That evening Lamorat encounters Gawain, who is abducting a maiden, and begs him to let her go. Gawain threatens to kill Lamorat to avenge the death of his father, King Lot, assassinated by Lamorat's father, King Pellinor. Gawain is unhorsed and rides off; the maiden has fled.

That night while Lamorat is lying by a ruined chapel, a knight appears and laments his unhappy love for Queen Guinevere. Lamorat does not recognize him and rides off next morning while the knight is still asleep. He meets a very big knight who unhorses him and wounds him in his breast; two knights he meets subsequently tell him it was King Arthur. They say they come from Wales, from the vicinity of the Castle of Fortune, and are looking for Lancelot to avenge their brother whom he had killed. At that moment they see Lancelot approach. Lamorat rides towards him full of joy, but the two knights do not dare to budge. Lamorat informs Lancelot that Tristan is in the forest and would be at the fountain in three days' time; Lancelot fully intends to go there. As they are talking, the knight arrives whom Lamorat had left at the chapel;

Lancelot identifies him as Meleagant, son of King Bademagu of Gorre;* then Lancelot departs.

Meleagant joins Lamorat and asks him whom he considers to be the most beautiful lady in any of the lands held by King Arthur. When Lamorat names the Queen of Orcanie, Meleagant attacks him for not having named Guinevere. Lancelot reappears with Blioberis and stops the battle, but when he learns the cause of it, he is so furious that he sets upon Lamorat, and only Blioberis's intervention manages to calm him. Thereupon Meleagant wants to resume his battle, but Lamorat, not wanting to irritate Lancelot, declares Guinevere to be the most beautiful lady. Lancelot and Blioberis ride off together; Meleagant and Lamorat go their separate ways.

Tristan for his part does not find any adventures on the first day, but the following day he meets Kay the Seneschal who insults him when he hears that he comes from Cornwall. They arrive at a bridge defended by a knight, and Tristan lets Kay fight him in the hope of seeing him vanquished; however, Kay is victorious. They spend the night at the house of a forester where they find Tor, the son of Ares, and Brandeliz; the 'Cornish knight' is the subject of much mockery. When Tristan leaves next morning, the three knights, wanting to test him, speed along a road which joins the one taken by Tristan, and as he approaches, Kay challenges him to joust. Tristan wounds him badly and unhorses both Tor and Brandeliz; then he rides off speedily, laughing to himself at their surprise. Tor and Brandeliz ride after him to discover his name, which he divulges, but he refuses their company. Kay is obliged to remain at the forester's house for over a month.

Round about midday Tristan meets a young girl in tears and offers to help her. She takes him to a meadow in front of a large tower where he sees two knights holding a third who is on the point of having his head cut off by a maiden. Tristan's companion exhorts him to save the threatened knight, for he is King Arthur. Tristan kills one of the knights, wounds the other, and seizes the maiden. King Arthur, thus freed, snatches the sword out of her hands and cuts off her head; then he kills the wounded knight. The King explains that the maiden had come to court while they were deploring the act of a foreign knight called Saliel who had murdered one of his relatives, and she had offered to take the King's champion to the knight to avenge this atrocity. King Arthur himself had followed her and had slain the knight. Then she had led him to this tower and placed a ring on his finger which had bewitched him. Fortunately one day he met one of the maidens of the Lady of the Lake who had removed the ring and made him promise to cut off the head of the enchantress. But as he was about to do so, she called her two brothers, and they were on the point of killing him when Tristan appeared to save him.

Arthur and Tristan meet Hestor of the Marshes who does not recognize them and challenges one of them to joust. Tristan badly wounds
him in the left arm, and then takes his leave of the King who has no idea
of his identity. Arthur makes himself known to Hestor, and they spend
two days in the house of an aged knight because of Hestor's wound. On
the second day Brandeliz arrives, who immediately realizes that it was
none other than Tristan who had saved the King. They all leave together
for Camelot.

Tristan finds Lamorat at the fountain as arranged, and admits to him,
albeit unwillingly, that it was he who had rescued King Arthur. Then he
rides off to join Kahedin and is pleased to find him fully recovered from
his wounds.

The following day Tristan and Kahedin started out and
travelled until they reached the sea, where they found their ship
still waiting for them. It would doubtless have set sail already, but
there had been no wind. When those who had been left behind
saw Tristan and Kahedin return, there is no need to ask whether
they were pleased. They ran to meet them and welcomed them
with great joy, and then disarmed them and asked them if they
were well.

'Yes, thank God,' they replied.

It was very fortunate for them that on the very day they returned
to the port they had such fair winds that they put to sea, and three
days later they landed right in front of Tintagel. As soon as they
had gone ashore and their horses were ready, they mounted, and
once they were on horseback, Tristan asked Brangain:

'Where shall we go? That is Tintagel before us! There was a
time when I was happier there than I am now.'

'Don't be dismayed,' she replied. 'It may yet happen that you'll
find the joy and pleasure that you most desire.'

'Ah! God,' he exclaimed, 'when will that be?'

'We won't go into Tintagel', said Brangain, 'because I
wouldn't want you to enter into King Mark's domain except on
Queen Iseut's advice.'

'Where shall we go, then?' he asked.

'We'll go to the castle of Dinas the Seneschal,' she answered.
'If we find him there, we can be sure that we'll be made very
welcome; and if he isn't at home, there will be many in his
household who will receive us with great joy and honour.'

'You're right,' he said.

Thereupon they set out, and it was quite dark before they reached Tintagel. Fortunately for them they found that Dinas was staying there because he had been a little indisposed. When he saw himself face to face with Brangain, he was as happy as could be and leapt towards her, hugging and embracing her.

'Brangain,' he said, 'what news do you bring me? Have you found out anything about Tristan yet?'

'Do you want to see Tristan very much?' asked Brangain.

'Yes, I do,' replied Dinas, 'as God is my witness, for I know what his life is like, I know that he is living in pain and torment, and that he's never had much happiness since he left Cornwall. And that's something I'm very upset about, since he was the knight I loved most in the world of all those not related to me.'

'Would you want him to be in this castle now, so help you God?' asked Brangain.

'As God is my witness,' he answered, 'I love him so much that if he were in this castle now, and King Mark were outside with his entire army, I would rather lose all the land I hold from King Mark than that Sir Tristan should come to harm because I failed to help him.'

'Truly?' she asked. 'Well, in that case I should tell you that he is here.'

'Ah! you're pulling my leg,' he said. 'I wish to God he were here!'

'By my faith, I'll take you to him straightaway. Come with me; he's out there in the garden because he didn't want anyone except you to see him come in.'

'May the Lord be praised for these tidings! Let's go to him quickly. I shall never be happy or joyful until I see him.'

Then they went straight to Tristan. As soon as Dinas saw him, he embraced and kissed him, and led him to a very beautiful and luxurious room in his tower, and said to him:

'Sir Tristan, you can stay here as long as you like. I place myself entirely at your disposal, both my person and my castle, and shall carry out your command without reserve.'

'Dinas,' he replied, 'I'm most grateful. Certainly, I never found anyone in the whole of Cornwall who loved me as you've always done. One day I shall reward you for it.'

'Thank you very much, sir,' said Dinas.

'Now someone ought to let my lady Iseut know that I'm in this country,' said Tristan.

'We'll see to that soon enough, sir. You rest here for a while, and in the meantime Kahedin and I will go to court, and I'll speak to my lady the Queen.'

'That's a good idea,' said Tristan.

Dinas and Kahedin went off to court. King Mark received Kahedin with much courtesy and honour, thinking he was a knight-errant; and he had the appearance of a man of great valour. That day and the next Kahedin saw the Queen; and such was his misfortune that as soon as he set eyes on her he fell so passionately and so madly in love with her that never thereafter could he stop loving her until he died.

Dinas told the Queen in private that Tristan was in Cornwall, and when she heard this she was delighted and overjoyed. She immediately instructed Dinas how Tristan could come to her, and he carried out her instructions. Thereafter Tristan did not delay in coming to King Mark's court and seeking out the Queen, so secretly that no one noticed him, neither King Mark nor anyone else. Thus Tristan went to find his pleasure, and he stayed with the Queen according to his wishes. He told her all about Kahedin, who he was and why he had come to Cornwall at this point.

In this way Tristan enjoyed the fulfilment of his desires. But the same was not true of Kahedin. His love for my lady Iseut was so overpowering that when he saw clearly that he could not have her, he fell ill and took to his bed, and his condition deteriorated from day to day. He was dying of love. What shall I tell you? Since Sir Tristan was able to have my lady Iseut, he did not care about the world to come, nor did he remember Kahedin whom he had brought to Cornwall to show him Iseut's beauty. He forgot every single thing. He had no idea about the great pain and the great grief which Kahedin endured for love of my lady Iseut, no idea how close his friend was to death, how he languished and suffered, how he was nearing his end in agony and anguish. Kahedin kept repeating day and night that it was in an evil hour he saw Iseut, in an evil hour he ever came to Cornwall to finish his life in torment. He could truly say without lying that he never found such ill-fated company as was that of Tristan. In an evil hour had he seen Tristan, in an evil hour had he seen Iseut, for these two would cause his death.

Sir Tristan was in the tower with my lady Iseut, happy and joyous, full of great pleasure and delight. Never at any point, so it seemed to him, did he have such a good time as he was having now. He sang together with Iseut and enjoyed himself with her in the way that lovers should enjoy themselves. But this enjoyment, this pleasure, this delight was being paid for very dearly by Kahedin. If Sir Tristan was singing, Kahedin was weeping; however happy Sir Tristan was, Kahedin for his part was even more unhappy and miserable. Ah! God, how he lamented, how he sighed from the depths of his heart! He cursed the misfortune which had ever made him come to Cornwall. He was now so weak and ill in every respect, so thin, so pale and so debilitated that he said to himself that henceforth he could not endure any more: he had come to his end, he knew it well.

While he was suffering such great anguish for love of my lady Iseut that he did not know what to do about it, he wrote her a letter and without long delay sent it to her as secretly as he could. In this letter he told her how unhappy he was and how overpoweringly he loved her and how he would undoubtedly die if she did not have pity on him. Would she be so kind as to reply to him as she wished to reply, for after her answer his fate would be sealed: either he would die then and there, or he would be cured in no time.

When the Queen saw the letter and had read it, and she realized how passionately Kahedin loved her, she was quite dismayed, for it would not have entered her mind that he would get himself into such a state, at least not in view of his friendship with Sir Tristan. However, because she knew that Sir Tristan loved Kahedin with all his heart, and that he would be very upset if his friend died in such circumstances, she thought to herself that in order to comfort Kahedin and alleviate his suffering she would write him a letter feigning to console him, and promise him such things as would never come to pass at any time. Once he had recovered, she would make him recognize his folly and persuade him, so she thought, to go back to Brittany and never return to Cornwall.

With this aim in mind and none other, Queen Iseut wrote the letter, more out of love for Tristan than for Kahedin, and told him to take heart and get better if he wanted to have her love; and he should know that thereafter she would deal with his love in such a way that he would consider himself comforted; he should not be in doubt or fear that she would let him die.

When Kahedin, who was almost on the point of death for love of my lady Iseut, saw the letter she had sent him, he really believed that it would come about as my lady Iseut had promised him in this letter, and that he would be given the reward for his love that is usually given to lovers; and he began to feel very much better. Because of the great joy he derived from her message, he said to himself:

'Truly, now I can't complain at all about the anguish I've suffered for love's sake. Since my lady has promised to have pity on me and to take action to deal with my malady, I am cured! Now no knight could be happier than I am, nor luckier, for every good fortune has befallen me at this point.'

As a result of these false words of comfort which the Queen had written to Kahedin because of her love for Tristan, Kahedin began to feel so much better that he was quite healed and cured, and became as handsome and noble in appearance as he had been when he first came to Cornwall.

What more shall I tell you? The Queen's words were enough to make Kahedin recover and regain his health. Were it not for this false hope which the Queen had given him, he would already have been dead and buried. But that did not happen on this occasion, for he could go to court whenever he felt like it. King Mark who was very fond of him always received him most courteously and took him along to see my lady Iseut. Wherever the King went to amuse himself, he took Kahedin with him. Kahedin was so much in the King's favour that he could see the Queen whenever he wanted. There was no one there so bold as to forbid him to enter the Queen's room: he saw her whenever he wished, and similarly Tristan. He had his pleasure and his entertainment with them, but lacked the courage to remind the Queen of the promise she had made him. He did not dare to speak of it, for he greatly feared her. [§§ 569–835 of vols. ii and iii]

XV

THE LOVERS' QUARREL

AT this time when Kahedin was seeing Sir Tristan and Queen Iseut at will, in such a way that no one raised any objections, it happened one day without fail that Tristan came upon the letter which the Queen had sent to Kahedin, for Kahedin had brought it along with him. When Sir Tristan found it, and he had read and reread it, never in his life had he been so angry that he was not even more angry now. As soon as he saw the letter, he was convinced that the Queen had left him for Kahedin and that she loved Kahedin with all her heart. Sir Tristan did not know what to do. He was consumed with grief and anger. He almost went mad with fury. And when he had pondered and reflected about the matter for a long time, he could not devise any plan other than that he said to himself that he would kill Kahedin who had stolen my lady Iseut's love from him. Kahedin had committed an act of such treachery towards him that he could not have committed any greater. At this point he would have to pay for it so dearly that never again would he perpetrate any treachery against a knight as valiant as Tristan of Leonois. Tristan blamed Kahedin for his anguish and for everything that had happened. He would get even with him for it all. Now Kahedin could truly say that he had no worse enemy on earth than Sir Tristan. If Sir Tristan could lay his hands on him, that would be the end of Kahedin. Let Kahedin beware, for his life was in danger. He would not be able to withstand Sir Tristan if Tristan were to get hold of him in his present state of suffering and sorrow, caused by his belief that Kahedin had taken my lady Iseut from him.

One day it happened that Kahedin was thinking about his love and going from one room to another in search of Tristan, since he was not on his guard against him. As soon as Tristan saw him coming, he did not waste any time but rushed at Kahedin, his naked sword in his hand, and said to him:

'Kahedin, I defy you.'

Kahedin knew Sir Tristan's strength from past experience and realized only too well that he would not have the power to hold

out against him; and so when he saw him charge towards him
holding his bare sword, he was not bold enough to wait for him
unarmed as he was, but took to his heels.

'Ah! Kahedin,' said Sir Tristan, 'it's no good running away.
You will have to die, that's for sure; you can't escape it.'

Kahedin did not feel too reassured when he heard the threat
uttered by Sir Tristan; he knew full well that he would be dead
if Sir Tristan was able to strike a single blow at him. For that
reason he fled as fast as he could and ran straight to a window
overlooking the garden; and the height of this window was more
than two lances from the ground.* And I should tell you that at
this point King Mark was playing chess with Queen Iseut in that
very garden, and there were many Cornish knights watching
their game. Kahedin came to the window, and he was in such a
state of terror that he never looked to see how high it was from
the ground, but jumped down; and it was lucky for him that he
landed quite near to King Mark.

Sir Tristan rushed in pursuit, wild with anger, and wanted to
jump out after him. But when he caught sight of King Mark and
Queen Iseut down below and the Cornish knights watching the
game, he stopped short instantly and drew back in order that the
King would not see him. If Kahedin, having landed down there,
were to inform them about him, Sir Tristan would be able to
hold out at a strongpoint in the tower, and moreover one so well
fortified that the King would find it very difficult to seize him
should he want to do so, because the tower was very strong and
built in such a well-protected place that he could defend it all by
himself against a large number of people for quite a long while.
All the same, he deemed it preferable that the King should not
see him rather than that he should. However, because he was not
altogether sure what would happen, and regardless of whether
the King found out the truth about his presence at this point or
not, he took some strong and fine armour, the best he could find
there, and armed himself as well as he could; and he said to
himself that if the King ordered him to be attacked in some way
or other, and the Cornish knights attempted to take him by force,
they would not find him unprepared, if he could help it.

When King Mark, who was playing chess with the Queen as I
have told you, saw Kahedin fall out of the window, he was quite

taken aback, and jumped up and went over to him; and so did all
the others who were there. They found Kahedin still so stunned
that he did not know where he was; nevertheless after a while he
came to and opened his eyes. The King asked him:

'How do you feel? Are you badly hurt?'

'Thank God, I'm not injured, my lord,' he replied.

'And how did you fall?' asked the King. 'Were you asleep?'

The Queen instantly leapt forward and said so loudly that
everyone there was able to hear it clearly:

'My lord, it could not have been otherwise. Kahedin must
have been asleep.'

When Kahedin heard the Queen's reply, he did not dare to
contradict her in any way, but said to the King:

'My lord, what my lady told you was quite true.'

'In God's name,' said the King, 'it's a miracle that you aren't
badly hurt, since you fell from a great height. You were fortunate. Take care you don't go to sleep in such a spot another
time.'

'I certainly will, my lord,' he replied.

The King resumed the game and so did the Queen. She had
spoken these words because she feared that Kahedin would say
something different. She had deduced that for some reason Kahedin
had angered Tristan who had forced him to make this jump; and
this greatly alarmed her, for she was afraid that Kahedin would
tell the King that Tristan was up in the tower. If the King found
this out, he was so evil and so cruel that he would kill her
without more ado, and Tristan would no longer have the chance
of escaping. For that reason she was very worried and uneasy as
she played chess with King Mark, much more than he suspected.

Kahedin for his part, angry and distressed as he was, wondered
what to do about this matter. He knew well that if he told the
King that Tristan was up in the tower, Tristan would be in great
danger and would be seized without fail, and after that would
have no chance whatever of escaping from death. On the other
hand, when he thought about it, he realized that if Sir Tristan
were found out, the Queen would be shamed and dishonoured,
and he did not want that to happen under any circumstances; he
loved her more than the whole world, more even than himself,
and he was sure that she would be the first one the King would

wreak vengeance on. In consideration of this he said to himself that it would be better for him to keep quiet than to say anything about it. If he spoke, he would lose his chance of having his lady and the favours she had promised him. For this reason King Mark was as yet unaware that Sir Tristan was in Cornwall, but believed implicitly that Kahedin had told him the truth about what had happened.

Sir Tristan who had remained up in the tower fully armed and equipped to defend himself if anyone came to attack him, often sighed and lamented to himself, and kept looking at the letter which the Queen had written with her own hand. And this filled his heart with such grief and such anguish that his only wish was to die, for that would put an end to his suffering.

That evening as darkness began to fall the Queen made her way up there in great fear, being all the while frightened that Kahedin would somehow inform the King of Sir Tristan's presence in the tower. When she saw Sir Tristan armed, she was quite taken aback, and asked him:

'What's the matter, Sir Tristan? Why are you armed? What are you afraid of?'

And he replied, so greatly upset that he almost went mad with grief:

'Lady, why have you betrayed the most loyal lover in the world, who was never false in his love nor broke his faith in any way whatever? Lady, I don't know what to say. I have lost my wits and my strength and all the gifts that you had bestowed upon me. I am so utterly confounded at this point that no one could in any way confound me more, and it is you and no one but you who have thus confounded me. You alone and only you have plunged me into despair and deprived me of the great happiness which you yourself had given me. I am the tree which you planted and endowed with good fruit and all other virtues, but now you have completely filled me with pain and anguish and grief. Lady, how was it possible that Queen Iseut of Cornwall could be untrue to Sir Tristan? Lady, since it has come about that you have betrayed my love, I no longer wish to live, but long for my death. I want to die, that's all I ask for, that's my most ardent desire. And in order to put an end to my great grief without delay, I shall kill myself with my own two hands.'

When the Queen heard these words and saw her beloved going demented and out of his mind with grief, it is not surprising if, due to her love for Tristan, she herself became distressed and upset. She wanted to justify herself and tell him the truth about the whole matter, but Tristan, who was so grief-stricken that he wished he were dead, did not allow her to excuse herself, but replied without mincing words:

'My lady, what could you say? Your defence is pointless. Here is the letter, here is the missive which you wrote with your own hand and sent to Kahedin. This is such clear evidence against you that your defence is worthless. Your own hand has proved you guilty of this letter which I saw in an evil hour, for it is killing me, it is causing my death and my destruction. If you had not written it with your own hand, I would have taken it as no more than a fabrication and a lie that you could have left Tristan for Kahedin. But since much to my misfortune and affliction there is no doubt that you have left Tristan for Kahedin, Tristan will depart at this point, so unhappy and so anguished, so grief-stricken and so sick at heart that I can confidently say that at the present time there is no unhappier knight in the world than I am. Tristan is departing in great pain; Kahedin remains with you who henceforth will be filled with joy. You have brought Kahedin back from death to life; and you have thrust Tristan from life to death, although you used to love him so much, as I recall. And in doing so you can truly say that you have destroyed the knight who would have been the best in the world, had he been allowed to live.'

When he had spoken these words he took his sword and left the room, saying:

'Lady, I commend you to God. You may be sure that no knight will ever look upon you who loves you as much as I do.'

Then he went to the palace despite the fact that King Mark was there with a great company of Cornish knights. But Sir Tristan was disguised at that point by the armour he was wearing, so that no one who saw him recognized him in the slightest, though they did wonder who he could be. However, they did not stop him, but let him pass amongst them, thinking he was one of their household. And Sir Tristan went down to the courtyard and mounted the first horse he could find, and rode through Tintagel as speedily as if the whole world were pursuing him. But no one ever saw a man more grief-stricken than he was.

While Sir Tristan was riding along lamenting in this way, and he had already left the city behind him, he happened to meet Giglain, Sir Gawain's son,* who had been newly knighted that year. He was without doubt a brave knight and liked to go in search of adventures far and wide, just as his father did; and it was to find adventures and to see marvels that he had come to the Kingdom of Cornwall. He caught sight of Sir Tristan coming out of Tintagel, and because anyone seeing him then would have considered it the greatest marvel in the world, Giglain went up to him, since he saw him riding all alone, and took his horse by the bridle and said to him:

'Sir Knight, I beg you in the name of courtliness and nobility, in such a manner as one knight can beg another, that you tell me the reason for your grief. I know well that you wouldn't be so grief-stricken without good cause, and I promise you that I shall do everything in my power to alleviate your unhappiness.'

Sir Tristan who was in great distress replied to the knight and said:

'Sir Knight, leave me alone and don't harass me at this point with your words, for it wouldn't be a courtly thing to do. I want you to know and I tell you herewith that there isn't a single knight in the world who could do anything to lessen my unhappiness. There's only one way and that would be to strike my heart dead. I wouldn't want to find any other way out except death; all I want to do is to die. For that reason I beg you, sir, as fervently as I can, not to detain me any longer but to let me go on my way; I assure you there is no knight on earth to whom I would reveal the reason for my unhappiness.'

'In God's name,' said Sir Giglain, 'it's very clear that you have little respect for me and for all the other knights in the world, since you won't tell anyone about it. I've met many knights since I first bore arms, but I can truthfully say that I haven't come across a knight as arrogant as you for a long time. But even if you are more arrogant than other knights, that won't get you out of telling me the reason for your unhappiness, or else you will have to fight me.'

'Sir Knight,' said Sir Tristan, 'let me inform you that since I see you behaving in such an outrageous manner towards me, I would fight you even if you were as brave a knight as Sir Lancelot of the Lake, who is considered to be the best knight in the world, rather than tell you a thing.'

'That's all right by me,' Giglain retorted. 'I'd rather find it out by force than in any other way.'

Thereupon they defied each other.

That is how the two knights came to engage in combat. Sir Tristan did not have his shield or lance at that point, but he was well equipped with all his other arms. When he realized that he could not escape from Giglain without a battle, he took hold of his sword with which he had dealt many a mighty blow, and prepared himself to strike as soon as his opponent came to attack him. And Giglain, who did not know or fear Sir Tristan, rushed towards him as fast as his horse would go and, holding his lance stretched out, he charged at him and struck him so fiercely on his breast that his lance shattered to pieces. He did no other harm to Sir Tristan, because the hauberk he was wearing protected him on this occasion.

When Sir Tristan felt himself struck in this way he was even angrier than he had been before, and rode up to Giglain who was on the point of passing beyond him to complete his charge, and gave him such a mighty blow on his helmet that the part he had hit was knocked to the ground. The blow was powerful and struck with great anger and great strength, since Tristan was full of fury. But Giglain leapt back a little, with the result that Tristan's sword slipped downwards and caught Giglain's horse in the neck and cut right through it without difficulty, for Sir Tristan was a very strong knight. The horse fell to the ground, dead, and the knight flew down beside it, without however being unduly hurt, as the blow had not struck home. Sir Tristan replaced his sword in the scabbard and, seeing that he was rid of Sir Giglain, he continued on his way and rode off towards the forest, lamenting so bitterly that anyone who heard him would have considered it a great marvel.

King Mark was standing by one of the windows of his palace when this blow was struck in such a manner, and he had seen distinctly how Giglain had stopped Sir Tristan and how Sir Tristan had rid himself of him by means of a single blow. The palace was quite near there so that he had a clear view of the incident; and he saw that Sir Tristan had ridden off towards the forest and Giglain had remained on foot in the middle of the road. He called a squire of his who was beside him and said to him:

'Go quickly and take one of my horses to that knight who has remained on foot and help him to mount; tell him that I wish him to come to me so that I can find out why he stopped the knight who is riding off there.'

The youth immediately carried out the King's command; he mounted without delay and took a good horse to Giglain, who was still quite stunned by the mighty blow he had received. And the youth straightaway said to him:

'Sir, my lord King Mark greets you and sends you this horse to replace your own which was struck dead, as he himself witnessed clearly. Mount and come to see him, for he would very much like you to do so.'

Giglain did not delay any longer, but mounted the horse without dawdling and thanked the king for this present. And the squire who saw the damaged helmet and the horse lying there dead, and all of it done by a single blow, was so amazed that he could not refrain from exclaiming:

'In God's name, Sir Knight, you were vigorously struck, and this blow was not dealt by a child! If the sword hadn't slipped, that would have been the end of you; and from what I can see I can truthfully say that anyone who waits for the blow of a knight whom he knows capable of striking as hard as that would not be very sensible. But what quarrel was there between you?'

Giglain who was still quite dazed as a result of the blow made no reply whatsoever, but went straight towards the city, and asked the squire where he could find the King. And he replied:

'In his palace amongst his barons.'

Thereupon Giglain set off and rode through Tintagel as far as the palace, and dismounted.

When he had come before the King, he greeted him, and the King returned his greeting very courteously, and received him with great honour, making him sit with the other knights; but, to be sure, prior to that he had ordered him to be disarmed. The King had the helmet brought before him, and when he had looked at it for a time he began to think, and then after a while he spoke and said that the knight had been dealt a fierce blow. And the squire stepped forward and said to the King:

'My lord, that's not all there is to it; you should know that with this same blow he cut right through the horse's neck all in one go without stopping.'

'Sir Knight,' said the King, 'is the squire telling the truth?'

'Yes, my lord,' replied Giglain, 'he's not lying at all. The blow was such, so help me God, that I'm still quite amazed at it.'

'Upon my word,' said the King, 'the blow was strong and weighty, and was not dealt by a child's hand. I declare openly and want everyone here to know it: Tristan, my nephew, struck this blow. There can be no doubt that he has been staying amongst us. We have not been sufficiently on our guard since he has been in our midst and we knew nothing about it. Nevertheless, Sir Knight, tell me, what caused the quarrel to break out between the two of you?'

And he told him everything word for word, concealing nothing. When King Mark heard that Tristan was riding off in this fashion and had parted from Queen Iseut greatly vexed, and that she had become angry with him for some reason, he was delighted and overjoyed. He would have been only too pleased if the Queen felt as much ill-will towards Sir Tristan as he himself did; then he would be able to avenge himself on him by some means and put him to death.

The King was pleased at the Queen's anger, but on the other hand he was very upset that Tristan had been in Tintagel without his knowing it. It was highly unlikely, so he thought to himself, that Tristan had not slept with the Queen, and King Mark felt shamed and humiliated thereby. He no longer knew what to do: he had truly thought that the Queen was so well guarded that it would have been impossible for Sir Tristan to get in without his knowing it. And since he had gained entry despite all the guards he had placed there, he no longer knew what to do. He could not see the point of his vigilance any more, since Sir Tristan was able to get in despite all the guards he had placed there.

King Mark was very distressed, all the more so because of his love for Queen Iseut, for he knew well that if Sir Tristan had parted from her in anger, she would be grief-stricken and unhappy. All those who were around him noticed straightaway that he was exceedingly upset, but no one dared to say a word to him or to offer him any comfort. He was very sorrowful and downcast at the realization that Sir Tristan had been with Queen Iseut, and it caused him great anguish and made him completely lose his mind, since he loved the Queen very deeply.

When Audret, who spoke to the King more frankly than any other Cornish knight, saw him so distressed, he went up to him and said in order to comfort him a little:

'My lord, why are you upsetting yourself? If Sir Tristan has been in our midst and we didn't know anything about it, we shouldn't be blamed: so many knights come to your court from this country and from others that it's only too easy for one who wanted to conceal himself to arrive among all the rest without being noticed. If you feel ill-will towards Sir Tristan, you can avenge yourself on him soon enough; he's not far from here. Were you to send ten knights after him, there's no way he could escape you. They would seize him by main force; he would be unable to defend himself. And once they've captured him and brought him back, you can put him to death by any means you wish. That's my advice; I can't see a better way of avenging yourself on Sir Tristan.'

When the King heard these words, he began to smile with displeasure, and after a while he spoke and said:

'Audret, you've caught Sir Tristan very quickly! Tristan has become a child for us to catch him as easily as you describe! By my faith, I don't think that even the gift of the whole of Cornwall would induce you to face Sir Tristan with ten of the best knights you could find there, all of you armed, if it were stipulated that you couldn't take to flight when you wanted, provided that Sir Tristan was well equipped with all his armour and mounted on horseback and holding his sword in his hand. What is he afraid of? He doesn't fear king or court; he doesn't fear any man alive. And why should I conceal it from you? I tell you openly that Tristan is the man for whom I feel the most mortal hatred in the world, and were I to say anything else, I would be telling a blatant lie. If anyone wanted to search the whole world, I don't think he would be able to find a knight as full of prowess as Tristan, with the exception of Lancelot of the Lake, the son of King Ban of Benoïc. He is at the present time

considered the best knight in the world and yet, so help me God,
I doubt whether he is as valiant as my nephew Tristan. What
more shall I say? It was a great misfortune and misadventure,
more for me than for anyone else, that such animosity and
rancour ever broke out between me and Sir Tristan. As God is
my witness, if Sir Tristan had as much regard for me and loved
me as much as he did on the day he killed the Morholt of Ireland
to redeem the tribute of Cornwall, I would truly think, on
account of his great valour and the noble chivalry which God has
bestowed on him more than on any other man, that I had the
whole world in my power just because of him, and I would fully
expect to place him in control of the whole world in my lifetime.
Now you can see what I've lost as a result of the discord between
us. He is an impoverished knight, and I am an unhappy king. The
day I married Iseut was when all my misfortunes befell me; she
caused the dissension between us, as you know well.'

After these words which the King spoke concerning his
nephew, there was none so bold as to talk about Sir Tristan,
except that everyone there agreed with what the King had said.
Audret kept quiet and made no comment at all, and bitterly
regretted ever having mentioned Tristan at that point, for he was
consumed with anguish and envy that the King had made such a
long speech about Tristan. There was no one on earth he hated
as much as Sir Tristan, although he was his first cousin; and this
hatred was not caused by anything Sir Tristan had done to
deserve it, but by Audret's jealousy because he saw that everyone
praised him for his chivalry and for all his other qualities.

As a result of the King's words about Sir Tristan, the rumour
spread throughout Tintagel that the Queen and Sir Tristan had
been together without the King's knowledge. The people of
Tintagel went in crowds to see the blow he had given the horse,
and when they had seen it they said that it was undoubtedly Sir
Tristan who had passed there.

As Tristan is riding through the forest weeping and lamenting, he meets
a messenger-girl sent to Cornwall by Palamedes who suspects that
Tristan has gone back there, since rumour had it that he had left Brittany.
If the maiden were to find him, Palamedes would go to Cornwall to do
battle with him in spite of the promise he had previously made Iseut not
to return while she was there. For more details concerning this episode,

one should consult the 'Story of Tristan' by Sir Luce of Gat Castle.*
Palamedes remembers his promise well, but such is his mortal hatred
of Tristan that he feels impelled to fight him to the death wherever he
may be.

The young girl, who does not recognize Tristan, greets him, but he
does not see her or hear a word she says until she has addressed him three
times. She tries in vain to comfort him and asks him who he is. He replies
that he is called Unhappy Wretch; this is the only name he can give her.
Before leaving him she enquires whether he can tell her any news about
Sir Tristan, King Mark's nephew. Tristan thinks she has been sent by
Lancelot, but when she denies this, he suspects that it must be Palamedes,
and tells her that Tristan is dead: he died three days ago, struck down by
Kahedin. Then he rides off at great speed.

The girl continues her journey to Tintagel to confirm the truth of this
news. When she comes near the city, she sees the dead horse and the
crowd of people who have come to look at it; they tell her that it was
Tristan who had just struck this blow and was riding off into the forest
on a black horse. She realizes at once that it was Tristan she had met. She
decides to spend the night in Tintagel, and to ride back into the forest in
the morning and look for Tristan until she finds him.

The story relates that after Sir Tristan had left the messenger-
girl, he continued on his way and rode as far as the thick of the
forest. There he dismounted, sighing from the depths of his heart,
so distraught that he nearly went out of his mind. He lamented
and wept and groaned out loud, and when he had stood for a
long while beside his horse, he said in tears:

'Ah! God, why was I born to spend all the days of my life in so
much grief and torment as I have endured until now? Ah! God,
was there ever a knight or a man who suffered such great pain and
anguish as I have suffered for love of my lady Iseut? And now she
has rewarded me by completely forsaking me and retaining
Kahedin! God! What made her do such a thing? What can I say?
I'm done for, without fail. Iseut is killing me on the one hand,
and, on the other, Love is totally hostile to me. Iseut and Love
are undoubtedly causing my death. I am mortally struck by a
twofold ill.'

When he had lamented for a long time, wailing and weeping
bitterly, he disarmed himself, throwing his helmet on one side
and his sword on the other, and said to himself that never on any
day of his life would he wear armour or do anything other than

grieve, so much so that it would cause his death within a short while. Only death was acceptable to him, for only by dying, so he said, could he alleviate his suffering. Sir Tristan was exceedingly distressed and upset. He grieved so much and lamented so bitterly that anyone who saw him at that point would have taken him for a madman. He cried and shrieked so loudly that the forest resounded with it far and wide. He cursed himself and scratched his face and called at the top of his voice:

'Come to me, death! Why are you delaying so long? Here is Tristan, the wretched, who begs you with all his heart to come and take him in order to put an end to his suffering, from which he cannot escape in any other way. Ah! death, don't keep me waiting! Relieve me of this pain which I have undoubtedly endured longer than was good for me.'

Sir Tristan grieved and lamented bitterly, as I have described. He shrieked and cried with such great force that the sound of it carried a long way.

At this point a knight was riding along the main road through the forest all by himself, mounted on a good horse and fully armed. He was making for Tintagel, and had in his company neither squire nor servant, lady nor maiden, but rode quite alone by the light of the moon, which had already risen and was shining brightly, much facilitating his journey. When he heard the sound of Sir Tristan lamenting so loudly, he stopped in the middle of the road in order to hear more clearly what it could be. After he had listened for a while he realized that it was a man who was wailing, or so it sounded to him, and he was sure that he was in dire need of help. Then he began to think what he should do, whether to go in search of the man who was lamenting or continue on his way towards Tintagel. In the end he decided to go and find out what it signified and why this man was wailing with such anguish, and he turned the head of his horse in that direction.

When he had come up to him, he saw that Sir Tristan had sat down under a tree and was still lamenting as loudly and as bitterly as before. The knight scrutinized him for a long time to see if he could make out who he was before he spoke to him. He could distinguish clearly from the way Sir Tristan was sitting that he was one of the biggest knights he had ever seen, but however hard he looked at him he was unable to recognize him. Then he stepped forward a bit, still on horseback, and spoke so loudly that Tristan could hear him distinctly:

'May God save you, Sir Knight, and send you joy and comfort, for, it seems to me, that's what you need more than anything else.'

Sir Tristan raised his head when he heard the knight's greeting, but he was very annoyed at having been found in this way: he would have wished to be in some place where no one would ever see him so that he could the sooner end his life in sorrow and in tears. After a while he replied, doleful and downcast, and not as courteously as he was wont:

'What do you want, Sir Knight? What are you asking of me? What are you looking for? Why have you come here?'

'Sir, your loud lamenting which I heard from far away made me come here to find out what it could be, for I assure you that anyone who heard your loud wails from afar would consider it a great marvel.'

'Sir Knight,' replied Sir Tristan, 'if I am lamenting bitterly, no one knowing my predicament ought to marvel at it. I should tell you that the reason for my grief is so marvellous that nothing on earth could alleviate my grief until I die. There is no comfort for my grief; it will never cease until the hour that my heart stops beating. Now I've told you all about my grief, and you can go off when you like; you won't learn anything else about it from me, now or at any other time.'

When the knight heard these words he felt even more sorry for Sir Tristan than before, since he realized that his great sorrow and distress and the excessive grief he felt made him say what he did. However, in order to see if he could give him a measure of comfort, he replied:

'Ah! Sir Knight, for the love of God and for pity's sake, don't take such great grief upon yourself—you could easily die of it; and if you were to die in this way, no knight in the world would ever have committed a more cowardly act, for I can think of no greater cravenness in any man than to let himself die of grief.'

'Sir Knight,' replied Sir Tristan, 'you speak with a sound mind; I can see that you have no idea of the anguish that grips my heart. You don't feel what I feel; if you did, you would speak differently.

May God in his mercy protect you from feeling the pain which fills my heart. We have had quite a lengthy conversation together, but it has been a strange one, since by the grace of God you are fit and well, and happy and joyful as a knight should be, whereas I am sorrowful and unhappy and my heart is filled with sadness; and moreover I am in the grip of such pain as will not leave me until I die. For God's sake, go away and let me carry on lamenting. The mere fact of seeing you here greatly annoys and irritates me. Go away! May God give you good fortune.'

When the knight heard these words he began to weep so bitterly that he was unable to reply or to say a word, so that Sir Tristan could not fail to realize that his tears were heartfelt. At this point Sir Tristan began to smile and replied:

'Upon my word, Sir Knight, I see you weeping, and I have to laugh. But, believe me, there was a time when I laughed and rejoiced at what is now making you weep. Your tears are caused by pity and compassion, but God alone knows what mine are caused by. You are weeping because you feel sorry for me, but that is not a very good reason for weeping. Your tears are merely superficial, but mine are so deep-rooted that no joy can affect them.* Nothing can allay them except death.'

Hearing these words, the knight recognized clearly that Sir Tristan was one of the most discerning knights he had come across for some time. Then he said to himself that he would dismount. Sir Tristan speedily ran towards him and said:

'Sir Knight, I beg you not to dismount. If you want to dismount, you can do so somewhere else. Leave me alone here where you found me to carry on my lamenting. And if you want to stay in this particular place so much that you feel you must, I shall straightaway mount my horse which is nearby, and you can stay. I'll go off to another place, and you'll remain here all alone, for you may as well know that at this point there is no company which pleases me.'

'Ah! for God's sake,' said the knight, 'don't move! I would rather not dismount than make you leave here because I had annoyed you. I promise I won't get off my horse.'

'Then I won't move from here,' said Sir Tristan.

Thereupon the knight stopped short and said that henceforth he would not dismount there since he did not want him to do so.

After a while the knight said to Sir Tristan:

'For the love of God, Sir Knight, why on earth won't you tell me the reason for your unhappiness, or take comfort from anything I've said to you, but rather are all set on wanting to die of grief and determined not to find any other way out or do anything to help yourself? Accordingly I say that this bitter grief you have taken upon yourself is one of the greatest marvels I've ever heard about. After leaving you I shall not see you again for a long time, to the best of my belief, and perhaps never. I therefore beg you as much as one knight can beg another that you tell me your name; and let me assure you that I've never before met a knight whom I so much wanted to know about as you. But because I've heard from your own lips that at his point I won't find out anything about what caused your grief, I shall refrain from asking you. If only you would tell me your name, I should consider myself well satisfied; that is all I ask of you.'

When Sir Tristan heard the knight speak to him so reasonably, he became less antagonistic towards him, for he realized that he had spoken thus out of genuine goodwill. Then he replied and said:

'Sir Knight, I see clearly that you marvel at my state more than at anything you've seen for a long while, and my reply to you is that I marvel at you no less, but more so. And indeed, my condition is such, and so greatly to be marvelled at, that when the news of it will spread throughout the world after my death, all those who hear of it and who will be told the news will say without reservation that never in the reign of King Arthur was there so great a marvel as befell me, and people throughout the world will lament about it for evermore; nor will any brave knight hear about my death in times to come who will not be upset about it. And I assure you that my enemies will be no less distressed by it than my friends.'

When the knight heard these words, he immediately replied and said to Sir Tristan:

'Sir, what shall I say? So help me God, the longer I hear you speak, the more eager I am to know who you are. For the love of God and out of courtesy, tell me your name, if you can divulge it to a foreign knight.'

'So help you God,' said Sir Tristan, 'who are you who want to know my name so much? Tell me yours first of all, and afterwards, when I know you better than I do now, I may find you such that I shall tell you mine, or, on the other hand, I may find you such that I won't tell it to you under any circumstances.'

The knight replied and said:

'I assure you, sir, that if I find out your name as soon as you will find out mine, I shall know it immediately. I'll tell you my name, since you wish to know it: let me inform you that I am called Fergus.'

This Fergus was without doubt a knight full of prowess, exceedingly brave and bold, and he had been Sir Tristan's companion at the time when Sir Tristan and Queen Iseut were led to the fire, when King Mark wanted to put them both to death. And whoever would like to know more about this incident* than I am telling you, how Fergus had been Sir Tristan's companion and how fond Sir Tristan was of him, he should read the 'Story of Sir Tristan'; there he will be able to find out everything about it.

When Sir Tristan heard that it was Fergus who was speaking to him, one of the knights in the world whom he had found to be most noble and courteous for as long as they had been companions together, he fell down backwards. He was unable to make any reply, good or bad, such was the great sorrow and the great distress which filled his heart. However, after a while he rose to his feet, sighing from the depths of his heart, and replied weeping very tenderly:

'Sir Fergus, dear friend, I wish you a very warm welcome! I want you to know that you're one of the men I most wished to see at this stage. It's been a long time since I last saw you. I'm very happy that you've come. Praise be to God who has brought you here at this point. What more shall I say? Since I see you here before me, so dear a friend and so loyal as you always were to me all the while we were together, my heart doesn't allow me to conceal my identity from you any longer and I have no wish to do so. I can say no more. I am Tristan, your friend, the most wretched knight who ever wore a shield. I am Tristan who was born in an evil hour, and in an evil hour set eyes on Iseut, for because of her I shall die before my time. I am Tristan who never experienced anything but sadness.* I have spent my life in sadness, and in sadness and sorrow I am living and ending my life. It was a great misfortune and a great sorrow that I was born to lead a life so full of anguish.'

After he had spoken these words, he began to lament again as bitterly as he had done before.

When Fergus heard that it was Sir Tristan who was lamenting so bitterly, the knight he loved most in the world and in whom he had found the greatest courtesy and kindness, he did not delay any longer, but threw his shield down on the path and his lance as well, and took his helmet off his head and threw that down. And when he had done this, he jumped off his horse and went straight up to Sir Tristan and kissed his leg which was still covered in armour, and began to weep so bitterly that no one who saw him would have said that his tears were not genuine; indeed, he was in such distress that he was unable to utter a word. After a while when he could speak, he said in tears:

'Ah! sir, what are you doing? Why are you upsetting yourself? Why are you inflicting this upon yourself? For the love of God and out of courtesy tell me what has caused this grief. Tell me what's wrong on the understanding that I shall do all I can to help you in accordance with your honour, if no other knight of my standing can help you.'

On hearing these words, Sir Tristan who was so upset that he almost burst with grief replied as best he could:

'Fergus,' he said, 'dear friend, there's no doubt that you're one of the men I love most in the world and one whom in the past I trusted most, and still trust and shall do until the end; and for that reason I shall tell you what you ask. I would have you know that this grief I'm suffering was caused by my lady Iseut whom I loved so much, as you are well aware, and for whom I've endured such great torment and pain and sorrow that to my knowledge there is not at the present time a single knight in the world who could endure so much to sustain his love. But now as a result of it I have come to my death, and for such a poor reason as I shall relate to you.'

However, as soon as he had spoken these words, he changed his mind about his intentions and said:

'Fergus, dear friend, I repent of having wanted to tell you this. It was a foolish thought I had in mind and a very base act I intended to commit—which would have gone against me more than against anyone else—that I ever wanted to speak ill of my lady Iseut whom I have loved with all my heart above all earthly things. God forbid that I should do such a thing! I would rather lose my head than say anything bad about her. If she has been guilty of a misdeed which she should not have done and has acted wrongly towards me, I readily forgive her. She may yet regret what she's done, more as a result of kindness on her part than any good that I may have in me. I shall stop talking about her now, for I won't speak ill of my lady under any circumstances. I shall bewail the misfortune I'm having to bear and keep up my plaint until my grief ceases somehow.'

'Ah! sir, for the love of God,' said Fergus, 'tell me what has caused this grief, and I assure you I shall find some means of alleviating it.'

'Fergus,' he replied, 'what is there to say? At this point I can't tell you anything more than that this grief is caused by Iseut; and you should know that it has gripped my heart so fiercely that it will remain lodged there until I die. Don't ask me anything else about my state because I won't tell you any more. If you can find an effective means of helping me after what I've told you, I shall be only too pleased.'

'Dear friend,' said Fergus, 'from what I've heard and understood, I can see that you're exceedingly distressed. Moreover, since you've made it clear to me that you won't tell me any more than you have done, I'm extremely upset about it, because I don't know how I can help you in this matter if you don't tell me the whole truth concerning your predicament. And I promise you', continued Fergus, 'that tomorrow before daybreak I shall see to it that I shall be told the whole truth, for I declare that I shall go straight from here to my lady Iseut who by her grace has such regard for me—not because of any merit on my part, but solely as a result of her nobility—that I don't think she'll conceal anything about this matter from me. Then I shall be able to help both you and her, which I can't do at present.'

Sir Tristan remained silent and said nothing when he heard these words. He would have wished that Fergus was already before Iseut in order to describe to her the lamentable state in which he, Fergus, had clearly seen Tristan to be. Fergus talked to Sir Tristan about many things, but he never replied, instead continuing to brood and to sigh often from the depths of his heart. Never thereafter for the rest of the night did he reply a single word, nor do anything other than think of the one he never forgot. He did not sleep all night, but kept on thinking in the way I have described. And Fergus, who had come upon him as the story has related, was not so bold as to address any words to him when he saw that he did not wish to answer. But in one respect Fergus had a very good effect on his friend in so far as Tristan stopped lamenting on account of him; otherwise he would have kept it up all night as he had begun. But in order that Fergus would not blame him for it he controlled himself as best he could.

At dawn next morning when the birds were beginning to sing here and there in the forest, Fergus said to Tristan:

'Sir, I want to leave here now and go to Tintagel to see Queen Iseut, and speak to her as you've asked me to do. You may be sure that I'll come back as soon as I can. For the love of God and out of courtesy I beg you to do one thing for me, and I entreat you to do it by the love you bear me, namely that you'll wait for me here all day long. I assure you I'll return this very day. And I tell you even more, for I promise you that I shall come back with definite news of my lady Queen Iseut, such as will bring you joy and comfort.'

'Fergus,' said Tristan, 'I know well that you love me greatly, and have done so for a very long time, not just now. Since you wish to go to Tintagel, go in God's name, and greet my lady on my behalf and tell her that she might have acted more loyally towards Tristan than she did. To the best of my knowledge I think you'll find me here, if you want to come back.'

And Fergus promised him faithfully that he would have little rest until he had returned. Thereupon he quickly went to his horse and mounted and rode off, and came to the highway which was not far from where Tristan was.

Tristan remained behind and started to lament again as soon as Fergus had left. Fergus sped along the main road through the forest, and as he was on the point of leaving the forest, he happened to meet the messenger-girl that Palamedes had sent to Cornwall, as the story has already related earlier on. When she saw Fergus approaching, she stopped in the middle of the road until he had come up to her. Then she greeted him, and he returned her greeting as politely as he knew how and asked her:

'Maiden, who are you?'

'Sir,' she replied, 'I'm a foreign maiden going about my business. But, for the love of God, could you tell me some news about a knight I'm seeking?'

'Maiden,' he said, 'who is this knight you're looking for?'

'He's a knight who's riding a black horse,' she answered. 'He left Tintagel last night and came into this forest, I'm sure of it. If you saw him somewhere, tell me for pity's sake, for I need to find him urgently.'

'Maiden,' said Fergus, 'what shield was the knight carrying?'

'Sir,' she replied, 'when I saw him he wasn't carrying a lance or a shield, I remember it well.'

Hearing this, Fergus realized that it was Tristan the young girl was looking for, and he truly thought that she was one of Queen Iseut's maidens and that the Queen had sent her into the forest to find Tristan. Fergus would have been delighted and overjoyed if this were the case. And because it really seemed to him that she must be one of Queen Iseut's maidens, he said to himself that he would do his best to instruct her how to find Tristan. Then he said to her:

'So help you God, maiden, do you know the identity of the knight you're asking about and looking for?'

'Why do you say that?' she enquired.

'Because', he replied, 'I fancy that I know who he is. I do believe it's Tristan you're seeking and think that my lady Queen Iseut is sending you with a message to him.'

'Whoever it is who's sending me as messenger,' said the young girl, 'I can confirm that it's Sir Tristan I'm seeking. For God's sake, if you know where he is, then tell me, for I need to find him urgently.'

'In God's name,' he answered, 'I shall direct you so well that you'll find him quite easily.'

Then he took her to a stream which led to a fountain not far away from there and said to her:

'Follow this stream until you come to the spot where the fountain rises, and you may be sure that this is where you'll find Sir Tristan, if he hasn't gone since I left him there a short while ago.

Now I've given you the information you wanted to have; now you for your part tell me what I'm going to ask you: shall I find King Mark in Tintagel when I get there?'

'No, you certainly won't. The King went hunting this morning in the Forest of Espinoie.* He didn't want to go into the Forest of Morroiz because he knows that Tristan is there at the moment, and his men advised him against it.'

Thereupon they parted from each other without any further delay. Fergus took the road straight to Tintagel, for he was very eager to speak to my lady Iseut. The young girl made her way into the forest following the instructions which Fergus had given her, and rode on until she came to the very spot where Tristan was sitting, so distressed that he almost died of sorrow. He lamented and grieved so bitterly that anyone who saw him then would have considered it a great marvel. As soon as the young girl caught sight of him, she dismounted as quietly as she could and attached her horse to a tree. Then she went up to Tristan and saw that he was so deep in thought that he was oblivious of everything except what was causing his unhappiness. The maiden stood in front of him for a long while, but he did not notice her and she did not dare to address him in case it made him angry. After a while he wept and wailed, and sighed repeatedly, wringing his hands. And when he had gone on like this for a long time without saying a word, he exclaimed in great anguish:

'Help me, oh God! How great is my despair! Was there ever a man as basely betrayed as I was at this point?'

And after he had said this he fell silent and started to brood again.

The girl, seeing him so grief-stricken, stepped forward a little in order to speak to him and to ascertain if she could rouse him from these painful thoughts which, as she realized, were not doing him any good. And I should tell you that she was standing so near to him that she could easily have taken him by the hand, had she wanted to, and still he had not noticed her. When she had looked at him closely for a long time, she said to herself that he really was the most handsome and well-built knight she had ever seen in her whole life; to the best of her belief, it did not seem to her that God had fashioned a knight as good-looking as this one since he first created man. But she was of the opinion that he would have been much more handsome were it not for his pitiable state and for the great sorrow which filled his heart. Judging by what she could see, she said to herself that if it were not for the grievous thoughts which had taken hold of him and for his doleful face which was wet and stained by the tears pouring from his eyes, he was by far the most handsome knight God had ever created. She felt very upset and troubled about this brooding which kept him so downcast and melancholy.

The maiden looked at Sir Tristan very carefully. It made her very sorrowful and distressed to see him so sad. And because she would have liked to give him some reason to cheer up, she said:

'May God save you, sir!'

Sir Tristan, whose thoughts at that point were not joyous, did not hear the young girl, since his heart was elsewhere. He made no reply whatever, but continued to brood as before. Thereupon the maiden repeated more loudly:

'Sir Knight, may God protect you!'

Sir Tristan paid no heed to anything the girl said to him, since his thoughts were far away. He neither moved nor looked at her any more than if he had been dead, but continued to think; and after a time he sighed deeply.

'Lord God!' said the maiden, 'what can I do? This knight is thinking so intensely that I believe he'll die of it, so help me God, if someone doesn't rouse him from these thoughts by some means.'

Then she took Sir Tristan by the hand as gently as she could, for she was very anxious and afraid that he would be angry with her.

'Sir,' said the young girl, 'please stop this thinking now. You've thought long enough! No good can come of these thoughts henceforth, that's quite clear.'

At this Sir Tristan gave a start just as though he had woken up; and as he moved, he uttered a deep sigh like a man suffering great anguish, and looked at the maiden with exceeding wrath and displeasure, very annoyed that she had interrupted his thoughts. However, when he saw that it was a young girl who was standing before him, he wondered what she wanted, and who had brought her there and who had sent her. If a knight or a squire had thus roused him from his meditation and deprived him of his thoughts as this maiden had done, he would have been extremely angry; but because she was a maiden he did not dare to say anything, except that he replied:

'Ah! maiden, it was wrong of you to disturb me in my meditation. Not that I don't wish I could already have ended it in some way, either through my death or through my life; I don't care which comes first, for henceforth I love one as much as the other.'

'Ah! sir,' said the young girl, 'it's not right for you to keep brooding like this. I can see plainly that these thoughts are so harmful to you that they could easily bring about your death, if you keep them up. For that reason I advise you to abandon them and to turn your heart to other things; it's not fitting for any worthy man to fill his heart with such thoughts as will make him die in shame. No man can commit an act of greater cowardice or foolishness than to kill himself in this way.'

'Maiden,' said Sir Tristan, 'I've heard clearly what you've said to me, and I see and know well that you're saying it for my good. But what use is it to me? No exhortation and no words that one could henceforth say to me could ever be of any use. These thoughts which have gripped my heart are so deeply engrained in me that they can never leave me until I die. Go away and continue your journey, so help you God, and I shall remain here and return to my thoughts and, please God, bring them to a conclusion, whatever that may be.'

When the maiden heard these words, she began to weep very tenderly; and Sir Tristan straightaway started thinking again as he had done before.

'My Lord God!' exclaimed the young girl, 'what's going to happen? Can't I shake this knight out of these anguished thoughts which keep him in such torment? Indeed, I shall, please God!'

Then she stepped forward once again and took Sir Tristan by the hand and said to him:

'Ah! sir, for the love of God, do stop this thinking now! You've kept it up long enough.'

'Maiden,' said Sir Tristan, 'so help me God, the way you're acting isn't right. You're trying to make me do something which God himself doesn't want. Upon my word, do you believe that God wishes me ever to have comfort? No, he definitely doesn't,

I assure you. For that reason I beg you, as much as a knight can beg a maiden, to leave me alone at this point and let me carry on my grieving.'

'Ah! I beseech you, noble knight,' said the girl, 'for the love of God, don't kill yourself in this way, but have pity on yourself.'

'Maiden,' said Sir Tristan, 'I see clearly that I can't hold out against you!'

Then he jumped up and went to his horse and mounted, and went off to a different part of the forest where he thought the maiden would not be able to find him. [§§ 836–63 of vol. iii]

XVI

TRISTAN'S MADNESS

THUS Sir Tristan rode on until he came to a tower near which was a very beautiful and pleasant fountain. And I should tell you that in front of this tower Sir Tristan formerly fought against Palamedes for love of my lady Iseut at the time when Palamedes had abducted Queen Iseut from King Mark's court, as Sir Luce de Gat relates in his book.* And whoever wants to find out about this event in detail, should consult the great 'Story of Sir Tristan', for there Sir Luce de Gat describes word for word how Sir Tristan fought with Palamedes and how Queen Iseut out of fear for Sir Tristan wisely stopped the battle and sent Palamedes to the Kingdom of Logres.

As soon as Sir Tristan came there and saw the tower where he had already been previously and where he had stayed three whole days* after his combat with Palamedes, he immediately recalled this fight.

'Ah! Palamedes,' he said, 'valiant knight, dauntless and bold, the best and the strongest against whom I ever did battle, this is the very spot where we fought each other. Here you undoubtedly showed me the full extent of your prowess. If I had died then, in that battle, at the hand of a brave knight like you, it would have been a better fate for me than anything that will ever happen to me now. That would have been an honour, whereas now I suffer great dishonour, and shall be forced to die of grief. I declare that this is the greatest misfortune which could ever befall a knight. What should I tell you, Palamedes? I can truly say that never on any day in my life did I feel such great joy and such great gladness as when my lady was delivered from your hands at this very spot. Here my happiness was fulfilled so completely that never before did I know with such certitude what happiness was; but here I knew it without fail. And because it seems to me that my joy was more complete in this spot than in any other, I declare that in this spot I shall end my grief, and here my body will have its last sleep and its last agony.'

Then Sir Tristan dismounted without any further delay and removed the bridle and the saddle from his horse and let it go off into the forest wherever it wanted, declaring that henceforth he would not mount a horse again. Then he took off his mail leggings which he was still wearing. And when he saw that he was completely unarmed, he went straight to the fountain and sat down there and started to lament again as bitterly and as ardently as before.

Tristan remains sitting there like this all day long, regretting Palamedes and Iseut. He has eaten no food for two days.

The maiden looks for Tristan everywhere, and that evening she comes upon him by the fountain. Once again she tries to comfort him, and once again Tristan tells her to leave him in peace. She decides to let him be for a while and goes to spend the night in the nearby tower where she is welcomed by a noble lady who is a widow.

Tristan continues to lament for eight whole days, neither eating nor drinking, although the girl regularly places food in front of him. She stays with him all day long, trying in vain to console him, but returns to the tower at night. When she goes to him on the morning of the eighth day she is alarmed to see that his skin has become as black and blue as if he had been beaten up in a tournament, and she fears for his life.

The previous evening the maiden had found a harp in one of the rooms of the tower and had begun to play. The lady tells her that it had been left by Tristan* when he had stayed there, and she could vouch for the fact that he could play better than anyone in the world. The maiden decides to play to him to see if that would comfort him. Tristan does indeed stop his wailing and asks her to sing his lays, of which he has written three, as she knows well: the 'Lay of Tears', composed in the boat after his battle with the Morholt; the 'Grievous Philtre', after he had drunk the potion; and the 'Joys of Love', written while the lovers were together in the Forest of Morroiz.* She sings the first two; Tristan compliments her on her skill and asks her to sing the third, but she makes him first promise to sing a lay himself after she has finished. He tells her to come back the following morning, then he will play to her, but not before; and the rest of that day he never says another word. She spends the night as usual with the widowed lady to whom she never reveals what she does during the day.

Next morning at daybreak the maiden, who had not forgotten what Sir Tristan had said and promised, rose and set out, and made her way to where Sir Tristan was still sitting as usual in front of the fountain. As soon as she came up to him, she wished him good day and good fortune, and he returned her greeting.

'Maiden,' he said, 'now I'm quite prepared to fulfil the promise I made you yesterday evening.'

'Sir,' she replied, 'many thanks.'

And immediately he took up his harp and began to tune it to the best of his ability. And when he had tuned it correctly to harmonize with the song he wanted to sing, he said to the girl:

'Maiden, did you ever hear anyone mention the "Mortal Lay"?'

'No, sir,' she answered, 'I didn't, so help me God. I never heard anyone speak of it.'

'That's not surprising, maiden,' he said, 'since no one but myself has ever sung it. I only composed it last night; it's about my suffering and my death. And because I wrote it in anticipation of my end, I called it "Mortal Lay"; I derived the name from the event.'

After he had said this, he began to weep very tenderly, and in the midst of his tears he began to play the harp so melodiously that anyone who heard it would have declared that it would be impossible to hear a sweeter melody. And weeping like this he started his lay as follows:*

> I've made many a song and lay
> But now abandon all I play.
> Here is my final legacy,
> This last lay, for Love's killing me.
>
> This is my very last lament.
> Clearly my flame of life is spent,
> My flesh bruised by grief's punishment
> As, singing, I voice my complaint.
>
> Joy has no place in this singing,
> Rather with sorrow beginning.
> Love treats me far too cruelly
> In taking harsh revenge on me.
>
> I rail against Iseut, oh she
> Whose service turns to slavery,
> Whose worship I regret, for I
> Now dying, don't deserve to die!

Those knights who're on adventure bent,
Don't suffer Love's predicament;
In love they're far more fortunate
Than Tristan, the disconsolate.

Yet Love for me's too much to bear,
Finishing life in black despair.
Love's the beginning and end of me,
Killed by my own heart's loyalty.

While others sing at ease, engrossed
In love, I weep; trapped by the boast
That now ensures my death: Tristan
Loved more than any other man.

Death and Love have laid me low,
And transformed my joy to woe.
Before day dawns they'll cause my end,
And helplessly my head will bend.

Alas, who cares that I must die?
None will recall me with a sigh.
My knightly deeds are swept away
By Death who holds me in his sway.

Though often I've escaped and run
When to help me there was none,
With Death and Love my bitter foes,
Even King Porrus had lesser woes.*

Ah Lancelot, my dear sweet friend,
It is my wish someone will send
This lay to you. Love has killed me,
Its promise broken utterly.

I feel I suffer, for Love's sake,
Like one who let a poor cold snake
Take refuge on his breast; and thence
Was given death in recompense.

I've welcomed from the very start
The love I've honoured in my heart:
No arrow kills me of hard wood
But rather Love's ingratitude.

The noble Guinevere is not
My bane, nor fever makes me hot.
It is Iseut who causes this,
No reason but her wantonness.*

How can I blame Love, how express
Reproach for causing my distress?—
When all too soon my lips are numb.
Love's deadly venom makes me dumb.

Against each leaf, however little,
Which lack of wind makes wet or brittle,*
Love wields its power. Please God let
Love, on my death, feel deep regret.

What paltry chivalry Love shows
When it attacks a corpse! God knows
My strength is gone, and all my beauty.
I'm dead. What can Love get from me?

There's little profit Love will gain
Out of either my death or pain.
Love knows that I do not pretend.
This last affliction is the end.*

All of my strength has diminished,
Sorrow by sorrow replenished,
My grief and pain is now complete.
Tristan is sounding the retreat.

In Love's harsh prison I now lie.
Its cruel judgments make me die.
Can Love do more? It's been my end.
What's left of me may God defend.

Adieu, Iseut! And Love, adieu!
I'll make no more protests to you.
Because I loved so well, death's near.
But I have nothing else to fear.

Iseut, who once was my delight,
As I engage in this grim fight,
I beg you, my sweet enemy,
After my death, remember me!

I give Iseut my benison,
I, Tristan, give it, who is gone,
Who would have risked his life and limb
To gratify Iseut's least whim.

But since Iseut has been untrue,
All that is good now fails me too.
Death pounces on me suddenly—
I feel its final grip on me!

Once I was used to venery,
Now I'm the quarry. Death hunts me.
Death is mirrored in my face.
Its last assault is taking place.

No man on earth loved more than I.
I still love more, and that is why
Death appears like a dark doorway
Opened to me by this 'Mortal Lay'.

Feeling and reason, ears and eyes,
Even the soul which never dies
I gave to Love, and so I am
A lion slaughtered by a lamb.

And all of you who pass this way*
Come here: so that each one can say
If there were ever woes like those
Of Tristan in his final throes.

Song and tears in a single breath
Bring me right to the point of death.
I sing and weep. To God the just
My soul and spirit I entrust.

When Tristan had finished singing his lay as I have described, so beautiful and so sweet that no one could find fault with it, he fell silent and said no more, and began to lament again as bitterly as before, saying:

'God, what am I waiting for? Why don't I kill myself here and now? Then my suffering would be finished at one go.'

And saying this, he stood up and looked all around him to see if he could find a sword with which to kill himself. When he realized that it was impossible, his heart was filled with such great rage and his head with such great madness that he lost his mind and his memory so completely that he did not know what he was doing. He no longer knew whether he was Tristan or not; he no longer remembered my lady Iseut nor King Mark, nor indeed anything he had ever done. He went running about through the Forest of Morroiz, now here, now there, crying and shrieking like a mad animal. And for that reason the maiden soon lost him, for she did not know which way he had gone, and this upset and distressed her greatly. She searched for him far and wide for a long time, but there was no likelihood of her finding him unless she discovered his whereabouts by a lucky chance.

She spent a whole fortnight looking for him all over the Morroiz, but when she realized that she would not find him, she said to herself that henceforth she would return to Logres and tell Palamedes all she knew about Tristan; and then he could decide whether he wanted to remain in the Kingdom of Logres or come to Cornwall.

The young girl returns to Logres and finds Palamedes near Camelot. She tells him all she has learnt about our hero: how the first time she did not recognize him and asked him for news of Tristan and he pretended that Tristan had been killed by Kahedin; then she describes in detail all her subsequent encounters with him, adding that she does not hold out much hope for his survival. As regards Iseut, the girl says she was told that the Queen was ill in bed and had done nothing but lament bitterly ever since Tristan's departure: many people thought she would die of grief. From what the girl has told him, Palamedes suspects that Kahedin is the cause of the lovers' disagreement, and decides to go to Cornwall to try and see the Queen. He sets out five days later, accompanied by a squire and by the same maiden. [§§ 864–75 of vol. iii]

XVII

ISEUT'S DESPAIR

IN this part the story relates that when Sir Tristan had left Queen Iseut, greatly distressed and upset as I have described, and when the Queen who loved him more than anyone else on earth, even herself, saw him part from her with such grief and anguish, no one who knows about love's torment should ask what it signifies.*

'Alas!' she exclaimed, 'what shall I do? Since I've lost Sir Tristan, my dear beloved, and for such a poor reason, all I ask of God is my death. Ah! Kahedin, you have utterly destroyed me. Your betrayal has broken my heart, for through you I've lost Sir Tristan whom I loved more than myself. God! how fortunate I was to have had my dear beloved here with me! He could have stayed indefinitely without anyone knowing about it, and now I've completely lost him! Ah! Kahedin, cursed be the hour that you ever came to Cornwall! Your arrival has been my undoing.'

The Queen, who was so anguished and distressed that she almost went mad with grief, did not know what to do. She found no other comfort than to revile and curse herself.

While she was lamenting in this way, Brangain appeared who was none too happy to see her display such sorrow. As soon as the Queen caught sight of her, she cried out like one deranged and demented:

'Brangain, I'm done for, this is the end of me! The worst has happened. Tristan, my beloved, has left me. What shall I say to you, Brangain? If I lose him like this, so help me God, I shall kill myself with my own two hands. There is no other way out that I can take.'

'Ah! for the love of God, I beseech you, my lady,' said Brangain, 'don't upset yourself so much, but tell me what's wrong; and if I can do anything to help, I will.'

Thereupon the Queen sat down and started tearing at her face. And when after a time she spoke and answered Brangain, she felt such anguish and such sorrow that she nearly went out of her mind with grief and suffering.

'Brangain, what shall I tell you? Do you remember the letter sent to me by Kahedin, the son of King Hoel of Brittany, he who loved me so much that he ended up ill in bed almost at death's door? I received the letter and read it and then showed it to you. I might well have been very angry about it, as you yourself were aware, and this would have got him into serious trouble; but I refrained for Sir Tristan's sake, whom I loved and still love more than all the rest of the world, because I knew for certain that Sir Tristan was very fond of Kahedin and would have been exceedingly distressed if he had died in this country. And since Sir Tristan had brought him here, I comforted him by means of the letter which I told you I would write; and you more or less advised me to write it. As a result of this letter which I sent Kahedin because I didn't want Sir Tristan, my beloved, to be upset, I am plunged into despair, and so broken-hearted and grief-stricken that I shall never feel happy again as long as I live. To my misfortune and sorrow Sir Tristan found this letter today, I don't know by what misadventure. When he saw it, he was sure I had written it out of love for Kahedin, and told me that this was the end of him, he was inconsolable and would never again have joy or pleasure on any day of his life now that I had left him for Kahedin. Then he parted from me like a madman. Alas, I know for certain that he loves me so greatly and with such a deep love that he will die of grief and sorrow on account of this, since the letter he found convinced him that I was guilty of this act. It will make him die, I'm sure of it. But immediately afterwards I'm going to kill myself, so help me God.'

And when she had said this, she began to lament as bitterly as if she could see Sir Tristan himself dead in front of her.

Brangain was extremely upset to witness the great distress which the Queen was suffering, for she undoubtedly loved her lady with all her heart.

'In God's name, my lady,' she exclaimed, 'don't torment yourself so grievously and don't kill yourself in this way! If Sir Tristan has gone from here, we'll find him by some means. You may be absolutely certain, my lady, that I shall never rest until I see him. I'm quite sure he won't leave the Forest of Morroiz and I shan't have to seek him for long before I find him. What can I say, my dear lady? I shall set out tomorrow morning and go

straight to the Morroiz and ride all through the forest with one
of my brothers until I find Sir Tristan; and then I shall tell him
the whole truth about this affair and what your intention was in
writing that letter. He is so discerning and wise and courtly in all
things, and has found me so trustworthy on numerous occasions
in the past, that I'm sure he'll believe all I tell him. Therefore, my
dear lady, you should take heart from what I've said and not be
so dismayed. I assure you that as soon as I've found Sir Tristan
your peace will be made and this great suffering will be relieved,
since the discord between you and him can't last for long.'

When the Queen heard what Brangain said to her, she took
heart and became less unhappy. After a while she spoke and
replied:

'Brangain,' she said, 'what shall I tell you? All this pain and this
grief I suffer night and day because of my love for Sir Tristan was
caused by you and Gorvenal, as you know well, that day when
we were at sea and you handed me and Sir Tristan the philtre.
You are responsible for this malady and this sorrow, and you
should bear the blame for it more than we ourselves should, for
never would Sir Tristan have loved Iseut nor Iseut Tristan had it
not been for the love potion which you gave us by your foolish
and careless mistake. Therefore, since this pain and this anguish
we suffer is your doing, see to it that our suffering is alleviated in
some measure by your actions. And if you can't bring this about,
I have no other comfort than to take my own life. And that is
what I shall do, so help me God, rather than go on suffering the
great pain and the great torment which I've endured until now
for love's sake. And if I were to kill myself for love, I wouldn't
be the first ever to have done so. Dido of Carthage killed herself
for love of Aeneas of Troy; and many other women, nobler than
she was, took their own life, as the ancient stories tell us. And so,
when I remember what I've suffered for love, I declare truthfully
and without any pretence that I would rather kill myself than
endlessly suffer such pain and such anguish. For this reason I say
that unless you can find some means of alleviating my suffering,
I intend to end it myself with my own hands.

'Think then, if you can, of all the ways in which you can find
Sir Tristan; and should you be unable to bring him back to me,
at least comfort him and free him from these mad thoughts which

he's got into his head. Even if I couldn't see him for some time I would nevertheless take heart and forget the greater part of my sorrow provided I was sure he was fit and well. But if I knew that he was all the while unhappy and as grief-stricken as he was when he parted from me, that would be the end of me, I would never again be happy. Quickly then, Brangain, for God's sake, ride to the Morroiz early tomorrow morning and comb the forest far and wide until you find Sir Tristan, my beloved. If you find him, you may be sure that I shall be cured; if you don't, never expect me to take comfort from anything except death, for, so help me God, I shall kill myself with my own two hands. I would rather take my life than go on languishing like this.'

'My lady,' replied Brangain, 'don't be so disheartened! I assure you that if Sir Tristan can be found in the Forest of Morroiz by any maiden, I shall find him there.'

'May God grant it!' said the Queen.

While they were talking like this, both of them greatly distressed, King Mark came in to join them. When the Queen heard him coming, she stopped grieving and tried to give the appearance of being composed, even though this did not correspond to her feelings. Her feelings were unchanged in so far as she was grief-stricken beyond measure, so much so that she almost went out of her mind. But her appearance did not betray it, for were anyone who was not aware of the great sorrow which filled her heart to have seen her at this point, he would not have thought that she was so exceedingly unhappy. She was undoubtedly a very wise lady for her age, which was why she was able to conceal her feelings so well when she saw King Mark approaching, and consequently he could not tell that she was sorrowful and upset.

Even though King Mark was consumed with anger and displeasure because he knew for certain that Sir Tristan had been with the Queen, he did not show too much sign of it as he came into the room, since he loved the Queen so much that he was not prepared under any circumstances, whatever facts or words he was told, to subject her to shame or dishonour. He was sure that Sir Tristan had been with her on this occasion, and he was as upset about it as any man could be; but because he loved the Queen scarcely less than himself he did not have the heart to take any other action.

The Queen, seeing him come, got up to greet him, and he returned her greeting very courteously without daring to say what he was thinking.

'Lady,' he said, 'how are you?'

'Very well, thank you, my lord, by the grace of God,' she replied; whereupon he said nothing else to her apart from:

'Lady, do sit down.'

Then he left the room, weeping bitterly and moaning because he knew that Sir Tristan had been there. If he could catch him at this point he affirmed to himself that he would take vengeance on him. What more shall I tell you? King Mark put up with the situation and did not say anything to the Queen at that time. She was so worried and so distressed and upset by Sir Tristan's departure that she barely slept all night.

At dawn the following morning King Mark went hunting with a large company of barons and knights. He did not go to the Forest of Morroiz because he was well aware that Sir Tristan was there, and knew his superior strength and great prowess from past experience. The King was also well aware that if Sir Tristan held him with all his might and his own defence depended entirely upon himself, it would go badly with him. And because he was sure that only harm could come from encountering Sir Tristan, either to him or to his men, he went hunting in the Forest of Espinoie and not in the Forest of Morroiz.

Brangain, who did not forget what she had promised her lady the Queen, mounted her horse early in the morning and rode out of Tintagel, and earnestly prayed to God that He would let her find Sir Tristan. Once she had left Tintagel behind her, she made straight for the Forest of Morroiz. But before she had reached the forest, it so happened that she met Fergus, fully armed as befitted a knight. He was riding alone and was going to see my lady Queen Iseut for the reason which the story related earlier on. He recognized Brangain as soon as he saw her, having often seen her before. He stopped when he came up to her and said:

'Welcome, maiden!'

And she likewise stopped, realizing that the knight had recognized her. She had no idea who he was; nevertheless she returned his greeting very courteously.

'Ah! damsel,' said Fergus, 'I can truthfully tell you that you are one of the maidens in the world I most wanted to see. For the love of God, how is my lady Queen Iseut?'

'Who are you, Sir Knight,' she asked, 'who know me so well and enquire about my lady Queen Iseut in this way?'

'Brangain,' replied Fergus, 'what shall I say? There's no need for concealment at this point. I could not hide my name from you! Let me tell you that I am Fergus. I was at one time Sir Tristan's companion, as you yourself know. You should still remember it well, since I stayed with Sir Tristan in Tintagel for over half a year.'

When Brangain heard what Fergus said, she was overjoyed, for she knew well that he loved Sir Tristan almost as much as himself.

'Sir Fergus,' said Brangain, 'I wish you a very warm welcome. I should tell you that I wanted to find you and speak to you very much indeed. I can see that you've come from the Forest of Morroiz. For the love of God, did you meet Sir Tristan?'

'To be sure, maiden,' he answered, 'I did indeed meet him. I left him back there beside a fountain. You should know that he sent me with a message to my lady Queen Iseut. For God's sake, my noble maiden, since you can speak to my lady whenever you like, return with me to Tintagel and be so kind as to arrange it that I can give my lady Queen Iseut the message which I was asked to deliver to her.'

Brangain was delighted and overjoyed at this news.

'Sir Fergus,' she said, 'because I'm not quite sure whether you're the Fergus who was Sir Tristan's one-time companion, I beg you, please, to take off your helmet so that I can verify if you're the Fergus we've been talking about.'

'Maiden,' he replied, 'since you're in doubt as to whether or not I'm the one you think, I shall do as you ask.'

Then he took off his helmet. And when Brangain saw him clearly, she said:

'To be sure, sir, you are indeed Fergus. Now I shall carry out your request to the best of my ability. But tell me, for heaven's sake, what is Sir Tristan doing?'

'Brangain,' replied Fergus, 'I won't hide it from you. I can vouch for it that never in your life did you see a more unhappy knight than Sir Tristan. All I ask of you is that out of courtesy and

kindness you enable me to speak to my lady Queen Iseut; I shall
give her full details as to why I've been sent to her.'

'Fergus,' said Brangain, 'I assure you I'll see to it that you can
speak to my lady Queen Iseut, and quite soon, if God protects us
from misadventure.'

Thereupon Brangain started out on her return journey, and she
did so without apprehension, for she knew well that King Mark
had gone hunting. And when they got as far as the outskirts of
Tintagel, Brangain took Fergus to the house of one of her
acquaintances, and ordered the latter in the name of Queen Iseut
to serve and honour Fergus to the best of his ability, no less than
if he were the King himself. Brangain did not dare to take Fergus
straight to the court for fear of encountering someone who
would tell King Mark; and on the other hand she wanted to speak
to Queen Iseut first before she brought him any further. Fergus
remained at the house of the worthy man who greatly honoured
and served him because of Brangain's request and in order to
comply with the command which she had so forcefully given
him. He wanted to disarm Fergus, but Fergus did not let him; he
said he would not take off his armour until he saw the maiden
return, and the worthy man did not insist when he realized what
the knight's wishes were. Brangain rode directly to the palace and
dismounted from her palfrey in the middle of the courtyard, and
went from room to room until she came to where she found the
Queen who was still lamenting Sir Tristan's departure which she
could not forget.

When Queen Iseut saw Brangain arrive, her heart leapt with
joy, and she took comfort, for she was sure Brangain would not
have come back so soon if she were not bringing her some good
news. The Queen who was lying in her bed rose with great
alacrity, exceedingly happy and pleased, and said:

'Welcome, Brangain! Why have you come back so soon? It
seems to me there must be a reason. I'm so glad you've returned.
Please God that you have some good news for me.'

'My lady,' Brangain replied, 'I shall tell you at once what news
I'm bringing you. After I left Tintagel this morning and entered
the Forest of Morroiz to see if God were willing to grant me the
good fortune of finding Sir Tristan, it so happened without fail
that I encountered Fergus. He had just parted from Sir Tristan,

who is sending him to you with a message. And because Fergus thought that the quickest way he would be able to speak to you, my lady, would be with my help, he asked me to return with him to Tintagel. For the moment I've made him stay with a friend of mine, and there he'll wait for me until I tell him your reply. Now you must work out how he can most easily come to see you, because he is very eager to do so.'

When the Queen heard this message, she was delighted and overjoyed.

'Ah!' she said, 'he's very welcome. Quick, Brangain, don't be afraid to bring him here, but do so as soon as you can in such a way that he won't be recognized.'

'My lady,' replied Brangain, 'I assure you that I shall do my best.'

Brangain promptly left the Queen and did not stop until she came to the house where Fergus was staying.

'Sir Fergus,' she said, 'my lady the Queen sends me to you. Come and speak to her! Take off your armour and put on a cloak so that you appear before the Queen in a more courtly fashion.'

Fergus did as Brangain instructed him. He disarmed himself and put on a very costly cloak which Brangain had brought him; and when he was attired, he mounted a palfrey which his host had asked someone to fetch for him and rode straight to the court. He was fortunate in that there was not a knight to be seen in the whole palace at that time: they had all gone to amuse and enjoy themselves near the forest, and the King had taken the majority of the knights with him that morning when he went hunting. Fergus came before the Queen, since he found no one there who forbade him to enter. The Queen was very fond of him and received him very warmly; she made him sit down beside her, and at once began to ask him for news of Sir Tristan.

'So help me God, my lady,' he said, 'I can truly say that never in all my life did I see a knight as grief-stricken and unhappy as Sir Tristan was when I left him just now.'

Then he started telling her how bitterly Sir Tristan had lamented and wept and grieved all night long and so ardently that he had never taken any rest.

'And I should tell you, my lady,' said Fergus, 'that if someone doesn't alleviate his suffering soon, he can't fail to die.'

When the Queen heard this and realized the extent of Sir Tristan's anguish, she wept very tenderly. After a while she answered Fergus in the midst of her tears and said:

'Fergus, dear friend, you may be sure that if Sir Tristan were as wise as I thought he was, he would never have given himself up to this grief. He is grieving and I for my part am likewise grieving, and in this way we're wasting our lives in sorrow and in tears, and there's no end to this unhappy state of affairs. Therefore, Sir Fergus, because you don't know what has caused this sudden great grief of his, I shall proceed to tell you.'

Then she began to relate to him word for word the whole business of Kahedin and how she had written the letter to save him, since otherwise he would have died.

'Sir Tristan subsequently found this letter, I don't know by what misfortune, and as soon as he saw it he really thought it was true that I loved Kahedin. Sir Fergus,' continued the Queen, 'this is why you see Sir Tristan in such distress. But how, in God's name, can he think that I would stop loving him, the handsomest knight in the world and the best and the most gracious in all things, and turn to Kahedin? Truly, I would be making a very bad exchange if I wanted to discard the gold and keep the lead for myself. Indeed, as much as the value of gold surpasses that of lead, so Sir Tristan surpasses Kahedin in every way. It was great folly for him to think like that, a folly which he may have to pay for very dearly, so help me God; and I for my part likewise feel the effects of this folly, for if he died I shall kill myself with my own two hands, as God is my witness. For that reason, Sir Fergus, I beg you to return to him immediately, if you know where he is, and tell him from me not to let anything in the world stop him from coming back to Tintagel. Once he is back, I shall bring it about somehow that we can see each other. For God's sake, hurry up, Sir Fergus, and don't delay here any longer.'

'Willingly, my lady,' he replied, 'so help me God. I assure you I can't wait to get back to where I left him. I shall never rest until I see him again.'

'Many thanks, Sir Fergus,' said the Queen. 'Make haste, then, sir, for the love of God, and see to this matter as quickly as you can.'

Fergus parted from the Queen in order to carry out her command, and he took Brangain with him who would be able to

tell Sir Tristan better than anyone the truth about this matter and
how it had happened, for no other maiden knew about it. As
soon as Fergus got back to his host's house, he took off his cloak
and fetched his armour and armed himself as well as he had been
when he first came there, and then set out together with Brangain.

Having left Tintagel, they rode without stopping till they
reached the Forest of Morroiz. Then they found the stream
which led to the fountain where Fergus had parted from Sir
Tristan that morning, and they rode on till they came to the very
spot where Sir Tristan had remained; he had been gone for a long
time on account of the messenger-girl sent by Palamedes and all
she had said to him, as I described to you earlier on. And that is
why they did not find him by the fountain where he had spent
the night; though they did find his hauberk and his helmet. As
soon as Brangain saw the helmet she recognized it, having often
seen it in the King's room, for it was indeed the King's own
helmet.

'Fergus,' said Brangain, 'this helmet is proof that Sir Tristan has
been here. Lord God! where has he gone? If we don't find him,
we're in real trouble.'

'Maiden,' Fergus answered, 'don't be so dismayed. I assure
you we'll find him quite soon, unless our sins prevent us from
doing so.'

Then they began to ride through the forest, hither and thither,
backwards and forwards, right and left and far and wide, but such
was their misfortune that they were unable to find him. They
searched for him a long time, but it was all to no avail; it got them
nowhere. They never came to the place where Sir Tristan was.
What more shall I tell you? They searched for such a long time
that they became quite exhausted. They looked everywhere for
twenty whole days. They spent their nights now here now there;
they slept in hermitages or monasteries, and wherever they went,
they asked for news of Sir Tristan, but they could find neither
man nor woman who was able to give them any information. If
the Forest of Morroiz had been small, they would not have stayed
there so long looking for him, but it took at least five full days to
cross it lengthwise and three days breadthways. That is why they
remained there so long seeking him, because they kept thinking

that if they looked for him long enough, in the end they would find him somehow or other.

One day Fergus and Brangain meet Palamedes riding through the forest with his squire and his maiden. He challenges Fergus to joust, but the latter refuses, asking him instead for news of Tristan. Palamedes feels he has seen Brangain before, and asks her who she is; when she tells him her name, he is delighted and instructs his maiden to divulge what she knows about Tristan. Brangain had heard the maiden address Palamedes by his name and wonders what had made him come to Cornwall, thus flouting Iseut's command.

The maiden takes them to the fountain where Tristan had spent a week, and tells them everything she knows; in her opinion Tristan is by now dead. Brangain feels it is henceforth pointless to continue her search, and decides to return to Tintagel. Fergus however is convinced that Tristan is still alive, and says he will not leave the forest until he finds out some definite news about him. The maiden shows Brangain Tristan's harp, and the lady of the tower allows her to take it back to Tintagel. Brangain then parts from Fergus with much sorrow, and arrives at court that night.

Early next morning King Mark rides out hunting. He still avoids the Forest of Morroiz, but is reassured by the fact that no one has seen his nephew: perhaps he is dead or has left Cornwall. Audret insists that Tristan is lying somewhere ill.

Brangain goes to see her lady and tells her all she has found out. The Queen does not want to believe that Tristan is dead, preferring to think that Audret is right. Full of resentment against Kahedin, she sends Brangain with a message ordering him to leave Cornwall at once on pain of death. Then she asks her to bring Tristan's harp so that she too can compose a lay; it was Tristan who had taught her to play the harp while they were in the forest together.

Kahedin, aware of the extent of the Queen's hatred, arms himself and leaves Tintagel all alone, having previously sent his squires to Brittany for news of his father and sister, both very ill. He wails and weeps and laments, and such is his anguish that he stands for hours motionless in front of the gates of the city, thinking he was going on his way. At nightfall two knights speak to him and rouse him from his torpor. Thereupon he hurries into the forest intending to spend the night in a monastery there, but his grief is so intense that he loses his way. He rides about in the forest a large part of the night, getting more and more lost. Then he hears the sound of a horn blown twice very loudly, and turning in that direction, he comes to a dilapidated house in front of which is a very beautiful fountain where he sees a horse grazing, but no sign of a knight. It was in fact King Mark who had blown the horn to call his men, for he too had completely lost his way in the forest. Seeing a knight approaching, he thinks it is Tristan who has tracked him down, and, terrified, he hides inside the house.

Kahedin lies down to sleep beside the fountain, but before long he is woken up by the arrival of another knight who sits down nearby without seeing him. The unknown knight sighs and weeps and wails, and then begins an extraordinarily long lament, in turn accusing Love of disloyalty, deceit, fickleness, ingratitude, favouritism, unpredictability and treachery, and then regretting what he has said and taking it all back.

Suddenly the horses whinny; the unknown knight looks around him and sees Kahedin. Although annoyed that his lament has been overheard, he reveals his identity: he is Palamedes; and Kahedin names himself in his turn. Palamedes immediately remembers what the messenger-girl had told him about Kahedin and that he was the cause of the lovers' discord, and he challenges him to a duel to punish him for Tristan's death. But Kahedin very eloquently dissuades him, saying that Tristan is not yet dead and that both of them are in the same boat, for their love is hopeless. The two knights converse for a long time. Kahedin tells Palamedes all about himself, how he had fallen in love with the Queen and how she had deceived him; Palamedes is quick to see the reason, and for the first time Kahedin is made to understand why Iseut had written him such a comforting letter. Palamedes then relates to Kahedin all he knows about Tristan.

King Mark meanwhile has remained in hiding and has listened to every word. Unfortunately for him he suddenly has a coughing fit, and the two knights find him. He pretends to have been fast asleep and tries to conceal his identity, but he is recognized by Kahedin. Thereupon Palamedes threatens to kill the King and then challenges him to fight, but he only wants to frighten him and in the end lets him be; indeed, he later apologizes and offers the King his services. The rest of the night the three of them talk together about King Arthur and about Tristan.

Next morning King Mark finds his bearings and takes the two knights to the highway. Here they part: Kahedin intends to return to Brittany; Palamedes decides to go back to Logres; and the King makes his way to Tintagel. He meets Dinas the Seneschal who has spent all night in the forest looking for Tristan, and they ride back together. King Mark tells him about his adventures during the night and praises Palamedes's courtesy and intelligence.

When the people of Tintagel saw King Mark return, they received him with much joy and honour. They had been very worried at having lost him like that in the forest; but now that

they saw him safe and sound, they were greatly relieved. As soon
as the King was back, he went to see Queen Iseut, for she was
never out of his mind. In fact, he loved her so much that he loved
her scarcely less than himself. When he came before her, he
found her quite alone; she had cleared the room of all her ladies
and maidens because she did not want anyone to hear the great
grief she was carrying on night and day, if she could help it. The
King entered the room so quietly that the Queen, who was
holding her harp in front of her and tuning it, did not hear him
come in; she was weeping as she was trying to set her lay to
music, and singing with tears running down her face while
sighing tenderly deep from her heart. And there can be no doubt
that she was a lady of exquisite beauty, endowed with all the
charms a woman could possess, so that it would have been difficult to find a lady as beautiful as she was anywhere in the world.
Nevertheless, the great suffering which filled her heart and her
continued lamenting detracted somewhat from her beauty, for
it had made her face look a bit pale and sallow, and had already
caused it to become quite thin; even the tears which kept
flowing from her eyes were detrimental to her beauty. Had it
not been for the fact that all this undermined her appearance at
this point, King Mark could safely have boasted that there was
not in the whole world at that time a lady as beautiful as the
Queen.

When the King entered the room and saw that Queen Iseut
was in there, holding her harp in front of her and singing in a low
voice whilst weeping bitterly, he stopped short and thought to
himself that since she had not noticed his arrival, she was bound
to make some unexpected remark and say something for which
he could then call her to account and with good cause. Thus the
King stopped short in order to hear what the Queen would say,
keeping quite still.

The Queen, who had no idea he was there and who was trying
to set the lay to music as best she could, often sighed from the
depths of her heart. She continued like this for a long time without uttering a word except when she was singing in order to
compose the music for her lay. Then she put her harp beside her
and began to weep very bitterly. And after weeping in this
manner for quite a while, she said:

'Ah! treacherous and cruel Love, disloyal and evil, full of spite and envy, devoid of all pity and moderation, why have you killed and destroyed the flower of all knighthood? God in his kindness and graciousness had placed in one single being all the qualities and natural graces which mortal chivalry should embody, and you, to your shame and dishonour, have annihilated this being and subjected him to torment and to death. Could you possibly have harmed the world more than by this death alone?'

When the Queen had spoken these words, she said no more, but for a long time remained silent, lost in thought. After a while she began to lament again as follows, saying:

'Ah! Tristan, would that I had never seen you and your love! This vile and shameful death which has thus carried you off is my undoing. As far as your love is concerned, I can openly say that it never brought me anything but good; it is this death which I complain about, since it has taken you from me; and I should rightly complain about it for evermore as long as I have a breath left in my body. This death has plunged me into such despair and has so broken my heart that I shall never find comfort except in one thing alone, and that will be my own death which will shortly bring my life to an end. In this way I shall make my suffering cease at one go.'

When she had said this, she raised her head and caught sight of King Mark standing not far away from her. The Queen, being convinced of Tristan's death, was in a state of exceeding distress; and because she realized that King Mark had heard everything she had said and that it would be quite useless for her to try and cover it up, she spoke like a madwoman, full of rage and anger, for it was all the same to her now whether she lived or died, and said:

'King Mark, did you hear what I said quite clearly?'

'Yes, lady,' he replied, 'quite clearly. You may be sure that these words can only bring you harm and vexation.'

'Indeed,' said the Queen, 'I couldn't care less. It's all the same to me now whether I lose or whether I win. Henceforth I have nothing to lose, for I've lost everything.'

'Lady,' said the King, 'it seems to me you still have one thing to lose, namely your life.'

'King Mark,' replied the Queen, 'so help me God, that's my least worry. Do you really think I'm afraid of death? Certainly not! I'm looking death straight in the face; it is closer to me than anything else. King Mark, why should I think otherwise? Death is my close relation. It was sent to me a short while ago, I don't know from what land. Do you know who sent it to me? Tristan! Tristan has sent me my death so that I should die after him. He is dead, and I too want to die, you may be sure of that. Nobody ever longed for death as fervently as I; I beseech and call upon death with clasped hands to end my suffering. I have no other desire, and for this reason it should be quite obvious that I don't fear death in the slightest; indeed, if it were going to keep me waiting too long, I myself would harbour it within me, because I would kill myself with my own two hands.'

When the Queen had spoken these words, she fell silent and said no more at this point; and after a while she began to lament again as bitterly and as ardently as before.

King Mark, hearing her speak like this, was even more distressed and upset than he had been previously. Now he did not know what to do, for the Queen's words had shown him and made him realize beyond any doubt that she wanted to commit suicide on account of her sorrow for Tristan, and that if she were not watched she would certainly take her life, and moreover quite soon, since it was clear to him that she was almost demented. The King loved the Queen so greatly that he did not want her to die on any account, whatever the circumstances; and because he was convinced that Tristan was dead and it seemed to him that henceforth he had no reason to fear him, he said to himself that he would send for Dinas the Seneschal. The Queen was very fond of him, and once she had his company, her great friendship for him would bring her some comfort, if she were ever going to be comforted. The King did not want to lose her in this way for anything as long as he had the chance of saving her.

What shall I tell you? He sent for Dinas who came without delay. The King at once drew him aside into one of the nearby rooms and described to him how bitterly the Queen was grieving; whereupon Dinas asked the King as though he knew nothing about it:

'My lord, what is the reason for this grief? Why is my lady so terribly unhappy?'

'Dinas,' said the King, 'I won't conceal the truth from a man like you. I'll tell you the reason and reveal my shame to you quite candidly. Tristan is definitely dead, I'm quite sure of it, and I have no doubt that you must have heard something about it. And because the Queen is convinced that Tristan is dead, she keeps lamenting so bitterly that never in all your life did you see such grief; and she openly affirms that she will kill herself without fail. But as I wouldn't wish her to die like this, I want you to stay with her the whole time and to comfort her in any way you can. I leave her in your care. Make sure she doesn't kill herself, for I shall hold you fully responsible.'

'My lord,' replied Dinas, 'since you're placing me in charge of the Queen, I promise you faithfully that I'll keep such a close watch on her hands that even if she wanted to kill herself with them she would be quite unable to do so.'

'That is what I order you to do,' said the King.

Thus the Queen remained in the care of Dinas the Seneschal, who was very distressed and sorrowful to hear about the great grief which she continued to display.

When Dinas came into the room which the Queen had not left, he found her holding her harp in front of her, and he greeted her as politely as he knew how. The Queen raised her head, and seeing that it was Dinas, she replied:

'Welcome, Dinas, dear friend. What news are you bringing me?'

'So help me God, my lady,' said Dinas, 'I don't know of any news at the present time.'

'But I know some at the present time which should rightly displease the whole world: Tristan, my beloved, is dead! He who surpassed the whole world in beauty, valour, wisdom and courtesy is dead, and for love of him I also want to die without fail, since I know for certain that he died for love of me.'

As soon as the Queen had said this, she began to weep very tenderly and to curse the hour she was born more than a thousand times, seeing that she had in this way lost a man such as Tristan. Dinas, hearing the Queen lament so bitterly, tried to comfort her, saying:

'My lady, what shall I tell you? I must say that never before did I see any lady behave in such an extraordinary fashion! As God is

my witness, up till now I considered you to be one of the wisest
ladies in the world, but seeing you behave in this way, it seems
to me that you are very much to blame when you say that Tristan
is dead. How ever do you know? How can you be so certain?
Have you spoken to anyone who saw him dead?'

'No, to be sure,' said the Queen, 'but the great fear which I
have fills my heart with such exceeding sorrow that I don't know
what to say. My sorrow plagues and torments me; my sorrow will
shortly cause my death, as well as the news which Brangain
brought me.'

'What news did Brangain bring you, then, my lady?' asked
Dinas.

'Upon my faith,' she answered, 'I'll tell you.'

Then she promptly began to relate to him word for word what
Brangain had told her about Tristan, and once she had done so,
Dinas lost no time in replying:

'My lady,' he said, 'I've heard the whole of your story as you
related it to me. Now I'll tell you mine as I know it and as King
Mark himself revealed it to me.'

Then he started telling her all about Palamedes and Kahedin,
and the argument and dispute that took place between them.
What more shall I say? He told her the entire story just as King
Mark had told it to him, and listening to it cheered the Queen
up a little. When he had finished his tale, the Queen spoke and
said:

'Dinas, so help me God, what is your opinion concerning
Tristan, then? Do you think he's more likely to be dead than
alive?'

'My lady,' answered Dinas, 'I want you to know in all truth
that Tristan is not dead, but very much alive, and in my opinion
you'll soon hear some definite news about him.'

'May God grant it by His mercy,' said the Queen, 'as I
desire it.'

As a result of the comforting words which Dinas said to the
Queen, she began to feel a bit better, and she would have felt
very much more so had it not been for Audret who hated her
because of Tristan. Audret had encountered a foreign maiden
who had recently come to Cornwall, and he drew her to one
side, saying:

'Maiden, if you were willing to do something for me which I'll explain to you, I would make it very worth your while; and I assure you that you could do this safely without incurring any harm or shame.'

The girl was poor and very desirous of improving her lot, if it was God's will; and when she found out that it was Audret she was speaking to, who, after King Mark was lord and master of Cornwall, as she knew well, she promptly replied:

'Sir Audret, there is nothing in the whole world I wouldn't gladly do for you provided I could do so in accordance with my honour and safety. Now tell me what you want me to do.'

'Gladly,' said Audret. 'I know for a fact that Tristan has recently met his death. I myself was there when the mortal blow was struck and saw him lying dead on the ground; and if I hadn't seen it as clearly as I did, I wouldn't believe any man who told me of his death. Thus it has come about that the Kingdom of Leonois, which is his by inheritance, has remained without an heir and has rightfully come down to King Mark, his uncle, who wouldn't however want to rule over two kingdoms at the same time, I'm sure. Once he's heard the news of Tristan's death, I'm convinced he'll willingly give me the Kingdom of Leonois without needing much persuasion. And if it were mine, I would consider myself a very fortunate man for the rest of my life, and I would say that the services I've rendered King Mark have been richly rewarded. And so, maiden, because King Mark will give more credence to the news of Tristan's death if he heard it from you rather than from me—for were I to tell him myself how I saw him killed, he would immediately think that it wasn't true and that I was only saying it out of a desire to have the Kingdom of Leonois—I want you to tell him; and I assure you that it will be of great benefit to you. And if he asks you where you saw him killed, you can safely say that it was in the Forest of Morroiz at the hands of one of King Arthur's companions.'

'In God's name,' said the young girl, 'it won't be my lack of skill in delivering this message that will debar you from having the Kingdom of Leonois! Leave it to me without fear. I shall know well enough how to tell the King what you want me to say. When it comes to speaking fluently and putting forward an argument, no maiden could surpass me.'

'Well, we shall see', said Audret, thus ending their conversation.

That evening as it was growing dark and the sun was setting, King Mark sat down to dinner in the great hall, after which the other knights also sat down. The first course had just been served when the maiden with whom Audret had had the conversation I related to you arrived at court. As soon as those inside saw her enter they said that she was without doubt a messenger-girl, and they took her to the King. When she had come before him, she greeted him as politely as she knew how and said:

'King Mark, may God save and protect you!'

'Maiden,' answered the King, 'God grant you good fortune. Where do you come from, and from what country? Are you from the Kingdom of Logres? If you are from that land, then let us hear your news.'

'King Mark,' said the girl, 'as a matter of fact I was born in the Kingdom of Logres and left there not long ago and came to Cornwall on an errand which was very close to my heart. Exactly three days ago to the hour I was riding through the Forest of Morroiz in the company of only one of my squires. While we were riding in the forest as I'm telling you, it so happened that we met a knight, and he was fully armed as befits a knight and had two squires with him. As soon as he saw us, he stopped, and when we had come up to him he said: "I beg you to go to a fountain which is just ahead of us, where you'll find a knight who was killed a short while ago. Either you bury him there, or you take him to a religious house to be buried. He was a man of such great nobility and valour that one shouldn't allow the beasts of the wood to devour him." Thereupon the knight parted from us without saying another word.

'We immediately set out and rode until we reached the fountain. There we found a knight lying who had been struck right through the body by a lance in such a way that the lance-head protruded at the back, and some of the wood as well. The knight wasn't yet dead, but he was very near to his death, and seeing this I dismounted in order to find out if I could elicit some response from him. When I had got off my horse and was leaning over him, he opened his eyes and said: "Ah! maiden, I beseech you for the love of God and for pity's sake to do something for me which won't cause you much trouble. I am Tristan, the nephew of King Mark of Cornwall, that's the truth, I assure you. I had fallen asleep by this fountain when a knight who was my mortal enemy—as he's clearly shown me at this point!—found me sleeping here by chance, and treacherously struck me as you can see. He's killed me; I already feel death gripping my heart. I won't live to see this night. And so, because I wouldn't want the Kingdom of Leonois, which was mine, to be without a ruler for long, I beg you to ask King Mark on my behalf to take over the country himself or to give it to some worthy man who will be capable of ruling it."

'Shortly after he had spoken these words he died in our presence. We then took his body and carried it to a hermitage which was nearby and had him buried there. That is how Tristan died. At his behest I've come to you, King Mark, and I'm repeating to you exactly what he told me. Now I shall go about my business, for I had nothing else to do at your court except to give you this message and to carry out Tristan's request.'

When the King heard this news, he was so greatly upset that he did not know what to say. He really thought that it had happened just as the maiden had described. One moment he was angry, the next he was sorrowful and dismayed and beside himself with grief. And I can vouch for it that in the entire hall there were not even four knights on this occasion who were not exceedingly distressed by Tristan's death, and they all declared with one accord that now one could unhesitatingly say that the best knight in the world was dead. What more shall I tell you? The grief in there was so great and so intense that a thunderbolt from heaven would have gone unnoticed. Even King Mark, though he did not like to give way to grief, lamented so bitterly that no one who saw him could have said it was not genuine. The Queen herself, who was in her room and who was beginning to feel a bit more cheerful on account of what Dinas had said and continued to say to her every day, heard the loud lamentation which was going on in the great hall, and she immediately jumped up like a mad-woman, saying:

'Quick, Dinas, go there and find out what they're all lamenting about. My heart tells me it's for Tristan, my beloved. They've had some bad news about him, I'm convinced of it.'

Dinas did not know what to say in reply to the Queen's words. Hearing the lamenting and the commotion which was going on in there, he at once realized that it must be for Tristan, and he delayed no longer, but made his way straight to the hall. And the Queen, who was so uneasy about it that no one could have been more so, was unable to hold out until Dinas's return, and therefore went into one of the nearby rooms in which she found two maidens who were weeping very tenderly. The Queen advanced towards one of them and said to her:

'Maiden, why are you weeping like this? Tell me at once, I order you.'

Thereupon the maiden began to weep even more loudly, but nevertheless because she was afraid of her lady and did not want to anger her, she replied:

'My lady, why should I conceal it from you? It would be pointless to do so. We are weeping on account of the news which has just been brought to court by a young girl who informed the King that Sir Tristan was undoubtedly dead. The King is grieving about it so bitterly that I never saw anybody grieve more, and everyone else at court likewise. We ourselves are lamenting as you can see.'

When the Queen heard this news, she made no reply at all, but returned to her room as quickly as ever she could and sat down by her bed without saying a word. After this it was not long before Dinas came back from the great hall and, seeing him, the Queen could not remain silent, but said to him, weeping:

'Dinas, he is dead!'

As soon as she had said this, she fainted and lay for a long while unconscious, so cold, so pale, and so weak that she looked as if she were lifeless. Faced with this situation, Dinas had no idea how he could possibly help her. He himself was so grief-stricken that nobody who saw him at this point would have questioned that he was genuinely upset at this disaster. He was heart-broken about Tristan. He no longer knew what to say. He was almost demented; he cursed God and the whole world.

After a while the Queen regained consciousness. And when she could speak, she said to Dinas:

'Dinas, he is dead! And since he who kept me alive has lost his life, my own life no longer matters to me. Henceforth it is time and it is right for me to end my life. After his death I should not stay alive.'

This is what the Queen said, and Dinas did not hear her utter another word that evening. What more shall I tell you? There was great grief and loud wailing and considerable sorrow throughout Tintagel. The King grieved so bitterly that it would have been impossible to grieve more, and so did the rest of his household.

Queen Iseut was completely overcome with sorrow by the news which Audret had asked the maiden to spread at King Mark's court, as I have described above. What shall I tell you? From that day onward she lost all desire to eat or drink, so that the King declared openly that she could not live for long; and all those who saw her said the same. And you should know that what kept her alive more than anything else was the fact that she was concentrating on playing her harp, and on finishing her lay and composing the music for it.

When she had completed the lay as well as the music, she said to herself that henceforth she wanted to die. And because she saw clearly that neither her fasting, nor her weeping nor her lamenting would cause her to die soon, she decided to end her life more quickly. How? She would kill herself with her own two hands, using Tristan's sword, the one with which he had killed the Morholt, her uncle. That is what she resolved and aspired to do, and that is how she said she would do it; and she thought about the matter all night long.

The King, who noticed and realized that the Queen was thinking more than usual and that she was not sleeping at all, wondered what this could mean. When he had reflected about it, he said to himself that the Queen's intention must be to do some grievous harm to herself, and it was essential, so he said, for him to find out where these thoughts of hers were going to lead. The King for his part was likewise thinking; she was thinking of her death and how she could kill herself without anyone seeing her; the King, who perceived that she was more pensive than usual, declared that he would discover, if at all possible, where these thoughts of hers were going to lead.

At dawn next morning the King got up very early and announced that he wanted to go riding; and this is what he did. But as soon as he had left Tintagel, he said to those who were in his company:

'Ride on as far as the forest and wait for me there. I wish to stay here for a little while.'

And they carried out his command and went off straight towards the forest. The King remained at the entrance of a large garden which led right up to his rooms, for without a doubt this garden stretched all the way as far as the Queen's chambers. When he saw that he was alone except for a squire whom he had kept with him, he dismounted and told the youth to take the horse into a nearby valley to some spot where he could not be seen; and the squire promised to do so. The King went into the garden which was very beautiful and green and full of small shrubby trees where the merry little birds were enjoying themselves singing their various songs. He walked through the garden so quietly that he was neither seen nor heard, till he reached the rooms, and stepped inside one of them from which it was possible to look more or less into the Queen's chamber; and it also gave one a good view of a large part of the garden. The King went over to the palace window facing the garden, and affirmed that now he had found the best possible position and that the Queen could do nothing which he would not see.

Thus the King stood by the window and listened to the birds who had already begun their day and were singing so melodiously that it should have made anyone who heard it rejoice. It was still very early in the morning and yet the sun had already risen in all its splendour, and was shining with such brightness and radiance that the whole world was illuminated by it. While the King was standing at the window as I have described, he looked and saw the Queen come out with her harp which she placed by a tree, and then she turned and went back into her room. Before long she appeared again carrying a sword, the fittings of which were very costly* in every way. As soon as the King saw it, he realized it was Tristan's sword, the one he had always loved the most. Then the King knew without fail that the Queen wanted to kill herself, moreover with this very sword, and it was therefore essential for him to prevent her from doing this, and to deflect her from her intention. He would not have wanted her to die so soon for anything in the world; however, he said to himself that he would not move just yet, but would wait a bit longer to see what she was going to do.

Once the Queen had brought out the sword as I have described, she leaned it against a small tree; then she returned to her room and remained in there for a while. And I should tell you that on this occasion she had asked all her ladies and maidens to leave her, even Dinas and Brangain, saying that she wished to sleep because she had spent a restless night. None of them suspected anything, and they would never have supposed that the Queen intended to take her life in this way unless someone had informed them of it,* so they had gone off, some in one direction, some in another, thinking she wanted to rest as she had told them. After they had left, she fastened the door of the room behind them so firmly that they would have been unable to come back in without her permission; and for this reason I tell you that Queen Iseut would certainly have killed herself that day had King Mark not prevented her.

When the Queen had remained in her room for some time, she returned once again to the garden; but now she was clothed and attired as richly as on the day of her coronation, for she was dressed in the very robe in which she had been crowned and anointed, and moreover she was wearing her golden crown on her head. She had said to herself that just as she was honourably attired when she was crowned in joy, so did she want to be adorned when she died of love.

The King, seeing her adorned and bedecked in this way, and quite alone, greatly marvelled as to what it could mean. He was much more alarmed than he had been before. The Queen, who did not see him nor suspect his presence, went straight towards her harp. The first thing she did was to kiss the hilt of the sword; she did not however draw it from the scabbard, but placed it in front of her and began to weep over it very tenderly and to mourn for Tristan. After she had lamented thus for some time, she took up her harp and started tuning it; then, having done so, she began to look all around her, and saw that it was a beautiful day, bright and very clear with the sun shining, and then again she heard the divers songs of the little birds who were rejoicing in the garden. When she had listened to their song and their melody for a long time, she remembered the Forest of

Morroiz where she had once been so happy with Tristan, and this
made her weep; and after she had stopped weeping, she tuned her
harp again to harmonize with her song, and began her lay as
follows:*

> The sun is shining clear and bright,
> I hear the bird-song with delight.
> Around me in the little trees
> They chirp their latest melodies.
>
> About these sweet songs which delight me,
> And Love, which has ensnared me tightly,
> I start my lay, I weave my tune,
> And hope death will relieve me soon.
>
> In grief I set down my distress,
> Compose a song against my death.
> In harmony I sing and play,
> Making a sweet and tuneful lay.
>
> About my death, approaching fast,
> I write a lay; its fame will last.
> All lovers will be made to sigh,
> For Love is causing me to die.
>
> Weeping and singing, sad and gay,
> To Love just as to God I pray.
> Oh lovers all, come quickly nigh,
> For Queen Iseut will shortly die.
>
> With song and tears my lay takes wing;
> I weep my lay, even as I sing.
> My song and tears bring me so low,
> I'll not recover from this woe.
>
> Tristan, my love, at your last breath
> My impulse is to curse that death
> Which makes the whole world mourn for you,
> Except if Death would take me too.
>
> You're dead: unless you can revive,
> I have no wish to stay alive.
> For you I shall die happily;
> The world will soon be rid of me.

Beloved, with your noble traits,
Above all men deserving praise,
Had Death forgotten you in fact
Then courteous would have been his act.

But you've been added to his score.
The world considers you're no more.
Both kings and nobles weep for you;
It's little wonder that they do.

Beloved, none will equal you
In deeds of valour brave and true.
Now only rogues and knaves remain,
And straw replaces wholesome grain.

Beloved, your great bravery
Rescued King Mark from slavery.
You killed my uncle, once so strong.
Now you are dead: that's surely wrong!

Beloved, in that mortal strife
You'd certainly have lost your life
Due to the poison's fatal power
Had I not cured you in my tower.

In Ireland at the tournament
Your prowess was quite evident.
Your boldness, everyone agreed,
Did Palamedes's far exceed.

After the jousting in that place
Segurades you had to face.
As a result Mark hated you,
But in our hearts a new love grew.

Never since the world began
Was greater love bestowed on man
Than ours; and neither word nor deed
Can ever to its severance lead.

When to the forest we had sped
Nothing but words of love we said.
And Love was well upheld there, too.
Now it has brought this doom on you,

When I recall life in the wood
Which I'd return to if I could,
Happy is she, I say, who's died
While lying at her lover's side.

Beloved, much did I lament;
My days in weeping have I spent.
For Love which I'd adored in vain
Has cleft my heart in two with pain.

In Love I placed my hope and trust,
Believing it was true and just.
To Love as to the Lord I gave
My faith; now for my death I crave.

Not even Adam suffered so
When he lost Eden long ago
As did Iseut: she ends her days
Whilst on the harp ten tunes she plays.

Beloved, since you've died for me
Dying for you's no misery.
But comfort for you have I none
Except to die as you have done.

Tristan, my love, beloved yet,
This heart of mine, which once I'd set
On loving you, shall now be slain,
By your own sword put out of pain.

Oh sword, you've dealt many a blow,
And laid a host of felons low,
Yet at this point your use shall be
To strike and put an end to me.

Sword, decorated with such art,
You'll soon be plunged into my heart.
My very blood will stain your blade;
Death's grip is on my body laid.

I am destroyed by love's fire burning,
Rousing in me such anguished yearning
That flesh and soul are both consumed.
Before my time I am entombed.

Tristan, my love, beloved still,
Let God so judge my act of will
That your soul close to mine may dwell
Whether in paradise or hell.

I'm dying, walking down some way;
Where to? Does it lead me astray?
Tristan is guiding me, I vow,
Towards Love's house he leads me now.

And so my lay's conclusion nears,
Iseut ends it in song and tears.
Dying for true love's sake is she.
No queen could die more worthily.

She ends her lay, but makes this plea
To all who love: 'Don't censure me!'
She loves and dies; she's not to blame.
Dying, she calls on Tristan's name.

When Iseut had quite finished singing her lay as I have described, so pleasantly and so sweetly that anyone listening to her
then would undoubtedly have been able to say that never before
had any lady on earth composed such a beautiful lay or sung it so
well, she placed her harp in front of her and began to brood. After
she had brooded like this for a long while, she said to herself,
loudly enough for King Mark to hear it without difficulty:

'Unhappy wretch!' she exclaimed, 'what am I waiting for, and
what is stopping me from killing myself? Why don't I end my
suffering?'

When she had spoken thus, she stood up and drew the sword,
naked, from its scabbard, and started kissing the hilt very tenderly, saying:

'Sir, Tristan, dear beloved, for love of you I am kissing my
death.'

Then she put the hilt of the sword in the hollow of a tree and
wedged it so firmly and so well that she could throw herself
against the point without it moving at all; she would be able to
kill herself by running, and at one go.

Having prepared herself in this way for her death, she flung
down her cloak on the ground and turned in order to hurl herself

against the sword. But King Mark who had seen all this clearly
and who would not for the world have wanted the Queen to take
her life, realized that now he was in danger of delaying too long,
and for that reason he jumped out of the window. The Queen,
hearing him land, looked round, and when she saw that it was
King Mark himself, she was so greatly alarmed and frightened—
for she was in constant fear of him—that she was powerless to do
any more, but stopped short in mid career, scared to death. The
King ran straight to the sword before he went to the Queen,
since he wanted to seize it first of all. Once he had taken hold of
it and put it in the scabbard, he said to the Queen:

'Lady, lady, what you are doing is wrong. You are committing
a grave misdeed. This is not the way for a queen to behave. All
those who were supposed to be guarding you have rightfully
deserved to die, for they've guarded you badly. Return to your
room and think of something other to do than taking your life:
such conduct does not befit a queen.'

The Queen was taken aback to such an extent that she did not
know what to say. The King had so clearly caught her in the act
that she had no possibility whatever of defending herself. She
returned to her room, sad and sorrowful that she had failed to
carry out her plan. She was very upset that the King had stopped
her, since by now she would have accomplished her deed and
ended all her suffering at one go. It really seemed to her that she
would by now have been together with Tristan.

The King sent for all the Queen's maidens and reprimanded
and upbraided them severely for having left their lady alone in
this way. Let them take care henceforth if they valued their lives
not to leave the Queen on her own, or he would have them all
put to death.

'By your grace, my lord,' said the maidens, 'you shouldn't in
all fairness blame us for that. It wasn't our fault that our lady
remained on her own.'

Thereupon they immediately told him how the Queen had
ordered them to leave the room because she wanted to rest after
having spent a sleepless night. Hearing this, the King was less
angry with the maidens than he had previously been. He then
ordered Dinas to come before him, and as soon as the latter heard
that the King wanted to see him, he went, taking Brangain with

him. The King led them straight to the garden where the Queen had left her harp and her cloak; and when he had brought them there, he addressed them:

'Dinas,' he said, 'and you Brangain, I have a good mind to put you both to death, so help me God, for that is what you deserve.'

'My lord, by your grace,' said Dinas, 'how have we deserved to die?'

'Did I not hand the Queen over to you,' the King then asked, 'and tell you to guard her in such a way that she was never without your company?'

'Yes, my lord,' Dinas replied. 'And haven't we guarded her well up till now?'

'You've guarded her so well,' said the King, 'that I have a good mind, so help me God, to put you both to death; that is what you deserve.'

'How, sir?' asked Dinas. 'I assure you I can't understand why, unless you explain it to us more clearly.'

'And I shall explain it to you,' said the King.

Then he began to tell them all about the Queen, how she had prepared her death and the manner in which she had done so, and that she would undoubtedly have killed herself if he had not been there to rescue her.'

When Dinas heard what had happened, he crossed himself, so amazed was he.

'By your grace, my lord,' Dinas said to the King, I can tell you truly that my lady the Queen deceived us this morning. After you left here, she told me that she had spent a sleepless night, and begged me as I valued her affection to clear the room of all the men and women who were in it at the time, including Brangain and myself, so as to enable her to rest that morning. In all truth, my lord, this is how my lady the Queen deceived us. It never occurred to me in any way whatever that she wanted to take her life.'

'I can vouch for it,' said the King, 'that if I hadn't been there, she would have killed herself. However, henceforth guard her properly, and so closely that she never leaves your company. In the end she must surely forget Tristan one way or another.'

'My lord,' replied Dinas, 'I promise you that henceforth she will be so closely guarded night and day that she wouldn't be able to carry out her intention under any circumstances without my seeing it.'

'Make sure about that,' said the King, 'as you value your life.'

And Dinas said he would not fail to carry out this command, if God saved him from misfortune; and Brangain said the same.

That is how King Mark saved Queen Iseut from committing suicide as a result of Tristan's death. Those whose duty it was to guard the Queen were now so careful and vigilant that she would not have had the power to take her life if she had wanted to, because they watched over her too well and too closely.

Shortly after this it happened one day that Dinas was riding through the Forest of Morroiz where the Queen had sent him to find some herbs. She had conceived the idea of doing an ill turn to those who were guarding her; not because she felt hostility towards any of them, but so as to have the possibility and the time to end her own life. And I should tell you that she wanted to brew a potion with which she could send them all to sleep, and then she would kill herself, for then, so it seemed to her, she would certainly have the opportunity and the power to do so.

While Dinas was riding about in the forest here and there seeking this herb which the Queen had asked him to get, and he was weeping very tenderly and lamenting the death of Tristan, he happened to meet Giglain, Sir Gawain's son, who was riding through the Morroiz all alone without any company, and fully armed. Dinas recognized him at once. As for Giglain, as soon as he saw Dinas the Seneschal going through the forest weeping very tenderly, armed only with his sword, he knew him straightaway, since he had often seen him at King Mark's court; but he marvelled greatly as to why he was weeping so much. Then he turned his horse towards him, and Dinas, seeing him approach, immediately left off lamenting and tried to look as cheerful as he could.

'Sir Dinas,' said Giglain, 'may God protect you!'

'Sir,' answered Dinas, 'God grant you good fortune!'

'Why are you grieving so bitterly, Sir Dinas?' asked Giglain.

'Sir,' replied Dinas, 'because my heart compels me to do so. And I can tell you, sir, that no worthy man should blame me for my grief, since there is a very good reason for it.'

'So help me God, Sir Dinas,' said Giglain, 'tell me the reason, and I shall do whatever a knight of my strength can do to help.'

'Sir,' said Dinas, 'I don't want you to start a quarrel with me as you did with Sir Tristan, not for a reason such as this, so I'll tell you at once what you ask me; I don't wish to incur your anger. You'd better know that I'm weeping because the bravest knight in the world is dead: namely Sir Tristan, the nephew of King Mark of Cornwall; and the one blow he dealt you shows you the sort of knight he was.'

'What?' asked Giglain, 'is Sir Tristan dead, then?'

'Yes, sir, there's no doubt about it.'

'And how do you know?' asked Giglain.

'Sir,' said Dinas, 'we know it for certain from a young girl who saw him die and came to court to bring us the news.'

And then he began to describe to him how the maiden had arrived at court and what she had said about Tristan.

'Now tell me, Sir Dinas,' said Giglain, 'how long ago was it that the young girl came to court with this news of Sir Tristan's death?'

'Sir,' replied Dinas, 'at least a fortnight ago or more. King Mark is so upset about it that he's almost going out of his mind with grief; and my lady the Queen is lying in bed nearly at the point of death.'

'Dinas,' said Giglain, 'I can assure you that you would have done a very good deed if you had killed the maiden who brought you this news of Sir Tristan's death, for you should know that every word she said to you was a lie. I tell you by the faith I owe to King Arthur who is my liege lord and to the one who begot me that I saw Sir Tristan in this forest less than four days ago, sound of limb, though undoubtedly he had been ill and is still a little unwell.'

When Dinas heard these words, he was so overjoyed that he found it very difficult to reply. After a while when he could speak he said, sighing:

'Ah! sir, for the love of God, is it really true that you saw Sir Tristan less than four days ago?'

'The oath I swore you about it', said Giglain, 'was such that I would be very loath to perjure myself. I can assure you that I saw him just as I said.'

'Ah! Sir Giglain,' exclaimed Dinas, 'for the love of God, would you be willing to do one of the kindest deeds you've ever done

in your whole life and which will win you the gratitude of the
worthy men of Cornwall?'

'Yes, indeed,' said Giglain, 'I should be very pleased to do
that.'

'Then I'll instruct you what to do, sir,' said Dinas. 'If you
please, go straight to Tintagel and tell my lady Queen Iseut what
you've told me. She's so distressed about Tristan that she's dying
of grief, but she'll recover as soon as she's heard this news. Go
there, sir, and save her from death for the love of God and out of
courtesy and kindness.'

'Dinas,' said Giglain, 'can I really bring such great comfort to
Queen Iseut with these tidings as you say?'

'Yes, sir, so help me God, and even more. I assure you I
wouldn't beg you as earnestly as I do but for the fact that she's
much more likely to believe you than me. If I myself were now
to tell her this news, she would immediately suspect that it was
just a lie and a story I'd made up to comfort her. For that reason
I beseech you, for the Lord's sake, to go there yourself.'

And Giglain promised him that he would do so. Thereupon
they parted from one another; Giglain at once started on his way,
and Dinas remained in the forest. Giglain rode so hard that he
arrived in Tintagel that very day, and took lodgings in the same
place where he had stayed before. As soon as he was disarmed, he
went to court without delay, for he could not wait to speak to
the Queen. He had certainly seen Tristan by a fountain in the
Forest of Morroiz, but he had seen him so mad, so deranged and
so out of his mind that anyone coming upon him like that would
have every reason to be very frightened. He had seen him in such
a state that he scarcely recognized him, and he felt very sorry that
his grief had thus made him go to pieces, and that he had so
completely lost his reason and his memory. But although Giglain
had seen him in such a bad way, he did not intend to mention
this to the Queen; on the contrary, he was very eager to comfort
her rather than to tell her the whole truth about the plight Tristan
was in when he saw him on that occasion.

When Giglain arrived at court, everyone there welcomed him
very warmly and showed him great kindness and honour, for
they had met him before and knew that King Mark had likewise
shown him great kindness and honour all the while that Giglain

had stayed at the King's court. He asked at once where he could find the Queen, and those who knew where she was said:

'Sir, my lady is lying in bed very ill and indisposed.'

'Ah! for the love of God,' he said, 'tell her that I've come here and that I'd very much like to speak to her before I leave, if it please her.'

The man to whom he had said this was a relative of Dinas; he could go in and out of the Queen's room freely and talk to her whenever he liked. He now went to see her and said rightaway:

'My lady, a knight-errant has arrived here who would very much like to speak to you, if it please you.'

'Who is he?' she asked.

'It's Giglain, my lady, Sir Gawain's son. We've often seen him at court, and you yourself have encountered him here.'

'That's true,' said the Queen, 'and since he wants to speak to me, I'm quite happy to see him. Bring him in.'

Then the Queen ordered all the men and women to leave the room with the sole exception of Brangain and another young girl. They promptly carried out her command and all left. Thereupon Giglain entered, greeting the Queen as soon as he came up to her, and she returned his greeting. She made him sit down in front of her and straightaway asked him for his news.

'So help me God, my lady,' he said, 'I have nothing but good news.'

'In God's name,' she retorted, 'we on the other hand have bad news here, such as is harmful to all the brave knights in the world, for we have reliable information that Tristan is dead, who was a knight of such prowess as you know; and moreover you know it from your own experience rather than from what you've been told.'

'My lady,' said Giglain, 'so help me God, I'm amazed to hear you say that Tristan is dead! You shouldn't make statements like that for anything unless you knew it for certain.'

'We know it,' she replied, 'from the very maiden who saw him dead. What greater certainty could we have?'

'My lady,' answered Giglain, 'I'm not saying anything against you, since it would not be right in so far as you're the most worthy lady in the world; but as regards the maiden who brought you this news, I affirm in all truthfulness that never in the whole of her life did she tell a greater lie than when she told you that Tristan was dead. I can vouch for it, my lady, that less than four days ago I left him in the Forest of Morroiz, sound of limb; he had been ill without doubt, but he was quite recovered and had made his preparations to go to the Kingdom of Logres; he himself told me that he was leaving Cornwall more on account of you than for any other reason: this is what he said to me before we parted.'

When the Queen heard these words, she was so exceedingly happy and overjoyed that she quite lost her power of speech. For a long while she remained as though unconscious. After a time when she could speak she said:

'Ah! Giglain, is it really true that you've seen Tristan?'

'Yes, my lady, as God is my witness, I saw him less than four days ago fit and well.'

'Ah! God,' exclaimed the Queen, 'Holy Mary, will the day ever dawn for me when I shall be able to see him?'

'Yes, my lady, of course you'll see him again,' replied Giglain. 'It could not be otherwise.'

'Ah! God,' she said, 'the maiden committed a grave misdeed in bringing us the news of his death! It was almost the end of me. I'm sure she did it more out of spite against me than for any other reason. And since it has transpired that he is still alive, praise be to God who is keeping him alive, for to be sure the whole world is enhanced by his existence and all chivalry is more revered throughout the world.'

As a result of the news which Giglain had brought the Queen, she began to feel much more cheerful, since she never doubted that he had told her anything but the truth, although in fact things were very different with Tristan than Giglain had led her to believe. None the less the Queen felt so comforted that she fully recovered and gradually regained her beauty. She forbade Giglain to disclose these tidings to anyone else at court, and he did as she asked. She preferred it that the Cornish people should consider Tristan to be dead rather than alive, for once she was sure that he had gone to the Kingdom of Logres, she would see to it somehow or other that she would follow him all the way there and stay with him for the rest of her life.

Thus the truth about Tristan was concealed at that point from all the Cornish people except Queen Iseut, Dinas, and Brangain.

Apart from these three no one knew he was alive. Everyone else in Cornwall was convinced that Tristan was dead and that the maiden whom Audret had sent to court with the news of Tristan's death as I have described above had told them the truth; but that was not the case.

Now the story stops talking about the Queen—she was comforted by Giglain's tidings—and returns to Kahedin in order to relate how he left King Mark, with whom he and Palamedes had conversed at such length, and how he came back to his country, and how he died for love of my lady Iseut, Queen of Cornwall. [§§ 876–940 of vol. iii]

XVIII

THE DEATH OF KAHEDIN

AFTER parting from Mark,* Kahedin and Palamedes ride for some hours through the Forest of Morroiz, having decided to leave Cornwall and to try and forget Iseut. They meet Segurades who badly wounds Kahedin in a joust. Palamedes cannot avenge his friend, as Segurades, having broken his lance, has no weapon. Segurades rides off and continues on his way to Tintagel; but before he gets there, one of Audret's squires tells him that Tristan is dead. He is so upset that he falls ill and has to stay in a nearby abbey for a long while.

Palamedes takes Kahedin to the Abbey of Gaunes to recuperate; this abbey was founded by King Boort of Gaunes to commemorate his victory at that very spot over a giant who had killed his relative Anchises. Palamedes then leaves Cornwall and returns to Logres, though he will continue to love Iseut till his dying day; Kahedin, on the other hand, repents of his fruitless feelings for the Queen.

At this time, the anniversary of King Mark's coronation is celebrated at the Abbey of Gaunes, and the King attends the festival with Iseut. Kahedin hears two knights praise her beauty and finds out that she is in the church. He rises from his sickbed to see the Queen, and no sooner does he set eyes on her than his passion is rekindled. Henceforth nothing can cure him of his love. He cannot stop thinking of Iseut day and night. He stays in the abbey until his wounds are healed; then he sets sail for Brittany.

A storm takes him to Logres, and he decides to spend six days in Camelot at King Arthur's court. He admires Queen Guinevere's beauty, but affirms to Hestor of the Marshes that Iseut is the most beautiful lady in the world and Tristan the best knight. Guinevere sends for Kahedin; he discloses his identity to her and tells her how he accompanied Tristan to Cornwall to see Iseut, and how, having witnessed her beauty, he cannot blame Tristan for leaving his sister. He does not mention his love for Iseut nor its disastrous consequences. He reiterates that he considers Tristan to be a better knight than Lancelot.

After this conversation Kahedin leaves the court and rides all day through the large Forest of Camelot. At midday two knights and two ladies invite him to join them for lunch by a fountain; in the late afternoon he lies down to sleep by a rock, and when he wakes up, night has fallen. He decides to ride on until he finds some house or town, but it is so dark that he can barely see where he is going. Hearing the whinnying of a horse, he turns in that direction and comes to a fountain. His horse is so thirsty that it jumps in, and Kahedin gets very wet. He decides to stay by the fountain till daybreak. The night is so pitch-black that he does not see Lancelot of the Lake or Palamedes who are also resting by the fountain. Lancelot had in vain pursued Breuz the Pitiless until nightfall; Palamedes, after fighting with Dodinel the Wild, had lost his way following the Howling Beast, and had come to the fountain without noticing Lancelot's presence.

Kahedin lies down on his shield and begins to sigh and to weep, and then, at great length, laments about his love for the most beautiful queen in the world. Hearing his words, Palamedes sits up; this alerts Kahedin to his presence, and he regrets having spoken as he did. Lancelot is very vexed, thinking he had been talking about Guinevere. Palamedes suspects he is referring to Iseut, and is no less angry; he challenges Kahedin and presses him until at last the latter admits that the queen he loves is indeed Iseut. At this, Palamedes threatens him with death; Kahedin mocks him, declaring that he is just as foolish as another knight who had previously challenged him to a duel for the same reason.* This makes Palamedes realize that he is talking to Kahedin, and once again he asks him to do battle, but Kahedin declines to fight for a love which has caused him nothing but pain, and Palamedes does not insist. Kahedin tells him about his visit to King Arthur's court, and repeats that he considers Tristan to be a better knight than Lancelot, and Iseut more beautiful than Guinevere.

Thereupon Lancelot can restrain himself no longer. He warns the two companions that if any of Queen Guinevere's knights heard them speak like this, they might well find themselves in grave danger; he admits to being one of her knights and declares himself ready to fight both of them for the honour of his lady. Fortunately Kahedin manages to defuse the situation. Palamedes and Kahedin reveal their identity to each other, and are delighted to have met again so soon.

At daybreak Lancelot, who wants to remain incognito, puts on his helmet and prepares to leave, and the other two follow suit, when Blioberis of Gaunes, Lancelot's cousin, appears. He asks whether any of them wish to joust; Kahedin offers and is unhorsed but not hurt, and Palamedes likewise. The latter has recognized Blioberis and challenges him to fight with the sword because he wants to measure himself against the knights of the lineage of Ban; however, Lancelot intervenes and offers to fight in his stead. Palamedes suspects that he is Lancelot, and when pressed Lancelot divulges his name, whereupon Palamedes withdraws his challenge. Both he and Kahedin apologize to Lancelot for anything they had inadvertently said to offend him. Then Lancelot and Blioberis leave together for King Arthur's court. The two companions part; Palamedes intends to go to the Kingdom of Gorre, and Kahedin, disdainful of a country where the only greeting knights seemed to know was to strike and maim and kill each other, makes his way to the sea.

Kahedin has not gone far when he meets Kay the Seneschal who challenges him to joust; but Kahedin refuses, making a spirited attack on the customs of Logres. Some time ago Kahedin had freed Kay from prison in Brittany, and when the two knights discover each other's identity, they are very pleased to have met again. As they are riding along they encounter Lamorat of Wales leading a young girl. Kay, who does not recognize Lamorat, wants the girl for himself, but Lamorat unhorses first Kay and then Kahedin before riding off with the maiden. They suspect that their adversary was Lamorat because he wore the coat of arms of the lineage of King Pellinor of Listenois* (a red shield with a white lion's hand), and this is confirmed by a squire and a maiden they subsequently encounter.

Soon Kay and Kahedin come to a river; this is spanned by a bridge which is protected by a strong tower. In the distance they can see a castle called Uther's Shame. This name can be explained as follows: After his marriage to Ygerne, Uther had fallen passionately in love with Dya- genne, the wife of a knight called Argan, and persuaded her to return his love. He purposely went hunting near Argan's castle and was received very honourably by the unsuspecting husband. But a nephew of Argan discovered the two lovers and warned his uncle. The following day, while King Uther and Argan were out hunting, the King outstripped the rest of the company and returned to the castle; but Argan was on his guard and followed him. Dyagenne's sister alerted the King who quickly armed himself and sped away on horseback. Argan pursued him and brought him back, vanquished, to his castle. He spared his life, since he had not taken his wife against her will, but he killed the latter. King Uther was not freed until he had built a castle for Argan, so strong that it could withstand any attack: this was named Uther's Shame. Shortly afterwards Argan remarried, but his second wife ran away with Hestor of the Marshes, who, when attacked by Argan, defeated him. The latter was so outraged that he had a bridge built over the river and a bright red tower by it so that he could guard it against any knights-errant who wanted to cross and come to his castle. After his death, his four sons carried on the custom in such a way that the bridge, called Red Tower Bridge, was always guarded by the knight who had defeated the guardian. This continued until one day King Hoel of Brittany, Kahedin's father, who had come to Logres to look for his son, arrived at the bridge and found Tor, the son of Ares, guarding it; and since he defeated Tor, the King was forced to swear that he would remain its guardian.

When Kay and Kahedin appear at the bridge, Hoel challenges them. He unhorses and wounds Kay. Then the father and the son fight fiercely without recognizing each other, and it is not until after the 'first assault' that they discover each other's identity.* To free the King of his oath, Kay suggests that they should all three overcome the four brothers who were in the tower, and compel them to release Hoel from his obligation; they succeed. To recover from their wounds they seek shelter in a monastery nearby; Kay, less injured, leaves them after two days.

After a month, father and son return to Brittany. Everyone there is very upset that Kahedin can tell them no news about Tristan; some suspect that he has killed him. Iseut of the White Hands is distraught, weeping day and night. As for Kahedin, he cannot forget Iseut of Cornwall; his passion is such that, waking and sleeping, his being is absorbed by her more than ever before.

At this time, while Kahedin continued to be so passionately in love with my lady Iseut, there arrived in Brittany a harpist who had recently left Cornwall where he had spent many hours in the company of Sir Tristan and Queen Iseut. Indeed, the Queen had sent him to Brittany at this point in order to ascertain whether Tristan had gone back there. Since she did not believe him to be in Cornwall, she said to herself that he must be either in the Kingdom of Logres or in Brittany with his wife Iseut of the White Hands. And so, because she wanted to discover the truth, she had sent one of her maidens secretly and privately to the Kingdom of Logres, and she had asked the harpist to go to Brittany to see if he could find Tristan there, or at least to hear some news about him.

When Kahedin saw the harpist whom he had so often seen before in Queen Iseut's room, there is no need to ask whether he received him with joy and honour. He could not have welcomed him more warmly than he did. As soon as he set eyes on him he guessed that he had come to Brittany to glean some information about Tristan and to find out if by any chance he had gone back there. Kahedin received his lady's harpist very joyfully, and did everything to serve and honour him that he thought would please him. He wrote couplets and verses,* and set them to music and sang them to the harpist, who complimented him greatly. Kahedin was delighted at the harpist's praise, and said to him:

'I would like to ask you to do something for me.'

'Indeed, sir, with pleasure,' replied the harpist. 'It would have to be a very arduous task for me to refuse to do it, if I could.'

'I would like you to learn these verses,' said Kahedin, 'in such a way that you know the words and the music by heart, and then I beg you very earnestly to sing them only when you come into Queen Iseut's presence; and even then don't sing them unless she is quite alone. That's my request and the favour I'm asking you.'

'So help me God,' the harpist answered, 'I shall be very pleased to do that.'

Then he learnt the verses which Kahedin had written, and afterwards the music. He stayed on in Brittany for as long as he liked, and when he left, Kahedin gave him whatever he wanted to take with him from Brittany, and even more.

Once the harpist had put to sea, it did not take him long to arrive in Cornwall. As soon as he had landed, he asked for King Mark's whereabouts, and he was told that the King could be found in Tintagel where he had been in residence for over two months. The harpist set out straightaway and went on till he reached the court. The Queen was overjoyed to see him. When she had eaten, she retired to her room and sent for him and made him sit by her, and then began to ask him for news of Brittany, and he replied:

'My lady, I went to Brittany as you commanded, and remained there at least two months to see if I could find out anything about Sir Tristan. I must tell you, my lady, that they know nothing about him, and they are very upset and distressed by this throughout Brittany. To be sure, my lady, I swear I'd never have thought it possible that any foreign knight could be so loved and so missed in a country which is not his own as Sir Tristan is in Brittany, just as though he were everyone's blood brother, my lady. I can't see that they could possibly feel any greater love for him than they all do.'

'By my faith,' said the Queen, 'if they love him as much as you say, that's not surprising! Tristan is so endowed with all virtues that wherever he might have gone in Brittany, he could not have failed to be loved more than any other knight, except of course by those who are envious of him. But now tell me, so help you God, did you see Iseut of the White Hands, the woman Tristan married some time ago?'

'Yes, my lady, so help me God,' replied the harpist.

'And what do you think of her? Is she as beautiful as many people say?'

'My lady,' he retorted, 'so help me God, she is certainly beautiful, but not of such great beauty that one couldn't easily find a more beautiful lady in some place or other. However, this much I can safely say about her: I don't think I've ever in all my life seen any lady who speaks more amiably and answers more courteously than she does. As God is my witness, it never displeased me to be in her company. May the Lord grant her good fortune!'

The Queen fell silent and said no more about this matter. She was very upset that she could not find out anything about Tristan. Since she had no definite news of him and he was not in Brittany, she assumed he must be in the Kingdom of Logres. The maiden she had sent there not long ago to discover the truth would surely bring her back some definite information; it could not be otherwise. And so the Queen spent her time waiting for the news that the maiden would bring her, for it seemed to her that she was bound to come back soon now; she could not delay much longer.

One day shortly afterwards it happened that King Mark was out enjoying himself hunting in the company of many knights. That same day after dinner the Queen was sitting privately in her room, and she had only Brangain and one other young girl with her. She was holding her harp in front of her and had tuned it correctly and was playing the lay which she had composed for love of Tristan when she wanted to kill herself, and King Mark had stopped her. At this moment the harpist—the one who had recently returned from Brittany—appeared outside the door of the room. The Queen, hearing that he was at the door and wanted to come in, ordered that the door should be opened to let him in, but not anyone else; and this was done. The harpist had heard the lay which the Queen was playing from outside and had understood it well; and as soon as he had come into her presence and had greeted her as one should greet one's lady, he said to her:

'It seems to me, my lady, that this is a new lay which you were harping just now.'

'Indeed,' she replied, 'you're quite right. Not even half a year has passed since it was composed.'

'In God's name, my lady, I can tell you that I know some verses which I think are more recent than this lay.'

'And who wrote them?' asked the Queen.

'Saving your grace, my lady, I won't tell you that at present, but I'll sing the verses to you and play them on the harp, if you wish to listen to them.'

'To be sure,' said the Queen, 'I'll listen to them gladly, since they're as recent as you say. Sit down here in front of me and take this harp and tune it so that it harmonizes with the music and the words you want to sing.'

Hearing his lady's command, the harpist did not delay any longer, but sat down and took the harp and began to tune it so as to make it synchronize with the song he wished to sing and in accordance with his knowledge of what was required. And when he had tuned it correctly, he began to sing his song as follows:

> To you does Kahedin complain
> Oh Love, about the deadly pain
> Caused by the lady for whose sake
> He cannot sleep, he cannot wake.
> All his actions have come to nought,
> In Death's firm grip he has been caught.
> His love was loyal; that is why
> To you, oh Love, he makes his cry:
> Take pity on him and be kind,
> Since he's been wronged, and try to find
> In her who causes him such ache
> Indulgence. In her heart make
> Her now feel pity for her slave.
> Indeed I'm hastening to my grave
> Because I love with a true heart,
> For ever since the very start
> When God first made the firmament
> No heart was ever more intent
> On loving well than is my own.
> For this, oh Love, do not condone
> My death; beg her whom I adore
> Who is my spirit evermore
> That Kahedin should not forego

His life, if it should please her so.
I commend her to God on high,
May He persuade her to put by
Her wrath, and give me all the bliss
That in the past she made me miss.

When the harpist had finished singing his verses which he had accompanied on the harp as best he could, he fell silent and added nothing more. As soon as the Queen heard Kahedin mentioned, she realized straightaway that it was Kahedin who had written these lines for love of her, particularly as the harpist had recently come back from Brittany. Consequently she considered Kahedin very much more foolish than she had ever done in the past, for these verses showed her clearly that he had not yet got over his love for her at all. He was completely out of his mind to hanker after something he could not obtain. She neither praised nor condemned the verses which the harpist had played on the harp, except in so far as she complimented him for having harped so well. She praised the harpist, but not the words or the poem.

After this it was not long before the maiden whom the Queen had sent to the Kingdom of Logres returned, and told her that she had looked and searched everywhere, but had found nothing of what she had gone to find.

'Tell me, maiden,' said the Queen, 'did you go to King Arthur's court?'

'Yes, indeed, my lady, I certainly did, and I spoke to Sir Lancelot of the Lake who was there at the time; however, I didn't tell him that I was in your service, nor did he know that I came from Cornwall. When I asked him whether he had heard any news about Sir Tristan, he replied that he knew nothing, except that he thought Tristan was in Brittany. That is all Sir Lancelot said to me; I couldn't elicit any other information from him about what I wanted to find out. After leaving King Arthur's court I met a knight-errant in the company of a single squire and a maiden. This knight, who gave me to understand that he had come from Brittany, told me that Tristan was definitely in Brittany, and had arrived there recently.'

Hearing this the Queen really believed that the young girl had told her the truth, and for that reason she thought she would send someone to Brittany a second time to find out if Tristan was actually there. It seemed to her that he simply must be in Brittany, since he was not in the Kingdom of Logres.

Then she composed a short lay which she intended to send to Kahedin, identical in form to his, and wrote it down with her own hand. Thereupon she sent for the harpist and gave it to him, and told him he must go back once again to Brittany to see if Tristan had returned there, for she had been given to understand that he had gone back. If he was able to find him, he would hand him a letter which she was sending him,* but if he could not find him, he must conceal the letter and bring it back to her. Also, as soon as he was alone together with Kahedin, he should sing these verses to him in the same key as he had used for the other lay and to the same melody.

'My lady,' said the harpist, 'I shall be very happy to do so. I wish I were already in Brittany, since it's your wish that I should go back there again.'

When the harpist had prepared himself for the journey, he took his leave of the Queen, and then departed from Cornwall and travelled until he came to Brittany. On arrival, he began to ask where he could find King Hoel, and he was told that the King was staying in one of his cities called Rednez, and he immediately set out on his way there. And wherever he went, he always asked for news of Tristan, but he found no one who could tell him anything about him; they all affirmed that Tristan had not returned to Brittany after leaving with Kahedin, the King's son. The harpist was most dismayed to hear this and said to himself that the maiden had undoubtedly given the Queen false information.

What more shall I tell you? The harpist travelled through Brittany until he reached King Hoel's court, and there can be no doubt that Kahedin was delighted to see him. He received him as honourably as he could for the sake of the one he loved more than himself. When Kahedin was alone with the harpist, he asked him if he had sung the verses which he had given him to learn before the Queen.

'Yes, indeed,' replied the harpist. 'You may be sure that I sung them before her.'

'So help you God,' continued Kahedin, 'tell me what my lady said about them.'

'As God is my witness,' answered the harpist, 'she said nothing about them, good or bad. She neither praised nor criticized them, but when I was on the point of leaving she gave me some verses written in the same metre and to the same music as were the ones you gave me.'

'Ah! for God's sake,' exclaimed Kahedin, 'sing them to me so that I can hear them!'

'Willingly, to be sure,' said the harpist.

Then he began to sing the verses as follows:

An act of folly will bring shame
On any vassal worth his name.
In such an action he will find
No good, so he should bear in mind
Right at the start what he will do
When he has seen his action through.
If he finds that it could harm him,
Such a deed should then alarm him.
To reap some good should be his aim;
All people will then praise his name.
A man who loves, and does surmise
That she loves not, is most unwise.
A love where there can be no gain
Has to be called futile and vain.
Whoever does his best to serve
Where he can patently observe
That nothing good or true he'll face
Is but intent on his disgrace.
A bird is in a sorry plight
That with an eagle tries to fight;
It makes the eagle so irate,
A speedy death is the bird's fate.
Likewise it is a foolish act
For any beast to have attacked
A lion, for its strength is vast;
It tears the beast and kills it fast,
If that is what it wants to do.
And any man is foolish too
To try and go where he can't get.

> If he should die, none should regret
> His death; he chose it on his own.
> For such a man one should not moan.

These were the very words contained in the poem which the Queen had sent to Kahedin, as I have told you. After he had listened to them and heard them, he made the harpist repeat them once again in order to understand them better. Thus, taking his time, he let them sink in, and when they were firmly fixed in his mind, he realized beyond any doubt that the Queen had written these cruel words out of hatred for him and ill-will; and since his lady felt such total animosity towards him, his fate was sealed and he was absolutely heart-broken. He no longer asked God for anything other than death. Love had so ensnared him, and dominated him so entirely that it deprived him of his mind and his soul, for although Kahedin was undoubtedly one of the wisest knights in the whole of Brittany considering his age, at this point he had so completely taken leave of his senses that he himself was bringing about his end. He had only himself to blame for his death; he was doing all he could to hasten its approach. He thought very hard and reflected at length what to do about this matter, but in the end he saw that there was no hope for him: he loved the Queen so deeply, so tenderly, so ardently and so passionately that there was no way in which he could drive this love from his heart.

What more shall I tell you? Kahedin was so absorbed by thoughts of his love that he stopped eating and drinking. He could not sleep or rest or do anything other than think about his love. He grew thin and became weaker from day to day. He shunned and avoided everyone's company so that he could the better dwell on his desires. It greatly annoyed him to see people. He wanted to be alone without interruption in order to concentrate his thoughts on the one whose beauty was mirrored and inscribed in his heart. Ah! God, what a sad end, what extraordinary grief, all on account of his love for my lady Iseut! He was dying such a strange death that no man ever died in sorrow as great as his. His suffering was constant. He abhorred all pleasures and abandoned all joy. Innumerable people tried to comfort him, but in vain: he was not willing or indeed able to be comforted.

He would never find any medicine for this illness except in death. Death pleased and appealed to him; he no longer wished for any other happiness.

What shall I tell you? Everyone who saw him and looked at him was in no doubt that he was suffering from a strange malady, but they did not know what caused it, for they had always known him to be a man of such wisdom that it would have been impossible anywhere to find a knight of his age who was wiser, in view of his good sense and his knightly qualities. They would never have thought that he could have been driven as mad by love as he was. Love had so completely deprived him of his reason that he did not know whether he was dead or alive. He could not sleep at all and ate so little that it was a wonder how he kept going. He led such a peculiar life that those around him were greatly amazed in what manner and by what means he stayed alive considering the amount of food he ate.

The Queen's harpist who was not aware of the nature of Kahedin's illness and who did not suspect the reason why he was languishing, nonetheless did his best to cheer him up, but to no avail: Kahedin laughed when people tried to comfort him, and made fun of it all and joked about it, and said that he would recover soon enough. But all the while his health declined, as everyone knew and witnessed clearly. When the harpist saw Kahedin so debilitated in every way, he said that he would return to Cornwall, for he had no wish to stay with someone who was getting worse from day to day.

'Ah! in the name of God,' said Kahedin, 'I beseech you for the Lord's sake not to part from me before you know the outcome of my illness. For the love of God, grant me this request; you will be bringing me great solace and doing me a great favour.'

The harpist agreed readily enough, since he saw that Kahedin begged him so earnestly and so insistently.

Kahedin spent two whole months in this way, languishing for love of my lady Iseut, becoming weaker every day. The King, his father, who loved him more than he loved anyone else in the world, wept and lamented bitterly, and so did Iseut of the White Hands. She was so exceedingly distressed that she never stopped grieving. She cried day and night for Kahedin whose condition was deteriorating so much that everyone who saw him said, either openly or in secret, that he could not fail to die. All the barons in Brittany, poor and rich alike, came to visit him and asked him what was wrong with him.

'What's wrong with me!' he said. 'It's quite obvious: I'm ill! But I'm sure I'll soon recover.'

They came to see Kahedin in great numbers, one and all, so much so that they annoyed him, and he said to himself that he would leave there and go somewhere else. Thereupon he had his horse saddled, and mounted, and took the harpist with him, and went off to a large forest which was nearby.

When he had come to the forest, he dismounted by a very beautiful and pleasant fountain situated in a small valley, and he made the harpist dismount in front of him; and once the two of them had got off their horses and had sat down beside the fountain, he addressed the harpist, weeping:

'Friend,' he said, 'my death draws near. I shall not live much longer. I've suffered and endured so much torment, sorrow, unhappiness and pain that I can bear no more. I shall die quite soon, and in your presence. If you want to stay here, you'll be able to see it. In an evil hour did I ever set foot in Cornwall, for all the misfortunes which are making me die in anguish stem from there. Friend, take this; it's my last lament set down in writing. I've composed it in all truthfulness to the best of my ability. I'm giving it to you; look after it well until you're back in Cornwall. When you come into the presence of my lady Iseut, you will hand it to her on my behalf and tell her that I'm sending it to her because she was the one I've loved beyond measure. In an evil hour did I ever see her or love her, for I'm dying in such torment and such anguish that to my knowledge no knight ever died in agony as great as mine. God grant that my lady Iseut may find out for herself the terrible suffering with which a human being ends his life when he dies of love's sorrow.'

No sooner had he spoken these words than he fainted as a result of the exceeding distress he felt, and lay unconscious for a long time. When he eventually came to, he looked so sickly, so pale and so feeble that anyone seeing him then would have said without hesitation that he was undoubtedly close to death and could not escape from it in any way. As soon as he had regained consciousness he began to lament all over again in an unrestrained and singular fashion, and with such fervour that the harpist who was watching him wept for pity.

Kahedin remained like this beside the fountain for three days without moving at all, nor did he take any food or drink. The harpist who stayed with him was extremely upset about it. He never left Kahedin except for one hour each day when he went to eat at an abbey which was nearby. On the fourth day as dawn was breaking, Kahedin said to the harpist:

'Friend, why should I conceal it from you? This very day you will see me die, provided you remain in this place. My heart is failing me, I know it well. Death is closing in on me. Here is the letter which you will take to my lady Queen Iseut. However, make sure that no one sees it before you have handed it to her. When you're in her presence, inform her of my death, and describe my end to her according to what you've heard and what you're about to see. And if by chance you come across Sir Tristan, you can safely say to him that Kahedin met him to his misfortune, and went with him to Cornwall in an evil hour, for this voyage caused Kahedin's death. This much you can tell him from me.'

Then he drew from his breast a letter which he himself had composed and written, and, seeing it, he began to weep very tenderly.

Kahedin reads the letter to the harpist; it is written in verse,* and tells Iseut at great length that he is dying for love of her, since he now realizes that his love is hopeless. He is not blaming her, but Love who has deceived him. He is dying in great anguish and is sending her the news of his death by this letter. May she never experience such agony.

When he has finished reading it, he folds it up and gives it to the harpist and asks him to present it to Iseut on his behalf, and to tell her of his death and of the great suffering which caused him to die. This said, he falls down backwards and expires shortly afterwards.

The harpist, afraid that he might be accused of having killed him, quickly rides away; he does however tell some shepherds he meets that Kahedin is lying dead by the fountain, and they take his body back to court. He is buried with great honour and deeply mourned throughout the whole of Brittany; King Hoel nearly kills himself so great is his grief.

In this part the story relates that on the day when Kahedin died in the manner I have described, Queen Iseut was residing in the

city of Tintagel in Cornwall. She could not understand why her
messenger was delaying so long in Brittany, and she said to herself
that there must be a good reason for it. She waited and waited,
often thinking about this matter, until at last the harpist returned.
When the Queen asked him for news of Tristan, he told her that
Tristan was not in Brittany and had not been there for a long
time, and that in his opinion he was more likely to be in his own
country, the Kingdom of Leonois, than in any other place.

'I think you're right,' said the Queen. 'I'll send someone to
Leonois shortly to find out if he's there or not. But now tell me,
what news are you bringing me from Brittany, and how are they
faring in that country?'

'As God is my witness, my lady,' replied the messenger, 'I can
tell you truthfully, I don't think that anywhere in the world
would one find such great sorrow as there is in Brittany at this
moment.'

'Good gracious!' said the Queen, 'why are they grieving so
much in that country as you give me to understand?'

'Because, my lady, Kahedin, the son of King Hoel of Brittany,
is dead.'

'Upon my faith!' exclaimed the Queen, 'how did he die? Was
he killed? So help you God, tell me how he met his death.'

'Willingly, my lady, to be sure,' said the harpist.

Then he began to relate to her everything that he had seen
happen, and how Kahedin's death was undoubtedly due to his
unhappy love. And when he had finished his tale and had
described to the Queen the manner in which Kahedin had died
and the exact circumstances, he added:

'My lady, at his death Kahedin gave me a letter which he wrote
with his own hand, and he begged me earnestly for the love of
God to hand it to you as soon as I found myself in your presence.
I herewith give it to you; take it.'

Thereupon he gave her the letter and the Queen took it and
unfolded it, and then began to read it. After she had read it from
beginning to end, she said to herself that Kahedin was a very
discerning and intelligent knight to be able to write about his
own death so cleverly and so well. She said nothing else about it;
however, although she said nothing, it grieved her that he had
died in this way as a result of his folly.

What more shall I tell you? This incident could not be so well concealed that King Mark did not find out about it, and so did the Cornish people. The word soon spread throughout Cornwall that Kahedin had died for love of my lady Iseut; likewise it became known in the Kingdom of Logres and in the Kingdom of Leonois. There remained at this time no kingdom in the world frequented by knights-errant where it was not common knowledge that Kahedin, the son of King Hoel of Brittany, had died for love of my lady Iseut, the Queen of Cornwall. But now the story stops talking about all these matters concerning King Mark, Queen Iseut and the Cornish people, and returns to Sir Tristan, for the story has now been silent about him for a long time; and it will relate how he was found with the shepherds by the fountain. [fos. 148a–173d of BN 750]

XIX

TRISTAN'S CURE

THE story now relates that after Tristan had left the messenger-girl sent by Palamedes, he so lost his reason and his memory that he did not know what he was doing. Like a madman he began to tear the clothes he wore, so that he went around the Forest of Morroiz more or less naked, crying and howling, leaping and running as though he were a mad beast. And if anyone were to ask me what he was living on, I would say that he existed on raw meat, for he spent his time catching animals here and there, and then ate them quite raw, flesh and hide. That is how he lived, and in this way he satisfied his hunger.

At this time he made the acquaintance of a number of shepherds who were tending sheep in the woods. He liked to be in their company because they gave him some of their bread, but at times they made him pay for it dearly, beating and striking him so hard that it was a wonder he put up with it. However, this did not stop him from frequenting them; he continued to go there because they often gave him food. At this point, due to the physical suffering he underwent as a result of hunger and cold, of sleeping rough and enduring all the hardships that a mortal man can sustain, he became so pale, so thin, so debilitated, so weather-beaten and so burnt by the heat of the sun that his whole appearance changed; indeed, he looked so different that even the closest kinsman he had in the world, were he to have seen him in that state, would not have recognized him nor believed it possible in any way that this was Tristan. And what most grossly disfigured him was the fact that the shepherds cut off his hair and stained his face with a different colour every day. And he suffered it all, not knowing what they were doing to him, and he never hit back, however much they beat him.

At this time when Tristan was reduced to such a sorry state, both as a result of his malady and because of the shepherds who were doing him all the harm they could, it happened one day that Sir Daguenet the Fool was riding through the Forest of Morroiz intent on enjoying himself, accompanied by two squires. And I should tell you that Sir Daguenet had come to Cornwall on this occasion from King Arthur's court to see Queen Iseut, and he had been sent there by those of the Kingdom of Logres for fun and merriment. And because he felt the urge to drink, he dismounted by a fountain, and so did the squires, and they left their mounts behind them. As soon as the horses, which were rested and fresh, felt themselves unencumbered, they immediately ran off into the forest, chasing one another, neighing and kicking, frolicking and frisking about. Their owners, by the fountain, were intent on their conversation and on the amusement they could derive from Daguenet's words, and did not notice this until the horses had gone a considerable distance and there was no trace of them anywhere. They followed in their wake as best they could, without however hearing or seeing them at all. They searched here and there, but were unable to find the animals, for they were already too far away.

Thus the three of them roamed through the forest until they came upon the fountain frequented by the shepherds who used to give food to Tristan, as I have told you. The shepherds were sitting by the fountain at this point, and Tristan was with them. One of the youths asked the shepherds:

'Did you see any horses passing near here?'

The shepherds were at this moment laughing very heartily because Tristan had taken hold of one of the shepherds and thrown him into the fountain, nearly drowning him; and he had only just done this, and the shepherds were still laughing about it amongst themselves. They were simple-minded and foolish, as one would expect woodland peasants to be, and they answered the squires, full of mirth:

'We don't know anything about your horses, young sirs.'

The squires, hearing their laughter, thought that the shepherds were mocking and scorning them, and that they knew perfectly well which way the horses had gone, or had hidden them. And so they fell upon the shepherds without more ado and began to beat them fiercely, saying that either they told them where the horses were or they would all be killed. When Sir Daguenet saw his squires beat up the shepherds like that—being such a wise knight as we have many a time described to you before!*—all he did was to put his hand on his sword and similarly fall upon the shepherds. He started to deal them the mightiest blows he could, so that he straightaway wounded four of them; and I should mention that they numbered twelve altogether.

The shepherds who had previously been rejoicing and making merry and laughing at what they had seen Tristan do, now began to cry out and to lament bitterly when they felt themselves treated like that, and fled in all directions as best they could, trying their hardest to escape. When Tristan heard the shepherds lament so loudly, even though he was not in possession of his reason or his good sense at this point, having gone completely out of his mind, he was exceedingly upset at their wails, in so far as his mental state allowed him to be so. For a long time he watched Daguenet beating, striking, and maltreating the shepherds, but then he could tolerate it no longer. He jumped up and ran towards Daguenet, in no way deterred by the sword which the latter was holding, and gripped him by the sides of his body with his two hands and lifted him into the air as easily as if he were a child. Then he flung him onto the ground with such force that Daguenet lacked the strength to get up, and lay there as though he were dead, so bruised and so confounded was he by this fall. Tristan immediately seized the bare sword which Daguenet was holding, and with it rushed at the squires, striking one of them so fiercely that he cut his arms right off.* The squire at once fell to the ground and fainted as a result of the great pain he experienced.

As soon as the other squire saw this blow, he did not feel too reassured, for he realized clearly that if he waited for the madman who was holding the sword, he would be killed without mercy. For that reason he took to his heels as fast as he could and left his companions in the fray. His only concern was to escape from this adventure without coming to any harm; never before in any place where he had been was he as frightened as on this occasion.

What more shall I tell you? He was so intent on fleeing that he managed to get away and out of Tristan's reach. Tristan pursued him for a long time, but was unable to catch up with him, because after all the hardship and discomfort he had suffered in the shepherd's company, he was not nearly as agile as he used to be. He did not return to the fountain, but made his way straight to the dwelling of a hermit who lived in the forest; and I can tell you that he often went to see this hermit, since he gave him some of the food that God provided for him. And this is in keeping with the habits and the behaviour of madmen: even though they may have lost their sense and their reason, they readily go to a place where they find compassion and kindness.

Tristan made for the hermitage, the naked sword in his hand, leaping and howling like a mad beast. The worthy man was outside his hermitage at that point saying his prayers in front of the door of the little house. When he saw Tristan coming towards him, mad and deranged as he knew him to be, and moreover holding a bare sword in his hand, he did not wait, but withdrew into the little house and locked the door very firmly behind him, for he was very scared and frightened that Tristan would put him to death if he seized hold of him.

As soon as Tristan reached the good man's abode, mad and demented as he was, he asked him for something to eat, crying as loudly as he could:

'Hey, man, give me some food!'

The worthy man, who felt very sorry for him, opened a tiny window and gave him a large quantity of bread, since he could not give him anything else on this occasion. And why could he not? Because he did not have anything else. Tristan ate, and once he had finished, he went to sleep outside the worthy man's door. When the good man saw and knew for certain that Tristan was fast asleep, he unlocked his door as softly as he could, and then stepped forward and took the sword away from him so that he would not be able to harm anyone he encountered.

Daguenet returns to King Mark's court on foot, quite distraught, still clutching the empty scabbard of his sword. No one can get any sense out of him; all he can tell them is to beware of the madman by the fountain. The King decides to wait for the return of Daguenet's two squires to find out what has happened. The one who escaped returns to court alone that evening, his companion, whose arms had been cut off, having died. He tells King Mark the whole adventure from beginning to end, and concludes by saying that the madman was a huge, giant-like figure. This makes one of the Cornish knights suggest that he must be the giant Mathan the Brown, who, according to the knight, had lost his reason three months previously. At the King's request he relates Mathan's story.

Some time ago a knight-errant bearing a black shield with a white lion had arrived at Mark's court and offered to relinquish the beautiful damsel who accompanied him to any knight who could unhorse him. Only Mathan had dared to take up the challenge and had won, and had taken the young girl back to his own country. All this the King himself remembered well. The Cornish knight then told him the rest of the story: Last May he himself was riding through the Forest of Morroiz with Mathan and the maiden when they met one of Arthur's knights, Gaheriet, who wanted the girl for himself. He knocked down both Mathan and himself with such violence that neither of them could move for a long time, and rode off with the maiden. Mathan, who loved her more than himself, was so distressed that he did not eat or drink for four days; then he succumbed to a strange malady and lost his reason.

Hearing this, King Mark asks his men to search the Forest of Morroiz for Mathan the Brown so that he can have him cured in Tintagel. As for Tristan, he is now treated more kindly by the shepherds.

Shortly after this incident, Tristan has another adventure. There was in the Forest of Morroiz a high mountain on which for the past two hundred years has stood a very strong castle, whose lord at the present time is a fierce and hostile giant. Tristan would have liked to rid Cornwall of this giant, but Iseut, fearful for his safety, has forbidden it. The giant has always been afraid of Tristan, but when he hears that Tristan is dead or at any rate has left Cornwall, he gives free rein to his fury against the Cornish knights for having killed his father outside the gates of Tintagel at the time of Mark's coronation.

One day this giant, called Taulas of the Mountain, comes to the fountain where the shepherds are sitting with Tristan. They have no idea who he is, and he sits down amongst them. While they are talking, a knight from King Mark's court arrives with a very beautiful maiden, and Taulas immediately hides behind a tree. They dismount and go to the fountain to drink. Taulas pounces on the knight, throws him to the ground, and threatens to kill him. The young girl, distraught, flees on foot into the forest. One of the shepherds reproaches Tristan for not helping the knight, but Tristan has enough reason left to protest that he has no weapon. Thereupon another shepherd seizes hold of the knight's sword and gives it to Tristan, telling him to strike the giant right on top of his head. Tristan has to be told a second time what to do, but then he runs up to Taulas and with a single blow makes his head fly to the ground. He wants to do the same to the knight; fortunately he is stopped in time by the shepherds.

The knight, out of gratitude, decides to take Tristan with him and to bring him back to health; however Tristan, still clutching the sword, tells him to go away if he does not want a blow on the head. The knight asks the shepherds to intercede, but Tristan insists that he wishes to stay in the Forest of Morroiz. Much to the shepherd's surprise, the knight then picks up Taulas's head; he explains to them who the giant is, and tells them that he is taking this proof of his death to King Mark, who will be overjoyed by this extraordinary adventure.

When the knight has found the maiden, he rides with her to Tintagel to spread the news. Taulas's head is hung on a post in the middle of the city for all to see, as this deed is the greatest good fortune that has befallen Cornwall since the Morholt's death. Mark is more eager than ever to find out if the madman is Mathan the Brown or not, and to bring him back to Tintagel to be cured.

One day not long after this adventure, so the story relates, King Mark went hunting in the Forest of Morroiz with a large company of barons and knights. That morning he pursued a very swift and nimble stag, and because he was better mounted than any of his companions, he outdistanced them all and undertook the chase by himself, always remaining within sight of the stag. The other knights were left behind, since they could not keep up with him, for their horses were not as good as his. Within a short while the King was so far ahead that he had no idea of their whereabouts nor could he hear them. The stag, which was very fast, ran in front and the dogs ran after it, and the King kept following; but not for long, since his horse could not sustain the pace. This is how King Mark fared that day: he lost his stag and his hounds which were going ahead at full speed, and his companions likewise who were trailing behind. He did not know what had become of them, nor in what direction the stag had gone.

Just then he happened to find a narrow, deserted path which was seldom used, and for that reason it was quite grassy; and as he was riding along thinking all the while of his lost prey and of his companions, it so happened that chance brought him straight to the fountain which Tristan and the shepherds were wont to frequent. Tristan was asleep at the time, looking such an ugly creature, so uncouth, so ill-clad and ragged that anyone who came upon him then would have had to feel sorry for him. When the King saw the shepherds by the fountain, he turned in that direction in order to find out if they could tell him something about his hunt; but also because he wanted to rest at the fountain for a while, and felt like a drink, being hot and covered with perspiration and very exhausted.

The shepherds, seeing him approach, came up to him and greeted him and held his stirrup until he had dismounted. The first thing he did was to go and drink in order to quench his thirst. When he had drunk, he noticed Tristan sleeping beside the fountain, and began to look at him, for he saw that he was tall and thin and ill-clad and ragged, and that, although pallid, he was burnt and tanned by the heat of the sun. And without a doubt, he was at this point so completely changed in every way that King Mark who could see him clearly and looked at him very attentively did not recognize him at all, which was not really surprising. There was not in the whole of Cornwall a man discerning and perceptive enough to have recognized him in that state however hard he looked at him.

The King asked the shepherds:

'Who is this man sleeping here?'

And they replied:

'He's a madman who keeps us company. We don't really know where he's come from, but ever since he came here he's hardly left us. And we can tell you that he's done many extraordinary things since he's been here, so much so that if King Mark knew about it, he would consider it very remarkable.'

'Pray tell me,' said the King, 'what has he done that should be regarded as so extraordinary?'

'Sir, he killed Taulas of the Mountain, the greatest enemy King Mark had in the whole of Cornwall, indeed in the whole world. If this Taulas of the Mountain had lived for long, he would in the end have destroyed King Mark and all of Cornwall.'

As soon as the King heard these words, he remembered what the knight had told him in Tintagel, and he realized that this was undoubtedly the man who had pursued Daguenet and his company so cruelly, as the story told earlier on. Thereupon the King began to examine him to see if he was Mathan the Brown, but after he had scrutinized him at length it was quite clear to him that this was not Mathan. He looked at Tristan for a long time, and yet he could not make out who he was at all, which distressed him greatly.

When the King saw that he would not recognize him, he sat down amongst the shepherds to rest a little and to have a pleasant chat with them. Then he began to ask the shepherds:

'Now tell me, young lads, can you give me any news about Tristan, the nephew of King Mark of Cornwall? It's actually being said in Tintagel that he's in the Forest of Morroiz and that he hasn't left here yet. Do you know anything about this?'

'To be sure, Sir Knight,' replied the shepherds, 'Sir Tristan isn't in the Morroiz, but rather in the Kingdom of Logres; the other day a knight-errant who had come from Logres told us so. Moreover, according to what's being said both by the Cornish and the foreign knights, if Tristan has indeed left the Kingdom of Cornwall, King Mark should consider himself a simpleton and a fool, for they all maintain that as long as Sir Tristan used to be in Cornwall, the country had no need to fear any man or any prince, because there was not in the whole world so powerful a prince or so bold as to invade Cornwall while he knew Tristan to be there. Consequently, Sir Knight, since it has come about that Tristan is no longer in Cornwall, you may be sure that Cornwall can no longer be without fear, nor will it be feared by its neighbours or by any other foreign people; and that's why they say it's ill-fated that Tristan left Cornwall, for in the end it will bring about Cornwall's shame and dishonour.'

'Now tell me, young lads,' said the King, 'what do the foreign knights say about King Mark, and how do they talk about him?'

'As God is our witness, sir,' answered the shepherds, 'they speak only ill of him. They claim that he's disagreeable, base, treacherous and untrustworthy. And that's not all: they say that if Tristan were to exert himself a little and consort with the Round Table companions as brave knights do, he would be able to drive King Mark out of Cornwall by main force, since the King could never defend himself against him and his friends.'

'Now tell me,' continued King Mark, 'what do they say about Tristan and Queen Iseut?'

'So help me God, sir,' replied one of the shepherds, 'you do seem very simple asking questions like that! What's going on between Tristan and Queen Iseut is known to everyone in the world, and King Mark himself is well aware of it. He's very wise not to make too much fuss about it; if he did, he would stand to lose more than he would gain.'

When the King heard these words he was so stunned that he did not know what to say. For a long time he remained silent, thinking, and giving no sign of the anger that he felt and that had been aroused in his heart. After a while he took his hunting- horn which was hanging round his neck and blew it as loudly as he could, so that his men would hear it if by chance they were near at hand, and come to him.

When Tristan who was sleeping by the fountain heard the noise and the sound of the horn, he jumped up and began to cry out the first words that came to his lips:

'Quick, Hudenc, catch it for me!'

As soon as the King heard the name Hudenc, he remembered his nephew Tristan. He looked at him, but did not recognize him at all, for he had completely changed. And what more than anything else made the King fail to recognize Tristan was the fact that his whole face was stained and blackened by coal and ashes; indeed, the way he was got up, no one could have realized at this point that he was Tristan. The shepherds who often used to maltreat him, seeing that he was awake and hearing him cry out like a huntsman, immediately started jostling and hitting him and causing him great harm. What shall I tell you? They hurt and abused him so much that he grew angry, which only made them ill-treat him more. They manhandled him to such an extent that he lost his temper, so much so that he snatched one of the shepherds' crooks and attacked them, mad as he was, and in no time crippled four of them so badly that they remained lying on the ground as though they were dead, nor did they have the power or the strength to move from there. The others, seeing their companions maimed in this way, ran off; they had no wish to be seized by Tristan, since he was clearly beset by one of his bouts of madness. What more shall I tell you? They speedily fled in all directions and left him to it. They were in no doubt whatever that it was not a good idea for them to be with him or to remain in his company.

When the King saw himself quite alone with this madman who would not hesitate to strike him should his frenzy induce him to do so, I can tell you that he did not feel too reassured, since he was not armed well enough to be able to defend himself if he were attacked, having none of his armour with him except his sword. The King looked at Tristan with great apprehension: he saw him so far removed from his reason that even the sword which the King was wearing would not stop the madman from assaulting him if the frenzy went to his head. None the less the King remained there to see what the man would do. And while he was waiting in this manner, saying to himself that if he came towards him he would strike him with his sword, just then Audret appeared with as many as ten companions, some of them knights, others squires. And he had come straight to this spot because he had heard the sound of the horn; and they all thought that the King had caught the stag, since he had sounded the horn for the kill.

As soon as they reached the fountain and saw the King on foot, they dismounted and asked him what he had done with his dogs; and he told them that he had lost both his dogs and the stag.

'I don't know what's happened to them all,' he said. 'I can't hear the dogs barking or yelping, and that's why I dismounted by this fountain when I chanced upon it, as I was exceedingly tired and exhausted at the time.'

Then they began to look at the shepherds whom Tristan had knocked down beside the fountain and who were still lying there as though they were dead; and I do believe they all died from these blows. They asked the King who had done this to the shepherds, and he pointed to Tristan still clutching the crook, and described how the madman had struck them down like that and why.

'And I myself, so help me God, didn't feel too happy just now when you came here,' said the King. 'I know him to be so strong and he's clearly so mad that I'm sure it would worry him very little to kill me or some other worthy man, if he felt like it.'

And they burst out laughing when they heard this, for they knew that what the King had said was quite true.

Thereupon Audret addressed the King:

'My lord, as God is my witness, I wish we could take him with us to Tintagel. He could be a source of great entertainment for us with his folly, provided he hadn't got anything in his hands!'

'By my faith,' replied the King, 'nothing would please me better if he were willing to come and if he were dispossessed of that crook he's holding so that he couldn't do any harm with it.'

And the others said they would bring him, if at all possible. Then they began to blow their horns amongst themselves in order to make the dogs return. King Mark said he wanted to stay there till the evening; he was exhausted and wished to rest all that day.

What shall I tell you? King Mark remained at this fountain the whole day with a large company of knights and squires. At nightfall he started on his way back to Tintagel. Tristan accompanied them very willingly, though I cannot explain what this willingness was due to. He went with them to Tintagel, to the court of his uncle, King Mark, clothed in the manner I have described, so thin, so pitiable, so worn out and so changed in every respect that no one in the world, however close a friend he might have been, would have known he was Tristan. Although he was undoubtedly amongst his friends and amongst his enemies, nobody realized who he was. He could remain there in all safety; as long as he was dressed like that and so completely disguised there was neither a wise man nor a fool at court who would have identified him as Tristan. The people of Tintagel saw him morning and night, but none of them had any idea it was Tristan. They all jostled him; some hit him, others beat him; they caused him great shame and treated him in a most unseemly fashion. They chased him through the city, crying after him:

'Look at the fool! Look at the fool!'

And when they had shouted at him from all sides and driven him to such a pass that he could endure no more, he fled straight back to King Mark and made his way into the court, because there he was less beaten than anywhere else. The King, who readily laughed at his folly and who also knew how strong he was, seeing they were all chasing him like that, would not allow him to be ill-treated in his presence.

Thus Tristan remained at the court of his uncle, King Mark, night and day without anyone realizing who he was. Nor do I think he would ever have been recognized there had it not been for Hudenc, his hound, who knew him the moment he saw him. The hound recognized him where men had failed to do so. The

Cornish people greatly marvelled at this: it was Hudenc and not their good sense that made them recognize Tristan.

After that King Mark had Tristan taken and put in one of his rooms which was quite private and secluded. The King was very distressed and grieved when he found out it was Tristan, his nephew, who had been brought to ruin and to misery in this way for love of my lady Iseut. What more shall I tell you? King Mark kept his nephew in his rooms for so long and had him so well cared for both by the Queen herself and by others that Tristan was cured of the great madness* which had held him in its grip for such a long time. [fos. 173d–180d of BN 750]

XX

TRISTAN'S DEPARTURE FOR LOGRES

WHEN Tristan was cured of his madness and had regained his
reason, his beauty and his strength, and he knew that he was in
the hands of King Mark without whose consent he could not
depart, he was so upset and distressed that if he had possessed any
arms at that moment with which to kill himself, he would have
done so without fail. King Mark subsequently sent for him and
made him swear on holy relics that he would leave Cornwall
within twelve days and never return without his permission.
Tristan obeyed the King's command, for he saw clearly that he
could not do anything else, since he was so completely in his
power that the King could put him to death without more ado if
he so wished. But in spite of this oath Tristan did not fail to
return to Cornwall, though it has to be said that it was at the
behest of King Mark who gave him leave to do so at King
Arthur's court itself.* There would be much more to say about
all this for someone who wanted to describe it word for word.
But because I now have to concentrate on another part of the
story I shall dwell no longer on this episode. Whoever would like
to look at it* and to know about it should take up the great 'Story
of Tristan', the very one which Sir Luce of Gat Castle wrote.
That book will tell you clearly all the things which I have
omitted at this point; and I, Helie de Boron, for my part, want to
proceed with my story which I cannot abandon, and I shall
continue as follows.

When Tristan had sworn to his uncle, the King, that he would
never return to Cornwall against his will, he remained at King
Mark's court for eleven whole days. He was full of anguish and
anxiety at not being able to see Iseut, his lady, even a single time
before his departure from Cornwall, for he did not think that
after this parting he would ever have the chance to set eyes on
her again. He racked his brains, but to no avail: on this occasion
there was no way in which he could see the Queen, as she was
too carefully and too closely guarded. He longed for what he
could not then attain under any circumstances whatever.

Throughout these eleven days Sir Tristan remained with his uncle, King Mark, without ever setting eyes on Queen Iseut, nor was he able to do so. And because he was sure that after this present parting he would never come face to face with his lady again, he was so distraught that there was nothing in the world he would not at this moment have done willingly on condition that he could have seen her or spoken to her a single time.

If Tristan for his part was anguished, the Queen for her part was no less so, because she knew for certain that her beloved had to leave Cornwall never to return. She cursed the hour that she was born when she found she was unable at this stage to see Tristan. And you should know that during this time she was so closely guarded that no one on earth was allowed to speak to her without the authorization of Audret or of the King himself.

While Tristan was in the custody and in the power of King Mark, Audret had often said to his uncle:

'My lord, you want to set Tristan free. Take great care what you do, for I can tell you that in the end nothing but harm will come to you if you let him go. You know yourself what a valiant knight he is. Once he's in the Kingdom of Logres—and I have no doubt he'll go straight there—do you realize what he'll be able to do? So help me God, King Arthur won't need much persuasion and he'll march on you with his assembled troops and he'll ruin and destroy you, and all Cornwall as well.'

And King Mark had answered Audret:

'Audret, since I promised Tristan that I would let him go at this stage, I shall let him go, whatever happens to me afterwards.'

Audret had replied to King Mark:

'My lord, I assure you it will be to your misfortune, and the time will yet come when you'll wish you'd taken my advice; but then it will be too late.'

This is what Audret had said to King Mark about setting Tristan free, and the King had answered in the way I have told you.

When King Mark saw that the time for Tristan's departure was drawing near, he ordered that a beautiful and costly ship be prepared and fitted out with all that was required. Tristan would board the ship and would have himself transported and taken wherever he wished, either to the Kingdom of Logres or to that of Leonois.

The day of the departure arrived; henceforth Tristan could delay no longer. Gorvenal was ready to accompany him; and I should tell you that he had stayed all this while with Dinas, the Seneschal, except when Tristan was mad and deranged; during that time Gorvenal had looked for him in all the places where he thought he might find him, and thus it had come about that he had heard no news of him anywhere until reliable information reached him that Tristan was in the hands of King Mark.

On the day that Tristan was due to leave, as I have described, the Cornish barons all came to Tintagel in great haste to see and to escort him, and to be present at his departure. King Mark himself said he would accompany him as far as the sea; and although it is true that Tintagel was built facing the sea on one side, the spot where ships usually landed was probably about an English league away. When the actual day and hour of Tristan's departure had come, he was so distressed that he felt his heart would burst with grief and sorrow at not being able to see Iseut, his lady. And because he did not want the Cornish people to perceive the floods of tears flowing from his eyes, he decided to leave Tintagel dressed in full armour, as befitted a knight, with his helmet on his head, so that no one could see his countenance. That is why he had himself fully armed before he came out of the room where he had stayed for twelve whole days.

Once he was armed, he went into the great hall, his helmet laced on his head and his sword girded. Everyone who saw him said that he certainly seemed a fine figure of a knight; and indeed Tristan looked so handsome in his armour that one could not find a comelier man in the whole world, and many noble men and many knights had said this in praise of Tristan on many occasions. When he had gone into the hall, he uttered not a word, for his heart was so full that it almost burst with sorrow. Most of the people there tried to engage him in conversation, but he made no reply: he did not have the power to do so; his heart was so heavy that he was unable to answer even a single word. He went straight into the middle of the courtyard and mounted Passe-bruel, his charger, which he loved so dearly. King Mark had looked after it for many a day; he wanted to keep it for himself, knowing it to be such a fine horse. As soon as the King saw

Tristan mount, he mounted as well, and so did all the others, and they started out towards the sea-shore without delay.

As they approach the shore, a knight-errant appears who, surprised to see such a large company, asks one of the squires for the reason. When he hears that Tristan is about to leave Cornwall he begs the squire to give him a message: since he had come from a foreign land with the express purpose of testing Tristan's chivalry, would Tristan have the courtesy to joust with him before embarking? Tristan agrees readily, and knocks the knight off his horse, badly wounding him. The knight can no longer doubt Tristan's prowess, and hearing that Tristan intends to go to King Arthur's court, begs to be allowed to accompany him. Tristan grants his request. They enter the boat; Gorvenal goes first with Tristan's two squires, then the knight with his squire and finally Tristan with his horse Passebruel. Tears are running down his face, but they are hidden by his helmet.

Once on board, he leans over the side of the ship and calls out to the Cornish people, reminding them of his exploits: firstly, his duel with the Morholt; secondly, his defeat of the King of Norgales who had invaded Cornwall and besieged Tintagel to avenge the death of his son killed by King Mark; thirdly, his victory over the King of the Hundred Knights who had so angered King Mark by unhorsing twelve Cornish knights, as well as Mark himself, that the Cornish king had twice seized him, and the King of the Hundred Knights was only saved by Tristan's intervention; he had however returned with a large army intending to destroy Cornwall, and had only withdrawn his men when he recognized Tristan as the adversary against whom he was fighting in single combat in front of the Fountain of Shade, and had subsequently forgiven Cornwall;* finally his triumph over the giant Taulas of the Mountain. And how, Tristan asks, are the Cornish people thanking him for all the services he has rendered them? By banishing him from Cornwall!

The Cornish people make no answer; nor does King Mark.

Tristan said to the sailors:

'My good men, let's be off now. I wish we were already in some place other than this.'

Hearing Tristan's command, they hoisted their sails, for they could see that the wind was fair and blowing in the right direction; and in no time they had left the shore. Then Tristan began to lament, though he did so as quietly as he could. He was so exceedingly upset that he almost took his life, and he said to himself that since he had left his lady, he would never again feel any joy, whatever happened.

King Mark was not as upset by Tristan's parting words as was Dinas, the Seneschal, nor were many others. Nevertheless, a lot of the knights there felt very distressed, and declared openly that the Cornish people would not be feared by their neighbours now that Tristan was no longer in Cornwall, for it was only Tristan's presence which had caused them to be feared. Numerous other knights who were there wept copiously when they saw Tristan depart, saying that henceforth Cornwall would have to admit that it had completely lost its strength and its power. Not a single man left in the country would cause it to be held in awe now that Tristan was gone who had saved it from so many perils, so many disasters and so many misfortunes.

What more shall I tell you? There were many knights in Cornwall who were happy at his departure, and many others who were unhappy. But whoever might have been distressed, King Mark was not sorry about it at all; on the contrary, he was very pleased indeed. He prayed to God that Tristan would never return, and so did Audret; these two undoubtedly wished that he would never come back again.

The same could not be said about Queen Iseut who had gone up into the tower with Brangain, for she wanted no other company; and from afar they watched the ship which was already out at sea. And when the Queen saw the ship moving away from the shore, and so speedily, she wrung her hands and called herself a miserable wretch. Then she began to lament very piteously. She wept and sighed, and all day long remained plunged in bitter and exceeding sorrow at her beloved's departure.

Tristan for his part was suffering because of her, and his anguish at their parting was no less great, indeed rather more so in my opinion, though it is true that he concealed his grief as far as possible on account of the foreign knight who was with him, who was as yet unknown to him.*

The sailors who were there said to Sir Tristan:

'Sir, where would you like us to land, provided that God sends us fair winds and fine weather?'

And he replied, so distressed that he almost went out of his mind:

'I don't know, my good men, so help me God. It's all the same to me now whether I remain on the sea or whether I land, for henceforth I can find no happiness either on land or at sea. However, since I know that ultimately you have to land, I want you to make for Great Britain if you can, and close to Camelot.'

The sailors said that the wind was blowing in the right direction to take them there.

What shall I tell you? That day and the whole of the night they remained at sea, and the next morning before sunrise they touched land. Tristan asked the sailors:

'My friends, where have we landed?'

'Sir,' they replied, 'you will be pleased to know that we've landed in Great Britain, close to Camelot, thank God, just as you desired.'

'The Lord be praised who has sent us this good fortune!' said Tristan.

Tristan left the ship since he did not wish to stay on board any longer, and saw to it that his horse and his armour were taken out. Then he had himself armed without delay, and so did the knight. Once Tristan was armed and had mounted on his horse, the knight addressed him, saying:

'Sir, which way do you intend to ride?'

And he replied:

'Wherever chance takes us, sir! I can't be sure yet, because henceforth I want to ride through the Kingdom of Logres as quietly and as covertly as I can, in the manner of a knight-errant; and I should tell you, Sir Knight, that I don't want to go to King Arthur's court just yet. No man of worth should make himself known at the court of such an illustrious man as King Arthur, where so many worthy men and brave knights dwell, if his prowess has not made him known there first.'

'As God is my witness,' said the knight, 'you've just spoken some of the most noble words that any knight has said for a long time, and I feel I shall be the better for them all my life. And I want you to know, sir, that if I esteemed you before, I now esteem you even more, for I know well that these words were inspired by your noble heart; and I promise faithfully that I won't ride away and leave you in the lurch, as long as I can keep you company.'

'That gives me great pleasure,' replied Tristan, 'since my company is agreeable to you.'

When they were on the point of parting from the sailors, Tristan addressed them, tears filling his eyes, such was his unhappiness—though of course they could not see them because of the helmet he had on his head:

'My good men,' he said, 'you're going back to Cornwall from where I've been quite wrongfully banished, as you yourselves are fully aware. Give my greetings to all those in Cornwall who wish me well. And you can tell my enemies that no good can come to them from my departure; and perhaps they will yet regret having driven me away, but then it may well be too late. And finally, this much you can tell my lady, that if she loves me, I can only benefit by it; and if for my sins she forgets me, then all blessings on earth will be denied to me.'

When he had spoken these words, he parted from the sailors without any further delay. [fos. 180d–184 of BN 750]

Once in Logres, Tristan fights innumerable battles and has countless adventures* which have no link whatever with the primitive legend. True to his decision, he does not at first go to King Arthur's court; but soon Lancelot and his lineage, full of admiration for the feats of this unknown knight whose identity they suspect, go in search of Tristan. This 'quest' culminates in a combat between the two heroes, both incognito, which ends when the two recognize each other with great joy. Lancelot takes Tristan to Camelot, where he becomes a companion of the Round Table and occupies the seat of the Morholt which had remained vacant for ten years and two months.

Meanwhile King Mark, frightened that Tristan will return to Cornwall and with Lancelot's help deprive him of his wife and his kingdom, decides to go to Logres in disguise and kill Tristan secretly. However, things go ill with him in that country, and after numerous adventures—including the murder of a knight called Bertelai—he ends up at King Arthur's court where he is forced by Lancelot to reveal his identity and admit his crime. Arthur makes Mark swear that he will forgive Tristan, never bear him ill-will again, and release him from his oath not to return to Cornwall. Mark stays at King Arthur's court for a month; then he decides to return to Cornwall with Tristan. Arthur threatens Mark with death if he ever finds out that he has broken his oath.

King Mark however does not waste much time in breaking it. He abandons Tristan on an island; Mark himself only manages to return to Cornwall after a long series of mishaps. Tristan is eventually rescued and returns to King Mark's court where the King pretends to welcome him with great joy. But he has Tristan watched, and Iseut is closely guarded by Audret in the Tower of Tintagel where Mark has placed her.

XXI

MARK IN THE LAUREL-TREE—AND THEREAFTER

WHAT shall I tell you? King Mark saw clearly and realized from the way Tristan looked at Iseut and she at him when they sat down at table that they were still as madly in love as ever; and it is true, they loved one another so passionately at this time that they had never desired each other as ardently as they did now. King Mark was so incensed about it that he was bursting with anger and ill-will. He felt such mortal hatred for Tristan that he was never happy for a single moment when he saw him. If he could have brought about his death by some means he would willingly have done so; but he did not see an easy way of achieving this, because Tristan was too good a knight and too brave.

Tristan enjoyed and amused himself, and was very much happier than he used to be, for the Queen* could not be so well guarded that he did not consort with her from time to time. The King was well aware of it, and it caused him such distress that he wished he were dead. And if anyone should ask me where they used to meet, since the tower was so well guarded that Tristan could not have got in without the greatest difficulty, I would say that they saw each other in a garden which was at the foot of the tower. It was a large and beautiful garden with many different kinds of trees; but amongst all the others there was a laurel, so splendid and so tall that in the whole of Cornwall one could not find such a lovely tree. Beneath this tree it was very pleasant, and the two lovers often came there at night-time when everyone was resting, and there they would talk together and do much of what they wished to do.

Audret, who was obsessed by this whole business and who was eager to bring about Tristan's death if ever he could, found out about it sooner than anyone else. He realized they met in the garden beneath that tree, and went to King Mark and told him. The King was very upset by this news; he was at a loss what to do, being too frightened to attack Tristan because of the prowess he knew him to possess. Nor would he have laid hands on Queen

Iseut, since he loved her no less than himself. And Audret kept saying to him:

'My lord, what are you going to do about it?'

'Leave it to me,' replied the King. 'I'm sure I can deal with it on my own, and in such a way that my honour will be fully protected.'

Audret did not pursue the matter when he heard King Mark answering him in this way. And the King asked him:

'Do you know under which tree they meet?'

'I think they meet under the laurel, my lord,' replied Audret.

'Well, keep quiet about it,' said the King. 'I'm sure I can deal with it on my own.'

King Mark said no more about this matter, but that evening once darkness had fallen, he took his bow and his quiver and his sword, and went into the garden all alone, and came to the tree and climbed up into it. And he said to himself that if by chance Tristan were to appear, he would kill him without question. Thus he climbed up into the tree and stayed there waiting for Tristan to come. He uttered fierce threats, full of anger and bitter ill-will towards him.

The moon was bright and beautiful, and lit up the whole garden. Tristan remained in his lodgings, very annoyed when he saw that the weather was so fine, for if it had been a bit darker, he would have gone more readily to speak to his beloved; but at this point he did not dare to go because he was apprehensive and fearful of being intercepted and recognized by someone. Nevertheless, he was filled with such desire for his lady whom he loved with all his heart that he found it quite impossible to delay, and so he left his lodgings all by himself as soon as he saw that everyone was asleep and the town had grown quiet; he was wearing no armour except for a habergeon* and his sword.

When he had reached the walls of the garden, he jumped over; and, once inside, he looked towards the laurel and saw that there was a man up in the tree. He could not make out who it was, but he thought it more likely to be King Mark than anyone else; and he was well aware that the King would have come for no other reason than to watch how he and Iseut were going to conduct themselves. Then Tristan was not too sure what to do, whether to kill his uncle or to let him be. If he were to kill him, he would be committing a base breach of faith; it seemed preferable to let him live. On the other hand, the fact that the King had clearly seen him enter the garden made him undecided how to act, whether to kill his uncle or not. It was certainly unfortunate that the King had discovered him there, but he would no doubt expect him to go away out of cowardice and fear; and once he had left the garden and Queen Iseut had arrived, who was bound to come any minute now, King Mark would climb down and perhaps attack the Queen, and not finding anyone there to defend her, he might well kill her without more ado, given his anger and ill-will. For this reason Tristan stayed in the garden and went to stand under the tree.

When the King saw Tristan so close to him, armed with his sword and his habergeon, he was filled with such dread and terror that he wished he were in some other place; but he did not think that Tristan was as yet aware of his presence. Tristan remained beneath the tree and waited for the arrival of my lady Iseut; and he thought that if she ordered him to kill King Mark, he would kill him then and there, and thus they would be rid of him.

After this it was not long before Queen Iseut arrived, joyous and happy in anticipation of finding her beloved. And as she was hastening towards Sir Tristan, it so happened that she looked at the tree and saw King Mark up there. She knew at once that it was he and that he had hidden himself in the tree to watch how she and Tristan would conduct themselves. The Queen stopped for a moment, wondering what to do; she would have liked to make some sign to Tristan which would enable him to notice King Mark, for she was convinced he had not yet noticed him. Then she slowly advanced and addressed him like a very angry woman:

'Sir Tristan,' she said, 'what do you want of me? It would seem that you asked me to come here in order to speak to me, and I've come, as you can see. What is it you want? Certainly, I've taken a great risk in coming here; you may be quite sure that if King Mark knew about it, he would put me to shame. He would suspect that I'd come here with ill rather than good intent, since the Cornish scandal-mongers keep telling him that I love you illicitly and you feel the same for me. I certainly do love you and shall love you all my life, but as a loyal lady should love a worthy knight in accordance with God and with her husband's honour. God knows the truth, and so do you, that I've loved you according to His will, and that you never sinned with me nor I with you.'

'My lady,' he replied, 'what you say is absolutely true. In your great kindness you've always shown me honour and more good-will than I've deserved, and all too often you've been ill-rewarded for the honour you've continued to show me, because evil and disloyal men made my uncle believe such things as I could not and would not do for half the Kingdom of Logres. God knows it well, He who knows and perceives everything, that I never had any thoughts of committing adultery with you, and never shall, please God; and yet my uncle, King Mark, is not prepared to believe me.'

'To be sure,' she said, 'if you loved me as wrongfully as he thinks, then you would be the most disloyal knight in the world!'

'That's true, my lady,' he replied. 'May the all-powerful God protect me from such deeds and such thoughts.'

'Now tell me,' she continued, 'why did you ask me to come and speak to you tonight?'

'I'll tell you, my lady,' he said. 'It's true that when my uncle left the Kingdom of Logres, he assured me that he would never harbour any ill feelings or any ill-will towards me in respect of what might have taken place between the two of us,* and that he no longer felt any anger towards me. But I've recently been given to understand that he's trying to bring about my death; and that is why I asked to see you in all good faith according to God and according to reason, and beg you to tell me, provided that you know, whether the King hates me as mortally as I've been in-formed, for in that case I would protect myself against it and leave this country. I would rather stay out of Cornwall for the rest of my life than kill my uncle, King Mark, by some misadventure.'

The Queen was very pleased and very happy when she heard these words, because she realized from what Sir Tristan was saying to her that he had noticed the King's presence up in the tree. After a moment she spoke and said:

'Sir Tristan, I can't reply with any certainty to what you ask me. You say you've been given to understand that King Mark is seeking your death with all his power: about that, I assure you, I know nothing whatever. But if he wishes you ill and feels animosity towards you, that's not very surprising, since the Cornish traitors, who are jealous because everyone considers you to be the best knight in the world, hate you so mortally that they do nothing but slander you. As a result the King feels a deadly hatred for you, so it seems to me, and that's very unfortunate and very distressing. If he knew the truth about your attitude to me and your love, as God knows it and as we ourselves know, he would cherish you more than any man on earth, and me more than all the ladies in the world. But that's not how it is. He hates you, and me no less, not because you deserve it, but because it pleases Our Lord.'

'My lady,' said Tristan, 'this hatred upsets me greatly, particularly as I haven't in any way deserved it.'

'To be sure,' replied the Queen, 'I'm equally upset about it, but as it cannot be otherwise, I have to put up with it and pay regard to the King's will and the destiny which God has meted out to me.'

'My lady,' said Tristan, 'since you tell me that King Mark hates me mortally, I shall leave Cornwall and go to the Kingdom of Logres.'

'Don't do that!' she answered. 'Wait awhile: the King will perhaps have second thoughts and no longer feel this hostility towards you. It would be very shameful for you to leave this country so soon: the Cornish traitors would then say that you'd left out of fear and cowardice; meanwhile God will send you some better counsel than you've had so far.'

'My lady,' he replied, 'in that case I'll stay a bit longer.'

'Yes, indeed,' she said, 'that's my advice.'

Thereupon they said no more to each other. Tristan left the Queen and went back to his lodgings, happy and gleeful that they had carried on a conversation like that in King Mark's presence. Henceforth the King would not be as ill-disposed as before: the Queen would not be so closely guarded, Tristan would be more loved by King Mark, and the traitors would be less readily believed. That would not stop Tristan from taking Queen Iseut out of Cornwall the very next day or thereafter if he had the chance, since the Queen was more than willing, and that gave him great comfort.

When the Queen had parted from Tristan, she returned to her room where she found Brangain waiting for her; all the other maidens, who knew nothing about this matter, were asleep.

'Brangain, Brangain!' cried Iseut, 'you've no idea what happened to us! You should know that the greatest good fortune which ever befell any lady happened to me this very night concerning King Mark himself.'

'For the love of God! my lady,' exclaimed Brangain, 'tell me!'

'I can tell you,' said the Queen, 'that King Mark came to spy on us, but by the grace of God, we were fortunate enough to notice him, and promptly changed our conduct and our words.'

And she told her how and in what fashion they saved the situation, 'for I'm quite certain that now King Mark no longer has any misgivings about the two of us, but has turned against all those who ever spoke to him about us. Henceforth you'll see Audret very badly received at court. King Mark won't feel too kindly disposed towards him for many a day; indeed, he'll hate him with all his heart. Tristan the fair will now be the winner and Audret the loser. Blessed be the hour that ushered in this night, for this night will allow us to live in joy for some time.'

Both the Queen and Brangain were overjoyed and in high spirits. After a while the King arrived, and when the Queen heard him coming, she lay down in bed and pretended to be fast asleep.

Next morning the King got up very early and went to hear mass in his chapel. Afterwards he returned to his palace, and as soon as he saw Audret he led him into a room. And Audret immediately said to him:

'My lord, what do you think of Tristan and the Queen?'

'I think,' said King Mark, 'and I now know for a fact from all I've seen, that you're the most disloyal knight and the worst traitor ever to have set foot in Cornwall. You gave me to understand and kept telling me that my nephew Tristan was shaming me with my wife. That's the greatest lie in the world! If Iseut is amiable towards Tristan and honours him, that's not because of any wrongful love she may feel for him, but primarily for the sake of God and out of courtesy and on account of my nephew's prowess. I've now found out so much about the two of them that I shall love Iseut and my nephew for evermore, and I shall hate you with all my heart for making me believe they were guilty of disloyalty. Tristan is the most loyal knight that I know and the best in the world, as everyone agrees, whereas you're the most disloyal knight in the whole of Cornwall. Therefore I affirm by all that I owe to God and to the code of chivalry that if you weren't related to me I would have you killed and not accept any ransom for you. Now leave my court, for I don't want to have anything further to do with you, nor to see you come here any more.'

There is no need to ask whether Audret was distressed and upset when he heard this. The King told him to go away, and he did so, since he feared him so much that he dared not stay any longer. Then the King sent for Tristan who was only too glad and happy to go to court, as he was sure he would hear news which would please him. The King spoke before all the members of his household, and said so loudly that everyone could hear him:

'Tristan, dear nephew, what shall I tell you? Up till now I hated you more than all the knights in the world, because I truly thought that you were a traitor and that you were shaming me with the being I love most after myself. But I have had such proof of your loyalty that I know for certain that you love me sincerely and have respected my honour to the best of your ability. All those who made me believe your disloyalty are liars; I wish them ill and shall do so all my life. As a result of their counsel and their advice I've caused you much shame which I now bitterly regret, and it is right that I regret it, for no man should cause shame to a knight as valiant as you are under any circumstances whatever. And since I've been foolish and wicked enough to have done so, I ask you to forgive me, and beg you to tell me how I can make amends for it according to your wishes.'

Hearing these words Sir Tristan replied and said:

'My lord, since you declare that the shame you so often caused me was done not so much by your own resolve as at the instigation of the Cornish traitors who made you believe lies about me, and you say that you regret your actions, I readily forgive you in the presence of all these noble men, on condition that you promise me here and now as king that you will not again bring about my dishonour or knowingly allow me to be harmed.'

And the King promised this faithfully.

Thus King Mark became reconciled with Tristan and Tristan with the King. Seeing this, all the noble barons of Cornwall were filled with great joy and great happiness. The traitors felt grief-stricken and angry about it, but the worthy men were pleased and delighted. Tristan had all he desired, since he could speak to his lady whenever he wished. He found no one who stopped him in any way. He was completely lord and master both of King Mark and Queen Iseut, and he was so feared in Cornwall that all his commands were carried out. The traitors were consumed with envy and vexation; they felt so distressed and so irate that they did not know what to say. Audret was now on such bad terms with the King that he dared not come to court, and there was no one who asked him, since they all knew full well that the King hated him with all his heart. Tristan had his joy in full measure, and so did Queen Iseut; henceforth they could do nothing which displeased the King. He trusted Tristan so much that he would not allow anyone else to guard Iseut. Now the two lovers had their pleasure and delight, and all good fortune. Never before had they been as contented as they were at present, for when they remembered the pain and the suffering they had endured, and they saw that now they were together and could do all they wanted, they said that they would be fortunate if they could live in such joy and happiness for the rest of their days. They would have renounced all claim to God's paradise, provided that they could live like this for evermore.

All too soon, alas, the lovers' blissful life comes to an abrupt end. One day King Mark loses his way while out hunting, and when he returns home early next morning he finds Tristan and Iseut asleep in each others' arms. He withdraws silently, but shortly afterwards has Tristan served with a sleeping draught, and then orders him to be seized and locked up in the old prison of Tintagel. There Tristan languishes for six months, served only with bread and water, until he is rescued by Lancelot, who forces King Mark to set him free. Lancelot intends to take Tristan to Logres, but Mark sends Audret after them with a hundred men. Leaving Lancelot for dead, they recapture Tristan and imprison him in Pine Castle. Lancelot is later found and cured, and returns to Logres, believing Tristan to have been killed. After many adventures Lancelot arrives at King Arthur's court in Camelot: hearing that Tristan's name is still inscribed on his seat at the Round Table, he realizes that he must be alive.*

All the knights of Lancelot's family agree to go to Cornwall with him to take vengeance on King Mark, but the expedition is prevented by Lancelot's madness, due to a misunderstanding between him and Queen Guinevere who banished him from her presence. The knights of his lineage set off on a quest for him, swearing not to return until they find him. The five sons of King Pellinor likewise go in search of Lancelot—Tor, Agloval, Driant, Lamorat, and the youngest, Perceval. We hear the adventures of these knights; also of Gaheriet and of Gawain, who is responsible for the death of Driant and Lamorat.

Agloval, after seeking Lancelot for six years, is joined by his young brother Perceval. They make their way to court where Perceval is knighted by King Arthur, much to Gawain's displeasure. Thereupon Perceval departs alone in search of Lancelot. The news of his many exploits reach the court and fill the King with joy. A maiden persuades Perceval to defer his quest for Lancelot until he has freed Tristan. Wherever Perceval goes he is welcomed like a saviour. One day he happens to see Mark and Audret passing; he attacks and overcomes them, and keeps them imprisoned in a castle belonging to Iseut's mother until Mark agrees to release Tristan who is still, after four years, incarcerated in Pine Castle. Thereafter Perceval resumes his quest for Lancelot, whom he will eventually find and rescue from the Isle of Joy where King Pelles's daughter has retained him.

Tristan endeavours to put an end to the war between King Mark and Dinas the Seneschal. Having taken refuge with Iseut in the Seneschal's castle which Mark is besieging, he manages during a battle to knock the King down, and takes him and Audret prisoner. Not long afterwards Tristan comes upon a magic boat sent, so a maiden tells him, to take the two lovers to Logres; he orders King Mark to be released if they do not return within six months.

After numerous adventures Tristan and Iseut arrive in Camelot, where Mordret tries in vain to force Tristan, who is riding incognito, to come to court. This results in our hero being attacked by twelve of Arthur's knights, all of whom he overcomes. He does however make himself known to Lancelot, who offers to shelter the lovers in the Joyous Guard, the strongest castle in Logres; here for a while Tristan and Iseut lead a happy life.

During this period Tristan has countless adventures with innumerable knights, including Dinadan and Palamedes who are both invited to the Joyous Guard. King Arthur, wishing to see Tristan and Iseut, arranges a magnificent tournament outside the Castle of Louvezerp in the hope that they will attend; the lovers leave for the castle together with Palamedes who intends to surpass his rival in order to impress Iseut. Palamedes does indeed carry off the prize on the first day, but Tristan wins on the second day, and on the third both Lancelot and Tristan are declared the victors. Palamedes's suffering and despair know no bounds. The lovers return to the Joyous Guard. The news of Tristan's exploits spread throughout Logres, and he almost eclipses Lancelot's fame. They remain at the Joyous Guard for the rest of that summer and the whole of the winter. At Whitsuntide Tristan sets off for King Arthur's court on his own to attend the festival, during which, it has been predicted, the Holy Grail will appear; Iseut has declined to accompany him.

Like all the other Round Table knights, Tristan swears to uphold the Quest of the Grail for one year and one day, and like all the other knights he embarks on endless exploits and adventures. Many episodes from the *Queste del Saint Graal* are included. The year has long passed before he is finally free to return to the Joyous Guard, accompanied by Brunor, another knight who is passionately in love with Iseut. Dinas and Dinadan are already there waiting for him, then Palamedes arrives, and later Lancelot and his brothers stay at the Joyous Guard for one month; Tristan goes back with them to King Arthur's court. Our hero agrees to help the King of Ireland against the King of Norgales; then he returns to the Joyous Guard where he stays with Iseut for a month. Soon he departs once again to rescue Palamedes from prison, and embarks on many other adventures which are interspersed with further episodes from the *Queste del Saint Graal*.

Meanwhile, in Cornwall, King Mark pines for Iseut who has been lost to him for two years. After hearing the false news that the Round Table companions have died in the Quest, and on the advice of Audret, he forms an alliance with the Saxons, and both armies invade the Kingdom of Logres. First of all Mark attacks the Joyous Guard, and since Tristan is not there—he is recovering from a serious wound in an abbey—the King carries off Iseut and sends her back to Cornwall. Then he marches on Camelot. In the ensuing battle Arthur is badly wounded by Mark and has to withdraw into the city; however, with the help of Galahad and later Palamedes, Arthur is able to defeat the enemy, and they flee. After numerous adventures Galahad and his companions arrive at the abbey where Tristan is still recuperating. When he hears the news of Iseut's abduction, he has a relapse and lies ill for over half a year. Cured at last, he makes his way to the coast which he reaches after many further adventures. He meets Sagremor and together they set sail for Cornwall, where they stay with Dinas the Seneschal. Tristan is able to see Iseut occasionally. [fos. 38c–260b of BN 757]

XXII

THE DEATH OF TRISTAN AND ISEUT

ONE day Tristan had gone to the Queen's room and was harping and singing a lay which he had composed some time ago. Audret heard it clearly and went to tell King Mark. Thereupon the King took such measures as he saw fit, and succeeded in striking Tristan with a poisoned lance which Morgan had once given him. Tristan was completely unarmed, so that the King dealt him a deadly blow in the spine; and once he had done this he turned away, not daring to stay in Tristan's presence any longer. As soon as Tristan felt himself struck like this, he realized that he had received a fatal injury. Since he could not catch up with the King, he went off in another direction, down to the courtyard, where he mounted the first horse he could find and rode out of Tintagel straight to Dinas's castle. There he immediately took to his bed, saying that this blow had mortally wounded him and would undoubtedly cause his death.

When Dinas heard these words, he was exceedingly upset; and Sagremor, who loved Tristan very much, wept bitterly. Tristan lamented day and night, for he suffered considerable anguish. The doctors came to see him, but not one of them knew what to do about this wound; they all said without exception that he was going to die. He became thin and ugly-looking, and his condition deteriorated beyond all measure. He grew so much worse that before a month had passed anyone who had seen him previously would have found it very difficult to recognize him now. He was no longer able to move; he cried and wailed like a man demented. His companions, knowing the great agony he was suffering, wept at his bedside day and night; they saw clearly that his fate was sealed, and he himself was well aware of it.

When King Mark heard that Tristan was definitely dying and was past recovery, he felt happier than he had done for a long time. Now he was full of joy and gladness, because he was sure that once Tristan was dead there would never be any man in Cornwall bold enough to rise up against him. Now he had all he desired, since he knew for certain that Tristan was going to die.

Every day he sent his men to find out how Tristan was faring, and they brought him back news which pleased him greatly, for they assured him that he was dying and could not live much longer. Never had he been as glad about anything that happened as he was about Tristan's death, and Audret was thrilled with joy; these two were altogether jubilant.

But whoever was happy and joyful, the Queen's heart was full of sorrow. She wept and lamented and declared that she would die of this grief; and if her grieving did not make her die, she would kill herself with her own two hands. She had no desire to remain alive after Tristan was gone, and she fervently hoped that God would spare her from this ordeal. She would not want to survive him; she would not want to be queen of the whole world if he was dead. Without him she had no wish or intention to live a single day. Thus King Mark and Queen Iseut reacted very differently: the King was overjoyed at Tristan's death, and the Queen was so grief-stricken that she almost died of sorrow.

However, in spite of the King's happiness, he said he would very much like to see Tristan before he died; and finally, when he heard in what anguish Tristan was and how he had so completely changed that no one would recognize him in his present state of decline, his heart was filled with pity, and he could not refrain from saying, with tears in his eyes:

'Tristan's death is a misfortune, to be sure, for to my knowledge no one in the world will ever wield a lance as well as he did. If only he had not acted with such disloyalty towards me, he would have been in all respects the most praiseworthy knight I've ever known.'

When the King knew for certain from those who went to see Tristan that his end was drawing near, he began to repent of what he had done, and said to himself that sooner or later Tristan's death was bound to have disastrous consequences. Now he bitterly regretted his action; now he wished he had not done it and had not believed Audret, since he was forced to admit that by killing Tristan he had killed the best knight in the world. Everyone would condemn and blame him for it. Even his own men, who had feared him because they were afraid of Tristan, would no longer fear him very much. These were King Mark's

thoughts; and he felt pity for his nephew, as well he might in
view of their kinship. Now he wished he had not done it.

The Queen, who was so unhappy that her only desire was to
die, lamented night and day. Nor did she conceal her grief from
the King; she would have been only too pleased if he had killed
her so that her suffering would cease. She herself noticed that the
King regretted what he had done to Tristan. When she was told
that Tristan was so close to his death that he could not live more
than three or four days, she replied without hesitation:

'Let him die whenever he wishes, for certainly I shall go with
him that very day! I'll kill myself, so help me God, and thereby
end my suffering.'

Those were the Queen's words on hearing that Tristan was
about to die. The King himself was more upset than he showed.

When Tristan felt within himself that he would not live much
longer, he said to Dinas:

'Send word to King Mark that he should come and see me. I
would very much like to see him before I die. I don't blame him
for my death as much as I do Audret. If he wishes to come, he
should make haste, for I shall die very soon.'

Dinas immediately sent word to the King; the messenger went
to Tintagel and told King Mark the news. As soon as the King
heard it, he began to weep and bowed his head, and said so
loudly that his words were clearly audible to all those present:

'Alas!' he exclaimed, 'what a misdeed I've committed by
killing the best knight on earth! I've brought shame on the whole
world.'

The King did not delay, but mounted his horse and took with
him enough men to assure his safety in Dinas's castle. Once he
had arrived at the castle and the gates were opened for him, he
entered, exceedingly distressed, and dismounted; then he climbed
up to the tower where Tristan was lying in such a state of decline
that the King scarcely recognized his nephew and started weeping bitterly at the sight of him. When Tristan saw the King
coming, he tried to sit up, but in vain; being too feeble, he lacked
the strength and therefore lay down again.

'Welcome, uncle!' he said. 'You've come to celebrate my
death which you've desired for so long. Now your joy is complete, since Tristan is near to his end. Tristan is done for! Soon

you'll have what you desire, for today or tomorrow you'll see him die. I can go no further; I've gone as far as I can. This is where death awaits me. Ah! King Mark, you desired my death so much and thought you were acting in your own best interests, but you've done yourself more harm than good. As God is my witness, the time will yet come when you would give half your kingdom not to have killed Tristan. However, what's done is done, and it can't be changed any more now.'

When he had said these words, he began to weep bitterly. The King, who realized that Tristan was past help and that he himself could not save him, started weeping as well. Tristan said to him:

'Don't weep! Your tears, which you're now shedding in sadness, will soon flow in earnest, so help me God! You'll lose much more by Tristan's death than you think! Uncle, I ask you to do one thing, for my sake and for pity's sake, namely that you let my lady Iseut come to my bedside so that I may see her at my death, and she may see me; and rest assured that I shall die today or tomorrow. The only wish I have is to see her at my death.'

'Nephew,' said the King, 'since you want the Queen to come to you, she shall come at once.'

Thereupon he sent for her. The Queen went there that very day, and I can tell you that she was more upset and sorrowful than she had been for quite some time past. Never did she long for her death as she did now, because she knew for certain that there was no hope for Tristan and that he must needs die. Now she too wanted to die; death would have been very sweet to her if it had taken her then. She asked nothing else of God but that death should come quickly so that she could die with Tristan.

When Tristan saw Iseut appear whom he had so loved and longed to see, he wanted to rise in order to greet her, but he was unable to do so. However, he did what he could do, that is, speak.

'Welcome, lady!' he said. 'You have come, but too late. Your coming can't help me any more now. What shall I tell you, dear lady? Tristan, your beloved, is done for! Today or tomorrow Tristan whom you loved so much will have to die; he won't survive after that. He fought as long as he could, but now he can't go on any longer. What more shall I say, dear lady? My fate is sealed, as you can see full well.'

The Queen, who was so grief-stricken and distressed that she could not have felt greater sorrow, wept from the depths of her heart. And when she was able to speak, she said:

'Tristan, beloved, are you really on the point of death?'

'Yes, lady,' he replied, 'there can be no doubt. This is where Tristan must die who had such power and such strength. Look at these arms, my dear lady! These are not Tristan's arms which used to strike such blows! They're the arms of a dead man; there's no longer any force or vigour in them. Henceforth the world should know that Tristan's end is near. All his exploits are over. He who had such power and was so honoured and so feared on earth is lying here as dead as an empty shell. All his strength is gone. Alas, how grievous was the blow which was aimed at me! The whole world will be debased and impoverished by it!'

Tristan groaned with the pain he felt. All that day he was in such a state that he said nothing else at all. No one could get a word out of him and no one uttered a word, but they all grieved in silence; there was not a single one who did not weep bitterly. The Queen, who was so sorrowful that she asked only for her death, remained with him that evening, as well as the whole of the night. It was light enough in there for everyone to see very clearly, except Tristan whose vision had become quite blurred.

The following morning as dawn broke and Tristan saw that the day was bright, he made a supreme effort to speak, and said so loudly that all those present heard it clearly:

'Ah!' he exclaimed, 'what can I say? This is my last day! Today I shall be forced to die; I shall never see another day. On this day Tristan will go to rest, he who once had so much power and honour. Ah! Lord God, why do you allow this to happen so soon?'

When he had spoken these words, everyone there began to lament with such bitterness and intensity that it would have been impossible to grieve more. Tristan himself wept copiously; he felt great pity for himself, knowing well that his end was near.

After a while he addressed Sagremor and said:

'Sagremor, dear friend, please bring me my sword and my shield; I want to see them again before my soul leaves my body'

Sagremor, who was so distressed that his heart almost failed him, brought the sword and the shield; and as soon as Tristan caught sight of the sword, he said to Sagremor:

'Friend, draw it out of the scabbard, so that I can see it more clearly.'

And Sagremor did as he was asked. When Tristan saw the sword which he knew to be so strong that he did not believe there was a better one in the world, he sighed from the depths of his heart, and then said in tears:

'Sword, what will you do from now on? At this point you're parting from your lord, and you certainly won't have as good a one hereafter. You'll never be feared as much as you were till now, for now you're losing your honour.'

Thereupon he began to weep very bitterly, and then he remained silent for a time. The grief was so loud in there that a thunderbolt from heaven would have gone unnoticed. After a while Tristan spoke again and said to Sagremor:

'Sagremor, dear friend, henceforth I bid farewell to chivalry and take my leave of it. Much have I exalted and revered chivalry, extolled it and put my trust in it; I've honoured it as long as I could, but now it will be honoured by Tristan no longer.'

Then he fell silent; but after a while he began again:

'Sagremor, dear friend, I have to say it, I can't conceal it any more. Do you want me to tell you what is undoubtedly the greatest marvel you could ever hear about? Alas! how shall I express it? I'm forced to do so, I can't go on like this. Sagremor, what shall I tell you? Tristan now has to say the most shameful words he ever uttered. Alas, how can I make them pass my lips?'

Thereupon he fell silent once more, and then spoke again:

'Sagremor, I can conceal it no longer: I am vanquished! Never before did such shameful words pass Tristan's lips.'

And when he had said this, he began to sob loudly and much more bitterly than before; and after weeping violently like this for a long while, he looked at Sagremor amidst his tears and said:

'Sagremor, since I'm vanquished, I might as well surrender my arms to you, and I herewith do so. What more shall I say? I surrender my chivalry; henceforth I must leave behind me all blows and all thrusts, all daring and all prowess, and I leave them against my will, for death is forcing me to do it. Alas! what great sorrow and great harm will be inflicted on the Round Table by the death of a single knight on this very day!

Palamedes, Palamedes, courteous and worthy knight, full of valour and merit, this is the end of our quarrel; never again will you strike a blow at Tristan nor Tristan at you. Our dispute is over! Palamedes, dear friend, Tristan is sounding the retreat. He'll never face you again, nor will you face him. The hostility between us will cease because of me, and nothing you'll see me do will ever make you feel aggrieved again. Death is now putting an end to the great conflict that existed between the two of us.

Ah! Dinadan, handsome knight and friend, this is the termination of our companionship. Now I'm being more cruelly mocked than you used to mock me. You won't be present at my death, but I know well that you'll lament me often; you'll be distressed and unhappy to hear that I'm dead.

Ah! Lancelot, today you're losing a good companion and a knight who loved you; today our friendship ends. Death which has no pity on me is forcibly ending it.

Ah! Sagremor, dear friend, these three whom I've just named before you, greet them for me and let them know that I'm dying in sadness and sorrow because our companionship has to break up so soon. And since now I can't present myself in person before the knights of the Round Table, please, for love of me, present my sword to them which I cherished so much, and beg all my companions to honour my sword seeing that they can't honour me. God knows full well that I loved them with all my heart and did my best to uphold the glory of the Round Table wherever I happened to be. For that reason it's only right that they should honour my arms which I send them as a token of my love. I'm not able to present myself, and therefore you will present my shield and my sword to them in my stead, and tell them that I'm sorrowful to be dying so soon, more for chivalry's sake than for my own.'

When he had spoken these words, he burst into tears, and then addressed Sagremor once again:

'Sagremor, bring my sword close to me so that I can see it.'

And Sagremor took it to him, and Tristan began to kiss the blade and the hilt, and then he kissed his shield, and thereafter he spoke again:

'Alas!' he said, 'how greatly it upsets me to part from my arms and to leave chivalry so soon! As God is my witness, it does not seem to me that more harm could be caused in this world by a single knight than will now be caused by me. Alas, why am I dying so soon?'

Then he kissed his sword once more and his shield likewise, and said weeping:

'Henceforth I bid you farewell, for I can look at you no longer; my heart is breaking with sorrow. Ah! Sagremor, now you can take my arms: I'm giving you my heart and my soul; honour them in my stead if ever you loved Tristan. Once you've arrived in Camelot, make sure they are put in a place where everyone can see them. There will be no one on earth who won't say when he hears about me and looks at my arms that the blow which King Mark dealt me was a grievous misfortune. The world is shamefully debased by it and all chivalry will have been dishonoured. Now I've told you everything I wanted to tell you. I commend you to God.'

When he had spoken these words, he turned towards King Mark and began to look at him, weeping, and then said:

'Uncle, so help me God, what do you think of me? Am I the Tristan you used to fear so much? Certainly not! I'm not that Tristan any more. I'm the Tristan who is taking his leave of chivalry and of the world. Henceforth you can be sure that Tristan won't cause you any more fear. Don't ever be afraid of me again! Today sees the end of the animosity and the rancour which for so long has existed between the two of us. Until now I've always fought in such a way that I never lost; but in this cruel battle which I'm fighting today I shall be vanquished. Here I can strike no blow with my lance or my sword which would save me; I've been completely overcome and defeated. My opponent is so unyielding that it's useless begging for mercy. I shall clearly have to die; at this stage begging or appealing for mercy is of no avail to me at all. Truly, I never to my knowledge overpowered any knight by dint of arms whom I did not spare if he implored or begged me to have mercy on him. But in this mortal battle which I've taken upon myself there's no point in begging for mercy. I must needs die, for I shall find no compassion. King Mark, on this grievous battlefield you inflicted the most cruel death upon me which was ever witnessed in Cornwall. But since I see that it can't be altered, I willingly forgive you; may God likewise forgive you.'

When he had said this to King Mark, he turned to the Queen and addressed her.

'Lady,' he said, 'I'm dying. The hour and the time has come when I can keep going no longer. To be sure, dear lady, I've struggled against death as long as I could. And now that I'm dying, what will you do after my death? Lady, how could Iseut possibly live without Tristan? It would be as great a marvel as a fish existing without water, or a body without a soul! Dear lady, now that I'm dying, what *will* you do? Won't you die with me? Then our souls will leave our bodies together. Ah! dear beloved, sweet lady whom I love more than myself, do what I ask and die with me so that we may die together. For the love of God, make sure that this is how it shall be.'

The Queen, who was so grief-stricken that her heart almost broke, did not know what to reply.

'Beloved,' she said, 'as God is my witness, there's nothing I would like better than to die with you and to be your companion in death, but I don't know how to set about it. If you know how, then tell me, and I'll do it at once. Were it possible for any lady to die of the grief and anguish she had in her heart, I swear I would have been dead many times over since I came here last night, for I don't think any lady could ever have been so upset that I'm not more upset still. So help me God, if I could have my own way, I would die here and now.'

'Ah! sweet lady,' said Tristan, 'does that mean that you would wish to die with your beloved?'

'Yes,' replied the Queen, 'as God is my judge, I never desired anything so much.'

'No?' he asked. 'That makes me very happy! Then it will come about, God willing. Certainly, in my opinion it would be shameful if Tristan were to die without Iseut, because they've always been one flesh, one heart and one soul. And since you want to die with me, sweet lady, we must needs die together, so help me God. Now, I pray you, embrace me, for my death is approaching fast. Tristan has come to his end!'

The Queen wept, and so did the King when he heard these words; he showed clearly beyond any doubt that he was exceedingly distressed by Tristan's death. Dinas was beside Tristan and lamented bitterly; no one who saw him would have questioned that he truly loved Tristan with all his heart, as indeed he did. Sagremor wept, and all the others likewise; there was not one who did not pray to God that death would claim the lovers soon, since they could see that Tristan was dying. They were all grief-stricken.

When Tristan realized that his end was drawing near and that he could not hold on any longer, he looked around him and said:

'My lord, I'm dying! I cannot continue to live. Death is already gripping my heart and will not let me stay alive. I commend you to God.'

After he had said these words, he spoke one more time:

'Iseut, beloved, embrace me so that I may die in your arms; in that way, it seems to me, I shall die happy.'

Iseut was bending over Tristan and, hearing his request, she lay down on his breast. Tristan took her in his arms and held her like this against his heart, and said loudly enough for everyone to hear it clearly:

'Now I don't mind any longer if I die, since I have my lady with me.'

Then he clasped her to his breast with all the strength he had in him, so that her heart stopped beating; and he himself died at that precise moment. Thus the two lovers died with their arms round each other and their lips touching. They remained lying like this in each other's embrace till everyone there, who at first thought they had fainted, realized they were dead and would never regain consciousness. They both died of love; there was no other comfort for them.

The lovers' death is mourned by everyone in Cornwall with the exception of Audret, even by those in other countries. King Mark is distraught at having lost both his nephew and the wife he loved. The Cornish barons fear that Cornwall will be shamed without Tristan to protect it. All who hear the news come to Dinas's castle, and when they see the two lovers lying dead in each other's arms, they declare that this is the greatest marvel that ever happened, and that as long as the world lasted people would talk about the extraordinary love of Tristan and Iseut. King Mark has the bodies taken to Tintagel and buried together with great honour right in the middle of the great church of Tintagel. He orders a most beautiful and costly sepulchre to be erected, at the foot of which are placed two life-size figures skilfully sculpted: that of a knight with a sword in his right hand and with his left hand placed on his heart, and that of a lady; the names of Tristan and Iseut are inscribed with gold lettering on their breasts.

Sagremor, after lamenting Tristan's death for a long time, leaves Cornwall with Tristan's shield and sword which he intends to take to Camelot; he carries the sword hanging round his neck. As he is riding through a forest in Logres towards King Arthur's court, he meets a knight coming from there who tells him that he had never seen the court in such despair: news had just arrived that Palamedes, King Bademagu and Erec, son of Lac, were dead, as well as countless other knights all of whom had died in the Grail Quest. Sagremor replies that he is the bearer of even worse news: the death of a knight of such exceptional valour that he cannot bring himself to put the knight's sword at his side, but wears it hanging round his neck. The revelation that this knight is none other than Tristan arouses great dismay in his companion. Sagremor is relieved to learn that Lancelot, Hestor and Blioberis of Gaunes have returned safely from the Quest.

Sagremor reaches Camelot one Monday morning and finds King Arthur very distressed at the terrible news which keeps coming to his court, and in particular at the death of Palamedes. He is pleased to see Sagremor, thinking that he must be the bearer of good tidings from Cornwall. Sagremor asks King Arthur to assemble all the Round Table companions, and is shocked to hear that more than forty of them have died in the Quest. The King asks a youth to blow a horn from the top of a tower so that it could be heard throughout the city; this was only ever done in order to summon the knights of the Round Table. Lancelot is the first to arrive; he too is exceedingly distressed that Palamedes is dead.

When all the Round Table companions who are in Camelot have assembled, Sagremor presents them with Tristan's shield and sword, and announces his death. The news calls forth such intense grief that never will greater be heard. Rich and poor alike grieve for Tristan; all the other knights whom they have previously mourned are forgotten. King Arthur wishes he could die and says he will never again feel joy; Lancelot, beside himself with sorrow, declares that the whole world should come to an end, since the death of Tristan meant the death of all chivalry. The mourning is maintained in King Arthur's court for one whole year. The King composes a lay for Tristan which he calls 'Royal Lay'; Queen Guinevere composes another, as well as Sir Lancelot and many other knights; and each day when they lament Tristan, these lays are recited. Everyone at court wears black clothes as a sign of mourning, and here we can see the origin of this custom. [fos. 260b–263a of BN 757]

EPILOGUE

I have put much effort into completing this book.* It has taken me a long time, and I have brought this extensive work to a successful conclusion by the grace of God who gave me the wisdom and the strength. I have told the story to the best of my ability in such a way as to give pleasure and delight. And since there are so many fine words contained therein, King Henry of England* has read it from beginning to end, and still reads it frequently, no doubt because he finds it so enjoyable; and for this reason, and also because he discovered much more in the Latin Book than the translators of it put into French, he asked and begged me, both in person and through other people, in writing as well as orally, on account of the fact that he found many things missing in this book which should be included in it but could no longer be added now, that I set to work again on another book which would contain everything which is missing in this one.

And since I would not dare to disregard the request and command of my lord, now that I have completed this book, and as soon as the cold winter has passed and we see the beginning of the pleasant season which we call spring, when I shall have rested a little after the strenuous toil of this book to which I have devoted one whole year* and left all knightly deeds and all other pleasures, I promise that I shall turn once again to the Latin Book, and also to the other works which have been translated into French; and I shall look through them from cover to cover, and from the material I find missing there but present in the Latin text, I shall make a new book. And, God willing, I shall incorporate in it whatever was omitted by us, that is, Master Luce de Gat who first began to translate, Master Walter Map* who wrote the original Book of Lancelot, Master Robert de Boron* and myself, called Helie de Boron,* provided that God allows me to live long enough to complete the said book.

And I for my part thank my lord King Henry very much for praising my work and for attributing to it such great merit.

Here ends the Book of Tristan. Thanks be to God and Our Lady. [fo. 263b of BN 757]

EXPLANATORY NOTES

3 *a knight of amorous and joyful disposition*: the OF text reads *chevaliers amoreus et envoisiez*. The author seems to feel that these attributes make him a suitable person to 'translate' this great love story, although strangely enough the subject-matter is not mentioned in the Prologue.

    translate: it was not unusual for authors to claim a Latin source, as this would raise the story in people's esteem. Originality was not considered of prime importance; cf. the *Queste del Saint Graal* which presents the supposed author Walter Map simply as a translator of the Latin original preserved in the library at Salisbury.

4 *Norholt*: Oliver Padel, the authority on Cornish place-names, assures me that there is no such place in Cornwall.

    born on Tuesday: the OF reading *au mardi fu nez et au mois de marz* is of course a pun on the King's name *Mars*, a pun which it is impossible to translate into English.

    Leonois: variants *Loenois, Lionois, Lyonois*. Probably *Lyonesse*, a prosperous kingdom widely thought to have been submerged between Cornwall and the Scilly Isles. It was described in early English chronicles as flourishing until its sudden disappearance beneath the sea.

    lady: the OF reading *demoisele* is usually a maiden or young girl, but can mean 'lady' and even refer to married women. In this context I have preferred to use the translation 'lady', since we see later that she is the owner of a beautiful tower.

7 *Tristan*: it is unfortunately impossible to translate into English the play on words *triste/tristor/tristesse/Tristan* of the original OF text.

9 *tutor*: the OF *mestre* is very difficult to translate. When it begins a sentence as a mode of address, I have sometimes rendered it by 'Master' or 'Sir'; in this instance the most appropriate word available seemed to be 'tutor' even though it does not perhaps quite cover the whole range of Gorvenal's duties and responsibilities.

10 *tribute*: this was established two hundred years previously when the Irish came to help Cornwall fight against the King of Leonois; each year the Cornish people had to hand over a hundred young girls and a hundred young boys, all 15 years old and of noble birth,

as well as a hundred valuable horses (see vol. i, § 142, 11 of my critical edition).

15 *swear on holy relics*: an oath was taken very seriously in the Middle Ages and was usually sworn on the Bible or on holy relics, i.e. the remains of parts of the body of holy persons or objects connected with them. The enormous popularity of relics and the completely uncritical attitude of medieval people in this respect led to many abuses.

16 *favour*. OF *don*. The convention of *doner un don* required the person to grant the request before knowing what it entailed.

18 *not a stone remained standing*: there is no trace of any of these events later on in the story.

    bier suitable for the horses to carry: the OF text has *biere chevaleresce*. This was a kind of stretcher or sedan chair with long poles so that it could be carried by two horses.

19 *except you*: this is a curious statement in view of his father's evident love for him.

20 *France*: the names *Gaul* and *France* are used synonymously in this text, although *Gaul* is more frequent. It is interesting to note that no sea crossing seems to be required from Leonois to France.

22 *the Morholt*: no one has ever satisfactorily explained the presence of the definite article which always precedes this name.

25 *daybreak*: the OF text has *ore de prime*, which was the first hour of the day, beginning either at sunrise, or at 6 a.m. throughout the year.

27 *not having told him earlier*. King Faramon reproaches Tristan especially because he says he is his *amis charniex*. This expression can mean 'kinsman' or 'close friend'; we have not been told that Tristan is related to King Faramon.

30 *Logres*: this is King Arthur's kingdom and seems to be synonymous with Great Britain.

35 *St Samson's Isle*: there is no island bearing this name off the coast of Cornwall. Tristan's victory over the Morholt on this island is mentioned also in Chrétien de Troyes's romance *Erec et Enide* (line 1243), but elsewhere the island is not given a name. As the Cornish people watch the battle from the shore (p. 38), the island must have been very near the coast, but we are not given any indication in the prose romance where King Mark is residing at the time. There is in fact no island off the north coast of Cornwall,

but there is a small islet in the south near Looe, called St George's Island; this may well have been the one referred to. It is less than half a mile from the coast and would fit in with the details we are given quite well. (See J. Loth, *Contributions à l'étude des Romans de la Table Ronde*, vi., *Le Cornwall et le Roman de Tristan*, *Revue Celtique*, 33 (1912), 274.)

36   *hauberk*: a long coat of chain-mail, reaching to below the knee, made up of as many as thirty thousand interlinked rings; it could be double or triple lined for extra safety.

      mail leggings: the OF *chauces* constituted the leg-piece of the armour, worn as a protective covering for the legs.

39   *litter*: a framework supporting a bed or couch used to transport the sick and wounded.

40   *rote*: a plucked instrument, a form of the ancient lyre, prevalent in Northern Europe from pre-Christian to medieval times, often having six strings.

44   *lance-head*: the lance was a weapon consisting of a long, wooden shaft which could be as long as ten to thirteen feet, and an iron or steel head. The knight held this horizontally, his hand level with his knee, in charging at full speed in order to unseat his mounted opponent.

45   *terrified*: it will be remembered that Gaheriet had accompanied the Morholt to Cornwall and had been very struck by Tristan; see above, pp. 35–6.

48   *Dolorous Guard*: this was a castle conquered by Lancelot. 'The castle was called the Dolorous Guard because every knight errant who ever went there was either killed, or at the very least was imprisoned there as soon as he was defeated; and all who went there were defeated' (*Lancelot of the Lake*, trans. Corin Corley (OUP, 1989), 104). The castle was renamed *Joyous Guard* after Lancelot had ended the enchantment.

50   *bath*: contrary to what is often believed, medieval people were well aware of the importance of hygiene and cleanliness, and by the thirteenth century there were many public baths in the towns; no less than twenty-six in Paris by the year 1292, according to E. Faral, *La Vie quotidienne au temps de Saint Louis* (Paris, 1942), 192. Taking a hot bath at home, however, was somewhat of a luxury, since the water had to be carried in from outside in buckets and heated in the fireplace. Only rarely was there a particular room in the house or castle reserved for this purpose, and privacy did not

seem to be a consideration. Indeed, the scene described here is quite a festive occasion, the enjoyment being shared by many.

57 *desire for him*: the OF text reads *quant ele voit qu'ele ne se porroit tenir de li parler en nule maniere*. The expression *parler a* when referring to a man and woman is in most cases a euphemism for sexual intercourse, and has been translated accordingly throughout the romance.

64 *fresh and new blood*: this scene in bed, interrupted by the arrival of the husband who finds the sheets blood-stained from Tristan's wound, is very reminiscent of Beroul's *Tristan*, lines 716 *et seq.*, though there the lady is Iseut herself and the husband is King Mark.

67 *Lady of Roestoc*: this episode occurs in the *Prose Lancelot*; see *Lancelot do Lac*, ed. E. Kennedy (Oxford, 1980), i. 374 *et seq.* There is no mention in that romance of Segurades's previous marriage.

74 *English league*: the league was a very ancient measure of length, estimated by the Romans at 1,500 paces, but varying from country to country. It was introduced into England by the Normans, and was equal to about three miles.

    Carduel in Wales: *Carduel* is the present-day Carlisle (Caer Luel of the Britons) the *d* being due to dissimilation of the first *l*. Carlisle is of course not in Wales, but in Cumberland, and Wales has to be taken here in a wider sense as including the territory once inhabited by the Welsh Celts who held the whole of Cumberland and almost all of the western half of England from the English Channel to the Firth of Clyde.

75 *this relationship*: Hestor is actually Lancelot's half-brother, being the illegitimate son of King Ban of Benoïc.

79 *his death*: the story of Merlin's fate at the hands of the Lady of the Lake (also known as Niniane) is first related in the *Prose Lancelot*; see *Lancelot do Lac*, ed. E. Kennedy, i. 23–4; it is also found in the Vulgate *Merlin Continuation* (*The Vulgate Version of the Arthurian Romances*, ed. H. Oskar Sommer, ii. *L'Estoire de Merlin* (1908), 451–2. Cf. *Les Prophécies de Merlin*, ed. Anne Berthelot (1992), 93–4).

    shield does indeed rejoin: the episode of the split shield is related in the *Prose Lancelot*; see *Lancelot do Lac*, ed. E. Kennedy, i. 401–3, where the shield arrives at court, and i. 547, where the shield rejoins.

lost him: for an account of Galehot's death because of his love for Lancelot, see *Lancelot do Lac*, ed. E. Kennedy, i. 612, and also *Lancelot: Roman en prose du XIIIe siècle*, ed. A. Micha (Paris–Geneva, 1978), i. 388–9.

86   *joy*: the MS reads *dolor*, but this is probably a corruption of *dolçor*.

87   *together*: this is followed in the MS by the words *et par linaige*, which do not really fit in this context.

89   *about the fair Tristan*: the OF text has *del bel Tristan*; the *bel* is a little unexpected and could be a mistake.

95   *chamberlain*: a knight appointed by a king to be in charge of his private chambers and attend to his personal affairs. At first chamberlains were of inferior rank, but gradually as a result of their close association with the king their position became much more important.

97   *serfs*: the social status of the serf was beneath that of the villein. A serf was attached to the land on which he lived, and cultivated the soil in return for the lord's protection. He differed from the slave in that he had certain rights and privileges, but he lacked personal freedom.

99   *lily*: in the versions of Eilhart and Gottfried, Brangain speaks of a white shift which she had lent the Queen. The prose author substitutes the lily, no doubt because this flower symbolizes chastity.

101 *palfrey*: a saddle-horse used by ladies and men for ordinary riding as distinct from a charger or war-horse.

112 *liege lord*: a lord to whom the vassal has sworn feudal allegiance and service.

     in the midst of a marsh: building on marshland was by no means unheard of in the Middle Ages; one only has to think of Winchester Cathedral where divers had to be used to repair the foundation! The buildings were usually constructed on brushwood and wood piling.

119 *Scarlet Cross*: a *Croix Vermeille* is also mentioned in the *Prose Erec* where it is a landmark, probably in Logres, at which Erec and Hector separate to seek adventures; cf. the *Croiz Roge* in Beroul's *Tristan* where the forester is told to wait for King Mark (line 1909) and where letters are attached (lines 2420, 2646).

129 *Fergus*: this knight, son of the rich *vilain* Soumilloit and a noble lady, is the hero of the *Roman de Fergus* by Guillaume le Clerc.

130   *The King had remained amongst his men*: in actual fact, all the King's
        men had fled; see above, p. 129.

131   *about nine o'clock*: the OF *hore de tierce* is literally the third hour of
        the day, ending at 9 a.m.

136   *Feast of St John (the Baptist)*: St John's Eve (23 June) was celebrated
        in the Middle Ages with song and dance. It is a very popular date
        in medieval romances.

137   *magic horn*: cf. the *Lai du Cor* by Robert Biket (end of 12th
        century); in this poem only the husbands or lovers of faithful
        women succeed in drinking from the horn.

        St Mary Magdalene: her feast is on 22 July.

142   *by tomorrow afternoon*: the OF text reads *dedenz demain none*;
        none is literally the ninth hour, that is three o'clock in the after-
        noon.

146   *Tristan who will bring sorrow on you*: the play on words of the OF
        text *Vez ci Tristan qui en tristece vos metra* can unfortunately not be
        translated into English; cf. the note to p. 7.

153   *by the porch*: the OF reads *envers les loges*. The word *loges* is often
        translated as 'gallery' or 'balcony', usually on an upper floor. But
        these *loges* are at the foot of the tower outside the door.

158   *eighty yards*: the OF text has *quarante toises*. The *toise* was an old
        measurement of length worth 1.949 metres, i.e. approximatively
        two yards.

164   *Forest of Morroiz*: already in the Domesday Book in 1086 we find
        a mention of the Manor of Moireis which owned an exception-
        ally large amount of woodland in the late 11th century—two
        hundred acres according to the Domesday Book. Later spell-
        ings are *Moreis c.*1175 and *Morres* 1205; it is known nowadays as the
        Manor of Moresk near Truro. The prose author could not
        have been very well acquainted with the geography of Cornwall,
        since the Forest of Morroiz is described as being near Tintagel
        (pp. 238 *et seq.*), though in this chapter it seems to be in the
        vicinity of Norholt (see pp. 167, 170, 173, 175). Cf. O. J. Padel,
        'The Cornish Background of the Tristan Stories', *Cambridge Medie-
        val Studies*, I (1981), 61–3.

171   *in the early evening*: the OF is *entor hore de vespres*. 'Vespers' was the
        sixth of the canonical hours of the breviary, said or sung towards
        evening.

        quiver: a case for holding arrows.

180 *end of their love*: as will be seen shortly, all this is just going on in Tristan's mind, since Queen Iseut was as yet quite unaware of his marriage.

184 *ship which took her to the Kingdom of Logres*: it is interesting to note that the maiden makes her way from Cornwall to Great Britain by boat. It was of course a long way to ride and probably less tiring to go by sea. Both routes were obviously used, as can be seen later (p. 194) when Tristan and Kahedin are in the Forest of Darvances in Great Britain, and Tristan tells his men to wait for him in Cornwall 'and he would make his way there either by land or by sea'.

189 *joy will return in the end*: the OF text reads *et que la fin ne retort a vie*. The meaning of this phrase is not clear, although it is the reading found in the majority of the MSS. However, one variant is *retourt a joie*, which seems more meaningful, and has been used in this translation.

191 *quarterstaff*: a long wooden pole tipped with iron used as a weapon of offence or defence.

     Land that Tristan Freed: the OF is *la Franchise Tristan*. The word *franchise* is clearly used here in its original sense of exemption from servitude or subjection, and the name is evidently given to the country in opposition to its earlier name of *País de Servaige*.

     lay: OF *lai*. This is a short lyric or narrative poem intended to be sung, probably to the accompaniment of a rote or viol, and later a harp.

     'Lay of the Land that Tristan Freed': This is followed in the OF text by a long account of the adventures of the *Vallet a la Cote Mautailliee*. This youth is the hero of an earlier verse romance, the *Roman du Vallet a la Cote Mal tailiee*, of which only 144 lines have come down to us (ed. P. Meyer and G. Paris, *Romania*, 26 (1897), 267–80). The interpolation of this romance in the *Prose Tristan* was probably an early development, but a careful consideration of all the evidence indicates that it was not present in the original (cf. my article, 'A Romance within a Romance: The Place of the Roman du Vallet a la Cote Mautailliee in the Prose Tristan', *Studies in Medieval Language and Literature presented to Brian Woledge* (Droz, 1987), 17–35). Since the story of the *Vallet* has nothing whatever to do with Tristan or Iseut, who indeed play no part in it, I have not included it in this translation. The same applies to the short account of Lamorat's adventures (§§ 617–35 of vol. ii) which precedes the story of the *Vallet*.

191 *in the same week*: the interval between Tristan's revelation of his
     love to Kahedin and the present episode must have been well over
     a week, for numerous adventures befall our hero in between (see
     pp. 190–1). This is a clear indication that these adventures were
     not present in the original, but were added by a redactor who
     forgot to adjust the text accordingly.

196 *Gorre*: the location of Gorre, the kingdom of Bademagu, varies
     from one OF text to another; a number of critics favour an
     identification with the peninsula of Gower in south-west Wales.
     Meleagant's abduction of Guinevere and her rescue by Lancelot
     from Gorre is the subject of Chrétien de Troyes's *Conte de la
     Charete*.

203 *two lances from the ground*: this could have been the equivalent of
     20 feet or more; see the note to p. 44.

207 *Giglain, Sir Gawain's son*: Giglain is Gawain's son by the fairy
     Blancemal according to the verse romance *Le Bel Inconnu*, of
     which Giglain (Guinglain) is the hero.

213 *'Story of Tristan' by Sir Luce of Gat Castle*: this is a reference to the
     episode related earlier, p. 124; a similar mention of Sir Luce occurs
     on p. 227, also referring to this episode (pp. 122 *et seq.*) These
     references would seem to suggest that a second author (Helie de
     Boron?) is speaking here and referring back to events related by a
     first author, Luce; see above, Introduction, 'The Authorship',
     pp. xvii *et seq.* Cf. also p. 218, where the 'Story of Tristan' is
     referred to without mention of Luce, and p. 298, where it is Helie
     himself who refers the reader to Luce.

216 *no joy can affect them*: the OF text *le mien plor est si fondez qu'il n'a
     cure de nul mal tens* does not make very good sense and is clearly
     corrupt. The reading of MS 750 *cure de joie* seems a bit more
     meaningful, and I have therefore used it in this translation. Unfor-
     tunately all the other MSS are very abridged at this point and do not
     contain Tristan's speech; see the 'Introduction' to vol. iii, p. xxxi.

218 *this incident*: see pp. 155 *et seq.* Cf. note to p. 213.

     sadness: the OF text reads *Je sui Tristanz qui onques n'ot se tristor
     non*. It is unfortunately impossible to translate into English the
     play on words *Tristanz/tristor* of the original; cf. notes to pp. 7
     and 146.

223 *Forest of Espinoie*: there is no forest of such a name in Cornwall,
     and this forest is not mentioned elsewhere in the *Tristan* legend.
     The OF *espinoie* means 'thicket'; cf. Beroul, line 4354.

227   *as Sir Luce de Gat relates in his book*: these events are related above
on pp. 122–5 *et seq.*; see note to p. 213.

     three whole days: in fact Tristan only stayed at the tower for two
days; see above, p. 125.

228   *left by Tristan*: no harp was mentioned when Tristan previously
stayed at the tower; see above, pp. 125 *et seq.* It would indeed have
been very surprising if Tristan had brought his harp, since at the
time he was pursuing Palamedes who had abducted Iseut.

     written while the lovers were together in the Forest of Morroiz: none of
the three lays which Tristan is said to have composed is included
or even mentioned when these episodes were related; see above,
pp. 40 *et seq.*, 74 *et seq.*, 86 *et seq.* The inconsistencies revealed in
the last few notes seem to suggest that this is no longer the first
author, Luce, who is writing; see above, Introduction, 'The Authorship', pp. xvii *et seq.*, and also note to p. 213.

229   *he started his lay as follows*: the inclusion of long lyrical compositions in a prose work is rare in the romances of that period; see
above, Introduction, pp. xxv *et seq.* I am greatly indebted to Katherine
Knight, organizer of the Poetry Writing Club at the City Literary
Institute and member of the Tristan Society of Great Britain, for
the verse rendering of Tristan's lay, based on my literal translation.

230   *Even King Porrus had lesser woes*: although the OF text has *Porru*,
this is probably a reference to the powerful Indian King Porrus
(Porus) who lived in the fourth century BC and is mentioned in
the twelfth-century *Roman d'Alexandre*. The 'woes' alluded to no
doubt refer to the Battle of Hydaspes in the summer of 327 BC
where Alexander the Great totally defeated the army of Porus.
The Indian losses were enormous and included two of Porus's sons
and many of his high officers. Porus himself was taken prisoner.
See *Cambridge Shorter History of India*, by J. Allan, Sir T. Wolseley
Haig, and H. H. Dodwell (Cambridge, 1934), 21 *et seq.*

231   *No reason but her wantonness*: the last two lines of this stanza have
been translated freely, since the last verse is not at all clear in the
OF: *Ençois m'ocist Yselt l'enrievre, | C'est cele ou ne gist pas le lievre.*
Cf. the modern French phrase *C'est là que gît le lièvre*, 'that's the
crux of the matter'.

     Which lack of wind makes wet or brittle: the order of all the other
MSS has here been adopted, placing the line second instead of last.
This makes the line a little more meaningful, although it is still far
from clear.

231   *This last affliction is the end*: literally *J'estuve ou derrien baig*, an idiom which is reminiscent of the modern French phrase *Quelle étuve!* 'What a mess!'.

232   *And all of you who pass this way*: an echo from the Bible; cf. the *Lamentation of Jeremiah*, 1: 12: 'all ye that pass by, behold, and see if there be any sorrow like unto my sorrow.'

234   *should ask what it signifies*: the OF text is corrupt at this point in all the MSS. I have tried in my translation to give the sentence some meaning.

256   *fittings of which were very costly*: the OF text is *espee mout richement appareillie*. The word *appareillie* is somewhat ambiguous. It could possibly refer to the decorations; but after having consulted *The Sword in the Age of Chivalry*, by R. Ewart Oakeshott (London, 1964), I feel it is more likely to be a question of the fittings, i.e. the grip and 'all the varying fittings which embellished, covered and completed' the sword (Oakeshott, 129), including of course the scabbard, an essential fitting, varying in embellishment according to the fashion of the time.

257   *unless someone had informed them of it*: this looks like an oversight on the part of the author, for Dinas *had* of course been 'informed of it' by the King (see above, p. 249).

258   *began her lay as follows*: in my attempt to transpose Iseut's lay into octosyllabic rhyming couplets, I have kept as close as possible to the original. I am greatly indebted to Katherine Knight for her helpful suggestions.

270   *After parting from Mark*: this chapter takes us to the beginning of vol. iv of my critical edition, which is as yet unpublished. Since the very superior manuscript, MS Carpentras 404 (*C*), on which the first three volumes of my critical edition are based, came to an end at this point, I have used for vol. iv another early manuscript, BN 750 (dated 1278) which shares a number of features with *C*.

271   *duel for the same reason*: see above, p. 245.

272   *lineage of King Pellinor of Listenois*: Lamorat was in fact King Pellinor's son.

273   *they discover each other's identity*: the folklore theme of a father fighting his son, each unaware of the other's identity, can be found in literature as far back as Greek antiquity. It was well known in the Middle Ages: see the epic *Gormont et Isembart*, where Isembart defeats his father Bernart (stanza 19), and Marie de France's lay

Milun. Cf. more recently, Matthew Arnold's poetic rendering of the Persian story *Sohrab and Rustum*.

couplets and verses: the OF is *couples et vers*. The meaning of *couple* is given in Tobler-Lommatzsch as 'Strophe' (stanza), but since Kahedin's verses are written in octosyllabic rhyming couplets, I feel that 'couplets' is a more satisfactory translation here, especially as the poem he then hands to the harpist is non-strophic.

278 *letter which she was sending him*: in some MSS the Queen is seen writing a letter to Tristan as well as a lay to Kahedin.

283 *it is written in verse*: Kahedin's letter consists of 34 stanzas, identical in form to the lays of Tristan and Iseut quoted earlier (pp. 229–32 and 258–61). It is published in T. Fotitch and R. Steiner, *Les Lais du Roman de Tristan en prose* (Munich, 1974), 50–62.

287 *many a time described to you before*: this is not actually true. Daguenet has only been mentioned once before, in the story of the *Vallet a la Cote Mautailliee*, where the *vallet* knocks him off his horse; see vol. ii, § 654, 3 *et seq.* Cf. note to p. 191.

288 *he cut his arms right off*: the OF text reads *il trenche les braz tot oltre*. The plural is not a mistake, for it is repeated on p. 289.

297 *Tristan was cured of the great madness*: after the innumerable pages dealing with Tristan's madness, the one sentence describing his cure strikes one as a little inadequate. It would seem that the author is not sure how one sets about curing a madman, which is not really surprising! Clearly he does not want to resort to the supernatural as did previous authors when faced with the same situation; cf. Chrétien de Troyes, *Yvain*, ed. Reid (Manchester University Press, 1942; repr. 1984), lines 2946 *et seq.*, and the *Prose Lancelot*, ed. Micha (Textes Littéraires Français, 6; 1980), 224. See R. L. Curtis, 'Tristan *forsené*: The Episode of the Hero's Madness in the Prose Tristan', *The Changing Face of Arthurian Romance*, ed. A. Adams, A. Diverres, K. Stern, and K. Varty (Arthurian Studies, 16; Cambridge, 1986), 10–22.

298 *at King Arthur's court itself*: MS 750 has *en la maison du roy March meïsmes*; this reading is a mistake.

Whoever would like to look at it: the following two sentences are found only in BN 750. However, there are several other references to the 'Story of Tristan' by Luce of Gat Castle, e.g. on pp. 213 and 227. On the subject of the dual authorship of the *Prose Tristan*, see R. L. Curtis, 'Who Wrote the Prose Tristan? A New Look at an Old Problem', *Neophilologus*, 67 (1983), 35–41.

301 *and had subsequently forgiven Cornwall*: Tristan's exploits against the
     King of Norgales and the King of the Hundred Knights have not
     previously been mentioned in the *Prose Tristan*.

302 *as yet unknown to him*: this knight, it transpires later, was Dinadan.

304 *countless adventures*: these adventures take us to the end of the
     thirteenth-century manuscript BN 750 (Löseth, § 203); after this I
     use BN 757 which, although a fourteenth-century text, is thought
     to contain the early version and is the base manuscript used by
     Löseth in his *Analyse*. The manuscripts of the so-called second
     version intercalate an even greater number of Arthurian adven-
     tures.

305 *the Queen*: literally 'the lady', which sounds very stilted in English.

306 *habergeon*: this was a sleeveless coat of mail, originally shorter and
     lighter than a hauberk; see note to p. 36.

308 *between the two of us*: the OF text *entre nos deus* does not make it
     clear whether this refers to Tristan and King Mark or Tristan and
     Iseut.

312 *he must be alive*: the Round Table was said to have seated 150
     knights, the name of each knight being inscribed on his seat at the
     Table. As soon as a Round Table knight died, the inscription
     disappeared from his seat.

326 *completing this book*: the Epilogue of the *Prose Tristan* is not written
     by Luce de Gat, author of the Prologue, but by Helie de Boron
     who refers to Luce as the one 'who first began to translate'
     (p. 326). This Epilogue by Helie is found in only twelve of the
     Prose Tristan manuscripts, many of them being incomplete at the
     end and others having no real epilogue at all. Four of the manu-
     scripts give the Epilogue in a longer form, without however
     altering its essential nature. The problems of the authorship of our
     romance are dealt with in the Introduction (pp. xvii *et seq.*); see
     also my two articles 'The Problems of the Authorship of the Prose
     Tristan', *Romania*, 79 (1958), 314–38, and 'Who Wrote the Prose
     Tristan? A New Look at an Old Problem', *Neophilologus*, 67
     (1983), 35–44.

     King Henry of England: if the claim for royal protection is legitim-
     ate, the king referred to is Henry III, born in Winchester in 1207
     and King of England from 1216–72.

     one whole year: a variant in some MSS is 'five years'.

     Walter Map: English scholar and writer (*c.*1135–1209) who fin-
     ished his studies in Paris and in 1162 entered the service of Henry

II Plantagenet; author of the *De Nugis Curialium* (1192–3). Also pretended author of the *Adventures of the Holy Grail*, the *Story of Lancelot* and the *Death of King Arthur*, according to the claims made at the beginning and end of the *Mort Artu* and the end of the *Queste del Saint Graal*. These claims to authorship are invalidated by the date of Walter's death (*c*.1209).

326 *Robert de Boron*: well-known author of the verse version of the *Story of the Holy Grail* and of a poem on Merlin (end of 12th century).

Helie de Boron: the reference to Helie is missing in MS 757, but is present in the other MSS. On Helie's relationship to Robert de Boron, see above, Introduction, p. xvii.

INDEX OF PROPER NAMES

THE numbers refer to pages. Names of persons are printed in SMALL CAPITALS, place-names are printed in *italics*. The index includes references to persons whose actual name is given in the preceding or following pages.

BLIOBERIS, knight of the Round Table, son of Nestor of Gaunes,
  67–70, 77, 196, 271, 325.
BOORT, King of Gaunes, knight of the Round Table and Lancelot's
  cousin, 111, 270.
BRANDELIZ, knight of the Round Table, 48, 196–7.
BRANGAIN, companion and lady-in-waiting of Iseut, 46–50, 54, 85–9,
  93–107, 133–5, 142, *et passim*.
BREUZ THE PITILESS, an evil, treacherous knight, 79, 217.
Brittany, 11, 174–7, 179–81, 187–8, 190–4, 200, 212, 235, 244–5, 270,
  272, 277–8, 282–5.
BRUNOR, father of Galehot, lord of the Distant Isles, 90.
BRUNOR, the real name of the Vallet a la Cote Mautailliee, 314.

Camelot, principal residence of Arthur, the finest city in Great Britain,
  74–5, 77–9, 184, 197, 233, 270, 303–4, 312–14, 322, 325.
CARADOS SHORTARM, a king and knight of the Round Table, 78.
Carduel, Carlisle, 74, 78. *See* note to p. 74.
Carthage, ancient city in North Africa, the capital of one of the most
  important empires of the ancient world, 236.
Castle in the Moors, castle in Ireland, 45, 102.
Castle of Fortune, castle in Wales, 195.
Castle of Tears, castle in the Distant Isles, 89, 90–1.
Castle of the Enchantress, castle in the Kingdom of Sorelois, 90.
Castle of the Giant's Rock, castle in the Distant Isles, 90–1.
Castle of the Pass, castle in Cornwall, 194.
CHRIST, *see* JESUS CHRIST.
CLAUDAS, King of the Deserted Land, 111.
Cornwall, 3, 4, 10, 17–18, 27–8, 30–4, 36–40, 45 *et passim*.
COTE MAUTAILLIEE, *see* VALLET A LA COTE MAUTAILLIEE.
COUNT OF NORHOLT, Cornish count slain by Tristan, 17–18.

DAGUENET, fool at King Arthur's court, 286–9, 292.
DAMSEL FROM CORNWALL, maiden sent by Iseut to Logres with a
  letter for Guinevere, 183–8.
DAMSEL FROM LOGRES, maiden who informs Iseut of Guinevere's
  love for Lancelot, 126–7.
Darvances, Forest of —, see *Forest of Darvances*.
DAVID, Old Testament hero, second king of united Israel, 149.
DELICE, sister of Galehot, 90.
DIALETES, giant, lord of the Giant's Isle, 90.
DIDO, in Roman mythology, queen and founder of Carthage, 236.
DINADAN, knight of the Round Table, 301–3, 313–14, 320.

SAXONS, THE —, 314.

Scarlet Cross, a landmark in Cornwall, 119. *See* note to p. 119.

SCOTLAND, KING OF —, *see* KING OF SCOTLAND.

SEGURADES, a knight from the Kingdom of Logres, 64–5, 67–8, 191, 259, 270.

SEGURADES'S WIFE, the most beautiful lady in Cornwall, daughter of a count, 56–60, 63–5, 67–70.

SHEPHERDS, companions of the mad Tristan, 286–8, 290–5.

SHEPHERDS, reveal Tristan's whereabouts to Mark, 169.

SOLOMON, third king of Israel, celebrated in the Old Testament for his wisdom and riches, 149.

Sorelois, kingdom in the vicinity of Norgales, 79, 90.

SUPINABEL, knight from Brittany, 187.

TAULAS OF THE MOUNTAIN, giant living on a high mountain in the Forest of Morroiz, 290–2, 301.

Thornbush Ford, a ford in Cornwall, 60–1, 66.

Tintagel, city in Cornwall, 55–7, 62, 65, 92–3, 136–7, 197–8, 206, *et passim.*

TOR, son of King Pellinor by the wife of the peasant Ares, half-brother of Lamorat, Driant, Agloval and Perceval, 197, 272, 313.

Tower of Tintagel, tower where King Mark keeps Iseut confined, 304.

TRISTAN, son of King Meliadus of Leonois and nephew of King Mark, 3, 7–76, 78–95, 106, 110–38, 141, *et passim.*

UTHER, King Uther Pendragon, Arthur's father, 272.

Uther's Shame, castle in Logres, belonging to Argan, 272.

VALLET A LA COTE MAUTAILLIEE, knight whose real name is Brun (Brunor), 314. *See* fourth note to p. 191.

Wales, 74, 76, 190, 195, 272.

WALTER MAP, English scholar and writer, *See* fourth note to p. 326.

Wise Damsel's Rock, rock in the Forest of Morroiz, 164.

WISE DAMSEL, maiden in Cornwall skilled in magic, 166, 169.

YGERNE, married to King Uther after the death of her first husband, the Duke of Tintagel, 272.

YVAIN, knight of the Round Table, 48.

THE WORLD'S CLASSICS

A Select List

JANE AUSTEN: Emma
Edited by James Kinsley and David Lodge

J. M. BARRIE: Peter Pan in Kensington Gardens & Peter and Wendy
Edited by Peter Hollindale

WILLIAM BECKFORD: Vathek
Edited by Roger Lonsdale

JOHN BUNYAN: The Pilgrim's Progress
Edited by N. H. Keeble

THOMAS CARLYLE: The French Revolution
Edited by K. J. Fielding and David Sorensen

GEOFFREY CHAUCER: The Canterbury Tales
Translated by David Wright

CHARLES DICKENS: Christmas Books
Edited by Ruth Glancy

MARIA EDGEWORTH: Castle Rackrent
Edited by George Watson

ELIZABETH GASKELL: Cousin Phillis and Other Tales
Edited by Angus Easson

THOMAS HARDY: A Pair of Blue Eyes
Edited by Alan Manford

HOMER: The Iliad
Translated by Robert Fitzgerald
Introduction by G. S. Kirk

HENRIK IBSEN: An Enemy of the People, The Wild Duck,
Rosmersholm
Edited and Translated by James McFarlane

HENRY JAMES: The Ambassadors
Edited by Christopher Butler

JOCELIN OF BRAKELOND:
Chronicle of the Abbey of Bury St. Edmunds
Translated by Diana Greenway and Jane Sayers

BEN JONSON: Five Plays
Edited by G. A. Wilkes

LEONARDO DA VINCI: Notebooks
Edited by Irma A. Richter

HERMAN MELVILLE: The Confidence-Man
Edited by Tony Tanner

PROSPER MÉRIMÉE: Carmen and Other Stories
Translated by Nicholas Jotcham

EDGAR ALLAN POE: Selected Tales
Edited by Julian Symons

MARY SHELLEY: Frankenstein
Edited by M. K. Joseph

BRAM STOKER: Dracula
Edited by A. N. Wilson

ANTHONY TROLLOPE: The American Senator
Edited by John Halperin

OSCAR WILDE: Complete Shorter Fiction
Edited by Isobel Murray

VIRGINIA WOOLF: Mrs Dalloway
Edited by Claire Tomalin

A complete list of Oxford Paperbacks, including The World's Classics, OPUS, Past Masters, Oxford Authors, Oxford Shakespeare, and Oxford Paperback Reference, is available in the UK from the Arts and Reference Publicity Department (BH), Oxford University Press, Walton Street, Oxford OX2 6DP.

In the USA, complete lists are available from the Paperbacks Marketing Manager, Oxford University Press, 200 Madison Avenue, New York, NY 10016.

Oxford Paperbacks are available from all good bookshops. In case of difficulty, customers in the UK can order direct from Oxford University Press Bookshop, Freepost, 116 High Street, Oxford, OX1 4BR, enclosing full payment. Please add 10 per cent of published price for postage and packing.